The Father's Son

A Novel

By Jim Sano

Full Quiver Publishing
Pakenham, Ontario

The Father's Son
copyright 2019
by James G. Sano

Published by Full Quiver Publishing
PO Box 244
Pakenham, Ontario K0A 2X0

ISBN Number: 978-1-987970-12-8
Printed and bound in the USA

The Light (photo), by Michael R. McGlothlen, mike-mcglothlen.pixels.com
Cover design: James Hrkach

NATIONAL LIBRARY OF CANADA
CATALOGUING IN PUBLICATION
ALL RIGHTS RESERVED

Published by FQ Publishing
A Division of Innate Productions

This book has received the
Catholic Writers Guild Seal of Approval

I would like to dedicate this book to:

My Irish mother, Rita Marie Doherty, and Italian father, Benjamin Joseph Sano, who taught us about love, dedication to family, faith and always seeing things from both sides.

My sisters, Florence and Cassie, and brothers, John and Jerry, whom I love dearly and have always been there for me in my life.

My two wonderful, precious, and beautiful daughters, Emily and Megan, who have been a blessing and a joy.

And most of all, my wife, Joanne, who has been my love and my life in the great adventure of marriage, friendship, and the journey of discovering ourselves and each other.

Thank you, God, for the precious gift of a loving family.

Chapter 1

Against his instincts, David entered the rear of the small wooden church and gazed beyond the vacant pews to the granite altar, the crucifix, and the Stations of the Cross depicted down each side. The silence of the empty church settled over him, and the dim glow of light entering through the multicolored stained-glass windows summoned an inner solace he struggled to resist. He breathed deeply and exhaled, letting go of the emotions of what he had to face.

The faint aroma of burnt wax candles drew his attention to the alcove to his left, to the very spot he had stood as a young boy, more than thirty years earlier. Now standing before the wood-carved statue of Mary, he could feel his eight-year-old hand securely in his father's rough but gentle grip. He was looking at Mary's gentle gaze as his father spoke to him. "David, whenever you are lost or need to be strong, always think of Mary. She trusted in God's plan for her. She knew he would give her the guidance and strength she needed to follow it."

He tensed. How had his father dared to lecture him about trust?

Anger shivered through him and shattered the church's spell. With three long strides, he rushed outside, blinded momentarily by the intense afternoon sunlight.

He circled around to the front of the tiny church and stood atop the steep hill looking over the harbor and islands of the humble fishing village known as Stonington, Maine. The sight was nothing less than breathtaking with the rugged coastline, the silhouettes of Isle of Haut and countless smaller pine-treed islands dotting the ocean water in the distance. Nowadays, the harbor teemed with lobster boats and old schooners docked for the night in the calm waters of the protected inlet. Off in the distance, he could hear the foghorn from the Mark Island lighthouse. As he walked down the steep grade of the road, familiar sights flooded him with memories he had long ago buried deep inside. The smell of the ocean air, the clang of the rigging slapping against the aluminum masts of the sailboats, and the rhythmic sound of the waves lapping against the rocky shore made as much an impression on him now as they had each summer when he had come as a young boy to this small town for vacation, until that last year.

His father had taken him to the church before they were to travel home, and little did he know it would be one of the last times he would ever see him.

In the center of the village, he passed the local newspaper office, two art galleries, Bartlett's grocery, the library where people were sitting on the small stoop, and a used book shop where he spotted his companion from his six-hour journey from Boston. With two gift bags in hand, she glanced up, and an infectiously big smile came over her face as she waved and shouted, "David!" In the late afternoon sunlight, her striking blonde hair and the brightly colored sundress that hugged her attractive figure made it clear that she was no town native.

Before Jillian could ask him whether he was successful with his mission, David placed his arm around her and kissed her. She was a worthy distraction for him and, for the moment, she forgot her question.

They stowed her packages in his car, spent the day together exploring the island, and the evening at the Inn on the Harbor in their room by a romantic fire and a stunning view of the quiet moonlit harbor. Jillian slept while David's mind was racing all night until the morning hours as uninvited memories forced their way into his thoughts.

By eight o'clock, David was dressed in a finely tailored suit as Jillian wore an attractive but appropriate black dress for the occasion. They grabbed breakfast at the Harbor View Cafe across the street and then headed to the cemetery on the edge of town. Jillian stood stiffly at David's side as he stared at the names on the gravestones. Next to his mother's freshly dug plot was his mother's twin sister, Marie. She'd died as a child, so he'd never met her, but his mother, Ann, had often talked about her. They were born on Easter Sunday, and Marie was the April Fools' joke that year because no one was expecting twins. Unfortunately, Marie was born with a rare lung disease that often kept her home in bed when breathing was particularly difficult.

Marie and David's mother were remarkably close, even for twins, and with no other siblings, they enjoyed each other's companionship more than any friend from school. When Marie's condition worsened to the point that she could no longer attend school, his mother had carried her books home from school and taught her the lessons. By that summer, Marie's condition had worsened. His mother had often dwelled on Marie's final day, when she had sat with her in bed, promising that she would never leave her side, but before the sun had set, Marie had drawn her last breath. His grandmother had pulled his mother out of Marie's room, tears streaming down her cheeks and body shaking. She'd often uttered the same thing she'd said to her mother that day: "How could God do this to Marie? She's only twelve years old!" Over time, her sorrow had given way to anger and the inability to forgive God for not taking care of Marie. His mother told him she'd made a vow to be buried with her, to be with her always. That was one promise she had been determined to keep, and now David was making certain she did.

Jillian reached out to David, drawing him back to the present. "Are you okay, David?"

David nodded several times. "Yes. Yes. I'm sorry. I was just thinking about this being the one thing my mother always wanted."

Other thoughts raged in his head. During his morning run, he had headed up a steep hill and picked a route that ran along the coastline which, with each turn, unburied another forgotten memory as he ran by homes and docks that had seemed barely altered by time. He had slowed to a standstill when he reached the house where his mother had grown up. He recalled spending hours sitting on the wraparound porch with his grandfather and his grandfather's old, adopted bloodhound, "Duke." Duke was named from the stories his grandfather, Pops, had recounted about the many years he'd spent on Captain John Duke's schooner, the Annie and Ruben, hauling large blocks of granite from the local quarry to Boston, New York, and Washington used to build schools, museums, and government buildings. Pops had a profound regard for Captain John and would think of him when he sat beside his dog.

David remembered evenings out on that porch with Pops and his father lighting up cigars and occasions when the entire family gathered telling stories and laughing loud enough for anybody on the harbor shore to hear. His older brothers, Jimmy and Bobby, his sister, Abbie, Pops and Grammy, any cousins that dropped by, and his dad and mom had carried on for hours at a time. He could still envision his mother throwing back her head, giggling and smiling as she glanced over at him or put her arm around his dad. He had forgotten that beaming smile and distinct and infectious laugh of his mother. Until that moment, the picture in his mind of his mom was of a distant, serious and often beaten, bitter expression that had seemed to represent her life after that fateful October afternoon in 1971, back home in Boston, where everything in his life fell apart.

He shook the thoughts away and turned to look at Jillian, startled to realize how exceedingly beautiful her facial features were. There in the unlikeliest of places, he stopped to drink them in as she blushed under his attentive gaze.

He took her hand in his. "I really shouldn't have asked you to come today. We hardly know each other, and I've dragged you six hours to a funeral for someone you've never met. I wasn't thinking or being fair to you."

"I'm honored that you asked me to come. I just want to be here for you." She stroked his hand.

"I haven't really talked about my mother to anyone. I don't know exactly what to say." He paused, embarrassed for what he was about to admit. "We may be the only ones that show up."

"Didn't you mention you have brothers and sisters?"

"My sister didn't think burying our mom warranted the flight and hassle of coming out from Minnesota, and my brother didn't return my calls or letters." He didn't tell her he hadn't even broken the news of his mother's death to his ex-wife or his two children, which had seemed like the best idea at the time, but now that the day was here, he was feeling differently about making the decision for them.

He pulled his hand away from her and shoved both of them in his pockets as he stared at the casket suspended over the covered grave. "Growing up, she took care of the three of us for years, working long hours at a job I know she hated but was glad to have. Then, she came home every evening to cook our meals, mend our clothes to get a few extra months out of them, and made sure we stayed in school and off the streets. I hardly ever saw her smile, and she rarely took the time for friends or fun. She took care of us in terms of physical needs, education, food, and shelter—and that was all she had to give. Emotionally she was not—" David paused, eyed the funeral attendants shuffling around by the limo, and said more softly, "I'm sorry, I'm going on too much."

Jillian jumped in. "Please don't apologize. You need someone to confide in about your feelings, or you just end up bottling them up—but never enough to stop them from coming back up."

They stood there awkwardly for a few minutes until Jillian spotted a heavy-set woman approaching.

The woman lumbered over to them, out of breath and wiping her forehead with a napkin. "You must be Annie's son."

David looked her up and down with no idea who she was. "Yes, I'm David Kelly."

"David John Kelly," the woman added before he could say anything more. "I guess you're wonderin' who I am." She paused to catch her breath. "Emma Brown. I was a close friend of your mom and her sister, Marie, and grew up next door to them in Green Head. I felt like a third sister to them and grieved with Annie when Marie died so young. You probably don't remember my coming over to visit with your mom and family on your grandpa's porch, but I remember you, the youngest of Annie's clan. I feel like I know you better than my very own. Your mother used to write me— oh, once or twice a month—and I would read all about you and Abbie and Bobby, and poor Jimmy. She was so heartbroken after the tragedy. I think it sadly opened the wounds from Marie's death too wide to heal. I kept telling her she had to be strong for you kids, but I constantly worried about her." Emma turned to Jillian and stretched out her hand. "It's so nice of you to come with David."

Jillian smiled. "I'm pleased to meet you too. I'm Jillian Miller."

David spotted John Colby, the funeral director, approaching them.

John patted David's back, shook his hand, and greeted him in a distinctive Maine accent with the hushed voice people reserve for sleeping babies and funerals. "David, I hope things have been set up to your satisfaction." Without waiting for a reply, he waved toward a huge spray of flowers. "Did you notice? From your friends at IMS."

David glanced at Jillian, knowing she'd shared the location with his secretary to ensure they would send something. She returned a half-guilty smile.

David collected himself. "Thank you, John."

After a brief welcome to the two women, John glanced around at the empty landscape, as if to check for anyone else climbing the hill to the funeral, then stepped up to the casket, cleared his throat, and stood more erectly—a sure sign he was ready to begin.

David had left the ceremony plans for the funeral home. Because his mother had long ago abandoned religion and God, as she had believed they both turned their back on her sister and herself, he had decided against anything tied to the Church. John read a short meditation on her behalf, and then David read a poem called "Remember Me" that was recited at Marie Kelly's funeral, one she had picked out before she died.

After the readings, David turned to the casket. "Mom, you can finally rest from all your years of sweat and heartache. You can be with your sister again, the one you loved most in this world and lost without ever knowing what the purpose was."

As they lowered the casket into the grave, he tossed a clump of soil and a rose on top then turned and walked away.

While Jillian stood by the gravesite deep in thought, Emma caught up with David under a honey locust tree. "David, I want you to know your Aunt Marie's life did have meaning and purpose, at least to me. I admired your aunt's strength and her incredibly positive spirit. Others would've been mired in lamenting that life was being robbed from them, but not Marie. She took the smallest things, and not only made us appreciate them but also realize how important they were: a smile when someone entered the room, the tiniest wildflowers along the path we would walk to pick blueberries or sitting to gaze at the view of the harbor from the hilltop. She would ask how I was, even when she was obviously having a difficult day herself or would help out the family down the road because she knew they had so little.

"Marie believed she had a purpose no matter how compromised or shortened her life would be, and she loved your mom more than herself until the end. Well, when I grew up and thought about what my life was going to be about, I thought of Marie. Her example made quite an impression on me. She is the reason I've spent the past fifty years helping to build a network of support shelters in Maine and several in Burundi and Nigeria, Africa. I'm not telling you this for egotistical reasons, but to let you know how much your aunt's life impacted mine. I cherished and loved Marie almost as much as your mom did."

He watched Emma's eyes as she spoke and surprised himself with how differently he viewed his mother as Emma's words unfolded.

Emma continued, "I also loved your mother like a true sister. She wrote to me as if I were the only one with whom she could share her struggles and feelings. Losing Marie was like losing half of her heart. Then losing her firstborn so tragically was plainly too much to bear. But your mom knew she had a job to do, to take care of and raise all you kids the best she could. She desperately wanted all three of you to have a better life, and she believed you, especially, had the strongest chance to fulfill that wish."

Emma gave David a hug and then pulled a tissue from her purse to wipe the tears from her face as Jillian approached. Emma said, "It was so good to see you again, and I do pray your mom is smiling once more with Marie." She turned to Jillian. "It was so very good to meet you too, Jillian. Maybe you'll come back this way someday under happier circumstances." Emma leaned in to whisper in Jillian's ear, "And your mate here may be a looker, but I believe deep down there's something there that would make him a keeper." She hugged Jillian, and then David, before turning to walk back to the funeral home for her car.

David watched till she disappeared down the hill, not realizing he'd been holding his breath. He let out a deep sigh and looked around him. The men from the funeral home were patiently standing off in the shade of an oak tree, waiting for David to leave so they could finish their work. Other than them, the place was empty. He shook his head—this was all his mother's life had amounted to. Mourning her sister and working herself to death to take care of her children on her own, with only one soul showing up to pay respects. Not even her other two children.

His mother had no idea how good life could be. The bitterness and sadness that had overshadowed her life robbed her of any chance of living it well.

He took Jillian's hand and started back towards his Porsche 911 GT2 convertible. As they walked, his thoughts drifted back to a summer night as a boy when he was playing street hockey with the neighborhood kids and an orange convertible sports car with a unique engine sound drove slowly down the street. Charlie Cassavette, wearing sunglasses, long sideburns, combed backed hair, and an opened polyester shirt with a gold chain glimpsing through, was driving the most distinctive car David had ever seen in a town where people could barely afford a third-hand, oversized car from the early sixties, often with one different colored passenger door and a hood that wouldn't entirely shut. Charlie was driving a 1973 Porsche 914 that rode low to the ground and had only two seats. The passenger side was occupied by an attractive girl David didn't recognize. Every kid had stopped playing to watch him driving through, their open-jawed mouths matching David's own expression, except David's was not jealous or envious, but rather determined that he would not only own a car like that someday but the moment as well. Charlie had called out to David, "Someday, Little DJ. Someday," and sped off into the early summer evening.

As he held the door for Jillian and glanced at her, her long legs, her flawless ivory skin, and soft blond flowing hair, he smiled.

David had exceeded even Charlie's imagination of success.

Chapter 2

Jillian nodded off for long stretches of the six-hour drive back to Boston, and David thought about his work schedule for the week to help push the resurfaced memories and emotions back into the dark grave where he had buried them. His mother, father, and oldest brother were now all gone. His brother, Bobby, had severed ties years ago, and his calls to his sister, Abbie, were more out of feeling responsible than seeking a close relationship. He had separated from his wife and their two children six years ago, and as his time commitment and frequent travel for his job grew, David had become more of an awkward stranger than a real father to his kids. Amy, now sixteen, was beginning to see her parents as more of a roadblock to life than wise and loving mentors on her way to maturity. James was just turning seven and asking more questions about the father he couldn't remember ever living with and knew he was missing.

David didn't see any of them now as being a natural part of his daily rhythm. The constant routine of work, exercise, and entertainment left little "free" time to sit and ponder the meaning or purpose of life, which he realized after the current day's reflections, may have been subconsciously by design.

Monday morning, David's alarm went off at five o'clock as it did every morning. The song playing was "Wake Up Little Susie," which only made him smile and mumble, "How about a little 'Rocky' or something to get me going?" He reached over the side of the bed and patted his yellow Labrador Retriever. He had found him on his doorstep six years ago with no owner tags nor signs of where he came from other than the name Topper on his tag that he changed to Trooper. He dressed and ran a five-mile loop along the Charles River, through the Commons, and up and down the neighboring streets before arriving back at the front door of his Beacon Street Brownstone apartment with a runner's high and salty sweat dripping down his forehead. The run helped him quiet down the emotions still playing through his mind. After a soothing, hot shower, he got dressed in one of his custom-made suits and headed off for his usual breakfast stop, the Eastside, on his way to work.

The walk from the Eastside to his Prudential Center office was only five minutes, and David would've taken the stairs up if his office were not on the forty-eighth floor of the tower. His secretary was a round Haitian woman named Izzie, short for Isadora. Her skin was dark, and she was attractive for a matronly built woman of forty years. After losing her husband, she had left Haiti to give her three children a chance at a better education and life, and she didn't hesitate to sacrifice her own wishes to make that happen. Izzie had been with David for ten years now and insisted on calling him "Mr. Kelly." She was always at work before David and today was no exception.

"Good morning, Mr. Kelly," greeted Izzie as her hand touched the crucifix that rested on her light blue blouse.

David looked her in the eyes. "And good morning to you, Izzie," he said as she handed him his mail neatly sorted in the order of importance from her perspective.

Behind him, he could hear familiar footsteps, the first of many people trying to grab a few minutes of his limited time. "DJ, got a minute?"

He glanced up at Izzie's smile and subtle nod. "Sure, Walshy. Come on in."

Kevin Walsh was one of his area managers who aggressively drove his sales numbers but enjoyed having a good time as well. Many of the sales reps and managers had come from local colleges such as Boston College, Northeastern, or Holy Cross. Several were ex-football players, but all had something in common: they came from very modest backgrounds, were willing to work hard and learn, and they were extremely loyal to both IMS and DJ Kelly. Everybody of importance seemed to have a nickname; Walshy, Sully, Quigs, DJ, Billy, OD, Paddy, Brendy, and Mickey. David knew he had walked in on the Irish Mafia of high-tech as soon as he had started at Information Management Systems.

David was hired by Kevin and started reporting to him early in his career at IMS. Kevin taught him the ins-and-outs of the company politics and how to win a deal by any means possible. David was never thoroughly comfortable with the process, but he was young and attracted by the opportunity to grow quickly at a company on the fast track. He spent as much time with all the top performers as he could to learn their tricks and best practices. He studied the technology, the competitors, and especially his customers. David was so talented at identifying opportunities and developing trusted relationships with the right people at the prospective customer that he "blew out" his revenue quota quarter after quarter after quarter. He was promoted to Senior Sales Rep, to District Sales Manager, and to Area Manager faster than anyone in company history and he was now the Divisional Vice President of Sales for Eastern US and Canada. Kevin was now working for David, which he had no issues at all with because he respected David's intelligence, incredible work ethic, and ability to win business.

Kevin stepped into David's spacious corner office furnished with a beautiful, cherry wood desk, a meeting table, and an area with a sofa and leather chairs. There were views of Beacon Hill, Boston Common and the Garden from other sides of the building, but David liked seeing Fenway, where the Red Sox played baseball from early April to September. Kevin sat down on one of the comfortable chairs and looked up at a photograph of the clubhouse porch at The Country Club in Brookline. Kevin pointed to the framed photo. "That was a great day, wasn't it, DJ?" The photo was a shot of eight of the top sales executives at IMS. Kevin Walsh, Billy O'Connell, Michael Shea, Patrick Harrigan, Sean Quigley, Kenny O'Donnell, Brendan O'Neill, and David were all standing on the porch of the elite clubhouse built in 1882. It had been a fun day of golf followed by an evening of drinks and dinner on the losers and gloating by the winners of that year's annual tournament.

David replied without hesitation, "It was a great day for the winners. I'm glad you enjoyed it too, but you'll have your chance again next week, Walshy."

In his thick Boston accent, Kevin said, "We will, and we're not lettin' Mickey cheat for you again this year. Ya know, I can recall feelin' on top of the world that day. We'd made more money than our wildest dreams could've imagined. We'd bought homes and cars we always wanted without flinchin' at the cost. We'd seen the world on first-class trips, attracted the most incredibly beautiful women lookin' for the best time money can buy, and we're looked up to like something better."

David's eyes squinted with curiosity. "What are you getting at, Kev?"

Kevin stared down through the glass coffee tabletop at the Oriental rug below. "Ya know, you and I were on a plane flyin' to a customer call in Atlanta just two weeks after that day of golf, watchin' those planes slam into one of the Twin Towers. We were just sittin' there and watchin' it happen in slow motion like it was a damn movie, and I'm thinkin' 'holy crap, we're goin' down too.' Nothin' I owned — money, cars, boats, my home on the water in Dennis – or could own, was worth anythin' at that moment. No power or position I had here mattered because I felt powerless. You remember when we landed, and I was in shock?"

David interjected, "Everyone was in shock, Kev. I don't think anyone wasn't on 9-11 or for days afterward."

"Really? You seemed to be pretty even-keeled afterward. Not that you didn't care, but you seemed calm and thinkin' about how everyone on our team could keep movin' forward. I keep goin' back and forth in my mind thinkin' about what's the point of my life."

David leaned over to put his hand on Kevin's left shoulder, and said in a slightly softer voice, "Do you need some time off to sort things out? Is there something I can do to help?"

Kevin kept looking down. "I really don't know, but I don't want to drag you down. I'll be fine. I probably just need to keep busier and think less."

As Kevin stood up to leave, David reached out and patted him on the back. "Take care of yourself, Kev. Let me know if you want to go out after work for a drink or something."

The rest of David's day was full of meetings and calls with his sales teams and customers. Izzie kept his calendar moving and prioritized who could sneak in to see him. He wouldn't run into Jillian today since she worked out of the Newton office, which was ten miles out of town. They had planned for dinner on Tuesday night in town, and she was getting exposed to restaurants and special dining rooms she didn't know even existed before seeing David. He never put on airs but knew how to move with ease around the inside track of the upper echelon where many of his customers' decisions were made. He left work around seven-thirty, making sure he said "good night" to the younger employees who were still working hard, and headed first to the gym for a workout and then home to make a late dinner and sit on the rooftop to relax and review proposals for the next day.

While David was an expert at compartmentalizing his feelings, his brief conversation with Kevin Walsh kept creeping into his thoughts. He vividly remembered experiencing that same sense of fear and the inability to control the situation as he helplessly watched those two planes, which had also flown out of the same Logan Airport as he and Kevin, explode into flames as they crashed into the towers. It opened up the vulnerability he felt when his oldest brother died, and his family was turned upside down forever. To help put these feelings back in storage, he dressed and went out for a quick run through the Common while listening to an Aerosmith lineup of songs on his iPod before walking back home and back in control of his emotions.

Chapter 3

The next day was a typically busy day, and he found getting back into the routine helped to silence the uncomfortable feelings that continued to haunt him.

Midafternoon, Jillian texted him. *Are we still on for dinner?*

David texted back: *Dinner is just the start of the evening I have planned.*

Jillian texted him a smile.

Trooper growled at the door, and David opened it for Jillian, who was carrying an overnight bag, a change of clothes, and a red dress that was a little more date-worthy. David told Trooper that Jillian was a friend as he held both of her hands and stepped back to admire her. "You look absolutely beautiful. Might you be interested in a night on the town with a desperate man?"

"I only date the most handsome, intelligent, successful, generous, and non-desperate men I happen to bump into."

David introduced Jillian to Trooper, and she squatted down to pat Trooper's head, rubbing his fur and peering into his brown eyes. "I didn't know you had a handsome roommate," said Jillian playfully, as she continued petting him.

"Sorry about the barking. He's very protective, but now I think I have a little competition for your attention."

Jillian stood back. "I think you've already lost that competition."

They drove only a mile and a half down Beacon Street to a restaurant called FuGaKyu, an older style Japanese restaurant where they removed their shoes. David bowed in greeting to the sushi chef and politely asked, "What fish is freshest? We would like to dine omakase tonight."

Jillian politely lowered herself to sit on the chairs with no legs and sat with her legs slightly sideways. "David, what is dining omakase?"

"The chef I spoke with is called the *itamae* or a highly skilled sushi chef. Greeting the *itamae* is a sign of respect and requesting omakase dining is a compliment to the chef since it gives him permission to serve us anything he chooses, but it assures us only the best and freshest sushi." He warned her not to insult the chef by ordering wine that would mask the taste of the sushi.

After dinner, as they walked towards the car, Jillian playfully nudged her shoulder against David's. "Next time let's splurge a wee bit and go to a place where they cook your food too. I have never, ever eaten raw fish before, but I will have to say I was pleasantly surprised."

"I'm glad you like surprises," he said as he opened the car door for her.

After a few turns toward downtown Boston, he pulled up in front of a building with an illuminated sign that read Dante's. There was a line outside, which surprised Jillian on a Tuesday night. A valet approached the car and opened the door for her before taking the keys from David.

Jillian took David's arm as they cruised past the line and into the nightclub entrance. A woman at the desk greeted them. "Good evening, Mr. Kelly. It's good to see you tonight." David returned the greeting, and Jillian turned her head toward him with an inquisitive stare. He pointed ahead toward the spacious dance floor jammed with hundreds of attractive people dancing to an infectious beat of an Italian nightclub sound. Jillian loved to dance, and her shoulders were already moving as she took in the layout of the place, the meeting areas and bars with engaging staff keeping people served and happy in between dances. Jillian pulled David onto the floor and was obviously impressed that he didn't hesitate and knew how to move on the floor as did she.

When they finally took a short break, Jillian said, "So?"

"So, what?"

"Sew buttons. You know darn well what I mean. How did you just walk in the front door without hesitation, and everybody knew who you were, Mr. Kelly—that's what?"

David just laughed. "It's either my natural charm or that they work for me and my partners in this small venture."

Jillian's eyes popped. "You own a nightclub! And this isn't just any dance hall by the looks of it." She noticed the neon sign over where they were standing read Purgatory and then peered up and down at the levels above and below them.

David said, "Yes, they are called—"

"—Heaven and Hell?" guessed Jillian.

David shook his head as the music played louder. "Close. Paradise and Inferno. Do you have a preference?"

"I think I'll stay here in the middle and enjoy. Can you tell me if it's okay to drink wine here or will we insult the chef?" David ordered Jillian a tall glass of expensive wine he thought she would appreciate and a glass of bourbon on-the-rocks for himself.

David knew staying too late at the club was not good for being up for early morning meetings or for romance, so after an hour, he was ready to leave. "Let me know when it's getting late for you on a school night." She put on a disappointed look and said goodbye to people she had met on the dance floor.

As David drove back home, Jillian said, "David, I don't want you to take this the wrong way, but do you think we could call it a night? I think I'm beginning to like you quite a bit, but I would like to think our evening was enough to be a great date. Am I making any sense?"

David mentally adjusted his expectations of a summer evening rooftop experience in the Jacuzzi under the stars. "Sure, it makes sense. We both have work early in the morning, and we did have a really nice evening, didn't we? Do you want to pick up your things or would you like me to take you home and get them later?"

"Maybe home would be best if you are okay with that."

"Home it is, fair maiden."

Without traffic, Jillian lived only about twenty minutes away, across the Charles River in an apartment in Watertown.

She shifted in her seat. "How have you been doing since coming back from Maine?"

David offered no more personal insights. "Thanks for asking, but I'm doing fine."

They pulled up in front of the two-family house on a quiet street perpendicular to the Charles River. He opened the door for her and reached out his hand to help her get out of the low sports car seat. When she stood up, she looked up into his eyes in a way he had only seen once before in his life. It was a gaze that went deep into his eyes. He put his arms around her and gave her a very long and enjoyable kiss. It was such a pleasant evening out that they strolled, arm in arm, onto a small bridge over the river. The moon was overhead, and they could see its shimmering reflection jumping back and forth on the moving water as they embraced and kissed again.

Jillian caressed his face. "I need to go home."

At her front stoop, he put his hand tenderly to Jillian's cheek, gazed into her eyes, and gave her another lengthy kiss.

"David, thank you for such a wonderful evening, and for being so understanding and a gentleman in every way."

"Good night, Jill, and sleep well. At least I do get to dream about you tonight." He watched her open the door to her apartment, safely get inside, and turn the light on before he glanced up at the moon through the leaves of the elm tree above and breathed in the fresh summer breeze. As he got back to his car to head home to sleep and start his routine in the morning, he realized he was enamored with Jillian but wasn't sure where their future was headed. He shrugged the thought away to concentrate on tomorrow's schedule of meetings and business appointments.

Chapter 4

At 5:00 a.m., David woke to the tune of Simon and Garfunkel's "The Boxer." He remembered listening to the song on the album *Bridge Over Troubled Water,* which he had played on his turntable over and over when he was young. The words echoed in his head as he recalled feeling beaten and abandoned by his family when he was a young boy. After all these years, this was the first time he noticed the line about a man hearing what he wanted to and disregarding the rest.

He laced up his running shoes. He remembered how difficult it was to sort everything out; surviving the unwelcoming kids in the new neighborhood his mother moved them to, understanding his mother's personality transformation, her distance when he needed her most, coping with losing his brother and father, and the overwhelming sense that everything was too much for him.

As he pulled on his favorite running shirt and the ballad continued to play, he envisioned himself still standing in the ring, despite being knocked down so often as a young boy. The fighter still remained.

Two hours later, showered and changed, David headed out the door for breakfast. His usual Eastside stop was unexpectedly closed for a few weeks due to underground electrical repairs, so he went to the Cafe Incontrare, one block over. When he asked the waiter what he recommended, the middle-aged Italian disappeared and came back a few minutes later with a cappuccino decorated on the top with an impressive design in the foam and a small plate with what he called a Sicilian-style Strata—a rustic mix of eggs, prosciutto, tomatoes, olives, parsley and scallions—and a glass bowl of fresh fruit. It was perfect.

As he raised the fork to his mouth, he glanced up and noticed a man in sweats and basketball shoes getting out of his beat-up, old Honda. The man opened the hatchback and took out several boxes and crates of food, some overloaded with vegetables and fruits, and others with wrapped meats and containers of milk and eggs.

For some reason, David was intrigued more by the man than what he was doing as he hoisted the first heavy crate into his arms and thumped with his foot against the door of the old brick building. The man was in good physical shape, probably in his late thirties, and about six feet tall, if not slightly taller than David. He was a good-looking man and seemed to be more than just a delivery man. A short, heavy black man with a dark beard and receding hairline opened the door and smiled with delight to see who had been banging. The man came back out with a friendly arm around another younger man who was wearing an old, worn apron on top of his jeans and tee-shirt. They both grabbed crates and boxes and brought them in until the car was empty.

After several minutes, the man in sweats came back out and picked up some trash lying on the sidewalk in front of the building. Then he walked over to a homeless man who was wearing a tattered trench coat, worn work shoes, an old Red Sox hat and a beard that hadn't been cut or groomed for some time. He put his hands on his shoulders as he spoke to him. Then he reached into the pockets of his sweats, pulled out a few bills and put them in the man's hand before waving goodbye. David thought the homeless man would probably waste whatever amount he was just given at the first pub or liquor store that would let him in. After finishing his breakfast and cappuccino, he left enough to cover the bill and a generous tip under his cup and walked the last short leg to the office. Passing by the mystery building, above the door he noticed a painted sign read: *My Brother's Table, Food Pantry Hours 11:30-1:00, 4:30-6:00.*

As David entered the Pru, he noticed his secretary, Izzie, standing inside the elevator with her large bags and a big smile on her face as she let the doors close before he could reach it. He laughed it off as he waited for the next elevator. He knew Izzie had an inexplicable need to beat him to the office every morning. As he passed her workstation, he heard her mumble, "Late evening last night, Mr. Kelly?"

"As a matter of fact, it was an early evening, if you're really interested."

He'd barely settled at his desk when his phone rang. It was his ex-wife, Kathleen. "David, why didn't you tell me your mother passed away? We should've been there. Are you doing all right?"

"I know. I know. It was a bad decision. I just wasn't thinking straight. I'm okay."

"Are you sure?"

"I am, Kat. I'm really okay and I appreciate you calling. I'm sorry about not telling you, but I need to run to a meeting. Say hello to the kids for me."

David hung up the phone, tapped his pen on his desk for a full minute while he stared blankly out the plate glass windows at the white clouds in the sky, then shrugged away the conflicting emotions. He turned to the business at hand. First, a series of meetings, then a lunch conference call with all his area sales managers to review the top deals on the table.

By midafternoon, he was buried in a four-hour working session to prepare for customer negotiations on a two-hundred-million-dollar multi-year disaster recovery deal that would take up the next several days and possibly the weekend in Virginia.

In the end, the work spilled over into Monday night and he didn't arrive back in Boston until mid-day Tuesday. He worked from home for the rest of that day and called Jillian to ask if she wanted to get together that evening. There was no hesitation on the other end of the line until David said to bring her "boating gear."

David ushered Jillian into his house, his gaze lingering on how her capri pants hugged her before noticing the elastic band in her hair that gave her an aura of innocence. They walked up the stairs to the kitchen, and he took her in his arms and gave her a long kiss.

Jillian rested her head on David's chest and said with an exhale, "I missed you the past too many days."

"Are you ready for a nice evening?"

She glanced at a small wicker picnic basket and checkered blanket sitting on top of the kitchen counter.

Trooper brushed against her leg, so she crouched down to pat him. "Hi, Trooper. I missed you more."

He grabbed the basket with one hand and her much smaller hand in his other with Trooper leashed in between. "Come on, then. Let's find out where this one leads us." They headed out the door to a beautiful, early evening summer night, and crossed the pedestrian bridge to the bank of the Charles River. After walking for a little over ten minutes, David stopped, let go of her hand, and put down the basket to unfold and snap out the blanket with both hands, letting it gently land on the grass for an evening picnic dinner. Jillian waited to be served as David opened the well-packed basket of homemade pesto chicken sandwiches, fruit, salad, wine, and a decadent looking dessert. Behind them was the bustling city full of people trying to get home. In front of them, the pleasant evening sun shone on the Charles as sailboats and crew teams passed by.

Jillian remarked, "As I said, I never know what to expect and—"

"And?"

"And no complaints here. I am completely spoiled, and I don't feel like I deserve it—but I love every minute of it!" Jillian kissed him.

With a mischievous smile, David replied, "I hope you don't think the evening is over yet."

After enjoying their picnic, they packed up the basket and walked further down the bank of the river past the Esplanade to the Community Boats, Inc. docks with small sailboats for members to take out. The organization had begun in 1941 to encourage sailing for everyone, making it accessible and affordable to rent sailboats, take lessons and enjoy the river.

David had become fairly proficient at it and literally showed her the ropes. It was a more-than-pleasant evening to be on the water with a gentle breeze to take them out for an experience he could tell that she and Trooper thoroughly enjoyed.

On the walk back to David's place, the setting sun was creating a dazzling show of red, orange and purple colors against the evening sky that was dotted at the horizon with a thin sheet of "mackerel" clouds. David felt how relaxed Jillian was as they held hands on their walk home and up to his rooftop garden to enjoy the evening transition into night. David waved towards the Jacuzzi tub, attractively set in stone and surrounded by garden roses, daylilies, and other plants to provide privacy. "Want to soak a bit?"

"It does look very inviting, but I didn't bring my bathing suit, and—"

David put his arms around her to give her a kiss and she reciprocated until she obviously realized that she might not be able to stop. "—and I do have an early day tomorrow."

He drove Jillian home and wished her sweet dreams. She told David how much she enjoyed the evening and how good it was to be with him, but by the time he reached home, David lost the warm feelings and was numb again when he lay his head on his pillow for the night.

Chapter 5

The next morning, he paused by the den window, coffee in hand, staring at the leaves bobbing in the gentle breeze and the men working on the street below. He recalled looking out the window as a boy but stopped himself short, set his coffee on the nearest table, and headed to the bathroom to shave.

David ran a different route across the bridge and through the Harvard Campus. He could always tell when he was in good shape by how good he felt at the end of his run, and today he felt great as he walked off the last yards to his door. He showered, dressed, and was off for his breakfast stop before work. The Eastside was closed again, so he went around the block to Cafe Incontrare, as he had the previous Wednesday. He liked the setup of the cafe. The interior was attractive, and the outdoor tables and plantings provided for an inviting stop as David sat at the same table as last week. The waiter recognized him with a nod and a smile and brought over a cappuccino before he had even ordered, which brought a smile to David's face.

As he checked out the daily menu specials, David noticed the same Honda hatchback pulling up to the My Brother's Table building. The same man got out of the car wearing Pony basketball shoes, black sweatpants, and a jersey that looked like he was ready to play. The man opened the hatchback and lifted the first crate of fresh vegetables when a worn leather basketball bounced out and rolled down the street towards the cafe. He looked to make sure it stopped in a good spot and proceeded to knock on the door with his foot. Without thinking about it, David got up and retrieved the ball, gave it a few bounces, and walked it over to the blue Honda. He liked the feel of the ball as it reminded him of spending hours playing basketball in any available gym in the winter or on an outdoor court in the summer when he was growing up in a city north of Boston called Lynn.

By the time David reached the car, the man in sweats had come back out. "You don't look like you're dressed to play, so I'm guessing you are bringing my runaway ball back? I appreciate it." He reached out his hand. "My name is Tom."

David held out the ball with his left while firmly shaking Tom's hand with his right. "Good to meet you. I'm David or DJ. I saw you here last week."

Tom smiled. "I normally come on Wednesdays and Thursdays, so I expect you to be here as well to guard my ball; it seems to want to escape more often than not."

"Do you need any help?"

Tom replied, "That would be great. My usual helper seems to have disappeared today." He put the ball back into the car and lifted a crate of fruit. David removed his Armani jacket, lifted a box of chicken, and followed Tom to the door now being held open by the same short-bearded man. Tom entered and turned his upper body. "Thanks. Sam, this is David or DJ."

Sam patted David's shoulder. "I will call you Mr. David or DJ."

David shook his head and carried his box into a large industrial kitchen, laying it on the metal island. Through the kitchen wall opening, he could see people setting up the serving stations and someone wet-mopping the floors around the tables with upside-down chairs on top. There was a sign above the opening that read: Whatever you did for one of the least of these, you did for me.

Tom was already back out to the car, and David quickly followed him, grabbing the next box. "That's quite an operation in there."

"Sam's done a great job putting a team together that gets what it's about. Can you grab the box with the meats to get them in the fridge?"

"Sure." By the time they had cleared out all the boxes and crates from the car and filled the kitchen, David was surprised by how much food had fit into Tom's old Honda. "It looks like enough food to feed an army."

Tom frowned. "Unfortunately, we need it."

As they walked outside, Sam reached his hand out. "Thank you, Mr. David or DJ. Many hands make light work, and it's much appreciated since Ari didn't show up this morning." Tom and David were left outside after Sam closed the door.

Tom reached into the back of the Honda to grab the basketball with one hand and turned to David. "David, thanks for helping out on the spur of the moment. I'm sure it wasn't part of your plans on your way to work. I really appreciate it."

David noticed something different in Tom's eyes and demeanor. He couldn't put his finger on it, but it intrigued him.

Tom flipped the ball up and down. "Do you play?"

"I love the game, but as you said, I am on my way to work right now."

"I just thought I would take advantage of playing you in those dress shoes. I usually try to play down at the Back Bay Fens courts around four thirty on Wednesdays if you're interested. I'd be curious to see what you've got."

David was not one to ignore a challenge and hadn't run into anyone for a while who talked to him with such initial ease. "It was my pleasure to help out. Maybe I'll surprise you someday."

Tom got back into the car and rolled down his window. "I think you could beat me—maybe one out of ten games," smiled and drove down the road past the working sewer crew until he was out of sight.

David shook his head and walked back to his cold cappuccino, left a ten-dollar bill on the table, and headed to work on an empty stomach.

The unexpected morning side trip had assured that Izzie beat David into the office again. She stared down at the papers she was working on. "Late night, Mr. Kelly?"

"As a matter of fact, it was another early night."

He poked his head back out of his office. "Would you mind getting me a coffee and something to eat from your secret source?"

She nodded and returned with coffee, fruit, a scone, and yogurt, which she placed on David's desk, along with a printout of his schedule for the day. David already knew the most important agenda item was a three to five o'clock meeting in Cambridge with a large, potential Bio-gen customer. He thrived on staying busy and being the main driver of decision-making during his day. He knew his instincts were good, and it felt good to be highly regarded and the center of attention in an area he could control and wasn't personal.

At two o'clock, he had a driver take him back to his house to pick up his car to drive to the meeting and then to dinner with the sales team and prospective customer in Cambridge. On his way across the bridge, his phone rang.

Izzie prattled into his ear. "—and he apologizes for needing to postpone until next week."

As he shoved the phone back into his suit pocket, he decided that since he was already this far across town, he'd work from home the rest of the day to keep Trooper company.

Changing into more casual clothes, he thought about Tom's invitation. Or was it a challenge? He looked at the clock. Three-thirty.

Why not? His meeting was canceled, and he needed a breather. Besides, he was curious about this guy. He changed into shorts, basketball sneakers and the faded blue tee-shirt he liked to wear when he played and headed out the door to the Back Bay Fens courts.

Chapter 6

The Back Bay Fens Park was part of the greenway "Emerald Necklace" and was less than a ten-minute run for David from his house. He was there a little early and noticed a three-on-three game being played on one court and a few people shooting around at the end of the other court. He started his routine of shooting by beginning with close layups and moving out until he was hitting three-pointers with consistent swishes. It always felt good when the ball went through the chain nets as opposed to the clang of a brick shot off the front of the rim. As he pulled up for a jump shot at the top of the key, another ball from behind him swished right through the net, making him miss. He heard a familiar voice from behind say, "Sorry about that. I didn't mean to interrupt your shooting rhythm, but I am glad you dropped by, David."

As David's ball bounced and rolled off to the side, he turned to see Tom standing in shorts, a basketball tee-shirt with the number thirteen and the name of the team sponsor J.C. and Co. printed on it, and the Pony basketball sneakers David had seen him wearing that morning.

David responded, "This morning, I think you said you could beat me nine out of ten games, and I wanted to come by to actually see that. Let's get those Ponys in gear and see what they can do."

Tom laughed. "Well, I did hit my shot to take the ball out first, but, since you seem a bit rusty, why don't you shoot first." He picked up his leather ball and handed it to David. "Game to eleven by two?"

"Okay," said David as he promptly pulled up for a jump shot and put it right through the net.

Tom retrieved the ball and handed it to David again. "You will need ten more of those, Hondo."

David laughed at the "Hondo" reference to his favorite Celtics player John Havlicek, then started up with a similar move, faked the shot and drove hard to his right for a layup, but Tom had spun around and blocked the shot before he could reach the basket and it bounced off David's leg.

David was impressed. He handed the ball to Tom at the top of the key. "Nice block, Bill," he said, referring to all-time great Bill Russell.

"It was at that!" He drove immediately to his left and elevated to lay the ball in the basket off the backboard. He also hit his next three shots. Tom seemed just as strong going to either side and was a great shot. David was able to steal the ball off Tom's dribble and bring it back out to the top of the key, making a quick burst to his left and under the basket to score on a reverse layup. Tom was beaten but still up in the game by a four to two score.

They both knew this would be a battle even as Tom extended his lead to a commanding ten to five before losing the ball off his foot. Most players did not have the killer instinct to finish a game, but David realized this was not an issue for Tom. Tom got the ball and backed David in close enough to the basket to shoot a favorite turnaround jump shot for the game winner, but just as he did, David was up in the air with Tom and tipped the ball out of bounds. Tom was taken by David's effort and determination to play the game to the end. Tom finally won the game, by only two points, on a generous bounce off the rim after a nice bank shot.

They were both breathing deeply and dripping with the sweat of a good game.

While trying to catch his breath, Tom said, "If the other nine games are going to be like that, this is going to be a long night!" They played four more games with Tom winning three out of the five total games. All the games were close and the last one went to a back and forth with a twenty-eight to twenty-seven score before Tom won by two points. More players showed up to play full court five-on-five games. They had been watching the battle of the last two games David and Tom played and were enjoying the competitive nature of the games and their talent.

One black player, with a black hat on backward, yelled out, "Hey, Tom. I think you have your hands full with this hustler. I can recognize one from a mile away. How much did he take you for tonight?"

David retorted, "If I'm a hustler, why am I buying him the beer tonight?"

The player shot at the basket. "You old guys are welcome to play full if you're interested and don't need your wheelchairs," he laughed in a friendly way.

Tom said, "We'll be back next week with our canes to whoop those butts of yours before those shorts drop to the ground. How do you keep those things up while you're playing, anyway?"

The player grinned while he kept shooting. "My shots are the only thing that's gonna drop tonight!"

Tom and David picked up their gear as they walked off the court and onto the surrounding grass.

Tom wiped his forehead. "That was some good basketball. I enjoyed playing with you. Are you interested in paying off the winner down the street?"

David was not going to avoid buying a beer for the winner, and he wasn't going to let Tom off the hook when he planned on beating him next time. As they walked, they were so absorbed in talking that David hadn't noticed the street they were on until they got closer to the bright lights over Fenway Park. The Red Sox were playing the Yankees tonight and needed to get on a roll if they were going to catch them. They had lost last night to the Yankees by a score of six to zero and hope was fading.

David said, "You'll never get tickets for this game. Let me call up to the IMS company box for—" Before he could finish, Tom was chatting with the guy at the ticket window, and David saw a hand slide two tickets to Tom under the window bars. David shrugged with curiosity as he walked into the stadium with Tom to two grandstand seats. David hadn't sat in the grandstands since he moved up at IMS Corp and started sitting in the corporate box to entertain important customers. They sat down in the best place to be in Boston on a summer night—Fenway. Pedro was warming up and had his game face on. David climbed the stairs to the back and bought two beers and two franks, then brought them back to their seats, handing Tom his championship prize.

Tom smiled broadly. "I cannot accept all the credit alone for this incredible win tonight. I have to give a lot of the credit to you, David, for helping me to win."

David chuckled and took a sip of beer from his thin plastic cup and a bite of his Fenway Frank. "Who do you know to get last minute tickets to a Yankees game?"

With half of his hot dog in his mouth and mustard on the corner of his lip, Tom smiled. "I have connections with someone very high up. I hope Petey has a good outing tonight. He pitched a great game against New York in May. I think he had at least ten strikeouts in that win when we were in first."

David nodded in agreement. The Sox were now down by eight games with their all too common drop off in late August despite a full house of almost thirty-four thousand fans.

As New York's second baseman, Soriano, led off, David observed, "If we can keep Soriano off the bases, we may have a chance." Just then Soriano hit the ball to third and on an error reached second base. Jeter bunted to move him over and Giambi grounded into a double play scoring Soriano to put the Yanks up by one run.

Tom rolled his eyes at David and feigned a smile. "What were you saying again?"

As a pitchers' duel was shaping up, they sat and enjoyed the summer evening, and talked about the baseball season, about basketball, about nothing in particular. David felt like a kid who had anxiously moved into a new neighborhood and then found a great new friend living next door. There was an ease to the conversation. At one point, David said, "You know, I don't even know your last name."

"Hey, I thought you were just superficially interested in my dashing good looks, my jump shot, and free Sox tickets. I didn't know you cared."

David laughed. "So?"

"It's Fitzpatrick, Mr. Kelly." David was more than puzzled because he hadn't mentioned his last name to Tom. David raised his eyebrows until Tom fessed up. "Well, I always check out people thoroughly before I play basketball for a beer. You never know what kind will just drop their breakfast to help out at a food pantry and then meet a complete stranger in the park."

"Come on. You are not getting off that easily. How did you know my name?"

Tom confessed. "Okay. I wasn't sure. When we were talking at the pantry, there was something about you that looked a little familiar. Then, when you were down nine to two—"

"You don't have to rub it in."

"—and you fought as hard as you did, that and the release of your jump shot reminded me of someone I watched play in high school. Also, when we were getting tickets, and you mentioned IMS Corp company seats, I was pretty sure who you were and thought I'd take a chance."

"Nothing you just said answered my question."

Tom laughed. "Okay. I played basketball for Hyde Park High, and in my junior year, we were in the State Tourney playoffs with a tough team. Unfortunately, we lost in a double overtime game to Chelsea, but I stayed to watch the other division games in the Garden. There was this small forward playing for the Lynn English Bulldogs. Lynn was down by twenty-eight points in the second half, but this player pushed his teammates to stay with it. He must have scored twenty-five points alone in the second half, diving after balls, and playing great defense against a much taller player. This player had a certain move to create separation and a quick release that was hard to defend. They lost their game by one point, but that desire to win and never give up attitude stuck with me."

"That would be pretty impressive if you could recall my name from a game played twenty-one years ago."

"Actually, when you mentioned the company you worked for, it clicked for me. I tried being a sales rep a few years out of college for a competitor of IMS Corp. They were fast growing and an aggressive nuisance in the market, and we had to figure out how to best beat the IMS sales teams at strategic customers. Everyone was aware of this hot-shot young sales manager at IMS who was making that task incredibly difficult. That guy was David Kelly, and when I first saw you this morning bouncing my ball in your three-thousand-dollar suit, I thought, only a very successful sales guy dresses that well, and there was something about all those puzzle pieces that made me think this may be that same guy. I took a chance, and now I would say you owe me another beer if I'm right."

Without saying a word, David stood up and climbed the stairs to get two more watered-down Fenway beers as the fourth inning started.

When he returned, Tom said, "Thank you, Mr. Kelly. Now let me ask you a question. What made a successful executive like you show up for one-on-one basketball with a perfect stranger?"

David paused for a second. "As my mother used to say, 'I haven't the foggiest.'" They both chuckled and returned to watching and critiquing the game. The Sox bats were flat, making the Yankees pitcher, Mussina, look stronger than he was. The Yankees scored four runs in the seventh and another two in the eighth to cruise to an embarrassing seven to nothing win over the hapless Sox.

David and Tom turned to each other at the same time and said in unison, "Hey, maybe next year," and shook their heads with a smile.

They filed out of the park with the remaining fans, holding their basketballs under an arm as they talked about the game. Back outside on Jersey street, Tom asked, "Which way is home for you?"

David pointed northeast. "Probably Brookline Ave to Beacon would be the fastest."

"Can you make it home without a proper escort, young lady? I have an early morning and am heading this-a-way."

"Yeah, me too. Despite losing in two sports tonight, I had fun. Maybe again sometime?"

Tom was already walking east on Van Ness Street with his back to David and his basketball spinning on his index finger like he was a Harlem Globetrotter. "Next Wednesday," he hollered, disappearing into the dark.

David shook his head, smiled and noticed that he felt happy in a very odd way. Normally after losing to someone, especially someone he recently met, he would've been obsessing about how to win the next time, and after a Sox loss to the Yankees, he would've been let down, but tonight he was neither focused on how to win nor feeling disappointed. He just enjoyed his evening and appreciated something about it he couldn't describe during his short walk home. After a quick shower and laying out his clothes for the morning, he was in bed and slept more soundly than he had for quite some time.

Chapter 7

That next morning, David was still feeling up from the basketball game and decided to play a joke on Izzy when he arrived before she did. He closed his office door to make her think she had beaten him in again. He waited until he heard her stirring around her desk, then opened his door and smirked at the expression on her face. She turned and walked off, returning ten minutes later, coffee and schedule in hand. "Mr. Kelly, did your mama ever tell you that you were—never mind. Here."

David took a sip of the hot coffee. "Thank you, Izzie. Let me know when that meeting in Cambridge is rescheduled." He thought about how much he liked and respected Izzie. As much as he had faced struggles in his own life, he could not imagine being a refugee from Haiti, a single mother of three living in Dorchester, and keeping it all together. He was glad he could help her with stock bonuses and once surprised her younger girls with a piano and lessons.

As Izzie closed the door slowly behind her, a call came in on his direct line. Jill. He hadn't called Jillian at all yesterday.

"I didn't hear a word from you all day after Tuesday night. What, did you meet someone else?"

He could hear the pout in her voice. "As a matter of fact, I did—" Then he heard a loud click on the other end of the line.

He called her back several times in a row. After the third attempt, he glanced at the time and had to get on with his day. He attended his meetings but continued to call her number during the day. He knew he hadn't done a single thing to undermine her trust and wasn't sure what she was feeling. Jillian had talked to David about the lack of affection from her father, whose constant negative and sometimes abusive critique eroded her feelings of self-worth. While they had both lifted themselves up from poor and emotionally difficult childhoods, he thought they both still had sensitive reactions to questions of trust.

Finally, he sent her a text message. *As far as I know, he was a manly kind of man.*

She texted back, *Sorry! Can I take you out tomorrow night? :) I have class tonight.*

David responded a few minutes later, *Nobody I'd rather be with than my girl Friday. :)*

David had meetings until late and ended up going out to a local pub for beers and dinner with several of his associates. Kevin seemed to be his normal self again. They talked about the major deals they were working to close the quarter and tried to top each other's stories about odd customer personalities, summer vacations, women they met on business trips, and how much money it would take to quit this great gig they had going. They had all risen in the company and enjoyed a high level of material wealth, prestige, and respect at work and with their "friends." They would never have to worry again about the basic necessities their parents had struggled with every day. The group laughed, sang, argued, and ragged on each other mercilessly. A few times, Kevin laughed loud enough to carry to the four corners of the pub, but then occasionally looked across the table at David with eyes that seemed somehow empty and distant.

As midnight approached, David wondered for the first time if any of them were really happy. They were now either divorced or periodically cheating on their wives and rarely seemed satisfied despite all that had come their way. Knowing they would be there until the doors shut, he picked up the tab and another round for the rest of the crew before heading out alone to the dark and practically empty street.

Back home, he was in bed, but sleep took longer than usual, and it reminded him of the restless nights he had when he was eight, nine, and ten years old.

The next day passed quickly. He finished up at six o'clock so he could meet Jillian at Columbus Park. Despite the great Italian restaurants and bakeries that dotted the streets of the North End of Boston, David didn't normally patronize them. His memories of living there and then abruptly leaving were not ones he cared to think about, so he avoided going back as much as possible. As David's thoughts roamed, Jillian came up silently behind him and placed both hands over his eyes saying in as deep a voice as she could muster, "If you want to come out of this alive, just turn around and put your hands—"

David interrupted, "—around your waist and give you a kiss?"

Jillian smiled. "Something like that." David held her tight and gave her a long kiss. "Okay, exactly like that. I feel like I haven't seen you for a month." They sat for a few minutes watching the docked boats and the sun lowering in the sky over the harbor while they talked about sailing on the Charles.

Jillian jumped up. "You aren't the only one on this team that can come up with date ideas, you know." Taking both of his hands, she pulled him up from the bench and walked away from the North End. Relieved, he took her hand and her lead.

They walked along Atlantic Avenue and came to Rowe's Wharf, where the Boston Harbor Hotel, with its magnificent multi-storied archway that opened onto the harbor. Jillian had reserved a table on the patio with a view of the harbor stage that held a large movie screen. The hotel sponsored free movies on Friday nights in the summer, and the restaurant made for a great spot to sit with a drink or have dinner while watching. The maître d' showed them to their table and held the chair for her as David sat with an impressed look on his face. Jillian inquired, "So, is this okay?"

David took her hand and said, "Okay? It's perfect. The table is perfect. The evening weather is, I assume, as ordered and the idea is wonderful. Thanks for asking me out!"

Jillian smiled and reached in to give him a kiss just as the waiter arrived at the table to ask if they would like anything to drink before ordering dinner.

Their drinks came, and they chatted about their day. Jillian questioned, "So. Who was your date on Wednesday?"

"What date? Oh, you mean who was the 'other man' I met?"

Jillian's eyes widened. "Was there more than one?"

Shaking his head, "No. No. It was really nothing. I was having breakfast at—"

"At the Eastside?"

"No. They had to close for a few weeks, so I tried a different place and noticed a man who drove up to what I thought was a vacant building. He started unloading crates and boxes of food to take in."

Jillian raised her eyebrows. "And?"

"And nothing, really. He drove off when he was done."

"That was it? That's why you couldn't call me that night?"

David shook his head. "No. That was the week before. The next Wednesday, I ended up going back to that same cafe for breakfast and this man, Tom—"

Jillian interrupted, "How did you know his name was Tom?"

David explained the course of events in detail before finally answering her question. "Then he invited me to come down to play basketball at the Back Bay Fens courts that afternoon."

"And you did?"

"Yeah. For some reason, that afternoon, I was pulled to go. There was something different about him. His ease and confidence intrigued me. We had a great set of games and the loser, yours truly, had to pay up. So, he took me to the Sox-Yankees game."

Jillian said, "Wait a minute. You had to pay up by letting him take you to the game?"

"Hey, I bought the beer and hot dogs! We just talked like we had known each other for years, and by the time the Sox had officially buried the season and I got home, it was pretty late. I'm sorry for not sending you a note or calling. There was just something—I don't think he is a rich guy by a long shot but—I don't know. I really can't put my finger on it."

When dinner came, and the sunset had finished painting the sky with shades of pink and purple that fascinated Jillian, the movie played. It was Jimmy Stewart and Jean Arthur in *You Can't Take It with You*, a fun, wacky kind of comedy classic in black and white. Jillian's eyes lit up as she watched it. The irony was not lost on David—enjoying the little things in life versus the pursuit of money, status, power, and prestige.

"That's it!" David blurted out, then quickly lowered his head as Jillian looked at him to see what happened.

"That's what? Are you okay?"

"Yeah. Yeah. Sorry. It just hit me what it is about Tom that's different."

"Well, what is it?"

He wrinkled his brow. "I'm not sure, but in the movie, Grandpa Vanderhof reminds me a little of Tom."

"Tom reminds you of a grandfather?"

David laughed. "No. What do you notice about Grandpa Vanderhof's character?"

"I like him. He seems to get it. He puts his granddaughter and daughter ahead of anything else. He seems free."

David said, again more loudly than he intended, "That's it! I think that's what hit me when I was talking with Tom. He seemed free from all the things that the rest of us have hanging around our necks like a heavy horse collar. He seemed present and at peace with himself and made me feel as if I were the only thing on his mind when he was with me." He waved a hand at the screen. "Vanderhof didn't seem to have any of the things that the guys I know spend their whole lives building, but he seemed happier."

"It's only a movie."

"I know. I know. It was just interesting knowing there was something I couldn't describe and then seeing something like it in action—well, in the movie."

With the movie over, they walked hand-in-hand around the harbor. It was getting late, and instead of walking back to his car, he called a number and within a few minutes a limo pulled up to the curb where they were standing. David held open the door and Jillian turned as she stepped in. "Hey, Mister. You know this is supposed to be my date night plan. No fair trying to top me on the same night."

David slid in beside her then turned to Jillian. "I couldn't think of a nicer evening or a more fun way to spend it. A-plus for you all the way. I loved every second."

She gave him a kiss and put her head on his shoulder for the ride home. He didn't ask to come in or stay. He told her how beautiful her eyes were and kissed her. He asked if she might be up for driving down to the Cape in the morning since the weather looked promising.

She nodded. "I'll be packed tonight," she said and headed toward the door of her apartment. He waited until she had gone into her apartment and turned on the lights before he headed home.

David was back early the next morning to pick up Jillian in a red Jeep to spend the weekend at his house in Dennis Port. Jillian loved how beautiful David's Cape-style house was located on the Bass River with lush landscaping and its own dock and boat. The weekend was fun spending time boating, swimming, playing golf, hiking the dunes, and playing games at night. Along the way, David had evaded questions from Jillian about his past, and part of him was almost relieved that they left early on Labor Day Monday for him to catch an evening flight for a Tuesday morning meeting in Chicago.

Chapter 8

Three days later, after a fruitful business trip followed by a day of in-house meetings, David woke up conflicted about following his rigid routine. The day moved quickly from meeting to meeting. There was a follow-up call with the Chicago team and the customer agreed to move forward with a formal proposal, a huge win for the company. Kevin Walsh dropped by and David glanced up at the clock that read ten minutes to four. "What can I do for you, Walshy?"

Kevin sat back on one of David's couches. "Nothing in particular. I had a break in my schedule and wanted to see how you were doing. You know what today is, don't you?"

"It's Wednesday as far as I know. If Oakland wins tonight, it would be a record twenty games in a row? The winner of *American Idol* is announced tonight. I give up, what day is it?"

Kevin stared at David as if he were looking through him. "It's September fourth. It's one week before the anniversary of September 11. I keep thinkin' about it and can't get it out of my mind. It keeps me up at night. Doesn't it keep you up at night?"

David knew this would be a long conversation he didn't want to start now. It was almost four. "Kev, how about if we go out tomorrow night, just you and I, and have a beer? This sounds like its weighing heavy on you."

"I'd appreciate that," Kevin replied as he pushed himself to stand. "Let's catch up tomorrow."

After a quick change into his basketball shorts, tee-shirt, and shoes, he reached the street and hurried toward the Back Bay Fens not knowing if Tom would even be there. He stretched then started his shouting routine while keeping an eye out for anyone sneaking up on him. Just as David thought his opponent wouldn't show, he saw Tom walking across the field toward the basketball courts. "Well, well, well. How many middle-aged businessmen have time to play basketball on a Wednesday afternoon? Good to see you again, David. Did you come by to watch me shoot or did you want to buy me another beer?"

David smiled, took a shot well beyond the three-point arc and was dead on. "Let me know when you're ready."

Tom took his shot from the same spot and swished it. "Ready."

David bounced the ball to Tom. "Your ball."

The game went back and forth. David was using several of the moves he worked on earlier and hit some tough shots to take a big lead that led to winning the first game. The second game was tight, but Tom won on the last shot. David kept taking mental notes of Tom's strengths and tendencies but there was always something new he hadn't seen before. Any action close to the basket was physical and aggressive as neither wanted to give up on any play or loose ball. They traded wins in the next two games and started the tie-breaker fifth game again. David was determined to win this game, despite an early deficit. Finally, Tom had the ball with a one-point lead. He drove hard toward the basket and went straight up against David's tough defensive attempt to block the shot, but it went through and Tom was the winner again.

There was unexpected applause from a bunch of guys who had been watching the contest with interest. Both Tom and David bowed, breathing deeply as the sweat dripped down off their brows.

Tom put his hand on David's shoulder. "Good game, David."

"And better game, Tom. I suppose you're thirsty."

As they walked off the court, a player watching said, "Hey, Trev. I thought these guys said they would come back this week and whup your butt. Didn't they?"

Trevon was holding his worn basketball and nodding his head. "I do recall something like that."

David was exhausted and a little disappointed when Tom jumped in. "I think it was exactly like that."

Trevon smiled, knowing he and any other player he picked would be half the age of these two tired old men. "So what ya willing to play for?"

Tom pointed to Trevon's ball. "One game to eleven, winner takes the other's ball and is King of the Fens."

Trevon called out to the best player, Big Russ. Big Russ was a half-foot taller than David, young, and agile.

Trevon stood at the top of the key with Tom's basketball in hand. He passed it to David with force, saying with a confident smile, "When you're ready."

Tom was leaning on Big Russ to make sure he did not get too close to the basket for an easy pass and dunk. Tom was ready to play, and the competitive juices energized David. He bounced the ball to Trevon, who shot past him like a lightning bolt and scooped a pass to Russ as Tom slid across to stop Trevon from getting an easy layup. Big Russ caught the floating pass and dunked the ball with ease and power through the metal net. Everyone watching made a loud cheer, and one person yelled out, "Ouch. New basketball for Trev!"

David checked the ball again to Trevon, who without hesitation, hoisted a jump shot and sank it. Tom whispered something in David's ear. David overplayed to Trevon's right, forcing Trevon to go to his weaker left side while trying to use Big Russ as a screen to take an easy shot. David rolled right behind Big Russ, and Tom shot out and stole the ball from Trevon. Tom cleared the ball and lobbed it to David under the basket for a quick layup just under Big Russ's block attempt.

After several exchanges, the score was tied nine to nine, and Tom seemed to notice the return of the frustration on Trevon's face and the ragging he was taking from the sidelines. This was important to Trevon in ways that Tom could see in his silent and focused determination not to let David score on him. David drove right and made a smooth pass back to Tom at the top of the key, but it went through Tom's open hands. Trevon quickly caught up to the loose ball and drove to the basket for a difficult layup that missed, but Big Russ had rebounded and dunked it in with two hands. Trevon coolly took the ball from David and nailed a quick jump shot without hesitation—to the cheers of the bystanders. Tom shook Trevon's hand and presented him with his favorite leather ball. Trevon looked at Tom with respect but didn't ask the question that was obviously on his mind as he then jumped up and down. "Big Russ, who are the Kings of the Fens? We are!"

Exhausted, David and Tom picked up their things and headed off the court. David said, "I still owe you a beer, even if you did miss that pass. Are you still thirsty, Mr. Fitzpatrick?"

"I am, indeed, Mr. Kelly. Very thirsty. I know a good pub a few streets over that should work."

As they walked out of the park, it struck David that his office overlooked the Back Bay Fens basketball courts. His eye had always skipped past the park to look over at Fenway, but there was the Pru Tower staring down at him from several blocks away. They stopped in front of a pub with the name Dempsey's over the green door. There were windows on each side of the door and the inside looked like an inviting pub. It didn't look like the many bars that David had passed on his walk home as a teenager from his summer job at General Electric. Those narrow bars were dark and without cheer as men came to drink until they drowned their worries and disappointments in the least expensive whiskey or rum available. While the doors might've been open for a curious peak, there was nothing David saw that ever made him want to enter and quietly sit for hours in one of these darkened sedation rooms.

Dempsey's had a different feel. The old wooden booths looked like they had hosted many celebrations and friendly debates. The owner stood behind the bar with a towel draped over his left shoulder and a smile on his face as he conversed with the three men sitting with half full Guinness drafts in front of them. Dempsey nodded to Tom as he entered, and Tom pointed to an empty booth around the corner from the door. As they settled their tired bodies into their respective sides of the booth, Dempsey came over. "Hello, Tom."

Tom responded with a bit of an Irish brogue, "Ah, it's Himself. Meet my good friend, David Kelly. He will be buyin' tonight."

Dempsey smiled. "Good to meet you, David Kelly. Your man here is a hard one to beat and has rarely had to spend a penny in this establishment over the years. So, what will you have?"

David said, "I know. I will have a half-and-half and Mr. Fitzpatrick can have whatever he pleases tonight."

Tom smiled. "Make that two, two for me that is."

David let the flavor of his first sip settle on his taste buds. "I could've sworn I had you tonight."

Tom enjoyed a long sip of his beer. "Now, I couldn't let that happen. If I did, you'd have no reason to come back next week since you'd have beaten me. You're too busy a man to be taking off to play games every Wednesday afternoon without incentive."

David let the cold beer slide down his throat, nodded and smiled. "Next time you are buying, and I'll be very thirsty indeed."

Tom replied, "Do you mean I should plan on bringing money next week?" He pulled his pockets inside out to show that he hadn't thought he needed to bring any tonight.

David smirked. "You don't have a basketball either since that pass slipped through your hands. We had that game. What was up with missing that pass? It almost looked like you missed it on purpose."

Tom shrugged. "Must've just been a bad pass."

"That pass was on the money, and from what I've seen, you don't miss good passes."

David liked the warm feeling and friendly atmosphere of the pub and he felt at home. There were posters on the wall about the Irish Sessions music on Thursday nights and Sunday afternoons, and pictures of places Dempsey had visited and sports teams he sponsored. David was in no rush to go anywhere as he and Tom talked and the Red Sox at the Yankees game played on the small TV over the bar. A loss tonight would pretty much seal the Sox's fate for another season. Of course, it had only been eighty-five years since the Red Sox had last won a World Series.

David looked off into space after turning away from the game. Tom smiled. "You are thinking about it, aren't you?"

David replied, "Thinking about what?"

"The game and names that won't be mentioned. Don't tell me you don't think about it every time we get to this time of the season and we have to wait through another long winter with hope for next year."

"How the heck did you know that?"

"I know the look."

David wondered what else he could tell about him without a word.

David said, "Okay, how about your favorite sports moments?"

Tom replied, "All right, I will give you one, then you give me one and we will see which one was the best. We are both about the same age, so the '67 Sox would be too early."

"I bet if Tony C hadn't been beaned and out for the season, they would've won for sure. You're still up."

"How about the Celtics beating the Suns in a finals triple overtime game?"

"When Havlicek hit that leaning jumper at the end of the second overtime, I was sure he won by one point and the game was over, but Richie Powers put one second back on the clock and was attacked by a fan."

Tom laughed, "Great memory."

"I will have to say the 1970 Bruins when Bobby Orr hit that winning shot against the St. Louis Blues. Bobby, Espo, Cheevers, Bucyk, Hodge, Smith, Cashman, and Stanfield."

"Game 6, 1975 World Series game in Fenway against the Cincinnati Reds. They were on the brink of losing in game six until Bernie Carbo hit the tying home run in the eighth, and then Fisk hits the walk-off home run over the Monster and just to the right of the foul pole."

David smiled. "Hard to argue. I loved watching Luis Tiant win Game Four in that series after throwing 173 pitches. Nobody does that anymore. I think you're in the lead again. How about either the 1986 Celtics, with Bird for a Celtics' championship, or wait, the 2002 first Patriots' Super Bowl win with Brady against the Rams that no one expected?"

Tom jumped in, "Hey, wait a minute, you can't just start throwing out multiple nominations in one turn," and then laughed. "We've been blessed with some great moments in Boston." They both turned to the Sox game on the TV and saw they were losing by a 3-1 score and said in unison, "And some not so great moments."

They talked more about their game as they drained their beers, then moved out of their comfortable seats to pay the bill.

David reached for his wallet and Dempsey put out his hand. "This is your first time in my home. No charge—" Then, after a hesitation, he continued, "—for your beers, but you still owe me for his." Everyone laughed. On their way out the door, they said goodbye to the remaining guys still watching the game.

Dempsey said, "Hey, you forgot something."

David and Tom turned to see what they were missing, and Dempsey said, "1980 Olympic Hockey team with Craig, Silk, O'Callahan, and Eruzone from Boston, Hagler-Hearns match in '85, and Marciano-Jersey Joe Walcott in '52."

Tom responded, "Demps, you aren't even old enough to remember 1952." He laughed and followed David out to the quiet sidewalk in front of the pub. The evening had cooled and there was a light sprinkle. Tom shook David's hand and patted him on the back. "I'm really glad you came by tonight, and no, not just for the free beers. I enjoy your company and your game. I may need you to help me get my ball back."

"Only if you hold onto my pass next time. Do you need a ride home?"

"No, no, no. Thanks, but I don't have far to go. You take care getting home yourself."

He headed north while David headed east to retrieve his car from the Pru parking lot.

The rain had picked up a little more and David was dripping on the floor when he stepped into his front foyer to be greeted by Trooper. David put his free hand on Trooper's frame, patting his fur. "Good job. Hey, we had a good evening tonight, even though we were not victorious against the great Tom." He showered, put his clothes out for work, and got ready for bed. He felt good and slept soundly, forgetting again to call or text Jillian good night.

Chapter 9

David took advantage of a rest day from his usual running routine and took Trooper for a morning walk before heading into the office.

"Good morning, Mr. Kelly. I hope you had a good afternoon and evening yesterday?"

"I did. Thanks for asking and how about yourself?"

"If you like cooking, cleaning, helping with homework, topped off with the best hugs ever from three darlings, then I had a great evening too."

David smiled and then paused before entering his office. "Izzie, did you ever hear of My Brother's Table?"

"Sure, Mr. Kelly. It's the food kitchen a few blocks away from here. Why do you ask?"

"Oh, no reason." He left Izzie looking confused and curious.

A few hours into the day, Sean Quigley poked his head into David's office. "Do you have a second, DJ?"

"Sure, Quigs. Come in. How've you been doing?"

"I was doing fine until I found out information about Jack Carusso last night. You know we lost two of our largest accounts, Diamond Tech and Brasco, earlier this quarter and now Fastler is showing signs of being shaky?"

"What does that have to do with Jack?"

"Both accounts went to the same competitor, InfoEdge. When I talked to execs at those accounts, it seemed like InfoEdge had too much information about us and knew just where to hit us to flip the account. Now some contacts at Fastler are bringing up the same issues. Well, last night, I found out that Jack has been talking with the management team at InfoEdge and working to steal those accounts before he moves over to them. I can't believe it. With all the investment and trust we put in him, he would turn on us like this."

David had no patience for disloyalty. Trust was not something David easily granted without building it over time. Within minutes David had given instructions to have Jack's systems and badge access shut down and his termination papers completed with his two-year non-compete clause highlighted. Thirty minutes later, Jack Carusso stood still on the sidewalk in his custom-tailored suit, expensive shoes, and gold jewelry. His large ego, dishonest methods, and greediness had driven a sense of invincibility for Jack, but it was the broken trust that ended his career at IMS for David.

Around six thirty, Kevin Walsh poked his head into David's office. "Are you still up for getting together after work for a beer?"

Still bothered by the situation with Jack and buried with work, David almost forgot about meeting with Kevin after work. "Sure. Sure. How about the Grille?" Kevin enjoyed going to the Capital Grille restaurant for its quality aged steaks, great drinks, and the atmosphere of an old men's smoking lounge with leather chairs, rich wood-paneled walls, and dimly lit tables and booths.

Both David and Kevin had been to the Grille many times with important customers, company functions, or just for drinks and dinner. The maitre d' at the desk beamed with immediate recognition. "Mr. Kelly. Mr. Walsh. How are you this evening? Would you like a table or prefer the lounge tonight?"

David offered, "Walshy, do you have time for dinner?"

Kevin seemed pleased. "I think I could be talked into it."

The restaurant was busy for a Thursday night, but the staff always held a few tables for valued customers. They ordered drinks and told the waiter they wanted time before putting in their dinner order. When the drinks came, Kevin raised his whiskey straight up to David's bourbon on the rocks. "Here's to us, good health and better days ahead."

David tapped his glass to Kevin's. "To us."

Kevin finished half of his drink in one swig. "I'm glad you had time to get together. I know I sounded a bit on the edge about things last time. I've been thinkin' a lot lately and have no outlet outside my own head. And we both know that is not a safe place for thoughts to be for Kevin Walsh."

David gave a slight smile as Kevin continued, "I guess I haven't spent much time, since we started this ride, to stop and think about things. I mean, we work so many hours, travel all the time, busy doing this and that and finding new ways to amuse ourselves. It's like I'm constantly consuming things but always feel empty. You'd think if I drink, I wouldn't feel thirstier or when I buy a new toy, I wouldn't feel like I instantly need to look for something else. The more money I make, the more I think I want to have, and the more women I sleep with, the lonelier I am. Am I talking crazy to you or do you know what I'm talkin' about?"

David took a sip to buy a few seconds before responding. He wasn't feeling any of what Kevin was describing. While he couldn't say he was satisfied, he didn't feel empty or sad. He was energized being busy with work. He enjoyed the things he had, his homes, his business, his cars, the respect and esteem he had within the company, his freedom to date women he desired, and generally doing whatever he wanted. It hit David that he was so busy, he never had time to question if he was truly happy or not.

He made eye contact with Kevin. "Walshy, I don't have the same feelings you're experiencing. Are you sure it's not just the stress of thinking too much about 9-11? Do you need some time off after the quarter to relax and enjoy life again?"

Kevin stared down into his glass at the shades of reddish gold liquor. "I don't think that'll help, DJ. I'm afraid that if I stop, I might just fall into that dark pit I'm constantly walkin' around the edge of. Look, I don't want to bring you down. I just thought, since we've been doin' and chasin' a lot of the same stuff, you might be having some of the same feelings. You know, I keep havin' this dream where I have all the money in the world and everyone is jealous of me, but I can't spend the money on anything that would make me happy."

David felt sincerely bad for Kevin. "Walshy, I'm not sure what to offer you. I'll have to think on it a bit."

"I was just lookin' for an understanding ear. I appreciate it, DJ. It's kind of funny but sad to think about things at the same time. No matter how incredibly gorgeous a woman I've been able to spend the night with, it's never stayed with me in any meaningful way like an afternoon spent with my five-year-old son fishin' or readin' a book to my three-year-old daughter while she's sittin' on my lap in her PJs after a bath. I don't have that anymore and I don't know what I thought I was gettin' in return. I was happier as a kid drivin' a beat-up car I bought and fixed up for two hundred bucks or just spendin' time with my brothers playin' baseball with a taped-up ball and a bat we made. I know we aren't kids anymore, but I wonder if we were smarter back then when it was all about the people we were with instead of the things we pile up or the people we hang out with because of what they can do for us?"

David whispered with a tone of concern, "Kev, you really have been thinking about this a lot. You're starting to worry me."

"Don't worry too much. I'll be okay, and I appreciate the support. I can tell you one thing I'm not gonna do. I'm not going to fly on any damn plane next Wednesday on 9-11, and I hope you don't either!"

"You can count on me. Now let's get some of those steaks."

They had a good dinner and David was able to get Kevin to laugh a bit, reminiscing about the fun times they had early in their careers at IMS, in and out of work.

Kevin drove David home after dinner. "I would walk you to the door, but I don't kiss on a first date, so you're on your own, sweetie. See you in the morning."

David waved to Kevin as he drove off. He walked up the stairs to see Trooper and took him for an evening stroll. Trooper was, as usual, happy to see him since he could relax from his guard duties and spend time with his owner. Maybe Walshy should get a dog. It might make him feel better. He gave Jillian a quick call to say goodnight and asked her if she was free the following evening. When his head hit the pillow, he wondered what was different about his life than Walshy's.

Chapter 10

Jillian came over Friday night, happy to be with David. He suggested several outings, but Jillian turned them all down in favor of making dinner together and playing a game. They had fun chopping and preparing the salad and the chicken as they enjoyed some Italian wine and assorted cheeses at the kitchen counter before taking everything up to the terrace. They grilled the chicken and sat at the table by patio garden boxes full of flowers and shrubs that provided a private garden setting.

As they sat for dinner, David fed Trooper a few pieces of chicken and asked Jillian if she was glad that the summer semester was over.

"I think I'm glad."

"You think you're glad?"

"Well, yeah. I was looking forward to it, but there's always a letdown after something ends and I don't know what to do."

David said, "I can't imagine you being down. You are always so positive and upbeat."

Jillian paused. "Well, I've been doing well lately, but I'm not always feeling either positive or upbeat. I wouldn't normally share this so early in a relationship, and I hope my sense you won't run away is accurate, but—"

"My feet and heart are going nowhere."

Jillian sighed. "I don't want to put a damper on the evening, but I've been fighting depression most of my life."

"We all get down from time to time."

"It's a little different from just getting down or sad once in a while. Sometimes, it's almost like being in a suit made of lead trying to move through quicksand. Like you don't have the energy or will to get yourself out of it."

David, himself, had experienced trauma and a feeling of hopeless emptiness at all too young an age, but he had put that far behind him, determined to never be controlled by those feelings again. It was hard for him to understand why everyone couldn't do the same and move on, so he didn't press her to explain. "Jill, I want you to always be free to tell me how you feel. I would hope that the two of us being together would make you happy."

"You're so right. With you, I can't help but feel perfectly content and happy. It's something I'm thankful for every day. Now let's eat this finely prepared meal before Trooper does."

The meal, the wine, and the cannoli were a feast for three as they sat and talked under the evening blanket of the moonless summer sky, lit by countless stars. Their earlier conversation seemed forgotten by Jillian as they kissed with the light evening breeze caressing their bodies. David could tell she felt chilly with her sleeveless top and light summer skirt, so they left the dishes and walked down the stairs from the roof into the apartment still kissing.

Neither Jillian nor David woke until the morning sunlight had filled the room. The alarm didn't go off. No music nor routine run. David slept in, and it was something he realized he hadn't done for many years.

Jillian was still nestled next to his body, and he watched her for a few minutes before it hit him that he was supposed to be picking up his daughter Amy in less than two hours.

He slid himself out of bed, leaving Jillian to sleep as he quietly crept into the bathroom to shave, shower, and dress. His shower wasn't a soothing one as he anxiously thought of how to entertain his maturing and increasingly distant daughter. He felt nervous about seeing Kathleen, even after six years of separation. David was used to feeling in charge and at ease, but he was feeling neither, at the moment, as he formulated how to tell Jillian that he'd forgotten about his day with Amy.

He woke up Jillian and apologized for the short notice. She understood, quickly got dressed, and readied to go. David had run out to get coffee and breakfast sandwiches for the drive to Jillian's before heading down the Southeast Expressway towards Hingham where he had once lived for almost ten years with his wife Kathleen.

Hingham was a charming old town on the shore south of Boston. Early in their relationship, David and Kathleen went sailing there with a friend of his. He could see the gleam in her eyes as she first drove through the quaint town with historic homes, comfortable neighborhoods, and access to the ocean that always made her smile. It wasn't hard to tell where she would love to live when they got married in September 1985.

Under David's usually confident and comfortable demeanor, his heart was pounding as he walked up to the entrance of his old residence, a beautiful 1905 Victorian home with a welcoming front porch, a large well-landscaped yard, and an easy walk into town and to the harbor. He'd felt his own uneasy anticipation as he lifted the brass shell knocker on the front door and knocked three times, trying to guess if Kathleen or his son James would open the door to answer. It was Kathleen O'Shea Kelly who opened the door and smiled at him while letting him know with her look he was late again. "Good afternoon, David."

David breathed in, resisting the temptation of getting lost in Kathleen's striking blue sapphire eyes.

She brushed back a shiny lock of shoulder-length dark brown hair, and David paused to recall how he loved caressing her hair at nineteen when its attractive length almost reached her waist. Despite the years that had passed, she was still beautiful in ways that seemed to radiate from deep within her soul. Whether she was wearing a little black dress, ready for an evening out, or no makeup, a tee-shirt, and a pair of jean Capris, David saw the same beautiful woman that attracted him to her many years ago. "How've you been?"

"I'm fine." She turned and hollered toward the upstairs. "Amy. Your dad's here."

A moment later, Amy came down the stairs wearing a pair of black jeans, an attractive top, and ballet-like shoes. Despite the distant and unenthusiastic greeting on her face, she was radiant with a pretty ribbon tied around her long, light-brown hair highlighted by the summer's sun. He hadn't noticed that Amy was becoming a grown woman and a beautiful one at that.

He tried to give Amy a hug, and while she didn't pull back, she didn't reciprocate. "Hey, Ames, I'm looking forward to our date today." He and Kathleen exchanged glances knowing Amy wasn't in a great place in the relationship with either of them right now but less so with her absent father.

As Amy shrugged, David noticed James coming in from the backyard. James was less than a year old when David moved out of the house. He had little sense of a real relationship with his father, but as he tilted his head up and looked so earnestly at David with his large brown eyes, it was painfully clear to see how much he wished for it. James had begun Little League baseball in the spring and was proudly wearing his Tigers team hat and tightly held the baseball in the glove that David had given to him for his seventh birthday. He was on the scrawny side and looked a lot like David had as a child.

David squatted down to eye level with James. "When I come by next week, do you promise to play ball with me?" James cautiously smiled and nodded as his father stood up and put his hand on James's head. David realized Amy was already sitting in the car, so he turned to Kathleen. "I'll have her back before eleven."

"She's been acting out and testing more, but I think she just needs to know we respect that she's growing up and that we care about her. Try to listen to her more. Sometimes people act very much the opposite of what they really want and need." David nodded and patted James on the head as he noticed that James was still looking up at him.

Amy was sitting in the car wearing the earphones from her iPod. He slid into the driver's seat and resisted saying the several sarcastic things that came to mind as he started the car. "I hear you have your learner's permit now. Do you want to drive?"

Amy pulled out one earphone. "As much as I would love to drive your car around town, I think I'll pass until I get the automatic down."

"Just thought I'd offer."

Amy sat silently for the next fifteen minutes of the drive and then snapped, "Why do you bother coming to get me for your obligatory monthly visit? I wasn't important enough for you to stay. There was always something more important than me in your life—and don't give me the usual stuff about your leaving had nothing to do with me, and it was only between you and Mom, so don't blame myself. You left all of us!"

He knew Amy struggled with the separation, but that was six years ago. He wasn't expecting the sudden outburst, and he wasn't sure how best to respond.

Suddenly, he pulled off the expressway exit and drove to Squantum Point Park, which was on the oceanfront in Quincy. The Boston skyline was right across the harbor from this park that once was a naval airfield and shipbuilding company. Today there was a two-mile river walk and dozens of species of wild birds to keep walkers entertained.

He drove the car up to a parking spot with a prime view of the harbor. "Ames, I know this hasn't been easy for you."

"I don't think you have any idea how hard this has been on James, on Mom, or on—" She stopped, closed her eyes, and breathed deeply to hold back her tears. He reached his hand over to touch her shoulder, but she pulled back. David got out of the car and leaned against it to collect himself. As she let out her years of emotions, he remembered feeling the same sense of abandonment, anger, and overall confusion when his own father was suddenly gone.

To avoid the flood of feelings he subconsciously knew were ready to overwhelm him, he took several deep breaths and moved his emotions into a safer compartment. He opened Amy's passenger door and put out his hand as if to ask for a dance. "Let's walk a little."

Amy took his hand, and together they started down the shoreline path in silence.

David let their footsteps calm their pounding hearts for a good five minutes before he spoke. "Amy, I would never want you to believe I don't care deeply about you. I love you and I'm so sorry that things with your mom and I didn't work out. It happens, and it's truly not your fault." They continued to stroll along the path as the fall sun warmed their faces. The sounds of the waves on the shore and the birds calling calmed his nerves.

Amy let the heavy silence build between them for the next quarter mile of the path. With her eyes cast down, she spoke in an emotion-packed whisper. "That doesn't make anything feel better. Even when you left, you'd see James and me for a full weekend every other week and now it's maybe for five to eight hours once a month. I can do the math and that's less than one percent of your time. We even have to wonder if you're going to call that off for something 'more important.'"

David still felt caught off guard and his normal ability to manage a conversation deserted him. "I never knew you felt that way. Most of the time, I get the feeling you wished I hadn't come and couldn't wait to get back home."

Amy looked out at the seagulls landing on the choppy ocean waves. "Maybe it's because I get that same feeling from you too." They walked the rest of the loop without saying much, not realizing how very much alike they were dealing with difficult feelings.

David drove Amy to his apartment, where he knew he could get her out of her shell with Trooper eagerly jumping up to let her hug him and rub his head. No matter how hard she tried not to smile, she couldn't help herself once the door opened and Trooper greeted her with his tail wagging.

"Do you want to take him for a walk? I'm sure he'd love it."

Amy nodded and retrieved his leash from the hall closet and the three of them walked down the Beacon Street brick sidewalks, weaving around the other walkers. The silence between them was less awkward with Trooper being the center of attention but her answers to his questions were still short and reserved.

Later David and Amy set out for Fenway Park, a short twenty-minute walk from his apartment. Amy liked going to Fenway, partly because it was a tradition and partly because she loved to people watch while the game was going on. Now that they sat in the executive suites and he was constantly being interrupted by people from the office or clients being taken out to the game, the experience wasn't so much fun. Today was no exception. David was pulled into several long side meetings at the inside bar with Amy left alone for long periods of time. He looked through the glass and, when seeing her sitting there by herself, worked to pull himself away from his conversation.

By the sixth inning, he knew it was time to go, and he apologized to her as they descended the back stairs and stopped into a local pub on the way home. Amy enjoyed the tennis game on the television as they ate but conversation remained awkward.

When it was time to take Amy home, she spent a few minutes hugging and patting Trooper, telling him she would see him soon. It was getting late, and they rode back to Hingham with the Saturday night countdown on the classic rock station playing softly in the background. She was tired and closed her eyes, falling asleep as he peered over periodically to look at her. She looked younger as she slept, almost as she had when he used to carry her in from the car to her bed when she was small. It made him smile and feel sad at the same time, thinking about how time had so quickly moved along and how little time they spent together.

When they pulled into the driveway of his old home, it was a few minutes before eleven o'clock and Amy was still fast asleep. David could see Kathleen's silhouette standing at the open front door. She came out to the car with her slippers on as he came around to open Amy's door slowly. Kathleen gazed down at her restful face, and then, without moving her head, Kathleen's eyes shifted up to exchange a smile with David. It didn't look like Amy would wake, so David gently reached down with both arms to lift her up and carried her into the house as Kathleen held the door and watched a familiar sight from the past ascend the stairs and lay Amy softly on her bed. They both watched her for a few more seconds before they heard, "Goodnight," as the door closed.

David and Kathleen quietly chuckled as they had many times when one of the kids said or did something cute. He opened the door to James' bedroom to look at him as the hall light shined into the room, and he saw James clutching a small, stuffed golden puppy dog that he had given him a few years ago. He didn't really know James and feared he may not grow up strong enough to face the trials of life.

David gently closed the door and felt awkward walking down the stairs from the bedrooms he hadn't been in for many years now. Kathleen looked up at David with no anger or animosity, even after his unilateral desertion of her and the children. He had seen that caring and admiring look on her face many times, which made him break the moment. "I will be by next Saturday to see James."

"Sure. Let me know when you'll be here. Amy has a tournament in the morning, and I know James would like to spend more than a few hours with you. He's at that age where he really needs that from you."

"I know. I know. Let me see if I can think of something fun to do together."

"He doesn't need to be entertained. He just wants to be with you. Does that make sense?"

David nodded and unconsciously started to give her a hug and kiss goodbye, catching himself but not before Kathleen noticed.

"It's good to see you too, Kat. I will call you later in the week. Tell Amy I had a good time and wish her luck in her tournament." He walked to the car as she stood in the doorway and watched him drive off again to his chosen life in the city.

Chapter 11

David planned on stopping at his usual Eastside breakfast stop, but as he approached the street, there were orange and white barrels blocking the road with a large sign that read: Road Closed. Please Seek Alternative Route. David pivoted and headed to his recent alternative morning spot, Café Incontrare. It was still nice enough to sit outside where he could observe the entrance to My Brother's Table. There were a few men sharing a smoke outside the door and wearing old clothes, one with a soiled Red Sox hat fitted tightly on his head with uncombed, long hair sticking out and the other man wearing a black winter hat. As he sat down, the waiter smiled in recognition and asked if he wanted a cappuccino.

"Yes, please. By the way, my name is David."

The waiter said in his broken accent, "Good to meet you, David. *Il mio nome e*—sorry, my name is Giovanni. I'm pleased to meet you."

David nodded. "Glad to meet you too, Giovanni. I'll have the breakfast special today, thank you."

"Very good, Signor David."

Giovanni came back with David's breakfast and a piece of paper. "There was a man that came by earlier this morning. I think from the food kitchen," he said as he pointed to the building. "He asked me to give this note to a well-dressed man named David Kelly. I think it may be for you, Signor David."

David opened the note as Giovanni arranged his plate and silverware on the small cafe table. The note read: *Good morning, Mr. Kelly. I hope you've been resting those tired bones of yours. I won't be able to play ball on Wednesday due to another commitment, but if you are interested, I was planning on going to the court on Tuesday instead. I hope you can make it so that you can buy me another beer! Ciao. Tom.*

He had planned on being in New York until late on Tuesday and arranged his busy schedule to play on Wednesday. He found himself feeling disappointed that he may need to pass this week.

Izzie greeted David with a wide smile as he passed her desk. "Good morning, Mr. Kelly. I hope your weekend was a good one. I have your tickets and travel plans on your desk."

David had been thinking about tomorrow. "Thanks, Izzie. Oh, could you do me a favor?"

"What do you need, Mr. Kelly?"

"I'd like to see if we can pull the schedule in to get more of the agenda completed today and, in the morning, so that I can catch an early afternoon flight back to Boston. I really appreciate it."

Despite the schedule changes and rush to accomplish everything, David had a successful trip and secured important customer orders for the end of the quarter. The driver had him home in time to change and be at the Back Bay Fens basketball courts by 4:30.

He felt a sense of freedom as he began to sink his first long jump shots. Just as he was taking a shot, Trevon lobbed a ball up to the basket and in came Big Russ to jam the ball through the basket. Trevon laughed with a "hee-hee-hee," and said, "What's ya doin' here on Tuesdee, man? We call you Mr. Hump Day, and now we got to come up with another name for you!"

Before David answered, they were off to the next court to high five the regulars.

He felt a presence directly behind him as he started shooting again, and his ball was blocked from behind as his hand futilely followed through on the shot.

"You can't trust anyone, can you?" Tom laughed as he retrieved David's basketball and sank it with an underhanded shot.

For most of his life, David hadn't allowed himself to fully trust anyone, but Tom was becoming someone he felt might be an exception to the constant vigilance with which he approached the world. David enjoyed his time with Tom and felt he was actually becoming a friend he looked forward to seeing. They played five intense games, each coming down to the "win by two points" difference in score, with most games going well beyond eleven points. David won the final game on a faked jump shot to get Tom off his feet and then a running one-handed shot off the backboard. This brought the other players to cheer as they stopped their game to watch and take bets on the final winner of the "old white guys who still think they can play" duel.

Both were bending down to catch their breath as sweat dripped off their tee-shirts and brows and onto the court. Still bent over, Tom reached out his hand to congratulate David. David was happy to finally win as he shook Tom's hand and waved his other to the cheering fans from the other court. David said, "I will let you buy me that beer now," and smiled from deep inside as he continued to recover from the all-out battle he had, at last, triumphed over.

It was much warmer than average for late September, which made for a comfortable walk over to Dempsey's Pub to collect the spoils of war from

Tom. He noticed that Tom showed a genuine interest in him as he asked questions about his week and how things were going.

When they walked into the pub, Dempsey looked up and said, "I wasn't expecting you two 'til tomorrow. So, what'll it be and more importantly who's paying tonight?"

Tom shifted his eyes towards David and bellowed, "What will you and everyone else in the house have tonight?"

There was a booth with three guys who were in the pub last Wednesday, and two other men sitting at the bar who instantly glanced over with a smile. After Dempsey brought everyone their drinks, the three men in the booth introduced themselves and asked David and Tom to sit with them. They sat and talked for a couple of hours about local and national politics, sports, the economy, and the disappointing baseball season with the Sox.

David was impressed with Tom's range of knowledge but even more in his ability to listen and argue a point without getting heated, so the conversation remained enjoyable despite any differences of opinion. He was trying to think of anyone in his life he respected and felt comfortable with. In a world where friendships were often measured more by personal benefit than plain friendship for its own sake, Tom seemed different and more sincere in his interactions with people. David hadn't thought much about that before, but Tom made him notice this as something that was missing in his life. As he watched Tom laughing and exchanging ideas, he was wondering if he'd ever had a true friend.

At times, during the lively conversation, David would be deep in thought and Tom would notice, giving him an affirming smile. David was thinking about how much of his time was spent with entertaining diversions, but tonight he was actually enjoying himself by being present. It made him smile back to let Tom know that things were good.

When they left the bar, the Red Sox were up 12 to 1 against the Rays. David had beaten Tom at a game they both loved, and summer was hanging on this warm September night as they walked home. When they hit the point where Tom was heading east and David north, they stopped and Tom said, "You played a great game tonight, but don't get too big a head because you only beat me."

"I would take you on my team any day of the week. Thanks for leaving the note at the cafe to let me know about the change in your schedule. Is everything okay for tomorrow?"

Tom said, "Oh sure. I just had a few things to attend to, nothing serious. Thanks for asking. How about yourself? You mentioned that you were flying over the city when the planes hit the towers in New York on 9-11. Are you going to be okay tomorrow? Are you flying?"

David answered, "No. No. I was in New York yesterday and flew back this afternoon."

Tom smirked. "I'm flattered that you flew in for the game and had the energy to play like you did. Very impressive."

"I was just thirsty and wanted that free beer."

They both laughed and headed off, each asking, "Next week?" and both responding, "Next week."

David got home to an excited Trooper, who stood and put his paws on David's chest to get a hug. David rubbed his head and stroked his back saying, "Hey, I saw you a few hours ago. Now, I did kind of run in and out on you after being gone for a few days, but I had a very important game, and do you know who won? That's right; this old man." After a shower, David gave Jillian a quick call to ask her if she was up for dinner the next evening and caught up on work emails before going to bed for a restful good night's sleep.

Chapter 12

There was no alarm that morning, and David slowly woke and looked over to see Trooper still sound asleep. "You certainly have the good life, don't you, boy?" David was feeling good. After a shorter run than usual, he showered and made scrambled eggs with spinach and mushrooms and sat with a cup of coffee at the table by the sunny kitchen window to read the *Globe*. The headline read: "The Nation Reflects, Solemn Rites Mark the Anniversary of Attacks," making David stop for a few minutes to reflect back to a year ago and about all those people who had died that day. He tried to reconcile the news with his own feelings of contentment this morning.

When 4:00 p.m. came around, he was still working, and Izzie popped her head into his office to remind him of the time. Since he wasn't leaving early this Wednesday, he thanked her and kept working until 6:30 p.m. before heading down to the lobby to meet Jillian.

Jillian seemed to take a chance that no one from work was looking and gave David a quick kiss before he asked her if she minded taking a walk before going to dinner.

"I'd love to, but first I'd like to know how I was lucky enough to see you on your mystery night."

David pulled his head back. "Mystery night? What do you mean by mystery night?"

Jillian answered, "Well, the last several Wednesdays you have been preoccupied with your new bud, and now here we are going out on Wednesday night, and you seem to be in a very good mood. What's the David Kelly scoop?"

David smiled. "We ended up playing basketball last night instead because Tom had something going on tonight. Why are you so interested, anyway?"

"I'm interested in everything about you and especially all your secret places."

They walked the loop around the Prudential and Copley Place and stopped near the fountains in front of the beautiful Christian Science Church. David sat down with Jillian on a stone bench and thought for a minute before responding. "I've been really enjoying myself, not only playing basketball, but spending time afterward just talking, debating, and having fun. I told you how I ran into Tom out of the blue. He seems to have a way about him, something that makes him easy to be around. I have been trying to understand it myself and it's hard to describe. I feel as if I could respect and trust him more than anyone I can think of. Am I making any sense?"

"I'm really happy for you and I'm glad you shared that with me." She reached over, her hand clutching his arm, and gave him a kiss on the cheek. She started to speak, stopped, and then started again. "David, I can't tell you how much I look forward to being with you. I know it's only been a few weeks, but I really love our time together. Trust me, a lot of women at work, including myself, would love to have caught you because you are very handsome, smart, successful, and rich, but none of those things seem to matter anymore. I enjoy being with David Kelly."

David blushed at the compliment but also because he wasn't sure where the conversation might go. "Well, this David Kelly is enjoying the company of a wonderful, talented and beautiful young woman who happens to go by the name of Jill Miller."

David sensed Jillian fighting her inclinations to shoot down each compliment he had just given her. She had told him she was still working hard to resist instinctively rejecting a positive view of herself, one she might envision possible for everyone else but herself. However, it was the expression on Jillian's face that made David realize her feelings for him may be more serious than he realized.

After sitting for a while and people-watching, David and Jillian continued their stroll down a side street with a neighborhood feel. They were talking about things they might like to do this fall as they came upon a large group of people holding candles, quietly walking up the stairs and in through the opened wooden doors of an attractive church. Jillian said, "I wonder if it's a memorial service or something for 9-11?"

Just as he was about to respond, his heart dropped. He shook his head and blinked to see if he was seeing what he thought he was seeing. Greeting and shaking hands with everyone entering the church was a man with a welcoming smile dressed in a priest's black cassock with a white collar. David felt frozen as he convinced himself that this was actually Tom. He felt somehow betrayed or lied to by someone he thought he could trust. Tom hadn't been upfront about who he was or even why he had canceled for tonight. He felt disoriented and more paralyzed than angry. His breathing was heavier, and he felt temporarily deaf to the sounds of the city around him and to Jillian's voice.

Jillian clutched his arm. "David, are you all right?"

Tom had turned to enter the church doors before he could notice David staring at him. "David, are you all right?" repeated Jillian a little louder.

He experienced the same waves of anxiety in his chest he remembered feeling days after his brother and father were gone from his life forever. Up until that time, there was no one he could admire as much as his brother and respect or trust as much as he did his father, and those things were buried and gone from his life until the very recent feelings he had just disclosed to Jillian. He started walking away from the church, a few steps faster than was comfortable for her.

Jillian rushed to keep up. "What's the matter, David? Please slow down and talk to me."

He stopped for her to catch up.

"Are you okay?"

"Jill, I'm sorry. I'm really sorry but—I don't think I can do this tonight. I really need to go. I'm sorry."

He left her stranded on the sidewalk and strode off towards his apartment alone.

When he finally got home, he changed into his running gear and ran for seven miles to push the flood of thoughts and emotion out of his body. After a long, hot shower, he sat in his leather chair and stared at the painting on the wall, a solitary sailboat on the choppy ocean off of Dennis Port Harbor with only the tip of Chatham and a few clouds off in the distance.

He sent a short text to Jillian apologizing for leaving her the way he did, saying that he needed some time. Knowing he had a full slate of meetings in the morning, he tried to get some sleep but only drifted into dreams. He was looking up at his father as he taught him how to hold and throw a baseball, then quickly shifted to closing a heavy door on his father as he tried to come into his room from a darkened hallway. A casket was being lowered into a black pit at a cemetery he didn't recognize, and then he saw himself sitting on the handlebars of his older brother's bike as Jimmy pedaled and laughed, before seeing him lying in a pool of blood on a cold floor. His dream shifted to boating with Jillian and then to dribbling past Tom with the basketball for a score, and then he was a boy again sitting alone in the pitch black of his room, which woke him suddenly as he found himself sitting up in bed and sweating in his own pitch-black room. Trooper slept soundly, and David was alone with the stillness of nothing— no sound, no light, no movement of air, no feeling at all.

Chapter 13

David fell asleep an hour before the alarm sounded, so he was surprised when the music on his clock radio began to play "My Sacrifice" by Creed. As he pushed off the blankets and swung his feet to the floor, he buried the notion that he had been sacrificing his authentic self and his relationships just to avoid the discomfort of doing otherwise. Without being aware of it, he mentally moved into a safer compartment that he had spent a lifetime building and started his routine. He ran, showered, went to the Eastside for breakfast, and then on to work.

He buried himself back into work, exercise and routine. He asked Izzie to schedule some customer and sales team visits he had been putting off. He would be out of town much of the remaining weeks of the quarter to close business and stay busy. Jillian had tried to text and call him, but she had no replies as David immersed himself in his meetings and readied for flights over the rest of the week to Atlanta, Washington, and Toronto. At work, he felt his best when he was focused and driven by his heavy work schedule and dealing with sales teams and customers.

Finally, David called Jillian to let her know that he was going to be straight out for a while but left her with no insight or sense of what was going on with him or even if it had to do with her. He could hear the concern in her voice but felt relieved that she wanted to give him whatever time he needed.

There was comfort and safety in his busy routine. Out on the road from Friday morning through Tuesday night, he was feeling more in control of his world as he headed back to Boston. On Wednesday morning, he was at work before Izzie, which didn't please her. "Did you sleep on the couch here last night, Mr. Kelly?"

David looked up from the work on his desk. "Oh hi, Izzie. No, I didn't sleep here last night. There's just a lot to do today."

She brought in a cup of coffee. "I know, Mr. Kelly. I have your calendar booked up until four o'clock."

David tilted his head, puzzled. "Izzie, you don't need to block off that time slot on Wednesdays any longer." She pursed her lips with concern but opened up his Wednesday afternoon calendar, which was quickly booked by Sean Quigley, who stopped by David's office at four-thirty sharp to talk about what they were doing for damage control on Jack's old accounts. While Sean was talking, David was standing at his large wall-length windows facing Fenway Park. As his eyes moved down the street several blocks, he could see the green of the Back Bay Fens and the river running through it. While he wanted to resist the temptation, his sights locked in the basketball courts where a full court game was starting up on one court and the other was empty.

Sean talked about the situation and opportunities with each account as David continued looking out the window and responding when necessary. He noticed someone walk onto the open court and start to shoot. With the distance, it was hard to make out exactly who anyone was, but from the moves he was making, he could tell it was Tom. He watched him shooting alone and then turn down offers from players to play games on the other court. He wasn't feeling much of anything at all as he watched from his spot high above the world, not anger nor a pull to go back. He just felt numb and preoccupied as he turned his full attention to Sean and the work at hand.

After work, David put on his running gear and headed out through the Fens and streets that he hadn't been down before. Near the end of his run, he found himself passing Dempsey's Pub, slowly enough to see a crowd of men conversing at the booth he had sat at with Tom more than a week before, but too fast to notice if Tom was sitting with them. He didn't turn back and ended up walking the last mile back home to sit with a beer and his faithful friend, Trooper.

Chapter 14

Tom woke at his usual time that morning, got showered and dressed. His day usually started with an hour of quiet prayer in a church pew or sitting in the back garden, which provided a peaceful setting. He strolled the brick walkways in the garden and thought about David. Several days ago, Jillian had surprisingly shown up at Tom's rectory door and relayed the events of the evening when David abruptly walked off and stopped seeing her. Tom could tell how distraught she was personally, but how much more concerned she was about David. He promised her that he would try to find out what happened and told her he thought David was strong and would be okay.

He knew there was something deep in David, but he had no idea what could've caused such a reaction. He prayed and asked for help and guidance on how best to be there for him if that was his role. He watched the bees float from one bloom to the next and listened for direction. Then, as a gentle breeze rolled through the roses and trees, he got a strong sense that it was a good idea to try to see David. What he didn't know was how and when to catch him.

At a few minutes after seven, he went into the church sacristy for 7:30 morning Mass. Normally the altar boy assisting at the Mass would already be there to light the candles, set out the Mass book on the altar, and help him get ready for Mass, but Tom knew who was serving today and wasn't surprised. He prepared the chalice and dressed in the white amice, alb, and then the more colorful stole and chasuble outer garments, reciting the appropriate short prayer as he donned each one. Tom approached his role in the Mass with reverence and humility, and always felt a sense of joy at this celebration because he saw the Mass was not a re-enactment of the Last Supper or Jesus's sacrifice on the cross but making those acts of love present in this moment to this community.

After Mass, Tom stood outside the front of the church and wished each parishioner a good day as they headed off to their jobs, school, and life. The altar boy stood next to Tom until the last parishioner left. "Father, I'm sorry for being late to help out before Mass again today."

"Tony, where would the mystery and fun be in life without you?"

Tony grinned as they walked back inside.

In addition to his pastoral duties, Tom had been taking care of the grounds and buildings with some volunteer help. At the end of July, a man started coming to Mass each morning at a church that needed serious attention. Soon afterward, doorknobs, broken windows, and the heating system were mysteriously fixed, the gardens were tended to, and things seemed cleaner and more organized. It was some time before Tom figured out who was responsible. Late one evening, he noticed lights on at the school and thinking it was the principal, Sister Helen, he walked over to convince her to call it a night. When Tom got closer to the side door window, he could see a short man dressed in work clothes and a baseball hat diligently mopping the floors. As Tom turned the knob on the door, he realized it was locked. The man looked up and then kept on mopping until it was evident that Tom wasn't going to leave. He went to the door. "Good evening, Father. How was your day today?"

Tom replied with amusement, "My day was fine, but what are you doing here mopping the floors?"

"They looked like they needed some attention."

"Like the doors and windows and boiler and gardens needed attention?"

The man nodded. "They sure did." He wasn't giving an inch to Tom, which amused him even more.

"How about if I tell you my name—"

"You're Father Fitzpatrick."

Tom smiled. "And your name?"

The man hesitated. "Angelo Salvato. I hope it's okay to help out."

Tom replied, "We certainly appreciate it. If you need a job, we, unfortunately, cannot afford to hire anyone to manage the property."

Angelo's eyes remained under the shadow of the brim of his hat. "I could use a job, but I don't need money, just a place to sleep at night."

"Well, I have a room in the rectory for visiting priests and family that's empty right now."

Angelo glanced over at the large green door to the utility room under the rectory. "If you're okay with it, I'd prefer to use this room."

Tom turned to the old door with narrow windows at the top leading to a supply room that was no larger than a nine by twelve-foot cellar-type room. "No, Angelo. I can't have you stay there!"

Angelo insisted as he had already been sleeping on a cot in the supply room for the past two months while taking care of things for the church. Tom learned that Angelo was also a good cook, and he would often cook up dinner and share it with Tom in the rectory kitchen before a very competitive game of chess.

Tom thought about David most of the day and decided to try to catch him after work. Dressed in his running gear, he walked over to the Prudential Center to wait for him in the lobby. He waited for some time and just after seven, Tom noticed David as one of the elevators opened, but David didn't recognize him under the cap and running clothes. As David headed out the door and started walking, Tom followed well behind until they turned onto Beacon Street.

*****

Just as David reached his home and climbed the steps to open the door, he heard a familiar voice behind him. "I knew you were a stand-up kind of guy, but I didn't think you would stand me up."

David hesitated, then slowly turned around to see Tom sitting on his steps with his back to him. David's instinct was to turn back around and go into his apartment, but instead, he quietly stepped down, put down his briefcase, and sat next to Tom.

Neither David nor Tom spoke for a few minutes as they watched the world passing them by on a pleasant mid-September evening. Staring ahead, David asked, "Why were you dishonest with me about who you were?"

Tom took a sharp breath in. "David, I'm really sorry for how you are feeling. I wouldn't want you to feel as if you couldn't trust me to be completely honest with you."

David quickly jumped in. "Then why did you do it? Why weren't you upfront with me?"

Tom said, "You never asked me what I did. It was good to develop a friendship based on who we were as people instead of acting differently because of our occupations—especially mine. I really enjoyed your company and felt like you could freely be yourself if I were just another guy."

David's forearms were across his knees and his hands holding up his head. "But you aren't just like anyone else." David stood up. "I need some time to think about things, Tom, or whatever your name is."

"Believe it or not, it is Tom, but you can call me whatever you like."

David turned the key to open his door and then turned toward Tom. "I don't know what to believe, so maybe I will just call you—"

Tom interrupted, perhaps thinking it could be any number of unpleasant names that could've come out of David's mouth, by suddenly tossing David the briefcase he had left sitting on the stoop. As David caught the briefcase, Tom gave him a hint of a smile in the eyes that showed nothing but genuine fondness.

Safely back in his apartment, David knew it was time he called Jillian and that he should be calling Kathleen to see if he could take James over the weekend, but he made neither call. He, instead, prepped for the morning's customer meetings. There was no Red Sox game on, so he played some old

Beatles and Who albums for background music while he worked at the kitchen table with a small glass of bourbon. As he pushed aside the morning's *Globe,* he noticed a headline on a lawsuit against members of the Catholic Church for sexual abuse cover-ups. The *Globe* had broken an explosive story in January about former priest John Geoghan and then later Rev. Paul Shanley. The allegations were that Church officials were aware of the abuse and knowingly moved the problem priests around instead of protecting the children. Boston Cardinal Bernard Law had apologized and offered his resignation but remained in office, and reports were pointing to his knowledge of complaints and problem priests.

These stories rocked Boston and the Catholic Church nationwide. It had shocked parishioners, as it did the community at large, who expected a higher standard of responsibility and trust from religious institutions and especially the dominant Church in the Boston area. Trust in the Church and church attendance itself fell off sharply during the year as more stories and allegations surfaced. People started to suspect every priest as a potential pedophile and believed no child should be in the company of a priest. The vast majority of cases seemed to be clustered around the late fifties to the early eighties, with the majority of victims being boys in their early- to mid-teens. Cases ranged from actual rape to inappropriate touching, and some priests were accused by over a hundred victims over those years.

There was no love lost with David when it came to the Catholic Church. While he had been baptized a Catholic, after his father's death, his mother never let him set foot in a Catholic Church again. David's mother had her own personal anger against the Church that she was more than vocal about with her three remaining children. David was too young to pay much attention to the details, but she would start ranting about how corrupt and evil the Church was. When this latest scandal had broken open, she would read every article out loud to David that confirmed her ardent opinion that the Church was a corrupt institution. While he had learned to tune her out many years ago, he certainly had no personal reason to defend the religion of a father who had broken his trust as a young boy. The current headline only provided a subconscious confirmation about his decision to dive deep into his work instead of a relationship with a priest.

He stayed busy with work and played golf with some of his team over the weekend. On Tuesday night, Trooper greeted him at the door looking like he could use an evening stroll, so David changed into more comfortable clothes for a walk and grabbed leftovers from the refrigerator. As he closed the refrigerator door and turned towards the kitchen table, he stopped for a second and turned back to look at the freezer door, which was covered with pictures of Amy and James, a few group golf pictures of the winning teams from the office, and a photo of him and Jillian that she had put there herself. He squinted as he noticed something else on the door that hadn't been there before. It looked like an old, faded fragment of paper with odd writing on both sides. Outside of Jillian or the dog walker, Lucy, David couldn't think of anyone who'd have access to his apartment and he definitely couldn't figure out what the writing meant or why it had been put there.

ΟΙ ΙΟΥΔΑΙ   ΗΜΕΥΤΟ ΓΕΓΕΝΝΗΜΑΙ

ΟΥΔΕΝΑ ΙΝΑ Ο Λ ΣΜΟΝ ΙΝΑ ΜΑΡΤΥ-

ΠΕΝ ΣΗΜΑΙΝΩ   ΕΚ ΤΗΣ ΑΛΗΘΕΙ

ΘΝΗΣΚΕΙΝ ΙΣ   ΛΕΓΕΙ ΑΥΤΩ

ΡΙΟΝ Ο Π ΑΙ ΤΟΥΤΟ

ΚΑΙ ΕΙΠΤΟΥΣ Ι

ΑΙΩ   ΕΜΙ

Underneath the strange message was a line, written in English, "The Perfect Answer to the Prefect Question."

Chapter 15

David slept off and on that night, dismissing the mystery riddle as a joke. After his quick morning walk around the block with Trooper, he inadvertently left the front door unlocked, and while he was in the shower, Trooper barked loudly. He stepped out of the bathroom half-dressed and opened the door to the staircase to see a man was exiting the building, scurrying down the street.

David patted Trooper for doing a good job as he calmed down. Leaving for work, he spotted a leaflet the 'intruder' must have left on the top step, the week's line-up at the Comedy Improv. He smiled to himself and headed to the office for a busy day.

That afternoon, David stood at the window behind his desk while he took a call on his speakerphone from the Chicago team. As the team talked back and forth about how to close the larger deals before quarter-end, he closed his eyes and felt the warmth of the sun coming in through the window on his face. When he opened his eyes, he found his gaze shift towards the Back Bay Fens basketball courts. He felt insulated but dazed over the past few weeks and flashed back to the sincere look in Tom's eyes when he had last seen him. He missed Tom's company, and he missed how he was starting to feel. David put the Chicago team on hold, poked his head out the door, and waited for Izzie to look up at him. Without raising her head, she said, "And what can I do for you, Mr. Kelly?"

"Please reschedule my meetings after four today. I might have to leave the office a little early today."

Izzie nodded approvingly as he slipped back into his office and closed the door. He didn't know why he had changed his plans. He still felt like Tom hadn't been upfront with him. Nevertheless, just before four o'clock, he went home to change and headed over to the basketball court with his ball and bag.

The court on the right was still empty when David arrived, so he started his shooting routine. The game on the other court had just finished up and a familiar voice shouted, "I think your bro missed you last week. He left teary-eyed and all."

David laughed, "Hey, Trev. He's a big boy. I'm sure he's recovered by now." He started to release a long shot, then felt a hand on his shoulder and turned to see Tom nodding with a welcoming smile.

David said, "I'm only here to beat your—"

Tom swatted the ball out of David's hands and drove to the basket for a pretty-looking layup. David played Tom harder than he had before as if part of him was playing against all those people he couldn't trust in his life.

Tom didn't complain. He matched David basket for basket throughout each of the first four games they split, and for the ten-to-ten tie in the deciding fifth game. Tom's attempt to drive past David for a layup was tipped by David, who retrieved the loose ball, dribbled quickly to the top of the key where he turned, squared with the basket, and hit the long-jump shot for a one-point lead. Tom grabbed the ball and handed it back to David, who didn't hesitate to drive to his right, and with a hard bump to Tom's chest, sent Tom to the ground as David hit a one-handed shot off the backboard for the win. David reached out his hand to help Tom back to his feet and Tom took it, shaking David's hand.

As they picked up their things, Tom, acted like a boy at the end of his first date with a girl as he scraped his toe on the ground in front of him. "Sooooooo—are you going to let me live up to my responsibilities as the clear loser here?"

David paused, "To tell you the truth, I hadn't really gotten that far."

"Maybe we should figure this out over a beer? What do you say?"

As they entered the pub, Dempsey was in his usual position behind the bar and smiled as he saw Tom and David coming in the door, waving as they made their way to an open booth and eased into seats across from each other.

Dempsey came over with cold beers in each hand for the resting warriors. "So, gentlemen, who's the generous benefactor of these refreshments tonight?" Tom raised his head and hung his head in shame as Dempsey placed the two beers in front of Tom, who slid one over to David and raised his mug to the winner.

"Demps," David said, "have you known that he was a—"

"Sure," Dempsey replied with a shrug before walking away.

Tom laughed. "So how are you really doing these days, Hondo?"

"I'm doing okay. It's been very busy."

"Busy by design?"

"It's end-of-quarter, so it's busy."

"But here you are with only five days left in the quarter. Do you want to tell me about anything that's been bothering you?"

David shook his head. "I think I'm good."

"Okay. I know you are a man who values complete honesty, so I'll trust you have no remaining feelings about this."

"I didn't say I had no feelings about it, but I'm okay with forgetting about it."

Tom tilted his head as he looked at David and sipped his beer, inviting David to say something more.

David took the bait. "Look, I felt like you were a straight-up guy and I respected you. When I saw you in your getup that night, I was surprised. I felt like you hadn't been completely honest with me."

"I want you to know that I've really enjoyed the short amount of time we've spent together. I would never want to undermine our friendship by being anything but honest with you. I apologize for not being more open and upfront about what I do with my days. People tend to act differently when they realize what I do, and I'll have to admit that I was enjoying just being ourselves. We may find out a lot about each other along the way, but I hope you can forgive me for any negative feelings I created."

David raised his mug to Tom. "I'll see what I can do."

"I'd like that. I have a feeling that this was a trigger to something else for you."

To change the subject, David reached into his bag and pulled out the piece of paper he kept concealed with his hand. "Could I ask you to look at something?"

Tom sat up. "Sure. What is it?"

David turned over his hand and showed him the paper with the odd writing. "I found this piece of paper in my apartment and can't for the life of me figure out what the heck it's about. I was curious if you had any clue."

Tom took the paper and closely examined the photocopy of the small fragment of an ancient Egyptian papyrus, only a few inches in size, showing the rough and aged texture with few legible characters.

David said, "I think there's a typo on the note on the back that should say, 'The Perfect Answer to the Perfect Question.' Any clue about what this means?"

"Where did this come from?"

David frowned, shaking his head.

"I have seen this fragment before. It's the earliest known actual manuscript of the New Testament Gospels ever found, and this small fragment of papyrus was found in Egypt in 1920. It now sits in John Rylands Library in Manchester, England. It's dated somewhere in the early part of the second century and the writing is in Greek. Do you know any Greek?"

Feeling more confused, David shook his head.

"It's from the Gospel of John and matches exactly parts of the Bible verses from John 18 on each side. Are you up on your Gospel?"

David kept shaking his head.

Tom ran his finger over the parts that were captured on the fragment to translate and then filled in the rest of the sentence.

"The Jews, 'For us it is not permitted to kill anyone,' so that the word of Jesus might be fulfilled, which he spoke signifying what kind of death he was going to die. Entered therefore again into the Praetorium Pilate and summoned Jesus and said to him, 'Thou art king of the Jews?'"

Tom turned over the paper and continued translating as David continued to look confused.

"'A King I am. For this I have been born and (for this) I have come into the world so that I would testify to the truth. Everyone who is of the truth hears of my voice.' Said to him Pilate, 'What is truth?' and this having said, again he went out unto the Jews and said to them, 'I find not one fault in him.'"

He turned to David. "Are you still interested in talking about this?"

David was ready to pass, but several guys from the pub had overheard the mystery translation and were now standing at their booth. David asked, "What does this have to do with the comment that was written on the back of this fairy tale? 'The Perfect Answer to the Perfect Question?'"

Tom jumped in, "I don't think there's a typo. I think it's correct the way it is written, 'The Prefect Question' might refer to Pilate who was the Prefect or Governor of Judaea around 26 AD to 36 AD. Pilate is interrogating Jesus to try him for the charges against him and cynically asks Jesus the rhetorical question, 'What is truth?'"

David's brow was furrowed. "That's it?"

*****

Tom sat back trying to decide where to take this as "basketball-friend Tom" as opposed to "Father Tom." He knew there was more to David's reaction to finding out he was a priest than just being upset about not being informed earlier of this fact.

One of the younger guys who had gathered around the booth leaned in with his half-filled beer mug. "I think the whole idea of truth is a myth, an outdated fiction that allowed religious institutions to have power and control over people by forcing their ideas of morality on them, nothing more."

Oh boy! Tom thought as he approached the young man, noting his long, unkempt hair and beard. "Hi, I'm Tom. What's your name?"

"You can call me Diogenes," said the young man. Tom smiled back at him.

Tom then glanced over to see how David was doing. He slid over on the bench allowing a few others to sit in the booth while others stood. With all eyes on him, Tom said, "I think Pilate's question is one of the two top questions going."

Diogenes asked, "Two?"

Tom answered, "Sure, 'What is Truth?' and once you answered that, the other is 'What are you going to do about it?'"

Diogenes reiterated, "I don't believe in absolute, inflexible, and unalterable definitions of truth. We're not slaves to someone else's ideas of what is true. How can you prove that your truth is any better than mine?"

Tom leaned back and hollered over to Dempsey, "I think we may need another round for the truth seekers here," hesitated and then added, "and for Diogenes as well!" He looked around the booth and asked, "Who here believes that absolute truths do not exist?" Diogenes and his friend Alex both raised their hands. He continued with his poll. "So, who here believes that absolute truth does exist?" Several of the guys raised their hands; this surprised Tom until he realized they were reaching for a beer off of the tray that Dempsey was holding. Tom grabbed his own beer and continued, "Okay. Who doesn't know or hasn't really thought about this?" Everyone, except for Diogenes and Alex, raised their hands. "What if I asked you if it's true all the time that three times two is six, that square circles never exist, and that the earth is both round and orbits the sun?"

Alex glanced at Diogenes. "Okay. Those types of things are always true because they can be validated objectively by mathematics or the scientific method."

Tom asked, "So you agree that absolute truths do exist?"

Diogenes answered, "Sure, but I'm talking about things we choose to do. No one's opinion is better than anyone else's, and it's wrong for you or any one institution to impose their 'truths' on anyone else. It's nothing more than an act of arrogance and oppressive to human freedom."

Alex nodded in full agreement.

Tom said, "So, you're saying that there are absolute truths about scientific and mathematical-type facts, but there is no such thing as absolute moral truth?"

"Exactly!"

David smirked as he watched Tom for his next move.

"There are no absolute truths," Diogenes continued, "and all truths are relative to each person's beliefs or feelings. I don't see any way you can logically disagree with that or prove me to be wrong."

Tom asked Diogenes, "If you just made a statement that contradicted itself, would you want to know?"

Diogenes looked at Alex. "What? I don't make self-contradicting statements, and I think most people feel that way."

Tom answered, "I think you are right that most people do feel that way, but you said, 'There are no absolute truths and all truths are relative.'"

Diogenes nodded. "Correct."

"That is a statement that contradicts itself. You made a statement that it's an absolute truth that 'there are no absolute truths' and by your own admission, there cannot be absolute truths."

Sam, who was sitting next to David, said, "Checkmate!"

*****

David thought about what Tom had just said and how Diogenes statement couldn't be true. While Diogenes was rubbing his forefinger across the top of his lip, he tried to counter the logic of Tom's comment. "Okay. Maybe there are some absolute moral truths, but most things are not absolute. You can't tell someone else how to think and what is right and wrong. People in one culture may have different morals from another."

Tom said, "Do you think that a person who takes a young child, tortures, and then kills that child for personal amusement would always be wrong?"

Diogenes answered, "Sure."

Tom continued, "Would it be wrong to impose your morals on Hitler and the Nazis if they personally felt what they were doing was morally right for them? If you believe all truth is relative and there are no absolute rights and wrongs, then how could you justify imposing your truths on them? They'd have the right to say to you, 'That's your truth, and this is my truth.'"

Everyone, including Alex, was staring at Diogenes for his response. "Okay. Maybe the truth is relative unless it hurts someone else. Other than that, people should have the right to do what they want and feel like. And maybe people have evolved to know that they need to get along with others to survive and that desire isn't some mystical absolute truth in the cosmos?"

Tom responded, "I absolutely agree that each person has the freedom to make choices on how to live his life. I do think that choice needs to be honest and informed, but the act of making that choice doesn't make it right or wrong. It is legal to make a choice about abortion, but the baby doesn't become or cease to be either human or living based on that choice or how we feel. The baby is objectively living and human, or not, regardless of how we may feel or what we personally believe."

Tom's tone was respectful as he continued to make his argument. "I agree we have instincts for survival that have developed, but it would only make sense that those are consistent with a natural and moral law that exists for our benefit. If someone took an animal into the woods and tortured it simply for amusement, it wouldn't hurt their social survival, but would we see it as right because they think it is? If the government systematically euthanized people who had medical defects, would that not improve the evolving species in the future? But in our heart of hearts, don't we all know that it's wrong?"

Diogenes didn't respond.

"Who thinks that truth is only relative to each person's feelings or desires? And who thinks absolute truths actually exist?" To that latter, most people raised their hands.

Sam mumbled, "I think my head hurts, but it's something to definitely think about. I mean, if everything were relative and there were no truths, it would seem as if nothing would really mean anything and no one could argue that it does if it's all about personal feelings."

Someone else said, "One thing I am sure of; you philosophers bantering back and forth aren't helping the Sox tonight!" and everyone chuckled.

They stood up to leave, saying goodnight to Dempsey and those who had regrouped at the bar for another round. Outside there was a slight mist, but the air was still warm. David stood outside the door staring at the ground as he held his sports bag.

"So," Tom asked, "how are you doing, David? You were very quiet tonight."

"Yeah. I don't know. I don't know what these crazy hieroglyphics are all about, and I still feel a bit strange about getting used to you being something different from what I thought."

Tom put his hand on David's shoulder. "I'm really sorry for not telling you something that made a difference to you. I hope that I'm still the person you've been playing ball with, and beating, and enjoying the company of because I've enjoyed your company. Sometimes when things become a little uncomfortable or we feel restless, there may be something there worth letting come to the surface. I don't know the context of the fragment in Greek that you showed me, but I think it's pointing to something to do with truth. I also sense that there's something deeper behind the intense feelings and reaction you had to seeing me in my working attire."

"Why do think that?"

"I could be wrong, but it's just a feeling I'm getting. One thing I learned along the way is that one of the hardest things to do in life is to look honestly at those things that are deep within us. 'To thine own self be true.'"

"Shakespeare, I suppose?"

Tom replied, "Billy boy himself. It is easier to read that line in *Hamlet* than to actually come to terms with it in real life."

"Sounds like a good thing to avoid at all costs then. So, what is truth? I get why this is the 'Prefect Question,' but why did it say, 'The Perfect Answer to the Prefect Question?'"

"I have a feeling you'll figure it out."

David frowned a moment, then started walking towards home. He waved his bag in the air and hollered back, "Thanks a lot, Padre."

Chapter 16

During the rest of the week, David found himself thinking about the line from Hamlet more often than he wanted. It struck him that it would take more courage to be completely honest with himself than to continue avoiding thinking seriously about it. He wasn't one to impose his views on how other people should live their lives, but he'd never thought about how honest he had been with himself or if he even knew anyone who was completely honest with themselves either.

On his way home from the office, he stopped at an old bookstore. He found an annotated version of Shakespeare's *Hamlet* and flipped to the section where Polonius gave his last advice to his son Laertes. *This above all: to thine own self be true, and it must follow, as the night the day, Thou canst not then be false to any man. Farewell, my blessing season this in thee!* To David, the idea of a "false" self we present to others and even to our own selves was a nagging thing to ponder, especially for a salesman like him.

With the company fiscal quarter-end on Monday, David worked through the weekend. He knew he had to call Jillian, and the longer he waited, the more difficult it became, anticipating what she felt and how she might respond to a call after this long, unexplained silence. In each meeting that he wasn't driving the discussion, he found himself drifting off, barely hearing what was being discussed. When he went out with the guys after a grueling day, the conversations and banter seemed more superficial and hollow to him. He had known these men for so many years, yet he didn't feel as if he really knew them at all.

As the surrounding men at the bar continued to talk, he glanced from face to face and realized he wasn't truly close to any of them. In fact, there hadn't ever been many people whom he ever really confided in. He had idolized his older brother Jimmy, who would take time out to teach him things, but he couldn't remember sharing many of his own thoughts with Jimmy. He remembered sitting with his dad as a young boy, his father listening to him go on and on about something he was excited about, or patiently answering question after question when he was curious about something. That attentiveness and genuine interest had made him feel as if he counted. After his father and brother were gone, his mother never seemed to have the time or energy for any deep conversations. As a young man, the only person he could trust and confide in was his first girlfriend, fiancée, and then wife, Kathleen.

Thinking of Kathleen drew his thoughts to his first freshman day at Northeastern University twenty-one years ago. He remembered being excited and nervous. He had rarely ventured out of his North Shore city except for sports events and had applied to Northeastern because of its Co-op program that allowed students to alternate academic semesters with full-time work at local companies, which helped to pay for school and also gain work experience and contacts. His first day was nerve-racking, riding the crowded subway and finally extricating himself from the trolley with only ten minutes to find his class on a campus he had never even visited.

David thought he could find the building, but after twenty minutes of scurrying from building to building and feeling panicked, he finally asked a girl if she knew where Lake Hall was. When she smiled and pointed to the building behind him, he turned beet red and thanked her as he hurried in to find classroom 305 for freshman English. When he reached the room, he saw only empty chairs and an older professor sitting in the front of the class wearing a tweed jacket and dark-rimmed glasses that sat on the end of his nose as he read through some notes. He looked up at David, who was out of breath. "Good morning, young man. Can I help you?"

David must've nervously appeared confused. "I was running late for my nine o'clock class but—"

A smile came to the right side of the professor's mouth as he replied, "You are more than welcome to join my freshman English class, but it doesn't start until nine-thirty."

David peered down at his schedule and noticed that he had nine o'clock classes on Monday, Wednesday and Friday but nine-thirty classes on Tuesday and Thursday. He had the right class but the wrong time and sat down near the back door. The awkward silence was broken as other students entered the classroom, including the girl who had helped this frantic student find his class. He busied himself, looking down at his empty notebook, but he could see out of the corner of his eye she was sitting down at the desk next to him.

She smirked. "I admire your commitment to getting to class on time."

David nodded, turned in his seat, and extended his hand to her. "David."

"No, it's Kathleen."

At that moment, he noticed how attractive Kathleen was, not just physically, but much more below the surface. He loved Kathleen's easy manner, her infectious smile, and her natural attractiveness that needed no makeup to enhance her long dark brown hair, fair skin, and her mesmerizingly beautiful blue sapphire eyes. On a campus where most of the female students were wearing jeans and a sweatshirt, Kathleen's simple but attractively feminine dress was a nice change.

It turned out that neither one of them had gotten breakfast before class, so they went to a small diner across from the campus, where they sat and talked for two hours. David found the conversation refreshingly comfortable and fun without the normally awkward beginning. Kathleen was an intelligent, witty, caring, deep, silly, and naturally nice person. She grew up in nearby Newton in a large Irish family and was the first to head off to college as a commuting student like David. At night Kathleen helped out with her younger siblings, did her own homework, and worked her part-time job waitressing at a local restaurant.

He never formally asked Kathleen out. They simply started dating and spending as much time together as they could. She was an English Lit major and was a great help to him in gaining writing skills. David was a business major and so he helped Kathleen with her statistics class. What struck him the most about their relationship was his ability to talk to her about anything without feeling guarded as he had for the previous ten years of his life. His relationship with Kathleen allowed him the freedom to be himself and have a place to share his thoughts, feelings, and dreams.

David had struggled through *Hamlet* in his freshman English class with Kathleen, who found Shakespeare's poetry and insights more beautiful and profound than he ever did. They would read the lines together, and Kathleen would try to explain to him what was going on. Polonius's advice to his son Laertes to be true to himself had passed right over his head. The last thing David felt he could ever do was to slow down long enough to be completely honest with himself about what he was feeling, what he feared most, and how devastated he was about the loss of his brother Jimmy and the complete betrayal of trust he had in his father. This was the one thing he could never share with anyone, including Kathleen. She had told him once that she was attracted to something intangible that she admired and cherished in him. She said that she knew, despite his faults, his obsessive focus on personal excellence and success, and his resistance to open up in areas she knew were painfully hidden deep in him, that he was a good person, and that he had the gift to be a great man.

He thought to himself, *Am I a great man? The men at work respected me. I've achieved great success in the business world. Why, then, do I feel empty and lost?*

That weekend, David reclined in his leather chair, exhausted from the end-of-quarter push at work, his reflections on life and success shoved into the recess of his mind as he flipped back and forth between the last Red Sox game of the season and the Patriots football game.

Finally, he turned the TV off and picked up his phone. It was time to give Jillian a call to at least see how she was doing and to apologize. He rang her cell phone, but she didn't answer. He decided to drive over to her apartment to see if she was there. She didn't answer the door, but he saw her yellow Volkswagen Beetle in the driveway. He texted that he and Trooper, whom he was smart enough to bring along, were sitting on her front steps and that they would understand if she didn't want to see them. A while later, Trooper stood up as the screen door squeaked open and Jillian walked out to sit next to David.

Jillian broke the silence. "I only came out to see Trooper."

He could tell she had been crying for some time.

Jillian said, "I've been so concerned about you, but you haven't called for so long that I haven't known what to think."

David put his hand on her shoulder. "Jill, please know it's all me and had nothing to do with you. I don't know what 'it' is exactly, but I just needed time to pull back a bit from everyone. I know it was really unfair to you not to have called and I am sorry. I don't expect you to trust me or forgive me, but I wanted to see how you were doing."

"Well, I'm not doing well. I tried to fight these feelings and kept saying to myself that you were hurt and needed time and would call the next day, but after a while, I just couldn't stop sinking into a bad place. What I do know is that I cannot survive another relationship that will—" She started crying and wiping her tears as quickly as she could, to no avail. "What I need you to do is to take care of yourself and figure out what you think you need and if we're going to have a relationship. I cannot do any sort of emotional roller coaster right now." She kissed him on the cheek and stood up and went back into the house before he could think of what to say. Trooper looked up at him with concern and disappointment.

David sat frozen for several minutes on the steps, truly not knowing what to think, what to feel or what to do. He knew about her father and difficult childhood, and she had also told him about being dumped after a long relationship with some guy she thought she was going to marry. He still didn't know what to do for her that wouldn't end up hurting her even more in the end. Finally, he stood up under the tree where he and Jillian had exchanged their first kiss and moment of connection together. Some leaves were turning brilliant yellow, orange, and red colors that would soon fill the New England autumn landscape. A few leaves had already fallen onto the sidewalk and his car as he let Trooper into the passenger side and readied himself to head somewhere, anywhere. Just as he started the car, his cell phone rang. David thought it might be Jillian but could see the caller ID and it was Kathleen. He turned off the car and answered. "Hi."

Kathleen seemed a little anxious. "David, did you get your messages yesterday?"

"No, I haven't listened to them yet. I was at work all day yesterday and this morning. Is everything all right with the kids? With you?"

Kathleen's voice got softer to not be overheard. "James was talking about missing his day with you. He was convinced you would've called him with a surprise this weekend because you had promised to take him to another Red Sox game before the end of the season, and today was the last game. He got very concerned about you and said, 'Dad would never break a promise. I think something must be wrong for him not to call.' I don't know how you want to handle this, but I wanted you to know and think you should talk with him."

David ran his free hand through his short brown hair to the back of his neck. "James is right. I did promise him to take him to a game, and I have been so wrapped up with work and my own self that I completely forgot. Jeez, he deserves better than that!"

"What are you doing this evening?"

"Nothing. What do you have in mind?"

"If you can be here before six, I have an idea that might help."

After dropping off Trooper, he drove to Hingham and pulled up at the house not knowing what to expect, but ready to play along with Kathleen's plan and somehow make this up to James. James was trying to play catch with himself in the front yard. He stopped when he saw David pulling up in his familiar sports car and yelled out, "Dad!" as Kathleen came out the door with an old glove of David's. James ran over to his father and was having a hard time getting his words out in his excitement. "Mom told me...that you wanted to take me to the game today but something important came up, but you still wanted to come down to see me and go to a movie together!"

David took the glove from Kathleen and quickly exchanged a thankful smile as he put his hand on James's back. "James, do you forgive me? How about if we play catch for a bit and then make a plan for just us tonight?"

Kathleen said, "Just for a few minutes." As James ran out to his spot to catch the ball, Kathleen leaned into David. "You can thank me later, but I think a pizza dinner here, and then a movie at the Loring and maybe an ice cream may save the day. Just don't keep him out too late. He has school tomorrow."

David played catch with James, showing him how to use his body to throw harder and how to catch fly balls and grounders. Some neighborhood kids slowed down on their bikes as they watched James. "Just playing catch with my dad," he yelled out.

When Kathleen called the ballplayers, David saw a look of disgust on Amy's face and deduced she was aware that he'd forgotten to take James to the game. Her greeting was reserved if not cold. Nevertheless, they all took seats at the table. It was the first time they had sat down as a family for dinner since James was in a highchair. Amy was generally quiet and gave only short answers to any questions from David or Kathleen, but she was attentive to James as he talked about whatever popped into his head.

While cleaning up, David joined Kathleen in the kitchen to wash the dishes by hand at the old soapstone kitchen sink. Kathleen handed him a dish to dry. "Thanks for coming on short notice. There is a movie called *The Rookie* playing at Loring Hall in town that I thought James might enjoy seeing since it's about baseball. I heard from neighbors it was pretty good. Maybe you could take him downtown and spend some time with him before and after the show?"

David smiled at Kathleen. "You are a really good mom, Kathleen O'Shea Kelly." He set the dried pizza pan to the side and picked up a plate. "How is Amy doing? She seems very quiet."

Kathleen shook her head in concern. "I don't know what's going on. Maybe it's just natural growing pains, though I feel as if we're losing her." She glanced over his shoulder at the old kitchen clock. "We'll have to talk about it later. Right now, you better head out if you want to have some real time with James."

David sighed and wasn't sure how to help with Amy. "Okay. We won't be too late."

He found James in the family room. Amy had already gone back upstairs. "Are you ready, Sport?"

As they walked out the front door, he paused to holler up the stairs. "Amy, we'll be back."

Kathleen was at the door holding the damp dish towel. "Have a nice time, boys."

As David walked with James, it struck him how small James still was, only four feet tall and as thin as he had been at his age. He also realized that he really didn't know him well outside of enjoying the idea of playing sports and craving his attention. They arrived in front of Loring Hall, a large, white Greek Revival structure with three arched doorways and wooden steps that people ascended as the line moved along to purchase tickets at the old style wooden ticket booth. As a young child, something seemed special about seeing a picture here and from the joy on James's face, he was sure James felt the same way.

After the movie, they walked to Brigham's Ice Cream Parlor, which was just a few doors down from the theater. He enjoyed watching James work on the large ice cream sundae covered with hot fudge and whipped cream as much as James enjoyed devouring it himself.

"You know, Dad, anytime you need someone to see a show with, I'm always available and I'm glad we didn't go to the last game today because it was against the Tampa Bay Devil Rays and I would've been rooting against us."

David laughed. "You're supposed to root for your team and not for the other team."

"But I like Tampa Bay now because, in the movie, Coach Morris got a chance to make his dream come true with them. Did you get to make your dreams come true, Dad? I hope you did but if you didn't, it looks like you still can."

He nodded, thinking the day with James had been saved, but as he gazed at his son, he wavered, unsettled by the question. Hadn't Kathleen and his children been part of that dream? This son at his side, whom he barely knew anymore, had been a dream come true, hadn't he?

Chapter 17

The next week stretched on with typical business issues: listening to sales managers explain why their taking a bad deal to make their quota was a good thing for the company, pulling together the wrap-up summary for the quarter, and dinner at the Capital Grille with the senior team at the Boston office to celebrate another record quarter. They celebrated, congratulated each other and toasted David, as they all knew that the morning would be all about game planning for another very strong fourth quarter to finish the year out.

That night, he sat at his kitchen table to look through the newspaper, but an odd feeling pulled at him and he turned to look at the freezer door. Nothing unusual this time. Just to make certain, he got up to examine each photograph and saw nothing out of place, which allowed him to relax. However, later in the evening, as he readied for bed, he noticed something sitting on his pillow—a rock. When he picked up the heavy stone, he noticed something written on the bottom that made no sense to him: *nihil fit ex nihilo*. How could it have gotten into his apartment? He knew it couldn't be Jillian, and Lucy, the dog walker, was out of town this week. No one else had a key. Also, Trooper would've been restless when he got home if anyone he didn't know and trust had entered the apartment. He made a note to call his security company to change the locks and check the alarms.

He didn't get to sleep until late and woke up an hour late, restless and unsure about playing basketball in the afternoon, but carried his sports bag with the stone he had found on his pillow to the office. He was noticeably off during the day.

"Mr. Kelly, I still have your schedule blocked after four o'clock. Don't you worry," said Izzie to him as he was taking one of the customer folders from her. "Are you all right, Mr. Kelly?"

David glanced up. "What? Oh sure. Everything's fine,"

By four o'clock, he felt too antsy to stay at the office. By the time he got down to the lobby, he decided that a little physical exercise might not be a bad thing today. He changed and headed over to the court where Tom was already shooting baskets with a few younger kids.

As David approached, Tom said, "Hey, these two NBA players want to take us on." The two young boys looked at each other, shook their heads and dribbled down to the other end of the court to play.

"I think they didn't want to waste their time playing us until we were ready."

Tom laughed. "You may be right. How have you been this past week?"

David started talking about all the end-of-quarter work, but Tom interrupted, "No. How have you been doing?"

David cocked an eyebrow at the thought that there was as difference. "Me? I'm fine. I spent some time with my son on Sunday, but I've been busy with work otherwise."

Tom let it go and started shooting with David before playing their usual set of games, only today David wasn't his usual intense self, winning only one game to Tom's three. It was a good workout but not the normal battle on each play. They stood for a few minutes, catching their breath and letting the early fall evening breeze cool them off.

Tom said, "Why don't I treat you tonight?"

David didn't argue. He picked up his bag and began the short walk to Dempsey's for a pint. As they entered the pub, Dempsey looked up and Tom held up two fingers as they made their way towards an empty booth. There was a rolled-up *Boston Globe* newspaper at the far side of the table. One of the headlines read, "For Church Counselor, A `Heartbreaking' Job." David noticed the life draining from Tom's face as he could tell that Tom knew it was another article on the sex abuse crisis.

Dempsey came over with two tall beers. "Boys, I hope these'll quench your thirst."

David held up his mug with a cold frost on the outside. "Cheers."

Tom tapped his mug against David's and took a few gulps.

"Do you mind looking at something for me?" asked David.

"The last time you said that I got into quite a debate." He noticed Diogenes, Alex, and two friends with MIT fraternity sweatshirts approaching the bar for drinks along with a few others who came into the pub for the evening.

David opened his bag and pulled out a smooth, dark gray stone and placed it on the table in front of Tom.

"Is this another riddle?" Tom asked.

David shrugged. "I wish I knew. I found this stone on my pillow last night. Another strange thing left in my apartment on two consecutive Tuesdays. I have no idea who's responsible, what to make of it, or how they got in."

Tom studied it for a few seconds. "I think I know what it is."

"What?"

"I may be out of my league on this, but my professional opinion is that I think this thing is definitely a— rock. No question about it, it's a rock. What else can I do for you?" A few people had noticed the rock sitting on the table and came over to see what was going on.

Diogenes shuffled over with his half-finished beer. "If you are going to try to convince me that this is a rock tonight, you win."

David reached out and turned over the stone to show Tom the letters marked on the bottom. Tom read it out loud, "*Nihil fit ex nihilo.*"

Diogenes said, "Is this more Greek mumbo jumbo?"

One of the MIT students, an imposing figure, tall and barrel-chested with dark bushy hair and beard, said, "That's in Latin, not Greek."

Tom nodded at the grad student. "That's right. Do you know what it says?"

The student answered, "Sure. It says, 'Nothing comes from nothing.' A Greek philosopher named Parmenides said it about twenty-five hundred years ago, arguing since nothing can come from nothing, the universe and all of reality couldn't have been created from nothing. Everything we know has always existed and is timeless and changeless. Hence, there was no creator and no god. Reality is 'what is' and couldn't have been created from nothing."

Tom nodded. "Impressive. I always thought it was just a line from *King Lear.*"

David said, "Sorry to break into this philosophical love fest, but what's this saying doing on a bottom of a stone?"

Diogenes blurted out, "Because the logic is rock solid and there's no silly, superstitious god that created that rock or the whole universe out of nothing."

David saw Tom noticing that there was more of a crowd around the booth and probably wondering how many directions this conversation could go tonight. "The clue might have to do with Aristotle. He was quoted as saying that 'Nothing is what rocks dream about,' which is truly 'nothing.' Aristotle believed that God had to exist for everything to come into existence from nothing. One reason he believed this was the concept of motion or change."

One of the observers blurted out, "What does motion or change have to do with God existing or not?"

Tom nodded. "Good question. We know that matter cannot begin its own motion or change or be the reason for its own existence. It must be acted on by another object or force. Since time had to have a beginning, there had to be a first cause of movement or an 'unmoved mover' to begin the process. That force is God."

One of the regular patrons was scratching his head. "Say what?"

Another said, "It makes total sense if you think about it. There had to be a beginning when nothing existed. Things can't create themselves, so it has to be God since no natural 'thing' could have existed to do it."

David hadn't expected to get into another deep conversation, but he knew a can of worms had been opened, so he didn't try to stop it.

The MIT student said, "That is a huge, irrational, and unscientific leap of nothing but faith. If you guys want to believe in your sky-god or invisible pink unicorns or flying—"

Tom interrupted, "Can I finish this familiar list? —the Flying Spaghetti Monster, Santa Claus, the Tooth Fairy, and the Easter Bunny. Did we leave anyone out?"

The student frowned. "I think you have it about right, and no intelligent person would believe in Zeus or any other god either."

"I'm Tom, by the way, and this is the owner of the rock and my good friend David. We met Diogenes and Alex last week."

"I'm Harris, and this is Richard. We are both grad students in Biochemical Engineering and I majored in philosophy and physics as an undergrad at a little technical institute across the river."

Tom reached out his hand. "Great to meet you, Harris and Richard. We only ask two things in our pub debates. One is to have some friendly fun, and the second is to do it respectfully. I will have to admit that mocking can be a very effective form of debate, but I haven't found it to be a very honest one. It tends to clog one's ears once you've decided that the person you are talking to is intellectually inferior to yourself. Challenge ideas all you want, but we would prefer to avoid either mocking or ridicule and have a healthy and respectful debate. Does everyone agree with that?"

Harris smiled. "Perfectly fine with me. No matter how illogical, silly, or stupid anyone's ideas sound, I promise not to go there."

Tom turned to David. "I don't suppose this was how you planned on spending your evening, is it?"

David waved him onward.

Harris asked, "So is it fair to say that the question on the table is, 'Could everything that exists have existed without a god somehow involved?'"

Tom said, "I think that's part of it, but the real question on the table is if anyone can present a reasoned argument that God exists?"

Diogenes said, "But it's impossible to use reason or science to show something exists if it doesn't exist."

To Diogenes's surprise, Tom replied, "I couldn't agree more. Have you heard of Procrustes's magical bed?"

Diogenes squinted skeptically at Tom for a trap. "Does it have anything to do with what we're talking about?"

"Just about how we think and listen. Procrustes had a house by the side of a road, and he offered his guests a delicious meal and a bed with a magical property in that its length would exactly match the length of any guest that lay down upon it."

81

Diogenes interrupted. "Are we only going to talk about magic and fiction tonight?"

Everyone else was listening intently as Tom continued, "What Procrustes did not reveal to his guests was how this magic occurred. When the guest would lie down, Procrustes would then proceed to stretch upon the rack any guest who was too short or cut the legs of those who were too tall until they perfectly fit the length of the bed."

Diogenes said, "I'll ask again, does this have anything to do with what we're talking about? Magic beds and people lopping off legs?"

David knew by now that anything Tom said had a specific purpose. "I think Tom is telling us that we tend not to be honest with ourselves and look only for what fits our belief of what the truth is. If it doesn't align, we cut off the parts that don't fit and stretch the things that almost fit to confirm our belief. I suppose believing in God is one of those subjects where intelligent people tend to do a lot of that kind of filtered listening and thinking."

Tom nodded. "What he said. Hopefully, the entire point is to get to an honest answer and not just to win a debate. Who can put forward the main arguments for holding that God does not exist, or that we can reason that God most likely does exist?"

Harris said, "I think I can summarize a reasonable position on that. First, people have always invented mythical beings and gods to explain what they didn't understand. Today, we have science to explain those things and there is no need to create or superstitiously believe in all-powerful gods of any kind. Those who do aren't thinking rationally. They don't fully understand that science can pretty much explain everything. Secondly—"

Tom interrupted, "Harris, do you mind if we take these one at a time to make sure that we are fully appreciating your positions?"

"Sure. Not at all."

To everyone else, Tom said, "Please jump in with any thoughts. I do agree with you that historically people didn't understand a lot about how the world worked and had plenty of fears and superstitions. My sense is people intuitively knew that there was something greater than themselves. They tried to put a name to it and understand it, but they didn't get it right with all the mythical gods of ancient times. I also agree that science has been a great gift to mankind. As great as science is, would you agree that it's limited in what it can observe and test by the scientific method?"

Diogenes folded his arms across his chest. "I don't think I would agree with that at all!"

Tom faced him. "Tell me this. Can the scientific method test moral truth or love between people? How about this one: can the scientific method test the claim that all truth claims must be testable with the scientific method to be valid? Science can only test things in the material world. Making the limiting assumption that only material reality exists would be based on blind faith and more like cutting off someone's legs to fit a short bed than real science. It's not valid reasoning to say because people once created mythical gods proves that an actual God does not exist, nor is it valid reasoning to limit God to only a material possibility."

There was a collective "Whoa" from observers as Harris was momentarily speechless while he tried to find fault with anything Tom had just said.

Finally, Harris said, "That still doesn't prove that your mythical god exists."

"And it doesn't yet prove that my God is mythical or unreasonable."

Harris huddled for a second with his MIT team while David exchanged glances with Tom. David didn't love the subject matter, but he was enjoying a verbal beat down of young, unearned confidence.

Harris came back, "I still don't think that an all-powerful, all-knowing, omnipresent, invisible god is reasonable, but let's move on. My second point is that I think the cosmological argument from ancient philosophers compared to the knowledge and intelligence of modern scientists is a very weak one, to say the least. There's no proof that the universe couldn't have existed eternally, and even if there were a beginning, there's no logical reasoning that would exclude the universe from creating itself from nothing.

"I can tell you that there's scientific proof that sub-atomic particles can spontaneously create themselves from nothing in a quantum vacuum. You say that whatever begins to exist must have a cause outside of itself. I say it is possible that the universe did not have a beginning, and there is proof that it did not need a cause. Even if you believed that there was a cause, and that cause was a god, you would have to explain what caused God and why there's been no scientific proof that God exists. I think there's more of Procrustes and magic beds in your belief than in my science."

Diogenes, Alex, and Richard seemed pleased and relieved to hear the comeback argument from Harris so easily articulated. The rest of the group listened in quiet anticipation as Tom exclaimed, "I think you may have me—"

A smile crept up on Harris's face under that unkempt beard. "—at the bottom of my beer. Fill 'em up, on me, Mr. Dempsey!"

The silent tension left the room as people laughed and drank down what was left in their mugs for the sponsored refill. David was looking at Tom with a level of respect and admiration that he wasn't used to feeling for others.

Tom took a sip from his topped off beer. "Now, where do we start, gentlemen? Where do we start? How about at the beginning? Many scientists have tried to argue that the universe has simply always existed; it is eternal without a beginning and without any need of a cause for its existence. I believe you young detectives lean toward this theory, correct?"

Harris nodded.

Tom said, "I like the line from Sherlock Holmes when he said, 'When you eliminate the impossible, whatever remains, however improbable must be the truth.' Hopefully, you agree with Mr. Holmes. I think it is safe to assume that you are familiar with the laws of thermodynamics?"

Harris slowly nodded with wary curiosity.

"Okay. Good. Let me know if I get this close to right: The first law holds that total energy in a system is what it is, it can neither be increased nor decreased but only changed. Basically, the total sum of matter and energy in the universe will remain the same."

"Okay," said Harris cautiously.

"The second law is the interesting one. It holds that the degree of disorder is always increasing in the universe, and available energy is always moving towards a state of being less unavailable. Basically, things are running down or decaying, and usable energy is running out over time."

Sam, who was listening intently, said, "Wait a minute, Tom. I might've lost you, but I thought you said that the amount of total energy can't go up or down, but now you are saying it's going down?"

Harris interjected, "Not to help anybody out in this debate, but he didn't say the energy was lost. He said it is changing into a less usable form, kind of like a hot cup of coffee in a room that begins to cool. The energy is not gone from the room but transferred to the cooler air in the room, warming it slightly. Eventually, the heat, or the available energy, from the coffee is gone as the coffee becomes the same temperature as the room and the heat or energy is now unavailable."

Tom said, "Great example. The coffee needs some external force to reheat it since it cannot heat itself. So, since the universe is moving towards disorder and energy is becoming increasingly unavailable, we know that it will eventually decay and die as does anything over time. Never mind that the concept of infinite time is not possible, the universe would've burned out long before now if there was no beginning point. Scientists have also shown that the universe has been expanding versus being in a steady state or collapsing. If we run the clock backward in time, we can see the reverse happening until we reach a single point in time, about 13.8 billion years ago when the Big Bang occurred and time, space, matter, energy, and the universe itself began. There is an overwhelming scientific consensus that the universe had a beginning and that before that event, nothing could have existed."

Harris stepped forward. "Why is the concept of infinite time not possible?"

"Think about it," Tom replied. "You can count seconds, hours, and days. If time went infinitely into the past, you would never get to today."

Alex said, "He's got a point," and Diogenes quickly hit him with his elbow.

Tom restated the hypothesis. "Everything that exists needs an explanation outside of itself. An infinite regression of causes of change or movement is not possible. So there needs to be an explanation, a cause that is external to the universe."

"I still don't buy it," Harris replied. "How do we know that the laws might not have applied before the Big Bang? Quantum physics shows us small sub-atomic particles have been seen to pop in and out of existence without a cause and from nothing, so I think that science will prove that no supernatural god is needed."

Tom took a sip from his beer mug as Harris's words settled on the group. "I agree that very small particles have been observed to act differently and seem to have spontaneously created themselves in a quantum vacuum, but empty space or a quantum vacuum is not actually nothing. It's actually something, and we're back to the same science discussion we just had. Isn't it interesting that nothing larger than these virtual particles or quarks have ever been observed by science to suddenly appear? If I had a missing leg, and I told you that it spontaneously appeared on its own, would you believe me?"

Harris hesitated. "Probably not."

"But you feel completely comfortable with the idea that from absolutely nothing, the entire immense universe spontaneously appeared?"

"I'm just saying that it may have or was the product of a multiverse."

"The multiverse or string theory would still have the same scientific issues we just discussed. So, Harris, you believe the most probable answer is that 'no one' plus 'no thing' equals everything?"

"I'm not sure I would say it that way. If you believe God created everything, then who created God?"

"That's kind of the point. God isn't matter or a thing to be created. If he were, then he would be part of the stuff we said could not have existed forever. God is instead the sheer act of being. To have created everything you see and the wonder of its beauty and incredible complexity, God would have to be supernatural, all-powerful, and the one that is uncreated, unmoved and unchanged.

"Harris, think about how incredibly fine-tuned this universe is and how unlikely or impossible it would be for just a random set of atoms to get the weakness of the gravitational force just right so that the stars didn't burn out, just the right nuclear force to ensure the perfect balance of free hydrogen, just the right density of matter in the universe that couldn't have been off by one quadrillion to support the galaxies or just the right expansion of the universe that was needed. The universe is so finely tuned that the odds of such a low level of disorder needed to support life, after the Big Bang, would have zeros stretched across the universe and be equal to your winning 10,000 lotteries in a row while getting struck by lightning each time you won. I don't know about you, but common-sense reasoning seems to point me to the only rational option."

Harris appeared to be trying to think of a quick response.

Tom said, "The facts seem to say it's impossible for the universe and everything in it not to have had a beginning. I can think of no possible explanation for change, movement or everything coming from nothing without a cause. Since we've ruled out the impossible, logic tells me that this cause had to be external to nature, eternal and powerful enough to create everything. We call that supernatural being God."

Harris scanned the expressions of Diogenes and everyone around the table. "I'm not agreeing with you on any of this, but even if I did, nothing you've said convinces me that this super-being is a personal god or just one power-hungry god."

Sam said, "I still think it seems pretty simple. There had to be a beginning when absolutely nothing existed, and you can't make all this stuff suddenly appear from nothing unless there was a cause outside of nature. If you honestly walk through the logic and follow it back to connect the dots, how do you come to any other conclusion?"

Tom asked an uncomfortable-looking David, "David. What do you think?"

David looked up, and all eyes were on him as he broke his silence, "The science seems to point logically to one answer. That seems clear and denying the facts to be contended with seems like a 'magical bed' exercise to dismiss what doesn't fit and too quickly accept what does fit the answer you want. I do have one issue believing in God though."

Tom listened intently as David spoke, "If God is supposed to be all-good, all-knowing, and all-powerful, then why is there so much senseless suffering and evil in the world? If he were all-loving and all-good, he would want to stop the suffering and if he were all-knowing and all-powerful, he would stop it. So, which is it? Is he all-powerful but doesn't care enough to stop it or is he not all-powerful and can't stop it?"

Harris exclaimed, "See! Another proof that God does not exist! By definition, God must be all-good, all-knowing, and all-powerful. A god that is all these things would want to and be capable of stopping evil and suffering. Evil and suffering exist, so God does not exist. Seems simpler than the Cosmological Argument and harder to dispute rationally."

A number of people in the pub were nodding and talking to each other as Tom responded, "I will admit that the problem of suffering and evil are the two things that trouble people the most. It is probably the number one reason why people stop believing in God and leave their faith consciously or unconsciously. Who here hasn't struggled with this one throughout your life?"

No one raised his hand or said a word. Tom continued, "9-11, a young child suffering in a cancer ward, sexual molestation by an adult or especially a priest, war, senseless torture, or a natural disaster. The list seems endless and downright cruel, so why wouldn't you ask yourself, 'What kind of God would allow this?' To be honest, I don't know if I can answer the question in a way that would make everyone feel good about it, but one thing I do know is that he is the kind of God that would love us enough to humble himself in Jesus who entered right into that suffering with us."

Sam murmured, "I never thought of it that way before. But why meaningless suffering?"

Tom scanned the attentive audience. Everyone was engaged in a conversation they probably never had an opportunity to have. "I know that some of you don't believe that God even exists, some of you may not think a lot about it, and some of you have a deep sense of God in your lives. I can only share what I've come to know in my life, which has ranged from having a strong conviction that there is no God, to being very angry at God, to having a life-changing relationship with the God I now know loves each one of us unconditionally and passionately.

"I thought freedom came from focusing on myself and what I wanted, but I found real freedom in God's plan and His love that never fails, never betrays, and never dies. I thought he was a god that didn't care about me, but He is constantly desiring a true relationship with each one of us, to pour out His love for us. It took a while for me to recognize that He wanted me where I was and gave me the gift of free will to return that love. If God were controlling all of our actions and decisions, we wouldn't have free will and that wouldn't be a loving relationship any more than it would be if we controlled everything in our relationships. However, the downside of free will is sin and evil acts that people do that hurt other people. I have had to learn to trust that God will take care of those injustices with an eternity of joy and love with him in heaven."

Tom paused for a few seconds. "Suffering from illness, injury or natural disasters were and still are a much tougher reality to understand. It can shake your faith to witness what seems like senseless and useless suffering, but that assumes that no good can come from suffering or evil, that God cannot turn those things into something with a purpose and a good. In the midst of suffering, I've seen great acts of personal compassion, courage and self-sacrificing love. People have received and passed on the gifts of patience, trust, empathy, and love when it comes to enduring suffering themselves or being there for those who suffer. I think there are times when our role on earth is to be an example to others.

"When it comes down to it, life isn't about us. When we slide into a self-focused and self-serving life and believe we have no need for God or His plans for us, we are missing the point and joy of life. My own mother was bedridden for almost twenty years with multiple sclerosis. Each day she had a smile on her face and set an incredible example for everyone who came to visit her. She trusted in God's plan for her. As I said, I don't think any one answer would fully address the struggle we have with this, but Jesus knew suffering. He lost His earthly father, His trusted friends betrayed Him, He was tortured and beaten to a point where He was almost unrecognizable, and then experienced a gruesome death, all so we could take our place in heaven. When we suffer, we can unite with Him in that act of self-giving love."

Sam said, "Thanks for sharing that, Tom. I have to ponder that one a bit more."

Tom responded, "Thank you for letting me share. This is a deep subject. People have written lots of great books on this that can help if you or anyone were interested."

While Tom had been talking, Diogenes and Alex had quietly slipped back to the bar, while Harris and the others had remained.

David found himself slipping into the discomfort of his own painful experience as a young boy but continued to pull himself out of the darkness of that pit.

Someone broke in with, "So, can we talk about the Pats?" and the response of laughter broke the thoughtful silence about a heavy topic. The Patriots had only beaten the Miami Dolphins twice out of the previous eight games, and there was plenty of anticipation going into Sunday's game in Miami.

People started to break into smaller groups and left Tom and David at their booth where the evening started. Tom gripped his mug. "Sorry about letting that turn into another debate. You had good questions, and I'm not sure you got the answers you were hoping for."

"Well, I don't know who the heck is leaving these messages, what they are trying to tell me, or why any god would let a young child—" He awkwardly stopped himself mid-sentence.

"I can't answer the first question about who, but it looks like someone is trying to get you to think about your life."

David's brow furrowed. "My life? Are they worried it's going too well?"

Tom smiled. "I could be wrong, so I apologize if I'm out of line, but something seems to be weighing on you pretty heavily. I'm guessing that it may be tied to trust somehow. The two clues so far—"

David cut Tom off. "So far? You mean there are more of these?"

"I don't know about that, but the two messages have been about believing in truth and believing in God. The answers to those two questions, for any man who has the courage, to be honest, can have a profound impact on his life. My guess is that it's probably someone looking out for you, not someone out to hurt you."

On the way out, Tom stopped at the bar, put his hand on Harris's shoulder and shook his hand with the other. "Harris, thanks for the lively debate. I appreciated the respectful conversation and back and forth. I hope you felt the same way."

Harris gave Tom a firm shake back and with a broad smile and a laugh. "Same here. Even if you got some wacky conclusions, you're all right in my book."

Tom looked directly at Harris. "Don't lose your curiosity just when things get interesting. That is what the fun of science and life is all about."

Harris smirked and nodded.

Outside the pub, David hunched his shoulders up to counter the cool evening air. "I have been a little restless lately, but I'm okay. Nothing to worry about."

"Well, that's great. Maybe next time you can come actually ready to play. I'd rather have you knocking me down than sleepwalking through the games like you did today!"

"Just setting you up for next week. Hey, you really believe all that stuff you said in there tonight? I guess you would, since it's your job."

"I might flip that around and say it's my job because I believe it. David, I think it's good to spend time thinking through things, but sometimes we can let thoughts and feelings roll-around in our own heads too much. We can be our own worst enemy by avoiding the real issues or answers. Let me know if you ever want to talk sometime without the pub mates."

"I think I'm good, but thanks for the offer. I was sorry to hear about your mom. How is she doing now?"

"Thanks for asking. I do miss her a great deal. She passed away two years ago this month. I used to visit her every Wednesday afternoon, and we'd have great conversations, so you can see that I'm depending on you now."

"That is a lot of pressure since we hardly know each other."

As they started heading in their respective directions, Tom said loudly, "Let's do something about that!"

Chapter 18

When David got home, Trooper was there to greet him at the door. He crouched down to pet him. "If I didn't provide you with a comfortable bed, food, water, and some attention, would you still want to be my best friend? I guess I'll never know for sure."

He found himself having similar thoughts about his relationships at work: Are we truly friends? Once the utility was gone from the relationship, would they stay? *Would I stay?* Tom was the first person he had known who seemed to truly want a friendship and expected nothing in exchange. He had the feeling that Tom would still want to know him even if he stopped playing basketball on Wednesdays. His relationship with Tom was new territory for him, and he wasn't sure how to manage it. What did Tom really mean when he had said, "Let's do something about that!" What did that "something" look like? How was it going to feel if Tom noticed areas of discomfort going on inside of him?

As he showered and readied for bed, he thought about Jillian. He knew she was hurting, and he felt frozen about the right thing to do. If he saw her without having his issues resolved, he'd be unfairly putting her on an emotional roller coaster. He needed to deal with an issue that he was desperately trying to avoid.

Next to the den cabinet sat a file box from his mom's apartment he had taken home after the funeral. Much of the contents of the box were things belonging to Jimmy or his father that his mom had packed up and put away for thirty years. One of the items was a diary that Jimmy started after high school. David took a breath and opened it for the first time.

January 1, 1971

A new year and ready to start my life now. Started a new job in the afternoons at Dunbar Security in Dot. When I'm eighteen next month, I can work loading and unloading armored cars—a lot better than cleaning and working the office with boss Bill. Once school is out in May, I can work full time and make my own decisions.

Dad still pushing for Community College in fall but done with school. If I can save up enough, hoping to move back to Savin Hill, but at least I can spend time now with my old friends and enjoy life.

Goals for New Year:
-Save to move out on my own and back to Dot
-Get into Bruins Stanley Cup game
-Don't get drafted (please don't get drafted)
-Have a year to remember!

And take DJ to a game this summer

David had built his own conception of his older brother, Jimmy. He idolized him and wanted to be just like him. As a young boy, he watched the way Jimmy dressed, the sports and music he liked, and the confidence he had, but he now realized that he really didn't know Jimmy, only the image he had created as a child. The diary gave an insight into Jimmy that he had never had before with entries from January 1, 1971, through the night before his tragic death on October 15 of that same year.

The family had moved to the North End in the summer of 1970. Jimmy was more than upset to be forced into a new neighborhood and a new school in his senior year of high school. This had created tension between Jimmy and his dad that raised tempers on a daily basis, often at dinner with all six of them crowded around the Formica kitchen table. Mom was trying to get used to the new surroundings, the neighborhood gossip, the smaller apartment, and the tighter budget. Above the hutch sat a picture of Giovanni or "Gianni" Fidele and Ann Elizabeth Kelly coming out of St. William's Church on a sun-filled September day in 1952, as husband and wife. What always struck David was the look of love and admiration his mother had as she was looking at her beaming bridegroom, with her arm around his and his other hand up in the air to shield the rice falling on their heads.

David's dad had served in the army from '48 to '51 and spent a year overseas in the Korean War. Ann met Gianni at a dance in town, and they dated and fell head over heels for each other before Gianni was shipped overseas. Ann had grown up living in a three-decker house on Sidney Street in the Savin Hill section of Dorchester, a primarily Irish Catholic neighborhood, although there were Polish, Italian, Swedish and Lithuanian families scattered throughout this neighborhood of Boston. Gianni had agreed to live upstairs in the house that Annie's parents, John and Carol Kelly, purchased when they moved down from Stonington, Maine after Marie's painful death. While they were Irish, they were staunchly Protestant and weren't thrilled with their daughter dating and then marrying a Catholic, never mind an Italian boy. In time, they did come to like and respect Gianni because he had served his country and more importantly, treated their daughter with loving devotion and respect. Setting foot inside a Catholic Church for the first time was one of the hardest things that they had done, but Annie had pleaded with them to celebrate the wedding and respect Gianni's only request. They agreed, as long as their own Presbyterian minister would co-officiate the wedding vows.

Gianni had grown up in a tight Sicilian neighborhood section of the North End of Boston. Moving to Savin Hill was a cultural shock, to say the least. Dorchester was divided into several sections and each into a parish defined by the local Catholic church. Just around the corner from Sidney Street was St. William's Church and Elementary School, where all four of their children attended.

Gianni got to know the neighbors well and was active in the local church activities, including coaching basketball for the younger boys at the school and the older boys in CYO. He learned to enjoy the Irish culture and the tight-knit community. After work at the construction warehouse, it was easy to stop by the North End, which he'd do at least twice a week to get some of his mom's cooking, especially her pasta with meatballs and perfectly simmered sauce seasoned with basil, oregano, onions, garlic, and lamb.

When Gianni would come home from visiting his family, Annie could always tell where he'd been even when he'd sit down for another full dinner with her and the kids. Gianni and Annie's family grew, beginning with Jimmy in '53, and then Bobby in '55, Abbie in '60 and finally David John in '63. Annie had lost two children before David was born, which had taken an emotional toll on her for some time. Gianni loved spending time with the entire family but also made a point to have one-on-one time with each of the kids. He also made sure that he and Annie went on a date once a week, even if only for a walk around the neighborhood. Gianni would always say that one of the best gifts you could give your children was the example of a strong and loving marriage.

As much as David had idolized his brother Jimmy, he admired his dad and the man he thought he was. His dad was up early six mornings a week to work hard at a manual labor job, but he was generally home early and was completely present with his family. He was a man of deep faith and loved his Church. He made sure that he and the kids went to Mass every Sunday and on holy days. David remembered his dad always tried to teach something new to the kids every day through his sayings on virtues like honesty, courage, patience, and love or reading sections from his favorite books. Despite Gianni ending his formal education at high school and joining the army, he never lost his love for learning and reading Homer's

Jim Sano

Iliad and *Odyssey*, Dante's *Divine Comedy*, or the Bible.

Annie tolerated Gianni's desire to raise the kids in his faith because it seemed to mean more to him than her faith personally meant to her. She was also okay with each of the kids attending St. William's Elementary because it was so close and offered a better education than the public school, and most of the kids in the neighborhood attended the local catholic school. Life for Gianni and Annie's family was good, and living upstairs above her parents helped them with raising four children on a tight budget.

Times were changing for the Boston neighborhoods of Roxbury, Dorchester, and parts of Mattapan, however, and for the heavy concentration of Catholic and Jewish families in these ethnic communities. To escape the continued oppression and racism still occurring in the South from the early 1900s through 1970, there was a great migration of African American blacks to cities like New York, Chicago, and Boston. With the Civil Rights movement of the sixties, there was a push to provide housing for poorer black families. Shortly after the assassination of Martin Luther King, Jr. in 1968, Mayor Kevin White announced the Boston Banks Renewal Group to help low-income, first-time African American buyers purchase homes with federally insured FHA mortgage loans. Twenty-two Boston area banks and local real estate agents got together to formulate a plan that ended up drawing a red line on the Boston map, only allowing these loans to be granted if the African American families applied within this marked area that included Roxbury, North Dorchester, and Mattapan, and denying loans outside of these areas. The belief was that the Jewish and Catholic families, who were heavily concentrated in these areas, wouldn't complain.

At the same time, unethical real estate agents were practicing a tactic called "blockbusting" by warning residents in these areas to sell their homes before their values declined anymore and that the neighborhoods and their daughters would be unsafe as black families moved in. These harmful tactics caused a great flight out of the area for the 90,000 Jewish families living there and many other families as well. Annie's parents couldn't afford the risk to the value of their home and broke the bad news to Annie and Gianni that they were going to sell and move back to Maine during that summer of 1970.

Gianni and Annie talked about the realistic options for where they could move in the city that would fit their finances and provide a good neighborhood atmosphere. Gianni found an apartment in the North End where he had grown up and had family and friends. Annie wasn't completely enthusiastic about moving out of Savin Hill but understood that the situation would probably only get worse rather than better and agreed that it was their best option for now. They knew that the toughest adjustment would be for Jimmy since he had a close group of friends and was entering his final year of high school. When he learned of the move, Jimmy said he'd live with friends in Savin Hill. Gianni took Jimmy for a walk to explain that he understood this was extremely difficult and unfair, but that family was more important, and they would be moving before school started that fall. This didn't sit well with Jimmy, but he knew that he didn't have an option and he resented it. Part of Gianni's decision to move out of Dorchester was his concerns for his seventeen-year-old son and the questionable associations he had developed around the neighborhood.

Gianni, Annie, and kids made the move back to Gianni's home neighborhood on August 13, 1970. It was a warm summer afternoon as they unloaded their furniture from the truck Gianni had borrowed from work and moved into the third-floor apartment on Lewis Street. The neighborhood was lively, and Annie played Sinatra classics as Gianni, Jimmy, and Bobby carried up the heavier furniture. Abbie and David did their share climbing the flights of stairs with packed boxes and other odds and ends. They took a break to eat their meal of Italian cold cut sandwiches and ice-cold ginger ale at the kitchen table as a well-used metal fan helped deliver a refreshing breeze.

By the time they had finished setting up the beds, positioning the furniture and unpacking most of the boxes, it was 6:30 p.m. and they were all about ready to collapse just as they heard sounds from the street below. David remembered racing to the open window first to see the small building across the street with the words Madonna Del Soccorso Society Fisherman's Club above the opened doors. A woman was singing "Ave Maria" as several men in white shirts and black pants carefully carried out a statue to the applause of a large crowd gathered in front of the club. David said, "Dad, there are a lot of people outside our house!" as everyone laughed and came to the window to watch.

Gianni said, "This is the Sicilian Fisherman's Feast, a tradition from the 16th century based on the devotion of the fishermen from a village called Sciacca to the Madonna del Soccorso or Our Lady of Help. They celebrate every year."

The air was filled with music and the smells of cooked sausage as confetti floated down from the apartments. The festive atmosphere intrigued David. "Can we go down to see her?"

Everyone hurried down the stairs, squeezing through the crowd to get a look. Gianni lifted David onto his shoulders so he could see the large statue and ornate platform held by large poles hoisted on the shoulders of several men while others held streamers coming from the top of the columns. They followed the procession through the streets of the North End and then to the Columbus Park Pier where the fishing waters were blessed.

While Gianni was used to the festivals in the North End, the vibrant neighborhood quickly felt like home to the rest of the family, except Jimmy, who was conspicuously absent as the evening celebration went on. Gianni looked at Annie as they sat at an outdoor table to share some grilled sausage sandwiches, fried calamari, and creamy sweet cannoli. Gianni smiled a smile that said he was happy to be home and that he was sharing this with his partner for life. They took a long walk around the neighborhood to enjoy the busy but quieter summer scene. They passed restaurants crowded with tourists looking for authentic Italian cooking and locals enjoying an evening out with friends. They passed churches, small groceries, barbershops, and brick and stone apartment buildings with residents hanging out the windows and groups of older Italians sitting outside their doors on the granite stoops or on old lawn chairs talking as much with their hands as with their mouths.

One man from that night stood out crystal clear to David. Mo Diavolo—black hair combed back with Brylcreem, dark glasses, and an open shirt exposing his thick gold chain against his dark, hairy chest—called out from across the street, "Johnny, are you back from Ireland?" Mo was standing outside the small establishment he had bought and renamed the River Styx Bar.

Gianni crossed the street and Mo gave him a big smile and a firm handshake while putting his other arm around his back. "Hey, Mo. Looks like business is going well. How have you been doing for yourself?" David could still feel the static rising between the two men despite the smiles on their faces. Annie knew that Gianni and Mo were very close friends growing up, but she also knew how Gianni felt about Mo these days. She didn't know the details, but she could tell by Gianni's body language that the conversation was going to be short. When Gianni crossed back over, Annie looked at his eyes to see how he was doing but couldn't read them.

The last stop on the walk was to visit Gianni's parents. The kids were used to visiting their grandparents, "Nonna" and "Nonno." Gianni was the youngest of their three children and the only remaining child as Gianni's brother had died in World War II, and his sister had lost a long battle with cancer. They were all tired after the move, so the visit tonight was more of a short hello. On the way out, Nonna handed Annie lasagna from the freezer. "Annie, we're glad you are all close by. Can you take a little something to help with meals while you are getting settled?" Annie took the dish and kissed Nonna on the top of her head since she was much shorter than

Annie but still taller than young David and headed home with Gianni, Bobby, Abbie, and David to start their new life.

Chapter 19

After their summer visit to their grandparents in Maine, David knew Jimmy wasn't looking forward to attending a new high school. Jimmy had made friends in the North End but took the subway back to Savin Hill frequently to spend time with his old gang and closest friends. He also knew Mo took a liking to Jimmy, let him into his bar with his friends, gave him tickets to Bruins or Celtics games, and encouraged Jimmy to work for the Dunbar Armored Truck Company located in Dorchester. By December, Jimmy was working part-time in the Dunbar security office along with his best friend from grade school, Tom Collins. Jimmy called him "Tommy C" after Tony C of the Red Sox. Tommy C was more energized than Jimmy to find ways to make money and enjoy life to the fullest. He had started school later than Jimmy and ended up staying back twice before sharing the same class with Jimmy in the sixth grade. Despite the three-year difference, he enjoyed Jimmy's company and friendship, especially since Jimmy never judged him as others had.

Tommy C was working on his certification to become an armored truck driver when he turned twenty-one in April. He couldn't wait to be driving that tank around Boston and carrying all that money. Mo had encouraged Tommy C to practice for the exams and his driving test. Mo also told him that he could help him to get a gun permit and handgun since drivers and guards had to supply their own weapons. Mo knew one of the managers at Dunbar and put in a good word for both Jimmy and Tommy C.

Tommy C loved showing Jimmy around the armored trucks during downtime. They were basically large, sealed metal boxes of hardened steel, chromium, and nickel, which created a dense, impenetrable casing. He showed Jimmy the gun ports in each door with spring-loaded plates you could only slide open from inside. He banged on the windows that were made up of several layers of automotive glass mixed with layers of bullet-resistant optical plastic and showed Jimmy how the windshield was at a 45-degree angle to aid deflection of bullets. The tires were armored and could run several miles even if flat. The steel ram bumpers and front grill also allowed the driver to push most vehicles out of the way. It seemed like nothing could penetrate this fortress. "The whole thing weighs 12,000 pounds and can carry 25,000. Pretty cool, huh?"

"Not really," Jimmy responded as he was sweating inside the hot, metal box.

Tommy C smiled and told Jimmy to sit on the passenger side that was separated by a steel bulkhead and was part of the cargo hold. "You are sitting where the second guard sits in what they call the 'hopper.' This door slams shut with an auto-lock and only the driver can reopen it electronically from the inside. For normal loads, I guess the hopper is the only one to leave the truck unless it's a large haul and then we might have two more guards riding in the cargo hold." Jimmy was impressed with his commitment to learning all the details of his future job and was thinking if he had done that in school, he may have even graduated on time.

At Christmas, Mo surprised Jimmy with Bruins tickets and a leather diary inscribed on the inside cover: *Jimmy, you are a great kid ready to start your own great life. Make sure it's your own and promise me you will fill this up with some great stories.* Styx. Even though he had long stopped believing in the reason for the holiday, Mo had the place decked out for Christmas to bring people in to celebrate. Jimmy knew he had to get home early for Christmas Eve dinner with the family, but Mo convinced him to stay a little while longer to get Jimmy's reaction to the entertainment for the evening. He had hired a beautiful, buxom blonde woman who was wearing a Santa hat, boots, and a skimpy red and white-trimmed outfit. Mo sent the Santa's helper over to Jimmy just long enough to get him lightheaded. Finally, Mo laughed and took her arm. "You have other stockings to fill, Natalia."

Jimmy told Mo he had to go and ran home just as Nonno, Nonna, some friends, and family were sitting down to enjoy the traditional Christmas Eve feast of seven fishes, including lobster, salt cod, shrimp, smelts, calamari, scallops, eel, and stuffed quahogs. Gianni glanced up at Jimmy as he was rushing in with sweat on his brow, smiling to let Jimmy know he was glad he was there. Annie and Abbie had spent the week decorating the apartment for the Christmas feast to their favorite Christmas music. Gianni had taken Bobby and David out earlier that day to pick out a tree from the Italian church a few streets over. They also brought home an assortment of desserts from the bakery that included Italian rum cake, cannoli, and Neapolitans to complement Nonna's biscotti cookies and ricotta pie, both lightly glazed with sugar and colorful sprinkles.

David could remember the adults toasting with limoncello while he sipped Italian lemon soda and enjoyed the festive atmosphere as the snow was lightly falling outside the apartment windows, creating a white blanket over the North End.

As the evening wore on, they sat and relaxed, opening one present each before going together to midnight Mass. David remembered opening up a harmonica, something he always wanted to play. Everyone except Mom got ready to go to Mass at St. Leonard's. The church, built by Italian immigrants and the Franciscans in 1873, was packed with parishioners from the North End and was lit only by candlelight. David could vaguely remember that it was hard to see very much, yet he vividly recalled all of his senses being filled by the Christmas hymns being sung, the incense, the decorations, and being in the middle of so many people gathered together to celebrate Christmas. Even at seven years old, as David felt his hand in his father's and looked around, he knew that home was not where he was living but the family he was surrounded by.

Chapter 20

As the bedroom alarm played, David woke up, still in the leather chair and Trooper on the floor next to him. He sat up to stretch out the kinks from being in an awkward position during the few hours he slept. He was exhausted more by the memories of his childhood than sleeping in the chair. He thought about the mysterious messages being left. As he shaved, David found himself talking to his reflection in the mirror. "Who the heck could it be and why? Changing the locks and the additional security should take care of the problem—I hope."

It was still misty this morning, and he decided to make himself and Trooper breakfast at home. While sitting at the table and wagging a dog bone at Trooper, David said, "You always get riled up when a stranger comes to the door and stay that way until I come home, right?" He didn't wait for a nod as he continued waving the bone as Trooper's head followed it. "And on neither day did you seem the least bit upset, did you? Lucy has the only key, and it wasn't her, right? Huh." He left for work troubled on both accounts and thought it was best to just bury himself in work than to keep thinking about it.

When David arrived at work, Izzie was sitting at her desk and said with a smile, "And good morning, Mr. Kelly. How was your evening?"

"It was okay and how was yours?"

Izzie shook her head. "I got my exercise getting home, going to the grocery store, cooking up some stew, helping one with a paper and listening to lines from a play for another, and then relaxing with washing and ironing. I bet you didn't have that much fun!"

David realized that this was a normal day for her, and he never heard her complain, only how blessed she was to have her children. He knew she meant it and that she wouldn't trade places with him for anything. It continually amazed him how upbeat Izzie always seemed, and he started seeing things around her workstation that he hadn't taken the time to notice before. Today he spotted a small picture of a girl sitting on the beach looking at the sunrise and the words, *Heaven is like diving into an ocean of infinite love*, written above. She always wore her cross and often went to the chapel at lunchtime or before coming to work. A very different life than his.

David made it through a few meetings, but he was getting more and more restless. Finally, he told Izzie to hold his next couple of calls and left the office. He had no idea where he was going. He just needed to get out of the office. He wandered several blocks and found himself walking down the street that had elicited such a strong response from him just three weeks earlier. As he walked past the church rectory, he noticed a short man replacing a broken church window. Several lengths down the sidewalk, he took a deep breath and then turned about-face and headed back to the church. When he got closer, he noticed the wooden sign in front of St. Anthony's Church with the schedule of Masses underneath. He stopped in front of where the man was on the ladder replacing a window. When the man's hammer dropped to the ground, David stepped over the small wrought iron fence around the garden and retrieved the hammer. "Can I help you with anything?"

The man looked down from the ladder at David. "Thank you, sir. I'm just finishing up, but I could use that rag in my toolbox to wipe clean the window putty. It's a shame when people's anger makes them throw rocks through a church window."

The handyman descended the step ladder and stood a good seven inches shorter than David but was sturdy and capable. His face reflected time-earned character with his rough, olive-colored skin and a large nose. He shook David's hand. The man's hands were larger and rougher than he had expected

"I appreciate the offer. Can I help you at all?"

David hesitated. "I, um, I'm looking for Tom or Father Tom, rather. Do you know if he's around?"

"He just finished taking a class of boys through the church, and I think he is back in the rectory. You can knock on the side door right over there."

David thanked him and headed towards the rectory but stopped and turned around. He reached out to give the man the hammer still in his left hand. "I don't want to have to go to confession too."

The man grinned.

Before David could knock, the door opened up and there Tom stood wearing his black shirt and the white clerical collar, with a dish towel in his hand. He greeted David with an Irish accent. "Now is it actually himself standing outside my door?"

David smiled. "Yes, it's me-self. I was just walking by and thought I'd stop in."

"Just walking by, huh? Do you have time to come in?"

David walked into Tom's kitchen. "You know, I'm still having a hard time seeing you in that," he said as he pointed to his collar.

Tom quickly swung the towel around his neck and smiled. "Does that help at all?"

"Not really."

Suddenly, there was a faint knock on the door. Tom reached out and opened the door to let in a student from St. Anthony's School. The boy was about thirteen years old and stood there sopping wet from head to toe. "Father Tom, Sister Helen wanted you to know that—"

"Let me guess, Michael, the sprinkler system went off again for no reason?"

Michael dripped and nodded.

"And Sister Helen was teaching a class in the room when this happened?"

Michael dripped, gulped, and nodded again.

Tom gave Michael a towel and walked him out to where the handyman, Angelo, was working. "Mr. Salvato, would you be able to bring some towels over to Sister Helen's class and see if we can take care of things?"

Angelo answered, "What makes you think I'm not any more afraid of a soaking wet nun than you are?" and headed off with Michael to face the situation.

David asked, "Tom, why don't you have someone come in to fix that?"

Tom motioned to David to take a seat at the kitchen table. "Sit down, David. Rest that weary head of yours. Would you like something to drink? Water? Tonic?"

David shook his head.

Tom took out bread that smelled freshly baked along with slices of turkey, cheese, tomato, lettuce, and spicy mustard. "Then what are you going to have with your sandwich?"

David glanced at the clock: 10:45. "It's a little early for lunch for me. Thanks, anyway."

"Well, I didn't have anything before morning Mass and won't be eating at noon, so this is my window, and you don't want to see me when I'm hungry. So, to what do I owe the pleasure of your first, well, second, visit to our home, which, as you can see, is in desperate need of repairs? I would love to call someone in for a new roof or to fix the sprinkler system and the heating system for that matter, but the budget's tight and getting tighter this year with all the sad news going on."

David curiously asked, "Sad news?"

Tom stopped making his sandwich. "I'm sure you are aware of the abuse scandal that's been on the front page of the *Globe* most days this year. It's more than sad for all those people who suffered what no child should suffer, and it's sad for the mission of the Church. A lot of people are obviously upset, and rightly so. Mass attendance has dropped off and so have contributions, so roofs leak more."

David wasn't sure if he should weigh in, but his disdain for all things Catholic got the better of him. "Why do you stay in a Church that condones abusing innocent kids? When I read about it, I keep thinking to myself that there is nothing worse. You don't seem like the kind of guy that would work for an outfit like that."

David could see by Tom's serious expression that this was an area of great conflict for him. Tom sat down at the table. "David, I have struggled to make sense of this all year. People have come by the church yelling names I won't repeat, warning the kids coming out of school to watch out for the dirty priests, and smashing the windows. They are angry, and I can understand why. I was so caught off guard when I found out that one of the accused priests had worked here when I started. Most people think that it's all going on right now, that most priests are pedophiles and that everyone knew what was happening."

David blurted, "How couldn't you?"

"The rate of sexual abuse and pedophilia is higher in public schools than by priests, but you don't hear much about it because those involved aren't talking. The kids are afraid or ashamed to talk and the abusers certainly aren't going to tell. At the time, I think there was a poor screening of candidates for the priesthood and a warped view of the sexual revolution but there was and still is, tragically, the abuse of children going on in all walks of society. Anyone working for the Church is and damn well should be held to the highest standard of expectations. You absolutely should be able to trust that your children are being protected by people doing God's work. Pedophilia is a real sickness, but there's no excuse for this tragedy.

"My heart has ached for those abused children, their pain, their shame, and I have cried many a night for them. The thing beyond comprehension is why the Church leaders, who knew about the abusers, didn't do everything possible to ensure it never happened again. I still don't know the details myself about those accused of knowingly moving priests around, but I'm more than pissed about it."

David shook his head. "I think they should be taken out and shot or hung. How could any human being not do everything they could to protect those kids? I mean, I'm reading about hundreds of cases and even though a lot of them were a while ago, that doesn't change anything. These people have had their lives destroyed, to protect what?"

Tom nodded. "You're right. I know the standard belief and guideline from psychiatrists was that this was a treatable illness. Many of those priests were sent for treatment and cleared, but that medical belief has changed dramatically. That doesn't, however, explain the priests whom you've read about in the paper or the leaders that let this continue. The percentage of priests involved in abuse is small and no higher than the general population but there shouldn't be any. I also feel sad for the 96 percent of good priests that are sickened by this and who are being looked at as potential pedophiles and sexual predators. It's a scandal and a stain on the Church, but each of those kids' lives was more important than any bad press exposing these offenders."

"So why do you stay?"

"I'm not sure how to explain this easily, but the Church is not a man-made organization that just went bad and should be abandoned. Jesus left us with His Church and it's not a building or a set of rules, but something profoundly more. The Church is also made up of imperfect sinners, who, throughout our entire history, have fallen, sinned and required constant renewal and cleansing. Those sins or stains do not change what the Church itself is, but it certainly doesn't live up to its mission to share the good news of Jesus and be a living example of his love.

"These crimes miss our mission completely and hurt the most innocent as a result. Jesus said that the Church he built would never die and would be the pillar of truth and love. What the rest of us have to do is help heal the injured, shine a light on the issues, and hope to bring people back to what the faith is all about. Remember, it isn't because these men followed the teachings of the Church, but precisely because they didn't follow them that we have all this pain and suffering. Maybe that doesn't make a lot of sense to you, but I believe in what the Church is really all about, even though I feel shame about this scandal every day."

David continued to shake his head. He wasn't processing everything Tom had said and realized that Tom himself was struggling to process this avalanche. "Sorry to get into all that. How are you doing with this yourself?"

"Well, my first priority is to make sure every one of those kids who comes to school or church is completely safe here and hopefully at home. It has made doing what I do a lot harder, but the parishioners have a right to know what the deal is and what's being done. I think I've moved from the denial phase into the angry phase, but I work to keep that feeling focused in the right place. Thanks for asking. How about yourself?"

David stared down and flipped a napkin on the table over and over, thinking of how to answer, unsure of why he even came. Finally, he said, "I'm not exactly sure how I am. You were right that something was triggered a few weeks ago, but I'm not sure what it is, and I'm confused with these messages that are being left at my place that only you seem to know how to decode."

"I'd be curious too. As I said, I don't think it could be anyone who wants to harm you."

"So, breaking into my house is a good thing?"

Tom laughed. "Well, if you have to be broken into, this isn't the worst result. Socrates said that 'The unexamined life is not worth living,' and there's no better place to start than believing that life has truth, purpose, and meaning, and that meaning comes from God. You were fairly quiet at those debates. How do you feel about objective truth?"

"I have no issues with there being things that are true and things that aren't true."

Tom made eye contact with David. "How are you about God? Do you think he is real?"

"I'm not so sure about God. If he does exist, I don't think he really cares—about me, anyway."

Tom's lips tightened as his expression towards David changed from curiosity to empathy. "How about your dad? Is he alive?"

David paused and asked, "No, he died when I was young. Why?"

"I talk with women who have issues with believing that a loving God exists, but the overwhelming number of people having a struggle are men, especially men that have had distant or difficult relationships with their dads. Sometimes losing your dad early on can create a sense of abandonment and a struggle to relate to any father figure unless you have a strong male mentor to step in early."

David was feeling uncomfortable with the conversation and that Tom had just knocked on a private door without an invitation to do so. Tom must have sensed this as he asked, "How about doing something different today?"

David was trying to adjust to the conversation's shift in gears. "Um. I'm not really off today. I just took a quick break from work. What exactly were you thinking of?"

"Here, eat half of my sandwich and just help me out with something. It is just a few blocks from here."

David hesitated but had a strong feeling that he didn't want to go back to work. "All right, but I won't have a lot of time."

As they got up to leave, David saw, through the window, a woman wearing a light gray head covering with a white band and a gray dress coming towards the door. As the door opened, it was obvious the woman wasn't completely dry and was holding a towel in her hand. David could tell from Tom's expression that it was too late to go out the front door. "How are we today, Sister Helen?"

Sister Helen was maybe five feet in height with a plain but attractive face and spoke with a slight Irish accent. David could tell that she was no pushover. She had a look in her eyes that was serious while playful at the same time. "Father, so towels is what we get when it is umbrellas that we need. You know that I'm not one to be asking for much, but a class without rain would be appreciated."

Tom smiled at her respectively, but he couldn't hold back a smile and a small laugh as he said, "Sister, I'm really sorry." David was waiting for the Sister to lose her patience with Tom, but her serious look turned into a smile and then a laugh of her own. Tom said, "I promise to see what we can do. By the way Sister, this is David Kelly, a good friend of mine who is coming over to My Brother's Table with me this morning. David, this damp lady is Sister Helen, the reason we have such a great school and great kids."

David shook Sister Helen's damp hand. "Pleased to meet you, Sister."

Sister Helen eyed him up and down. "If you dress that well to work in the food kitchen, I can't wait to see how you dress for church. I'll be looking out for you at Mass."

David said, "Ahh—"

Tom jumped to the rescue. "David doesn't go to this parish, but maybe someday he will visit us. Is there anything else I can do right now before we go?"

Sister Helen turned to David and shook her head. "What manner of speaking is that? Doesn't he have to do something first before he can do something else?" and then left mumbling to herself as she walked back to the school.

David raised his eyebrows. "The food kitchen? I don't know."

"I know you don't, but at least help me take a few things in?" They walked out to Tom's old Honda hatchback and David gave it an amused smile.

Tom chuckled. "I hope you don't mind riding in style today." He opened his door to get in. David checked out the seat to see if he was going to get anything on his suit and then slid into a car that was unlike anything he had sat in for many a year. My Brother's Table was only a few streets over, and they pulled up to the front door where he had first spotted Tom that morning in August. David grabbed one of the crates as Tom held another and knocked on the door with his foot.

Sam answered the door and enthusiastically greeted David. "Hello again, Mr. David or DJ. Good to see you back, and in another fine-looking suit." Sam's skin was dark, his beard was full, and his head mostly bald. He stood about 5 feet, 5 inches, round in shape, which went well with his broad genuine smile. He glanced at Tom. "We need some help today." Both Tom and Sam looked over at David with a smile in their eyes as well as on their faces. David stood there like the remaining man in a lineup after everyone else had taken a step backward when a volunteer request was made.

Tom said, "We definitely need you, David, but I can understand if you have more important places to be."

David peered up at the sky and pressed his lips tightly together as he searched for a good response. Based more on impulse than thought, David said, "Okay, but my rates aren't cheap." Sam put his arm around David as the three walked into the pantry kitchen through the metal alley door.

Inside the kitchen and out in the dining room were a number of men working to get things ready for the lunchtime guests. Sam said that most of the volunteers were men who had been in the meal line themselves at one time or another and were working their way out or giving back for the help that they had received. Sam handed David an apron to help keep his expensive shirt and pants clean and asked if he'd cut up the chicken for the dish.

Out in the dining room, Tom worked with some men to get the serving stations ready. David was struck by the level of respect Tom showed each man and how completely present he was with them. Sam placed the chicken in large skillets, sprinkled them with salt and black pepper; then added cooked sausage and some oil to them. In another large pan, he cooked up peppers, celery, and garlic. Sam asked David to start adding the chicken and sausage to the vegetables and then to stir in the rice which had been cooking on the other stove. Next, Sam then added broth, paprika, and thyme, then covered each pan to let it simmer while David prepped shrimp and scallions to be added last.

All this time Sam was talking about his family while Father Tom and the other men worked in the dining room. One man, whom David recognized from last time with the long hair and old Red Sox hat, came in with bread to be sliced.

Sam asked, "David, do you remember Ritter?"

Ritter turned to David. "Hey, man, the guy with the suit. Good seeing you again, bro." As Ritter sliced bread, he chatted about taking a trip to Vermont or maybe Mexico or maybe Rhode Island, to start seeing the world. He knew some people in Pawtucket, Rhode Island, so he'd have a place to crash. David just smiled as Ritter went back and forth with Sam about the advantages of Rhode Island over Mexico, and how good bread is when it comes right out of the oven, but how hard it is to cut.

Sam was making up enough jambalaya to feed an army, and it smelled tasty. David surmised that Sam always made sure he served food that he would want to eat and picked dishes where he could include vegetables and other ingredients that were good for the guests.

David noticed guests were coming in from the line that had been forming outside the door for the past thirty minutes. Tom greeted each guest with the respect and dignity they deserved even if they didn't believe it themselves. None were allowed in if they had been visibly drinking. Many had hair that looked like it hadn't been combed or well-worn clothes that hadn't been washed while others came in looking like anyone you might see in town, well-groomed and reasonably well-dressed.

David helped Sam and Ritter bring out the large pans of the jambalaya and bread from the kitchen to be served with the salad already at the serving stations.

Tom said to David, "How is it going, chef?"

David replied, "It's going fine. The food smells better than I would've expected."

"Sam takes a lot of pride in his cooking and serves the best he can for people who often had little sleep and no breakfast. Are you up for serving a bit?"

David peered out at a large number of men that had taken their seats in the dining hall and were queuing up at the serving stations, table by table. As they came up, most of them would smile with or without all their teeth, and ask if David was new, what was on the menu, or if they could take two pieces of bread. Some said, "Thank you," while others silently stared at him while holding out their plate. Tom was good at engaging with the guests, taking the time to say something sociable to those who were less gregarious. Tom was a natural, and David could tell that he had developed relationships with the majority of men who came through the line. Tom joked back and forth with David and included the person they were serving in the friendly exchange.

After everyone had filed through the line, David went around with coffee to fill up cups and enter into conversations. Sometimes he had to find a polite way to extricate himself from conversations that wouldn't have ended otherwise. Many of the men stayed to help clean the dining room and put the chairs upside down on the tables to allow sweepers to clean the floors. Cleaning the serving stations and the kitchen was fairly quick and fun with the personalities of all those helping out. The comradery felt comforting to David. Sam thanked him for all his work and hoped he didn't get anything on his clothes. David shook his hand. "Sam, you are a first-rate chef. Do you do this every week?"

Sam smiled. "We will be getting ready for dinner in a bit, and we do this twice a day, every day, so you are welcome here anytime, Mr. David or DJ."

David smiled and took off his apron to find that one spot did manage its way onto his hand-tailored shirt but somehow he didn't mind. Walking out the door with Tom, he was feeling a level of contentment that was different for him.

Tom seemed to notice the expression on his face and grinned.

David furrowed his brow and asked, "What?"

"I was just thinking."

David got back into Tom's car. "Come on. Thinking of what?"

"Okay. You did ask for it. I was thinking of the reading this morning at Mass. It was the story about a widow who was down to her last meal with her son. She meets Elijah, and he asks her to bring him water and a morsel of bread. The widow explains that she has nothing baked and only a handful of meal in her jar and a little oil. Elijah told her not to fear and to make a little cake for him and then for her and her son. Even though it was all she had, and she knew she'd have nothing left to eat, she did as he said. Because of her faith, Elijah told her that God would not let the meal in the jar nor the container of oil ever go empty, and it did not, as she and her son ate for many years."

"That is a charming story, but what made you think of that just now?"

"I saw that look on your face when you came out. You gave your time and yourself. If you had to sum up the entire Bible, you might say that it's about trusting in God and giving everything you have in love, and you will always be filled and never run out. But, when you cling to things other than God, they can never satisfy. You can hoard and save as much wealth, power or pleasure as you can, but it will never be enough."

Just then, David remembered what Kevin Walsh had been telling him at dinner a few weeks back. It connected with what Tom was saying.

"I know you don't feel connected to God right now," Tom said, "and it would be a major league leap to trust him completely right away but think about this. God is pure love and love is not something you can keep but only give, only pass on to another. When you are giving to others, especially those who are in need, giving of yourself without any expectation for something in return, you are linked with God. You'll feel filled and free. Widows at the time of that story had no means of income and there weren't any support systems around, so when the widow said she was down to her last bit of meal and oil, she knew she and her son would soon die of hunger, yet she trusted in God and he didn't fail her."

They pulled up back into St. Anthony's driveway. David said, "Still a nice story, but thanks for inviting me today. It was good."

As David was about to walk back to the office, a young man came out of the side door of the rectory. He looked to be about nineteen or twenty, slim and about 5 feet, 10 inches, with longish dark hair with some curl to it. He was wearing jeans, a black tee-shirt with an open button-down collar shirt on top.

Tom grinned, and called out, "Luke, did you get yourself something to eat?"

As Luke reached Tom and David, he was still chewing something in his mouth. "Nope." He extended his hand to David. "How are you doing? I'm Luke."

David liked the confidence in Luke's voice. "Glad to meet you. I'm David."

Luke glanced at Tom. "Ah. So, this is the guy who can't beat an old man like you at b-ball?"

David laughed. "What?"

Tom smirked. "Meet my little brother and trouble-maker extraordinaire. Luke, tell David that I never said anything even remotely close to that."

Luke chuckled. "Brother, you know I'd do anything for you, but you also told me lying wasn't a good thing to do, so I am conflicted."

"Maybe I should leave now to practice my pathetic game for next week," David said, "Good meeting you, Luke. Tom, good seeing you today."

Tom said, "I'm really glad you came and helped out. I'm sure it was appreciated by many."

When David arrived back at his office, Izzie inspected him and nodded. "Mmmhmm, and it's good to see you again today, Mr. Kelly. I hope you enjoyed your lunch today."

Remembering the stain, David looked down at his shirt. "No, Izzie, I'm not a sloppy eater. I was just helping out a friend, at uh, at My Brother's Table."

Izzie's eyes lit up with surprise and approval as her lower lip curled and she gave an approving nod.

As David entered his office, he could hear her mumbling, "Today is a good day."

Chapter 21

Tom put his arm around Luke as they walked back into the rectory. "It's not safe out here. There are damp nuns on the lookout for me."

Luke curiously shook his head.

"So, to what do I owe the pleasure of your company?"

"Can't I visit my only brother when I want?"

Tom peered at him, knowing there was more. Luke was attending Boston University on a partial scholarship, which didn't even cover all the high tuition, never mind the room and board, so he found different places to stay and was clearly in between.

"Do you need a place to stay?"

"That's a very kind invitation, and I wouldn't want you to be lonely."

"Luke, I'm not Dad or Mom, but they aren't here now, and I do worry about you."

"You were on your own at my age and you didn't worry about you, did you?"

"No, I didn't, which is precisely why I worry about you. I thought I knew pretty much everything I needed to know at nineteen. Dad used to say to us over and over, 'The more you know, the more you know you don't know.' So, imagine how much I really knew when I thought I knew everything. Noodle that one for a while. I don't want to overprotect you or put out that fire you have. I love your passion, your curiosity, your sense of adventure, and your sense of humor. Don't lose any of those, but try not to be swept up into a culture that is lost in terms of what life is all about and what being a man means. What we do has real effects on others and our own soul."

Luke grabbed the other half of the sandwich he had made, and with his mouth full, said, "I know you care, and I know that you love me. I need to figure out who I am and not just try to be you."

"You definitely don't want to be me. Just try to follow things all the way through until you get to the truth. Even though most people don't bother or have the courage to seek the truth, it can actually be the easiest part. Facing and following it is what a true man will do and will never regret."

"I know. The truth will set you free, right?"

Tom nodded. "Most people I run into would like to avoid the truth because they believe they have to give something up, but once you stop resisting it, you begin to feel a tug towards it. I think Chesterton said it 'begins a great love affair.' Luke, I have great faith in you and know deep down you have something really special in you. I know it has been tough with Mom's illness and losing Dad."

"I'm fine. Don't worry about me. Okay?"

With a loving gaze, Tom said, "I'll just worry a little."

While Luke worked on a philosophy paper, Tom was taking care of paperwork and thinking about his homily for Sunday Mass. They played a game of chess and kept the conversation light as Luke reached checkmate after a long chase of Tom's king. They enjoyed each other's company, despite Luke being exactly half his brother's age.

Luke cast Tom a serious look. "When I was a one-year-old, you were twenty times my age. When I was ten, you were less than three times my age."

"Yes, Einstein. That is correct."

"And now you're only twice my age, sooo—I think that my math is telling me that we will be the same age at some point!"

Tom grinned.

"Unless you actually follow it through." Tom got that this was Luke's way of telling him that he understood his earlier point, that while something feels like it is true, the facts may actually be very different in life.

Tom helped Luke make up the bed in the small spare room then patted him on the back to say good night. He knew Luke would be up for many more hours, but Tom had an early morning.

Tom was up early to get ready for morning Mass. Tony Cappolla was serving again today and was running in just before the start of Mass carrying the tall crucifix. Tom, a Jesuit priest, which made him a member of the Society of Jesus that was started by Saint Ignatius, tried to always celebrate each Mass as if it were his first Mass, his only Mass, and his last Mass. Eight years of study, community life, and apostolic work helped Tom to find the deeper meaning in his role as a priest.

After Mass, Tom mustered up his courage to go over to the school to see the damage done by the sprinkler system. Angelo had everything cleaned up and moved out of the room. The school wasn't large enough to lose a classroom, but Tom wasn't sure how he'd be able to fix the issue. As he was scanning the room, he could feel a unique presence behind him, then heard a voice saying, "So now he comes over. Father, I will be using the church basement for my classes until we can solve this problem. It is getting too chilly out to have the children running around soaking wet."

Tom turned around, slowly tilting his head down to look at Sister Helen. "Well, while you're in the church, you might want to pray for a miracle since I'm not sure what else we can do right now."

Sister Helen was a gift straight from heaven when Tom had started at St. Anthony's four years earlier. Being a Franciscan religious, she wasn't happy to see a Jesuit taking the helm at St. Anthony's of all places. Nevertheless, they quickly learned they had a similar passion and approach to making the school something special again. Sister Helen was able to attract many quality teachers and let the students know they were loved and welcomed in a school that was caring, disciplined, and excelled academically. Despite the tight budget, Sister Helen brought music, art, and drama into the experience. Tom appreciated her strengths. He knew his lay elsewhere, in sports and the classics. He taught several classes a week to help each student learn about God, how much they were loved by him, and that each one of them had strengths, gifts, and a purpose in life. He knew together they were a good team.

When Tom returned to the rectory, Luke had already gone off to his classes for the day. He rolled his eyes when he noticed that Luke left his cereal bowl and spoon on the table instead of cleaning up. He lifted the bowl and saw a paper underneath with the words, "Once in a while you will stumble upon the truth, but most of us manage to pick ourselves up and hurry along as if nothing had happened - Winston Churchill." On the other side of the paper, Luke wrote, "I will stumble, but I will not hurry along. Luke."

On the first Friday of each month, Tom ran a coffeehouse with a question-and-answer night in the church basement. He believed good teaching informed the mind but also moved the heart. The audience was mainly college students from several of the local colleges in the area, who were tired of trying to have fun by getting drunk or smoking pot and were looking for something different. The monthly Friday night gathering was fun as young men and women came in and greeted each other with a hug or a smile. Different students would take turns playing songs on a guitar, fiddle, or singing something meaningful or fun, and everyone would join in as they learned the choruses. Tom kept things friendly and comfortable for people, so they could share their faith experiences or any struggles they may have. He liked to encourage questions as they sat around in a large circle two to three deep on good nights. Luke wasn't one to show up for these gatherings, but he wandered over tonight when he came back for the evening and sat on the steps out of sight.

A student with long bushy hair and a beard, who went by the name "Beetle" and attended periodically, raised his hand in the back of the room. He usually asked questions that were deliberately confrontational, but Tom merely treated these types of questions as opportunities because he knew that many of the students had these same questions. He'd rather they talked them out here with accurate information. "Beetle, it's good to see you. What do you have for us tonight?"

"Father Tom, why is it that the Church has so many rules and regulations? Doesn't seem like Jesus would operate that way. Doesn't it just get in the way of important stuff like love and freedom?"

"That's a great question." He scanned the room, inviting the other students to join the conversation. "Tell me, what is a sport that you like to play or watch?"

The students called out, "Baseball. Hockey. Golf—"

"Okay. Good. Now take any one of those sports and then remove all rules of the game. Play baseball where there are no rules. You don't have to run on the base paths. There is no limit to the number of strikes or outs. You can swing the bat at someone trying to tag you out."

Everyone started laughing. Tom continued, "How about hockey? Sometimes it looks like there are no rules but actually, there are some. If an offensive player could just stay in the opponent's end of the rink or you could have as many men on the ice as you wanted. Take the game of golf and say you could throw the ball as far as you wanted when out of bounds or maybe put your foot in front of the cup when your opponent is putting. It sounds kind of fun, but it wouldn't be baseball or hockey or golf after a while. What about school? Say you studied hard and got every answer right on your test, but the teacher gave you a failing grade and then gave someone who never came to class an A? No rules. No complaints. Anything we care about, we put rules around to make the game what it is and to understand what is fair to expect."

Beetle interjected, "Okay, but what does that have to do with all the Church rules and regulations?"

"Jesus gave the Pharisees a hard time for focusing too much on the letter of the laws too, so it is always a good question to ask."

Beetle nodded as he scanned the room and puffed up with pride.

"But he also loved the law because of what it was. What do you think that was?"

One girl said, "The commandments?"

"Excellent, but what are the commandments?"

Another student said, "They are God's laws."

"Okay. Laws for whom?"

The student answered, "For us?"

"Correct. Now, do we see these laws as a loving guide to help us know and understand God's ideas of what is healthy and good for us or are they an imposition, a set of unreasonable laws whose only intention is to stop us from having real joy and fun in life?"

The girl said, "Well, what are they again?"

"There are Ten Commandments, and no, Moses didn't drop five of them on the way down the mountain. Jesus summed them up as two commandments of love. 'You shall love the Lord your God with all your heart and with all your soul and with all your mind. This is the greatest and first commandment.' And a second is like it: 'you shall love your neighbor as yourself.' Basically, God loves each one of us unconditionally and without fail. He has a loving plan for us that will always be incredibly better than our own plan, and that will give us a life of true love, true freedom, and knowing our true self. Think about laws and truth like banks of a river that give it direction and power. Without them, it just becomes a lazy lake."

Another student said, "Father Tom, it makes sense to have rules to keep things moving along but I don't see why we need religion to be spiritual."

Tom respectfully asked, "So, you might say you are 'spiritual but not religious?'"

"Yeah. That makes more sense to me and more like what Jesus would want."

Tom asked, "How many people feel that same way?"

Most of the students raised their hands.

Tom continued, "I guess the first thing to consider is if Jesus was who He said He was. If you believe He was the Son of God, then what He actually said and did become our best guide to the right answer. Although Jesus chided the Pharisees for following the letter of the law instead of the heart of the law when someone asked him how they could love Him, Jesus said, 'Follow my commandments,' and said He came not to abolish the law, but 'to fulfill it.' Jesus was actually very religious, knowing and following His faith and the scriptures. He railed against money changers for not respecting the holy temple, and when He was in His last days with His apostles, He told Peter, 'You are Peter, and on this rock, I will build my Church, and the gates of hell will not prevail against it.' Jesus knew we would need community and a church to guide people in the fullness of truth. He trained the apostles to teach with authority as He had, to forgive sins as He had, to heal the sick as He had, and to celebrate the thanksgiving of the Mass through the Eucharist and in the instructions to 'Do this in memory of me.' The apostles were at first afraid and didn't understand, until the Holy Spirit, whom Jesus promised, descended upon them, and then they were transformed, unafraid and inspired to share the good news even in the face of the agonizing death all but one of them experienced.

"When someone says they are spiritual but not religious, ask them how it's going. If someone is religious but not spiritual, ask them how it's going. Generally, not well nor with the fullness of what Jesus intended. Spirituality without religion or religion without spirituality provides only some of what we need, but not what Jesus has in store for us."

A thin girl up front spoke. "What is religion then?"

"The word religion means to 'bind back to God' or a relationship with God. Life is all about relationships and nothing else in my mind. We start with our relationship with God. We then have a relationship with ourselves, accepting and loving the true person God created in His image, loves infinitely, and has a unique plan for. Once we get that, we can see that our purpose for being here is to offer ourselves in self-giving love to others. Religion is all about those relationships and having a place we can trust for the fullness of truth through God's word and graces.

"Jesus said that 'Where two or more of you are gathered,' He will be there. We aren't meant to be alone or to be islands unto ourselves. We are meant to know and love God, trust in His love and His plan for us, and go out and give that love to others. Religion should teach us and inspire us to have the courage to let go, trust God and be free in giving that love to others fully. Religion is about learning and passing on what we believe, how we pray and how we live for God and each other. On our own, we easily get lost or lose sight of God's truth and replace it with our own version. Today, you can see almost forty-thousand Christian churches that all have different ideas of the truth, but God only has one version, and that is why he gave us one holy Church to be part of and to guide us individually but also as a community of love.

"Now, what I just said is a lot of words. You have to live it and experience it to know what I mean. It can't hurt to try it, and it can bring you to a great place if you do. Remember that God loves you enough to give you free will, but he also shows you the path to joy and happiness if you are open."

Luke got up from the back stairs and headed out the open door and back to the rectory while the Friday night coffeehouse continued with social time and music. When people started to break up, Tom talked to each student, even if to just say hello and thank them for coming. He stayed afterward for anyone who wanted to talk one-on-one about anything, and one of the young women came to him after everyone had left. Her eyes were misty, but once she started speaking the tears streamed down her face. "Father Tom, I don't know where to turn. I feel ashamed and scared about what has happened. I can't tell my parents I'm pregnant. My boyfriend seemed supportive when he found out, but as the days have passed, he has become more distant, and today we had a huge fight. I'm just not ready for this. I'm too young and have nowhere to go."

Tom put his arm around her, and she leaned forward into his consoling hug. As she regained enough of her composure, she separated and looked up into Tom's eyes that showed no sense of judgment or disappointment, only loving concern. Tom said, "It's Marie, right?" She nodded, and Tom continued, "Marie, why don't you come by the rectory next door. I might have someone who can help with some options."

"I thought with you guys there were no options, no choices?"

"There are options. There is also a place that can help you with things along the way. They are comfortable people and very good at helping where you need help." Marie followed Tom into the rectory and noticed Luke sitting at the kitchen table cutting an apple into slices and eating them one by one. Marie's eyes caught Luke's for a second and Tom said, "Luke, this is Marie. Marie, this is my smarter and more handsome brother, Luke."

Luke stood up and reached out his hand to Marie and chatted as Tom grabbed a card from his office. Tom came back out. "Marie, I would give them a call. They are close by and very easy to talk to. On the back of the card is my number, and I'd be more than happy to have a talk anytime if that would help. You will be okay, even with your parents." Marie thanked Tom, leaving with a look of emotional exhaustion as she closed the door.

Tom was thinking of what Marie was facing in the years ahead. The easy fix wasn't really so easy nor one of the options in Tom's mind. The card he had given Marie was for an Order that donated half of the convent to communal living and support services for young, pregnant women searching for help and direction.

He turned his attention to his brother. "Luke, you need something more than that for dinner. Let me cook you up some chicken cutlets and rice while you tell me how your day went."

"You really believe this stuff, don't you?"

"Believe what stuff?"

"You really believe that your Church and Jesus are the same things and that we can be happy if we just trust and follow."

"I guess that is one way to summarize it. Why do you ask?"

"I don't know. I guess I don't want to end up being a lazy lake."

Tom always knew there was more to his brother than he often let on, and Luke always found a way to surprise him.

Chapter 22

David had plenty of ways to keep himself busy, but none satisfied this odd stirring within him this morning. He ran several miles in the morning along the Charles River. The warm weather brought people onto the banks of the Charles to sit on the grass and watch the crew teams row. Many bikers and runners were also out to enjoy a late taste of summer.

When he returned to his apartment, it felt empty and uncomfortably quiet. For the first time in many years, he felt alone and even lonely.

He remembered sitting in the dark of his room when he was eight, traumatized and incredibly alone after the sudden loss of his brother and father from his life. It had taken him a while to process the fact that they would never be back. He had to adapt somehow to cope with the overwhelming feelings of loss and the anxiety about life in front of him. Over time, he adapted his mindset and energies to protect himself from those feelings—the same feelings that were again beginning to seep in through the costly walls of his personal fortress. He had learned well to operate outside of those walls, but no one was allowed inside. Kathleen had come the closest. Jillian was heading in that direction, and now Tom was knocking on those large thick fortress doors, and to his surprise, David saw himself beginning to open the sealed doors a crack to answer.

It was too inviting a day to be inside, and while Trooper looked as if he couldn't care less, David thought it would be good to take him for a long walk and maybe even play in the park.

Once outside, the sun felt good to both of them as Trooper walked alongside rather than in front of him. He found himself walking past the street of Tom's parish and stopped with Trooper. "What do you think, boy? Trooper didn't hesitate and sprang down the street before David could convince him to head in the other direction. As St. Anthony's Church came into view, he saw Tom come out with two folding chairs and a sandwich board, setting them up on the sidewalk in front of the church. David made out the words on the board that read: Got questions, comments or issues?

Tom sat waiting for a passerby to stop and talk. David wasn't surprised that Tom would do something out-of-the-box like this to provide people with an opportunity to ask questions in a way that was convenient and comfortable for them.

David held back with Trooper to see if anyone would stop. Soon a young student with a backpack, wearing a beard, stopped to read the sign and then chatted with Tom. Tom motioned him to sit. For a while, they talked and gestured back and forth. Several other people stopped and asked questions and then moved along.

Just when David was ready to start walking again, he noticed a man approaching Tom, and instead of shaking his hand, the man spit in Tom's face and made an angry gesture before moving on. Tom stood up and pulled a white handkerchief out of his back pocket to wipe off his face. David waited for him to yell something back at the man, but he never did. He felt both sad for Tom and angry at the man, but also wondered what it was about – the abuse scandal or a personal experience that he was taking out on Tom? David thought he had plenty of gripes with the Church, but Tom was now a real person to him, maybe even a friend. Not wanting to embarrass Tom, despite Trooper's pull to walk towards the church, David turned around and walked down another street to return home.

He kept thinking about the incident and decided to give Tom a call at the rectory.

Tom answered the phone on the second ring. "St. Anthony's. This is Father Tom. How can I help you?"

"Hey, Tom. It's David."

"Hey, I'm glad you called. I hope you are enjoying our 'summer' weather!"

David thought he was more upset with what happened than Tom seemed to be himself. "I am. How about yourself?"

"Great. So, what's up?"

David wasn't sure exactly why he called. "I was wondering if you might be free for dinner tonight. Just something casual."

"That sounds good. Normally, I'd be celebrating Mass tonight, but we have a visiting priest helping out and he'll be on duty. I was planning on seeing my brother. You met Luke the other day. Would it be okay if he joined us?"

"Absolutely. Hopefully, I'm not encroaching on your time with him."

"Not at all. The more the merrier. I'm meeting him down at the corner of Hanover and Richmond at six o'clock if that works for you. It should be a perfect night for the North End, don't you think?"

David could almost hear his heart beating in his chest. He felt frozen for a second, picturing the streets he tried to avoid, even when prospective customers pushed for some Italian food. Nevertheless, he gave in. "Sure. I'll see you there."

Hours later, David felt like a young boy walking the neighborhood streets that made such an impression on him in the sixteen short months he had lived in the North End. He was early and walked up and down streets he had almost forgotten. The North End was always bustling with people out for dinner at one of its many restaurants or just out for a stroll. David had forgotten the distinctive faces and corner conversations between residents, young and old, and it felt like more of a protected neighborhood than other parts of Boston.

As David turned down Prince Street, he saw St. Leonard's Italian Church with its gardens still in bloom. One street down was Richmond, and David spotted Tom with his black shirt and collar talking and laughing with a group of young people. The students moved along and said goodbye as Tom glanced up, caught a glimpse of David, and beamed. David gave a nod of recognition before working his way through the crowded sidewalk to where Tom was standing.

David was surprised Tom was showing no signs of being upset about his afternoon experience.

While they were talking, someone came up behind Tom and pulled on the back of his collar—Luke. "Hey, Tommy, the streets are buzzing tonight." He turned to David. "It's David, right? Did I remember correctly? What are three Irish guys doing in the North End?"

Tom shrugged. "Since it's so nice out, we could walk a bit and see if any place grabs us."

"Dinner is on me tonight," David said, "so take advantage of it!"

They walked up and down the old, narrow streets and enjoyed both the ambiance and the eclectic group of people they were sharing it with on a beautiful, warm summer-like night. People were in a good mood as the threesome moved from busy streets to some quieter sections where residents were sitting outside conversing, playing cards, or selling homemade lasagna and pastries.

Luke paused at the aroma. "I would love to live here. It smells like it would be great."

David resisted the impulse to reveal that he had lived there at one time and just agreed with Luke.

They ended up back on Hanover Street and Luke pointed to the Florentine Café across the street with its open windows and lively looking atmosphere at the bar. "I vote for grabbing a table by the window there and watching the world go by." He put his name in for a table, and they waited outside the open cafe entrance where they could see an Italian soccer match on the bar screen with a group that had congregated to cheer their team on.

While they were watching, the sidewalk up ahead seemed to part like the Red Sea as a woman made her way between the mesmerized onlookers. She wore a cream-colored dress with blue lace fringe that hugged her sculpted figure and accentuated her very feminine waist, hips, and full breasts. Each stride of her high-heeled shapely legs moved with sensual confidence, and as she passed the Florentine Café, she gazed into the eyes of David and then Luke in a way that said she agreed with them—she was worth the attention. Continuing down the sidewalk, it was clear that this woman had owned that moment in the North End as every man and most women had stopped to watch her. David was waving his hand like a fan in front of Luke's face, which was a bit flushed at the moment, then turned to Tom. "I can't believe you weren't averting your eyes with that collar on."

"It's perfectly okay for any man to admire beauty, even a priest. The question is if you treated her with dignity and respect in your thoughts or if you simply used her as an object for your own pleasure. Which would a real man do?"

David smirked. "Come on, Tom. I can't believe you didn't feel tempted a small bit."

"Sure. I'm human and I am a male, but I've also worked at seeing more than the outside of any person I meet, even if she did have really beautiful legs."

The young woman at the desk had overheard the conversation and smirked as she told them their table was ready. The inside of the café was an intimate size with an attractive wooden bar and large, open windows that made diners feel as if they were sitting in an outdoor café. They sat at a small table by a window and watched the myriad of people walking by, some across the street coming out of Mike's Pastry with their pastries and cups of cappuccino, and others going into the Peace Garden at St. Leonard's Church. David ordered a bottle of Brunello di Montalcino for Tom and himself while Luke settled for Italian soda.

Tom raised his glass. "Perfect spot, Luke, on a summerlike evening, and thanks to David for inviting us."

"My pleasure. I'm glad you had the night off. Now, Luke, have you cooled off from the look that woman gave you?"

"David." Tom said, "I was hoping you might be more help here than that."

"Help with what? It is natural for a young man to appreciate an attractive woman."

Luke frowned. "I think he's worried I'll do something stupid in my youth that I'll regret."

"Tom, are you worried about Luke liking girls?"

"No." he replied. "Actually, I hope he finds a girl he can really like and have a great relationship with."

"But I'm not supposed to do anything dangerous with her," Luke said. "The Church has an oppressive and unnatural view on sex. It's bad and only for making lots of babies."

David shrugged. "I'm not sure how I can help. I think he kind of has it right."

"Luke can and should make his own decisions, but I would like him to have the right information to make those decisions. I want him to be a man that understands what true love and responsibility are, a man that treats women with the dignity they deserve, and someone who actually gets what the full reality of sex is. More importantly, I want him and his future spouse to have the fullness of what a truly loving friendship and marriage have to offer. If he trusts and follows the guidance God gives us, he will be in good shape. If he tries to figure it out from scratch, based on the culture he is surrounded by, then he has the responsibility to know what he is doing and how it impacts more than just himself."

Luke narrowed his eyes. "But why is the Church so against something as natural to people as sex? It's just a physical expression of love, something that makes people feel closer and happier. Everything seems like a big 'No' just when people are ready to live life fully."

"Would it surprise you if I said the Church doesn't believe what you think it does? Would you want to know?"

Luke said, "Sure, but it would take a lot of convincing. David, what do you think?"

David sipped his wine. "I think I'm supposed to be quiet on this."

"Absolutely not," Tom said. "All opinions are out on the table for discussion."

David waited a moment while the waiter approached and placed warm bread, seasoned dipping oil, and antipasto on the table. "Well, sorry to side with Luke, but I think consenting adults should be able to have a mature relationship without guilt, and as long as no one is hurt, sex is part of it. We are built for sex and pleasure, and it's a natural, healthy desire for both men and women. I'm not sure why it would be otherwise."

"I agree with a number of things that you said, David, but I would add a few things if you don't mind. First, the Church's view is far from the antiquated or puritanical view of sex that you may be assuming. Actually, very far from it. The Church doesn't see sex as dirty, bad, shameful or even sinful. It sees sex as a beautiful expression of love that is a sincere and mutual gift of self in an act that is both intimately bonding and life-giving. It is a gift a committed couple gives to each other and part of a miracle when you come to think of it."

David said, "That sounds nice but how does that relate to the Church saying no sex or fun until you are married?"

Luke added, "It sounds like a naïve and unnatural constraint."

"Okay. You believe sex outside of marriage shouldn't be a problem because it's natural and a good thing for both you and the woman you are dating. Do I have that correct?"

Luke nodded.

"Then let's talk about what is natural. What is the natural meaning and purpose of our attractions and our desire for sex?"

David glanced out the window at several attractive women passing by, thinking about how hard it was not to take it in and about how much pleasure it brought most men. "I haven't really thought about it a lot; it just seems instinctive. Why do we need to analyze it if it's natural and if it's good?"

Tom was enjoying a piece of the artisan bread he had dipped in olive oil. "Sometimes, when we understand the meaning and purpose of things, it can make all the difference in the world. Yes, we have natural instincts. I think the two main ones are: first to survive as an individual, so we do what it takes to make sure we have food and shelter and can defend ourselves; and secondly, to survive as a species, so we have a strong desire to have children and take care of them. Oh yeah, and third, we have a strong desire for the Red Sox to win a World Series someday, but I think we should stick with first two as our basic and overriding instincts."

Luke and David smiled at each other, nodding in general agreement. Tom continued, "So, the second instinct drives us to mate."

"I think pleasure and the desire to be connected to someone drives us to have a relationship, and sex is a natural part of that," said Luke.

Tom swallowed a bite of the bread. "I don't disagree with that, but you talked about what is natural. When you see a woman, like that woman we saw this evening, that you find beautiful and attractive, why do you find her so irresistibly attractive?"

David laughed. "Which girl? I must have missed her."

Tom joined his laughter. "Let me help you: long beautiful hair, big eyes, pink cheeks, red lips, a dress that let you see that she had a thin waist, attractive hips and long legs, high heels and, what else was it?—oh yes, an ample pair of—um, you know."

David smirked. "Earrings?"

"Sure. Men's brain centers are the sexual command center, and when they see an attractive woman, the neurotransmitter dopamine lights up areas deep in the brain triggering pleasure motivation like a drug. Your heart beats quicker, and the brain releases a chemical that speeds up the flow of information to the brain to quickly assess the woman's physical features that we are all drawn to so instinctively. But why do we find these things so attractive?"

David and Luke exchanged glances, agreeing that neither had really thought much about why certain features made a woman attractive, they just knew what they were. Tom urged them onward. "Think of some examples. Larger breasts are a sign of higher levels of the estrogen hormone and fertility as is the perfect hip-waist ratio that a man's brain is capable of calculating with high accuracy in a fraction of a second. Breasts are larger, lips and cheeks are fuller and redder with the increased flow of blood closer to ovulation. Symmetrically shaped faces are a sign of healthy genes and long, full hair, smooth skin, and height are the signs of a healthy woman. The dark limbal ring around the eyes is a sign of youth and fertility."

David said, "Stop. Stop. What are you saying, Tom?"

Tom answered, "Every feature a man finds to be physically attractive in a woman is tied directly to her fertility or the health of her genes and immune system, all aimed at increasing the chances of creating a healthy child. When a man sees the perfect mate, most of his thinking brain is turned off, and he is in instinct mode. And guess what? She instinctively knows just what buttons to push to compete for his attention. Why do you think women become so driven to be physically attractive? She wears a padded bra, red lipstick, and blush for her cheeks, liner around her eyes, spends hours on her hair and skin, and wears high heels to look taller and clothes to emphasize these specific features. What we find beautiful and attractive has a reason and a purpose."

Luke paused. "I don't think all women do that intentionally, and they don't want us just for our looks."

"I didn't say people are fully aware of how sophisticated our biology and senses are to find a fertile and healthy mate. Women tend to have a much more sophisticated sense of smell. Did you ever notice when you hold a woman, how she will breathe in the scent of your shirt? Women aren't only aroused by the chemical that occurs in men's sweat, hair, and skin but they can actually determine if the man's DNA is a good match and is just dissimilar enough from her own to produce offspring with a stronger immune system. She will look for someone tall, for health and status; dark, for testosterone level; and handsome with symmetrical and masculine facial features as signs of genetic health. She is also more social, interested, and physically ready for sex the closer she is to her ovulation."

David nodded. "Exactly! Doesn't that tell you she is willing and interested? It's only natural for two consenting adults to do what is natural."

"Sure," replied Tom, "but I think we're back to the same questions we had at the beginning of the conversation. What is the purpose of sex? What is true love? And how does a man treat a woman? When it relates to sex, our entire biology and brain are geared to being attracted to men or women who are healthy and fertile mates. The act of sexual intercourse creates incredible bonding. It's also geared toward creating life and staying together to care for that family. Why is the ultimate drive for a man to deliver his boys, so to speak? Once he does, there's a change in desire and a chemical release that makes him want to stay and sleep."

Luke lowered his voice to a whisper. "Tommy, do you honestly believe we are supposed to make a baby every time we have sex?"

"No. You never know when that miracle will happen, but not acknowledging the full meaning of the act makes it less than it is. Real men are thinking about what is absolutely best for their mate, preserving her integrity and dignity. He gives himself completely to her in self-sacrificing love and wants the best for her throughout her life and beyond. When we are more interested in the pleasure for the short term, or when you treat her natural fertility as a disease and you need to neuter her with birth control, we are basically reducing her to raw materials for pleasure, even if you are two consenting adults. How often do you hear guys ask each other, 'Did you get some?' or 'Did she put out?' Or worse? Jesus emptied himself out of love for us. A real man doesn't fill himself by using and emptying her. That's backward. That's taking instead of giving. She should be worth waiting for and that gift of life-giving intimacy is intended for her future husband."

Luke put down his bread and leaned back. "I still don't get what the big deal is if you are both in love and are both happy."

"Luke, love is so much more than a feeling. Love is an act of the will, a deep desire for the absolute best for the other—even at the expense of your own benefit. You mentioned what is natural. Before 1972, when there was little access to birth control, what was the natural outcome of sex?"

Luke didn't respond immediately. Tom continued. "And what do you believe that baby deserves from both the mother and the father? A truly committed relationship or two people dating who are trying to figure things out?"

Luke glanced downward. "You want me to say that an honest man, a real man, wouldn't put temporary pleasure with someone he wasn't ready to spend his life with ahead of the entire life of a child that deserves a family and loving parents—right? I agree, but we now have the technology. We have medical discoveries so that the situation won't occur. It gives us the freedom to love without being irresponsible."

Tom said, "I like that you care about the child, a lot. That's a good sign of maturity. But I have two questions for you. Is that the natural design? And did you know that there is no birth control that is one hundred percent effective?"

Luke appeared confused by the question as Tom continued, "In practice, there's a forty-seven percent failure rate for young people in their first year of having sex. Even after that, CDC statistics show that condoms fail fifteen percent of the time and birth control pills about nine percent of the time. Do you think those odds, or any odds, are okay to take when it comes to another human's life?"

Luke was quiet and so was David.

Tom continued, "Did you know the Pill is a Group 1 carcinogen? When you tell her to take the pill, you are asking her to take artificial hormones, to lower her immune system that protects against STDs, to significantly increase her risk of cervical and breast cancer, heart disease, and stroke, to increase risks of nutrient deficiencies and depression, and to risk future fertility issues, as well as often asking her to take an abortifacient. The pill is also called the divorce pill because it actually changes the pheromones that allow her to pick a compatible mate so that when she goes off of the pill, she is no longer attracted to the man she is with. When you tell a woman that her natural fertility that attracted you to her is a problem, what are you really saying to her?

"Did you know that the more partners a woman has, the more difficult it is for her to conceive when she is married because of the multiple adjustments to her immune system—the body knows something is wrong? And couples who live together are much less likely to marry and much more likely to divorce. There are also twenty million new cases of STDs every year, most not preventable by condoms. Is any of that really willing the best for her?"

Luke exhaled. "Is there any more good news here?"

David agreed. "I'm feeling depressed myself right now."

"Sure, there is. This isn't really about a 'No,' but a much bigger 'Yes' that should be more than good news for both men and women. Yes, to what marriage and sex were designed for. Yes, to a deeply intimate and bonding act of becoming one for life. Yes, to completely and truly giving yourself to another in love that is life-giving with a commitment to build a family together. Yes, to the plan God has for each of you. When you start having sex before you're married and truly committed, you are telling someone with your body that you are giving your whole self to them, but that's really not the truth if you aren't really committed to them and not actually giving yourself to them. John Paul II once wrote, 'The dignity of every woman is the duty of every man.' Was he right?"

The waiter came back to the table to see if they were ready to order dinner. To break the quiet, Luke said, "We just had three full courses of food for thought, so I think we're ready for some food for the stomach now."

David and Tom laughed as the waiter squinted at them, confused while taking their orders. Tom apologized for going on so long and so passionately, but Luke said, "Tommy, you don't have to apologize to me. You gave me, at least, some things to think about. And you wouldn't be much of a friend if you didn't challenge me to become a man even my brother would be proud of."

David fiddled with his napkin, then grinned. "So where were you when I was growing up?"

Tom said, "Hey, we'll all be learning how to be men until our last day."

"Yeah, sure," David replied, "but it is pretty embarrassing when the priest knows more about women and sex than the eligible bachelors at the table."

They clinked their glasses together as Tom grinned.

The rest of the dinner was enjoyable as the conversation was fun and friendly. It was a good sign they could mix serious and sensitive subjects with lighter humor and banter without ever assuming anything but the best of intentions from each other. The authentic Italian food and comfortable evening didn't hurt either.

Chapter 23

David thought back on last night's conversation as he sat with his morning coffee. He respected Tom's perspective, insights, and his desire for the best interests of others. He was starting to open up to the possibility that Tom was a real friend.

As he mulled over all Tom had said, he thought about Jillian. Had he treated her with dignity? Wasn't she worth waiting for and had he thought about her heart as he pursued the relationship and then dropped her off of the Grand Canyon when he needed to pull back?

He wondered if she might not have sunk back into the depression she had once tried to explain to him. He had talked with the salespeople at the Newton office, but they weren't able to tell him much since Jillian had pulled back socially at the office. David felt stuck, not knowing what to do without hurting Jillian more. She didn't want to see him until he was ready to move forward in the relationship. If he saw her, would he hurt her more? Would he be doing it to make himself feel better?

On Sunday night, Kathleen called to talk about Amy. Her friends seemed to be changing and not for the better. Her attitude was becoming concerning. Kathleen was honest when she said that she wasn't sure if David's lifestyle was helping. As David hung up, the perspective on being a true man Tom talked about flashed through his mind.

Monday and Tuesday were busy days finalizing game plans for the quarter. David got back too late from a meeting at headquarters, so he drove to his apartment instead of going back to his office. The door locks had all been changed, the windows secured from the inside, and alarms were set. Having someone breaking into his apartment on two Tuesdays in a row was concerning and perplexing. He used his new key and the key code to enter the apartment. Trooper was hunkered down on the rug in front of the sunniest window and all appeared to be the same as David had left it. He fixed beef tenderloin steaks for the two of them; they dined by the fire in the den as he started at Jimmy's diary sitting on the bookshelf. He didn't remember leaving the diary there and was sure he had put it back in the box from his mother's house.

The room suddenly felt quieter, except for his own heartbeat, as he tried to figure out how it got there. He looked carefully around each room and checked doors and windows to see if anything appeared to be tampered with. He saw nothing unusual, nothing different except the diary.

As David sat back down in his leather chair, he stared at the diary for some time. He didn't want to read it tonight but knew something was up. The diary was sitting in front of an antique clock that his grandfather had given him for his eighth birthday. Nonno noticed that David was always admiring the small wooden clock with the painted face, brass hands, and a tick-tock for each second being passed. He had kept the clock all these years but had never wound it up since that fall in 1971. The hands were always set at 10:15, except for tonight; the hands were now on the nine and the four for 9:20. Thirty-one years, those hands had been fixed in place and now they had been moved. He got up from his chair to examine the old clock. Just holding it put him back to an earlier, freer time in his life, but the idea that someone else had handled it was unsettling. When he put down the clock, he picked up Jimmy's leather-bound diary thinking Jimmy had held this in his own hands. He sank back into his chair and opened the book up to the first entry.

As he flipped through the pages of the diary trying to figure out what was going on, David found something in the book after Jimmy's last entry that he hadn't seen before—a photo postcard. On the front was a picture of a three-story building with a white facade, a central entrance with windows on each side, and on the back were letters that didn't make any sense to him. At the top was the name "Luke" but the rest, "H A U W ? T" didn't relate to anything he could think of.

Luke

H   A

U

W   ?   T

David's adrenalin increased as he walked around each room again to see if he had missed anything else. He was more perplexed than ever how anyone could've possibly gotten into his apartment. All windows were locked from the inside. He was the only one to have the key to all the newly reinforced locks, and Trooper showed no signs that an intruder had been there. He sat back down, and Trooper made himself comfortable again next to the leather chair. The only "Luke" that he could think of was Tom's brother. He had been moving into an unfamiliar place of respect and even trust with Tom, but this seemed too coincidental, as did the subject matter of the last two messages.

David had worked so hard and for so long to protect himself from the world and to be in control. He tried to be a good person while building his fortress with success, position, wealth, esteem, power, and possessions. He was independent, self-sufficient, and self-satisfied. As the master of his bounded self, he could manipulate his world, but sitting in front of him was a small picture postcard that seemed to represent an uncontrolled intrusion into his self-manufactured world that unknowingly lacked integrity, values, trust, and love. If he had to really stop to think, that haunting feeling of loss, rejection, abandonment, and emptiness would come crashing in. It had taken many years to learn to sleep again as a child because of the nightmare lurking to meet him, a nightmare where David was awakened from a comfortable bed and pushed into the darkness of a bottomless empty pit, no light, no warmth, and no love. As he fell, David felt overwhelmed with hopelessness as the pit grew even darker and colder, until he woke in a sweat and a sense of panic throughout his being.

Chapter 24

David opened Jimmy's diary again to the first entry: *A new year and ready to start my life now.*

As David read the entries, his thoughts drifted away from the journal to his own memories of that year. Jimmy wanted to be with his friends, back in Savin Hill where he felt at home, to be on his own, and working at Dunbar Security helped. David, on the other hand, remembered becoming comfortable at school, and both Bobby and Abbie seemed content with the new surroundings. His most vivid memory of the year was wanting a toboggan. He had written to Santa twice and asked him in person at Jordan Marsh in Downtown Crossing that December. On Christmas morning, after opening his smaller gifts, clothes, and underwear, he had thought he must've done something wrong since there was no sled at all under the tree. Finally, Gianni said, "I think I saw something behind the couch," and sadness turned into joyous energy as David tore through all the red and green wrapping paper that covered a toboggan long enough to hold all six of them.

When they had a good snowfall that January, everyone bundled up, putting on their boots, coats, hats, and gloves except for Jimmy. Gianni motioned to Jimmy, who was planning on seeing his friends that afternoon. Within a few minutes, Jimmy was putting on his coat and hat and the entire family was heading over to Flagstaff Hill in Boston Common to test out David's Christmas present. At the top of the hill, David got into the front, then Abbie, Bobby, Jimmy, Annie. Finally, Gianni pushed and jumped on the back of the toboggan and down the hill they went, dodging other families flying down the long hill that ended at the snow-covered baseball diamond. David recalled the snow flying up into his face, how much he loved being in the front to watch the action, and how much more he enjoyed his whole family having fun together. A little more than halfway down the hill, a dog ran in front of the toboggan's path. Everyone leaned to the right to avoid hitting it and ended up toppling over into the fresh snow. Looking back and seeing his mother laughing and the big smile on his dad's face was a happy memory. After a good snowball fight that left them soaked, they all trudged home through the snow to enjoy homemade hot chocolate piled high with whipped cream.

Jimmy's diary for the rest of January was composed of short entries about working weekends and a few afternoons after school. He talked about becoming eighteen soon and counting down the days until school was finally through. All this time David remembered enjoying his small world of school and family in the North End while his oldest brother was feeling antsy and ready for something bigger and more exciting.

Jimmy wrote, "*I don't feel any different today than I did yesterday, but I'm officially a man. I can't walk into a bar through the front door and I can't vote but I can go to war and die. I hope that doesn't happen. I can't imagine dying before I get a chance to even live. It's a scary thought. I just need to convince Dad to trust me with my own life.*

"*I met Tommy C at Mo's place to celebrate. The rest of the guys were there in the back, and we had fun. Mo had four tickets to the Celtics-Lakers game that he gave me for a present and it was a great win 116-98. It was a great start to a year to remember!*"

David flipped the diary pages to March '71 and didn't see a lot of personal comments from his brother except, "*I think a lot about the war in Vietnam now. Every night the news shows pictures and film of this never-ending war and the casualties of men no older than me. I don't even know what they are actually fighting for and it is hitting me for the first time that I could be drafted and be one of them soon.*"

March 8. "*Great fight tonight between Ali and Frazier at Madison on the radio. Frazier is tough but didn't think he'd win.*"

March 10: "*It's official. I can vote. Small consolation for being able to fight and die.*"

March 20: "*B's win 13th straight! I'm smelling Stanley Cup repeat!*"

David skipped down to the last entry of the month, March 31st: "*Another month gone. Time seems to be going by fast with all these hours at Dunbar. Need to slow it down and live it!*"

David felt like he was only getting a small peek at who his oldest brother was. He never realized how much the war weighed on Jimmy, but it wasn't going to be the war that would take the life of David's idolized brother away. He fell asleep in his chair as his thoughts and feelings drifted back to a time when his family was still all together.

The morning had come early for David when he awoke in his den chair. Although he packed his basketball and clothes in his sports bag, he was thinking about not playing. The air was getting cool for outdoor basketball, and he wasn't sure if he was up for confronting Tom with yet another mysterious message.

At four o'clock, Izzie interrupted, "Mr. Kelly, I have your calendar blocked off for the rest of the day. I hope I have that right for today?"

David really didn't know what to do. In any event, he was feeling as if he needed to get out of the office. "Thanks, Izzie. I appreciate the reminder.

Why don't you leave early yourself to avoid the rush and spend time with your family?"

Izzie thanked him as he headed downstairs with his bag in hand.

When David reached the lobby, he saw Tom sitting on one of the couches dressed for playing but with his jacket on.

Tom waved and came over. "I didn't know what you were planning on, but with the cooler weather, I thought I'd see if you were up to playing indoors?"

David was actually glad to see Tom and appreciated that he made the effort to wait for him.

They walked the few blocks to St. Anthony's and into the churchyard, toward a door of the school. School had been let out for the day, but there were still students finishing up projects, helping out with chores around the school, or waiting for their parents to pick them up. As they passed each student, Tom greeted each one by name.

When they got to the gym, the late afternoon sun was streaming in through the windows and onto the well-used floor. David loved the feel of older gyms that reminded him of playing on the old courts in Lynn where he first came to love the game. The sound of the basketball pounding on the old wooden floor and the swish of the net as Tom sank shot after shot had a different feel, sound, and smell than playing on an outdoor court. Both had their advantages, but David loved playing indoors where memories of practices and tense games flooded his senses.

When David was ready, Tom made a two-handed chest pass to him that he caught and turned into a quick jump shot without touching iron.

"So, what do you think?"

David smiled because he knew just what Tom was asking and took the ball to the basket for a reverse layup shot. "I think I like it. I didn't know you had your own court. No wonder you come so ready to beat me each week."

"First of all, it isn't my court, and what would a respectable Catholic church be without a basketball gym? Secondly, I don't get time to practice, so you can get that thought out of your head."

Two of the high school players showed up and challenged them to a series of competitive games. Afterwards, David and Tom sat on the floor with their backs to the wall, forearms resting on their kneecaps, and the sun on their faces as the good feeling of sweat dripped down their foreheads. Staring forward, Tom said, "Now what are we going to do?"

David asked, "About what?"

Tom's smile went to one side of his face. "Those boys have worn us out and we haven't even played to see who's buying tonight."

David nodded. "Ahhh, that is a problem because, right now, I would just roll the ball out on the court and let you win."

Tom said, "Sounds good. I'll take the win and a nice cold Guinness."

Luckily the pub was only a few blocks over, and David put up two fingers as he nodded to Dempsey. The two of them made their way to their favorite booth to rest their weary bones.

Dempsey came over with two beers and teriyaki wings on the house. "You boys look like you could use nourishment."

They raised their glasses to Dempsey and then clanged them together before taking that first soothing sip.

"That was hard work but fun today," David said. "Those boys must've been well coached by someone. Should I guess who that might be?"

"I could use some help coaching the younger boys' team this year if you are ever interested."

The idea intrigued David, but he didn't know how practical it would be with his schedule.

"Think about it. We will be having tryouts after Thanksgiving before starting practices."

David took another sip and said he'd think about it, but that he was thinking about something else as well.

Tom leaned forward, stared at David with interest and asked with an Irish accent, "Now, what is it that is troubling you, David?"

David was quiet for a minute and then pulled out the picture postcard but didn't display it as he spoke. "Tom, I had questioned you before about the last two notes and I don't want to do that again, but last night—"

Tom interrupted, "You got another one? Who has access to your place?"

David said, "I did and no one else should have access since I had all the locks changed. The only reason I'm showing you this one is because of the name on the top."

David slid the postcard across the table to Tom, who looked at it with great interest. "I assume you mean the name 'Luke' and you think it may have some connection to my little brother?"

David said, "I really don't know what to think anymore. Somehow, someway, someone is playing a game with me, and for the life of me, I can't figure out what it's about. It seemed to start after we met, and the first two messages seemed to have something more to do with your job than mine, and now the name 'Luke' appears in the third one? Can you think of anything? Because I've racked my brain on this one."

Tom studied the cryptic set of letters:

Luke

H   A

U

W   ?   T

Tom was struggling to figure the message out but was coming up short. "Well, it's clear that the name at the top is 'Luke' but the rest is a mystery. Did you find anything else besides the note? The building on the front of the postcard seems like a nondescript white building, not new and nothing fancy. Does it look familiar?"

"Nope and there was nothing else. Oh, wait a minute. The only other weird thing was that my clock was moved."

"Moved to where?"

"They didn't move the clock, but the hands were moved. It is an old clock that hasn't worked for over thirty years, so the hands have always been in the same position, 10:15."

"Huh. What were the hands moved to?"

David looked down at the picture. "The hour hand was on the nine and the minute hand on the four. I don't know why they would bother."

Tom was nodding his head and said, "I don't think they would unless it was connected. So, it was 10:15, and they moved it to 9:04?"

"No, the minute hand was on the number four, so it was set to 9:20."

"Okay. I think the question mark means it's asking a question versus a missing letter because no letter would make sense. Also, the 'U' is bold, so I think it's separate from the other letters. If we were to remove the Luke, the 'U' and the question mark, the remaining letters say—"

David said, "H A W T. Maybe it's just someone from Hyde Park who spells the way he talks—like 'It's wicked hawt out'?"

Tom laughed. "I'm glad you're keeping a sense of humor. You can see that the W and T are placed further out, so I think it's W H A T and the letters are around the letter U and then a question mark."

David scratched his head. "So, it says, 'Luke, what around you?'"

Tom was thinking and then muttering, "Luke, what around you? Or Luke, what about you? That probably makes more sense. 9:20? Luke 9:20. Luke 9:20, and then, "What about you?'"

David felt more perplexed. "Okay. I still don't know what it means."

"I hate to tell you this, but it's one of the key verses in the New Testament from Luke, not my brother Luke, but the Greek physician that followed Paul and wrote one of the four Gospels and the Acts of the Apostles. Jesus was asking the apostles who people were saying he was, and the apostles said that people were saying he was John the Baptist or Elijah or another great prophet come back to life. Then in Luke 9:20, Jesus asks his apostles, "But what about you? Who do you say I am?'"

"So, what did they say?"

A few of the other guys in the next booth started listening for the answer.

"If you read through the Gospels, it's amazing to see how often the apostles admitted to not really understanding everything Jesus was saying or the full extent of who he was. Jesus was now looking at each of them and asking them who they thought he was. Peter was the only one to answer the question, 'You are the Christ, the Son of the Living God.' This is when Jesus knew that Peter would be the rock he would build His Church on. He looked at Peter and said, 'Blessed are you, Simon son of Jonah! For flesh and blood has not revealed this to you, but my Father who is in heaven. And I say also to you, that you are Peter, and on this rock, I will build my church; and the gates of hell shall not prevail against it. And I will give to you the keys of the kingdom of heaven: and whatever you shall bind on earth shall be bound in heaven: and whatever you shall loose on earth shall be loosed in heaven.' Jesus then told all of them what He had to do and what would happen to Him in Jerusalem."

David gazed at him. "And you know that all off the top of your head?"

"Well, I have studied it, and I recently read the passage for a talk I gave on the same topic. It's a pretty pivotal reading of the Gospel. The real question for us is, 'Who do we say that Jesus is?' The message may be just that: What about you?"

"It's not really something I've thought much about or something that I've really wanted to think much about."

One of the guys in the booth behind them got up and asked, "Hey, how do we even know that Jesus existed?"

Tom replied, "Well, the overwhelming majority of historians have looked at the evidence, the Gospel witnesses, Paul's letters, references by the Roman historian Tacitus and Jewish historian Josephus, writings by governor Pliny the Younger, Justin Martyr, an ossuary stone box from the first century referencing Jesus, and the very strong oral tradition of that time and era. Many of these writers would've run into some major criticism from witnesses and others of the time who had a stake in not letting the story of Jesus gain traction."

The man said, "But you can't trust that the gospels were actually written anywhere near the time of Jesus or that the writers didn't just concoct a myth."

Tom agreed. "There have been a lot of conspiracy theories such as Constantine actually creating the myth of Jesus in the fourth century and writing the gospels then or at least cherry picking the writings he liked.

How interested are you in the truth about this?"

The man said, "I'd like to know. I'm always open, more than most, anyway."

"Okay, good," Tom responded. "Historians have found fragments of gospel writings from the first or early second century that match exactly to current Bible writings. No other ancient writing has more numerous and earlier copies to validate its accuracy. The very early Church fathers and writers talked about the practices and gospels of the Church long before Constantine made Christianity legal in the Roman Empire. Until that time, Christians had been oppressed and killed. You would need to study oral tradition at that time, but it was strong and valid as a passed-down source of truth. Expert translations have confirmed that the Gospels were written fairly early based on the eyewitnesses and those that followed them.

"It's important to note that, despite years of teaching by Jesus before his death, the apostles were still afraid and not that enlightened. Jesus said that he would send the Holy Spirit to fill them with the truth and the courage to go out and teach as Jesus taught, to forgive sins, to heal the sick, and to spread the truth with an inspired understanding of His good news. After they were breathed on by the Holy Spirit, these men went from hiding and fearing for their lives to speaking in languages they didn't know, performing miracles and being willing to suffer imprisonment, torture, and gruesome deaths to spread the Gospel. Does it make any sense that all these apostles would've done this if they all knew it was a lie?"

By this time, several others gathered around the booth. One of the men said, "It doesn't make sense that they would all do that, and it wouldn't make sense for secular historians of the time to reference someone who didn't exist, but what makes you think that Jesus was anything but a man who happened to have a gift?"

Tom said to the rest of the men, "Any thoughts?"

Someone who was standing said, "Well, it's safer and easier to believe he wasn't actually God because, if he were, then we would have to seriously pay attention to what he said and did."

Tom said, "Well said. The answer to this question is a really big deal for each one of us. No lunatic showed the level of wisdom that Jesus did, but if He wasn't who He said He was, He'd have to be a lunatic or a liar to claim to be one with God Himself. The founder of no other faith has made that claim. Jesus said, 'I and the Father are one,' 'before Abraham was, I am,' and 'He who sees me sees the Father.'

"Lunatics and liars don't perform the many miracles that Jesus did. There are about fifty pretty amazing miracles in the Gospels, but I think that being resurrected from the dead and then being witnessed by more than five hundred people might be worth taking note. How could all these people be so willing to give everything up for a lie that could be refuted by so many people? You have to decide if you truly believe that Jesus was a liar, a crazy man, or who He said He was. Better than that, take time just to read through the four Gospels and see what you think. I guarantee you that it's the most surprising and profound true story you will ever read."

Sam said, "Let me ask a question. You two guys have come into this pub for the past several weeks with the authentic-looking sweat of a couple of regular guys, but you bring in these debates that you never hear in a pub or most any other place. Truth, God, Jesus."

David said, "Is there a question in there?"

Sam said, "Well, is this some type of devious way to get us into adult religion classes or something?"

Tom laughed. "Not by us, but maybe Dempsey has been planting these clues because he is worried about you guys."

Dempsey, who was always paying attention to everything going on in his pub, loudly cleared his throat. "I'd be charging tuition if this was my doing."

Someone yelled out, "Hopefully, you are making enough off of the concessions," and everyone laughed.

Tom said, "The two questions I always ask myself are, 'If it were true, would I want to know?' and if it is, 'What would I do about it?' For me, I found that Jesus is the answer to all the important questions in life and about what being a man really means. Most of us are drifting through life, too busy to stop and think about what it's really all about until we retire. Then we've lived most of our lives without meaning, without purpose, and without real love and joy."

Sam said, "You really believe that?"

Tom said, "I do."

Someone else said, "Do you believe it enough to die for it?"

Tom said, "I do." This made David look up at Tom, and it was as if he got a peek inside Tom's soul for a second, which was a new experience for David.

David and Tom finished up their beers and said goodnight to Dempsey. On the way out. Dempsey said, "We have a pool going to try to guess next week's surprise topic lesson. Did you want to get in on it?"

David said, "Dempsey, if we can have them break into your house to leave you the clues, then I'm definitely in."

Outside the pub, Tom said to David, "With the break-ins, are you concerned about going back to your apartment?"

"Maybe I should be concerned, but I think I'll be good."

"Okay, but you can stay at my place anytime. Do you think you should call the police?"

David replied, "It probably makes sense, but like you had said before, they probably aren't trying to do me any harm. I'd just like to figure out who it is and how the heck they are getting in and out without a trace."

"Maybe it's a miracle?"

David didn't take the bait.

Tom patted him on the shoulder. "Have a good one, and nice playing tonight. I hope the evening was a good one for you."

"It was good," David said and started walking towards Beacon Street.

Tom's voice drifted to him: "And think about the coaching too. You would be a great teacher."

Chapter 25

When Tom got back to the rectory, he took a shower, relaxed, and attended to the readings for the morning. The house was quiet as he got ready for sleep and left the side door open for Luke, in case he was staying that night. At some point in the night, he heard Luke coming in, but he also thought he heard whispering as well. When there was more movement than one person would make, Tom got up and gave a gentle rap on the guestroom door. Luke cracked opened the door. "Hey, Tom. I hope you don't mind if I stay here tonight."

Tom said, "You know I don't mind at all."

Luke said, "Thanks. I really appreciate it. Sleep well," and closed the door until it hit Tom's foot that had slid into place to keep the door open.

Tom whispered, "Like I said, I don't mind your staying but—" and he opened the door to see a girl sitting on a comforter on the floor. "Hello, Miss. I'm Luke's brother, Tom, and unfortunately, the nasty landlord."

"It isn't what it looks like," Luke said. "This is Gabby, and she just needs a place to stay for tonight."

The girl glanced up at Tom, her huge brown eyes brimming with tears she was desperately trying to hold back. "Hi. I hope I'm not imposing."

"I don't want to put you out on the street on a cold night, but unfortunately you cannot stay here with Luke, nor is a young woman leaving a priest's residence early in the morning a great idea either."

Luke stepped closer. "She really needs a place to stay, and we weren't sleeping together."

"I think you meant that you were only sleeping together. Gabby, if you really have nowhere to go, I can see if you can stay with Sister Helen tonight."

Luke rolled his eyes. "She doesn't want to become a nun."

Tom ignored the comment and waved the two of them toward the door. Sister Helen lived with several of the other sisters just a block away from the school in a portion of the old convent that had been subdivided into affordable housing for poorer families. Two of the sisters also taught at St. Anthony's School, others worked at the local hospital, and one at a pregnancy crisis center. Tom got dressed and walked Gabby and Luke down to the sisters' house, tapping lightly on the door. While most of the sisters were early to bed, he knew Sister Helen was a night owl and seemed to maintain high energy on only five hours of sleep a night. He knocked gently again and could see the hall light come on through the window. When Sister Helen saw Father Tom's face, she rolled her eyes and opened the door. "So, what in heaven brings a group like you to my door in the middle of the night? Come in before you catch your death."

Tom explained the situation to Sister Helen, and she put her arm around Gabby and took her down the hall to show her a spare room. When she came back, she said, "Luke, what happened that this girl doesn't have a place to stay on a night like this?"

Luke shifted left, then right. "She had a falling out with her roommates and just needed somewhere to go."

Sister Helen tilted her head. "Roommates?"

"I meant roommate."

"And would this ex-roommate be a she or a he?"

Luke didn't respond, and Sister Helen didn't ask again.

On the way back home, Luke broke the uncomfortable silence. "I know what you're thinking, but Gabby isn't one of those girls. She doesn't sleep around. She thought she loved this guy. She just couldn't see that she was in love with a total idiot."

"So, what is Gabby like? What's her family situation?"

Luke's hands sank deeper into his pockets. "Gabby's dad left when she was ten or eleven. I'm not sure, but there may have been abuse of some sort going on. When her mom started dating different guys, Gabby felt as if she was very much in the way. I think living at school was a good way to get out of the situation. She's really a great girl, but I'm not sure she believes it, and she still thinks she loves this guy she moved in with over the summer."

"It sounds like there's a lot going on there. You're trying to be a good friend—or is she more than that to you?"

Luke stared ahead.

"Obviously, I don't know her whole story, but when kids don't feel loved or affirmed growing up, their sense of self-worth can get seriously undermined."

"When we talk, I always try to build up her self-esteem, but she always pushes back and rejects any compliment I give her and any notion she should be treated better."

"Luke, no intent to get into semantics, but there may be an important distinction between self-esteem and self-worth to consider."

"Is there a difference? Aren't they both about feeling good about yourself instead of beating yourself up?"

"You are right that self-esteem is feeling good about yourself, but that sometimes leads us to build a false self that we can get other people to like, admire, and be accepted for. People can become narcissistic out of fear of being rejected for their true self and start to need others to build their self-esteem. They can still be empty inside and all the time frantically working to hide their true selves. We all do it to some extent but the more we know and accept who we really are, the healthier and more at peace we can be."

"So then how is self-worth different?"

"Self-worth is something deeper at our core, it's recognizing our intrinsic value as a person. This's why affirmation from parents is so important to help a child feel truly loved, to feel valued and essential. That gleam in a mother's or father's eye mirrors back to the child his inner goodness, beauty, and value as a person—not just in words but with a felt experience. When a person deep down knows his worth, he has a sense of emotional security that so many of us lack and a willingness to bear the trials of life for growth. We're not perfect by a long shot, but I think we were fortunate to have parents that gave us that gift every day."

Luke nodded. "I really do miss them. Sometimes you don't know how much impact a parent can have on a kid, do you?"

"One reason I was talking about the importance of sex in a truly committed relationship is because—"

"Because those kids deserve and need to be treated as more than a mistake, or something like that?"

Tom smiled. "Something like that."

Luke stopped and turned to Tom. "Can you tell me something? When I try to tell Gabby how wonderful a person she is, why does she push back and fight it so hard? It is almost as if any compliment I give her is a bad thing and she instantly rejects it. Why doesn't she trust me even a little?"

Tom's lips pressed together as he thought about this common experience in his counseling sessions with people young and old. "There's a theory on what you are experiencing with Gabby called 'self-verification.'"

Luke turned. "Self-verification? What's that?"

"It's an interesting dynamic I think has a lot of merits, from my experience. People need to be able to process the world coming at them or else they can feel very overwhelmed and stressed. When life experiences lead them to a negative view of themselves, this self-view, even though it's negative and false, still provides them with a sense of self-coherence and a means for understanding and responding to the world."

Luke stood with his hands in his pockets. "Huh. So, a person, even when she has an unhealthy negative image of herself, will want to maintain that perception in order to process and cope with the world coming at her?"

"You got it. They will seek out or create confirming negative feedback to maintain the distorted perception of themselves or else they'll feel lost, disoriented, and not have a secure basis for knowing the world. Their core sense of self, their very existence is threatened, and they can actually feel a high level of anxiety and fear when there are moments of hope. We tend to infer who we are by observing how others react to us, so we will create or seek a social environment that confirms and reinforces our own self-view."

"So, when I tell Gabby that she's beautiful, worthwhile or a good person inside, it might be creating a moment of anxiety or panic for her. I get that. But it can't make sense for her to stay with such a negative perception of herself. What's the best thing to do as a friend?"

They started walking again. "It's a great question and not an easy one to answer. We all have to be able to tolerate some level of discomfort in order to grow, but it needs to be only what we can handle. Take a woman who has been beaten or abused by her dad, and she continually dates or marries abusive men. She obviously believes in her negative self-view and that this is all she deserves. She may even believe it's her fault. She has sought out the environment that confirms her perceptions of herself and will make excuses to anyone who tries to tell her she deserves better. It's clearly not better for her to stay in that situation, even if it's uncomfortable to leave it and believe something better about herself. The best thing is to get her into an environment that's healthy and safe and to work slowly with her over time to unwind those 'truths' and replace them with the real truths of her true self and self-worth. It takes patience, love, understanding and, many times, professional therapy."

"You do a lot of counseling, Tom. Do you think you could talk to her and help her?"

"I would be more than happy to talk with her if she's ready to do that. As I said, I know very little about her personal situation, so much will depend on how open and ready she is to dig into areas that most of her will want to avoid or keep secret. Let's see if she is open to talking."

"Thanks for talking and for offering to help out. I know you're a busy guy."

Tom put his hand on Luke's shoulder as they walked the last few yards back to the rectory. "This is the kind of stuff that I'm here to be busy with."

Chapter 26

For the past thirty-one years, Columbus Day weekend has always been a long weekend during which David deliberately busied himself. He had a standing golf outing planned each year down the Cape, and he was looking forward to having the guys from the office down this year to drink, play golf, eat, and have fun. The conversation this year seemed more superficial and less interesting to him than he had remembered. There was laughing, joking, and drinking but he wondered if anyone was really having any fun. The golf was good, and the dinners were great, but he felt almost alone in the middle of constant interaction with his longtime acquaintances.

When he got home on Sunday night, he sat back in his favorite chair with Trooper next to him. David was just letting thoughts come to him, a change from so many years of making a conscious or maybe unconscious decision about what thoughts he'd allow into his mind.

Jimmy's diary was still sitting on the cabinet in front of him. He stared at it, trying hard to resist opening it.

Finally, he reached over and held the leather diary in his hand again and then opened it up to the marker he left in the book for the month of April 1971.

April 1: *Mo asked me to come over to Styx tomorrow. No clue what he wants. Just two months left of school! Freedom!*

April 2: *Mo met with me and Tommy C in his office. He said that there was a really good opportunity and thought he could use us if we were interested. He said that working at Dunbar was great but would never pay what they could make, and this opportunity could open up some real possibilities for us. Not sure what it is, but trust that Mo usually has a good nose for these things. Nice thing was that he gave me three tickets to the Sox opening day game against the Yanks.*

April 6: *Gave Dad tickets to the Sox game so that he can take David. Glad that he could see a win against the Yanks to start the season.*

David still had vivid memories of his first game at Fenway. He got a note to get out of school early that Tuesday and Gianni took a half day. His mom wasn't as excited about him getting out of school to see a game but didn't argue about it. They took the Green Line subway line to Kenmore Square and then walked to the park with over 34,000 other fans. Outside the park were the peanut and pretzel vendors singing out in their distinctive voices,

"Peanuts here! Get your fresh-roasted peanuts! Peanuts here!" Gianni bought two brown bags of the warm, roasted peanuts, and they strolled into the park. The tickets were for better seats than Gianni had ever gotten himself, grandstand seats on the first base side where lots of foul balls were hit. They moved through the crowds and up the ramp for David's first glimpse of the immaculate stadium with the colorful crowds, all that beautifully cut green grass, the large green scoreboard that was taller than he had imagined, and the baseball diamond itself with players tossing balls to warm up. David couldn't believe how incredibly awesome this was, and Gianni enjoyed watching the expressions on his face as they made their way to their seats.

He hadn't thought about that day in many years, but it remained one of his most cherished memories of his youth.

He scanned the page, over other menial entries, then turned the page and stopped.

April 15: *Met with Tommy C and Mo in the Common. He said he has the go-ahead to start planning something, but he wants to know if he can count on us and that we will keep working at Dunbar during the year. He said it was big but if well planned, it would be safe. I'm feeling a little nervous about this, but I think we can trust Mo.*

Watch B's lose 6th game 8-3. They need to take the final game in Boston.

April 18: *B's lose final game and out of playoffs. This sucks!*

May 12: *Went to Music Hall with Tommy C and Brian Murphy to see J. Geils Band. Wolf had the place rocking. Whammer Jammer, Looking for A Love. Fun time.*

The pieces were beginning to fit together. David could see from an adult perspective what he hadn't understood as a child.

Jimmy had started hanging out more in Savin Hill after work and bothering less with schoolwork now that he was in the homestretch. Tommy C was able to secure a quality fake Mass ID for Jimmy, so James J. Fidele was now "21 years old" when he needed to be. Jimmy was happy to be spending more time back in his old neighborhood, and a couple of those hangout spots included Connors Tavern and the Bulldog Lounge across the street. Both bars were owned by Eddie Connors, an ex-Marine and ex-hard-hitting professional boxer who won twenty-two fights, eighteen by knockout. Eddie did get a shot at the New England middleweight title but lost to Willie Green. Eddie had no issues with his bars being hangouts for mob criminals, bookmakers, and loan sharks and was known to be tight with Howie Winter, the boss of the Winter Hill Gang headquartered in

Somerville, Massachusetts. There was a large, fat man standing in the door frame who gave a quick glance at Jimmy's ID before he finally entered the tavern for the first time. The interior was black and smelled of stale beer as Jimmy noticed the cheap color TV over the bar and Eddie, who looked a lot like Rocky Marciano, standing behind the bar talking with some tough looking patrons.

Jimmy wanted to talk with Tommy C about Mo's offer to get in on his plan. Mo hadn't given out any details to either Jimmy or Tommy C but wanted to make sure they stayed working at Dunbar Security, jobs he had secured for both of them. Jimmy thought it must have something to do with the armored trucks or the lockboxes that were handled at the office. He wasn't feeling comfortable with the whole idea, but Tommy C wanted to see what the plan was before backing out on their commitment to stay at Dunbar. The more they hung around at the Tavern and got familiar with guys they knew were involved with less than legal activities, the less the idea of finding out what Mo had up his sleeve seemed like a bad idea.

On one occasion, Tommy subtly pointed out one of the patrons who came and talked with Eddie—Donald Killeen, the head of the dominant Irish mob in Southie at that time. Tommy C kept his voice down and told Jimmy about the mob war between Killeen's gang and the rival Mullen gang run by Paulie McGonagle. Donald owned a bar called the Transit Café just off Broadway Street in Southie. Tommy C said the rumor was that Donald's younger brother Kenneth had a fight outside the bar with Mickey Dwyer, a member of the Mullen gang. This led to Kenneth trying to empty his gun into Mickey but only hitting him once in the arm. Tommy C said, "Get this. When he was out of bullets, he jumped Mickey and ended up biting off his nose and sent him running to the hospital, while Kenneth stood there and spit his nose out. Supposedly, Donald retrieved the nose, washed it off, wrapped it and put it on ice to send to the hospital, but the war was on. I wonder what he's talking about to Connors?" Jimmy didn't know, but it wasn't making him feel comfortable about being there, as he finished up his beer while trying not to stare at Donald Killeen.

Living in the neighborhood, Tommy C became more and more acquainted with the regulars at the Tavern and was feeling as if he belonged to something bigger than himself. Jimmy was uncomfortable with the idea of not knowing what and whom he was dealing with. He went to talk with Mo about the plans he was working on that would involve Tommy C and himself. Mo told him to be patient because he was still working on getting "the okay" and that it would take a great deal of planning to pull it off smoothly.

Mo took Jimmy and Tommy C to one of the meetings at Twin Donuts donut shop in Union Square in Allston. Inside was a fifties-style diner, Mo told Tommy C and Jimmy to sit at a table near the front window while he met with two guys who were already sitting in a booth in the back. Tommy C sat with his coffee and a few chocolate-coconut donuts until Mo waved them to come to the back.

Mo introduced the two guys who both looked to be hard-nosed lads in their late twenties. "This is Jimmy and Tommy, both from Savin Hill. Guys this is Gino and Mac from Eastie and Southie. I think we have the makings of a solid team, but I need to know that each of you is all in. I'm still working on the nod and financing before we get into detailed plans, so let's keep this tight. I promise you a smooth and professional operation that can set you all up for time to come, but I need your commitment to every aspect." Everyone nodded and shook hands.

Jimmy felt like things were moving fast. He spent more and more time with Mo or at Connors Tavern and sometimes at The Transit in Southie, so the players didn't seem as intimidating unless someone got out of line. He'd seen the New England mafia boss, Gennaro "Jerry" Angiulo in the Styx lounge with a few of his soldiers and lots of the Killeen and Winter Hill gang members at the Transit. Tommy C loved the sense of action and the respect these players seemed to get, oblivious to the fact that he and Jimmy were now being safely protected as two of Mo's boys. Most of the gang activities seemed harmless since it involved bookmaking, loan sharking, and hijacking activities. They saw little of the extortion for protection or robberies and were unaware of the murders outside of the gang war-related confrontations. Off and on, they ran into Kenneth and Edward Killeen, Jack Curran, and Billy O'Sullivan and sometimes made a few bucks by running deliveries for the bookmaking business.

One night Jimmy went to the movies with Tommy C at the old Orient Theater on Blue Hill Avenue in Mattapan Square. Afterward, they drove over to the Transit Café for a beer before heading back home. Donald and Kenneth Killeen were there as was Billy O'Sullivan who was talking at the end of the bar with a guy who Jimmy didn't recognize. Tommy C told Jimmy not to look over at the bar. He whispered to Jimmy, "I think he grew up in the Old Harbor Village public housing project in Southie and spent a bunch of years in prison, including a stint in Alcatraz. I heard he volunteered for LSD experiments, and I'm not sure if that made him a little unpredictable or if he was always that way. He has a brother in politics and, growing up, his nickname was 'Whitey,' but they said to never call him that because he likes to be called Jimmy, so you two should get along well."

Tommy C laughed while Jimmy tried to catch a glimpse of the man with the tinted glasses and receding hairline. To Jimmy, the man seemed a little more under control and self-aware than the other members of the gang, but in other ways, he seemed more dangerous. Outside of the Tavern, Jimmy and Tommy C stood with their hands in their pockets making plans for the week. Jimmy made his way home thinking about what he was getting himself into, first slowly and now more quickly. When he got home, Gianni was sitting up at the kitchen table folding a piece of paper and then unfolding it and repeating the process to pass time. It was late as usual, and Gianni wanted to talk with Jimmy, but Jimmy wasn't in the mood for a lengthy lecture and Gianni didn't want to push it since everyone else was asleep.

Chapter 27

David thought about Jimmy on his brisk sunny morning run. He could see Jimmy moving into dangerous territory on his own in the diary at a time when he was only a few years older than his own daughter, Amy, was now. His mother had told him and his siblings the hard reality about their father being the influence that took their brother away from them and destroyed their family.

He forced himself to put any deep thoughts about Jimmy and his father on hold during his business trip. On a flight home Tuesday evening, his stomach clenched as he thought about Jillian, Amy, James, and even Kathleen. All the casualties of his own life caused by his own hypocrisy and hidden life, just as his father's secrets had broken his childhood. How was he being any better a man than his father to the people in his life? He was angry at his father for not living up to what he had wanted him to be.

He was tired when he got back to his apartment, which felt empty without Trooper, who'd been left with Lucy while he was away on business.

Thankfully, there weren't any riddles or clues left to greet him. His fortress had held and there was not a sign of intrusion or any messages left for him to decipher.

He hadn't exercised while he was away and wanted to go for a short run on the treadmill to loosen up but first went over to pick up Trooper at Lucy's. Trooper bounded into the house, happy to be home. David changed and went into the exercise room to run a few easy miles on the treadmill, then he would shower and relax with Trooper before bed. He ended up running longer than he had planned, and he walked out with a good sweat to show Trooper, then he noticed something on the dining room table. He stepped quickly to the door to open it up to see if anyone was on the staircase and then checked all the other doors and windows. Everything appeared tight and untouched. He checked on Trooper, who seemed more amused at watching him run around than phased by an intruder.

David walked over to the table to see a fine, lace-type material laid on the table. He knew that it wasn't there when he left, nor was it anything he'd ever seen before. As he stared down at the translucent cloth, he noticed something underneath and wasn't sure if he wanted to lift it to find out what it was. He asked Trooper what he would do, but Trooper offered no advice.

Sitting down at the table, he realized that it was October 15. He remembered his mother sitting him down at the table in their North End apartment to give him the devastating news she had already given to Bobby and Abbie. She was in a state of shock but knew she had to tell them before others did. He didn't comprehend anything she was telling him. Nothing she was relaying seemed possible, and nothing was translating into anything he could process. She went off to her room for days, sobbing and wailing, even when people had come over to console them.

David, Bobby, and Abbie spent time at Nonno and Nonna's while Annie spent hours at the police station answering the same questions over and over from different police officers and detectives. When it finally hit him that he would never see his brother or father again, he couldn't process the concept at eight years old but felt completely numb in between the crying and unanswered questions to his mom. He now stood up to break the anticipation that he was going to get sucked back into that black pit and pulled the veil off of the table to find a piece of paper underneath with something in a foreign language written on it. He quickly covered it back over and took a long, hot shower, hoping the veil and paper would be gone once he got out.

Εἰς μίαν
Καθολικὴν Ἐκκλησίαν Ἀποστολικὴν
Ἁγίαν

In the morning, after dressing, David walked by the dining room table and stared at the cloth and paper, still sitting where he left them. He wasn't sure if he would ask Tom about this fourth riddle but stuffed both articles in his bag to give him time to decide.

At the office, he was restless and almost a little testy during the day. At 4:00 p.m. Izzie entered his office and cleaned up his desk while he worked. When he asked what she was doing, she kept humming. David got the hint when she closed the folder he was perusing and scooped it up before he could say a word. Then Izzie turned and smiled at him as she flicked off the lights in his office. He grabbed his bag. "Goodnight, Izzie—and thank you."

"Goodnight, Mr. Kelly, and say hello."

He turned with curiosity. "Say hello?"

She shook as she chuckled, "To whoever you see, say hello for me."

He walked to the church, and instead of going to the rectory, he headed to the school gym to see if anyone was there. At the door was Sister Helen. "We don't just let people walk in off the street into the school without being accompanied. What were your plans, Mr. Kelly?"

Tom came up from behind him. "It's okay, Sister. David has a pass and will be helping to coach the boys' basketball team this year, so I can vouch for him."

David smiled at Sister Helen as he stepped into the hallway and then turned to Tom. "What was that you signed me up for?"

Tom grinned. "It got you into a nice, dry basketball court now, didn't it?"

Sister Helen called out, "I will still be watching him, Father."

When Tom opened the gym door to let David in first, David was surprised to see a group of boys in practice clothes and sneakers standing around at center court. They had no basketballs and appeared to be a rag-tag group, to say the least. He glanced over to Tom, but Tom had already proceeded to center court to talk to the boys.

"Boys. I assume you are all interested in trying out for the team in November?" All the boys nodded. Tom waved David over. "Boys, this is Coach Kelly. He may be helping out with teaching you boys if we have a team this year." He turned to David. "Coach Kelly, official tryouts aren't for a few weeks, but these are some boys who'd like to have a chance to play and could use help learning some basics."

Tom asked David if he would agree to split up the boys and do basic skills drills to see where players were with dribbling, passing, shooting and rebounding skills. They started doing basic drills with defense, boxing out, and running a fast break to see if they could pick up the concepts. Finally, they played a game, which was as sloppy a game as he had seen in a long time, but a few of the boys did stand out as potential players.

After practice, Tom picked up the remaining ball and put it in the bag as he walked over to David. "I'm sorry for springing that on you. I hope you didn't mind, and if you did, then I owe you a game." David reached into the mesh bag and grabbed one of the balls out and shot it one-handed towards the basket and sank it. Tom dropped the bag of balls, retrieved the ball and began bouncing it at the top of the key. They played a back-and-forth game until it was tied at thirteen each, then David hit two straight pull-up jump shots to win.

Tom shook David's hand. "Nice game. You know, some of the boys don't have dads around to teach them, and the boys really took to you today. Maybe you can become a player-coach for the team? How about I buy you a drink and we discuss your contract?"

David hesitated for a second, thinking about how James had said he wanted to learn how to play. When they got to Dempsey's, a few booths were filled with some regular guys and some new men playing darts. Dempsey brought over two half-and-half beers and asked if they wanted anything to munch on as well. They each ordered a burger and then caught up on the past few days.

Tom looked over at David's bag and then back at David. "Any more messages lately?"

Dempsey put down their plates and David took a bite before he said, "Yes."

Tom's mouth was full as well, but he managed to mumble, "Yes, what?"

David, still chewing, said, "Yes, I'm a victim yet again, and who else would I come to? So last night, it's always a Tuesday night, someone left something in my apartment while I was taking a shower, and I don't think it's my dog, even though he seems like the only possible candidate."

Tom was holding his beer in both hands as he was thinking. "And you don't have any clue as to how they are getting in?"

"Not a one. It may be time to call in a detective."

"So, what was the surprise this time?"

David scanned the tavern first and then pulled out the sheer lace cloth and held the paper under it, placing it on the table between them. Tom stared at the material for several moments. "It looks like a veil of some sort."

David asked, "A veil? What do you mean?"

"Women used to wear head coverings as a veil. I can see markings underneath it." Tom lifted the veil to see the odd writings. It didn't take Tom long to recognize the Greek lettering but took a few minutes to decipher the words behind the lettering.

David chuckled. "Hey, it's all Greek to me as well."

"It has been a while, but these are not unfamiliar words. I'm just trying to tell why they are laid out like this."

Εἰς μίαν

Καθολικὴν Ἐκκλησίαν Ἀποστολικὴν

Ἁγίαν

"Laid out like what?"

"Like the Cross. The top essentially says 'one.' The next row says, 'catholic' then 'church' and then 'apostolic.' Oh, okay, the bottom says 'holy.' These are the four marks of the Church Christ founded."

"But there are five terms, not four."

Tom tapped the paper. "The one in the middle is protected and defined by the four others that are laid out like the Sign of the Cross. At the top is 'one' and then at the bottom is 'holy' and then on the left 'catholic' and on the right 'apostolic' and finally at the heart is what Christ left us, 'his Church.'"

David rubbed both hands on the sides of his forehead. "Okay, religious again. And again, you didn't have anything to do with it, but each time the messages were left the night before I'm going to see you, so these have to be left by someone who knows both of us."

"That makes a lot of sense. Who are the potential candidates?"

David thought of the potential candidates. "Luke?"

"Luke didn't know you before the first message, and neither did Sister Helen for that matter. And I promise you, Luke has no knowledge of Greek."

"Let's just make sure. How about—? No, you wouldn't even know Jillian. There's no one at my office who knows where I go. It has to be someone who comes to this bar or at My Brother's Table. Or one of us?"

"No one stands out to me as having had the interest or the capabilities to be a prime suspect. It's definitely a mystery."

"Okay. I get the Greek but what about the cloth on top?"

Tom paused. "Hmm. A veil is used to protect something that is sacred. In the Jewish temple, there was a large curtain or veil between the people and the 'Holy of Holies' that was reserved for the presence of God. Only the High Priest could enter this chamber once a year on the Day of Atonement. A veil is also used in the Mass to protect the Eucharist or the real presence of Christ. And a veil is used for another situation that most people are familiar with."

David answered, "The only thing I can think of would be at a wedding."

Tom nodded. "Sure. The bride wears a veil to signify her honor and purity in coming to the relationship. Lifting the veil is a sign that they have permission to consummate the relationship in an intimate way as they become one while remaining two individuals. Marriage is thought to reveal the nature of God as a communion of love of three persons in one God."

"Okay. This is getting a little deep for me. Why the veil over these words then?"

"Oh, that's simple. The Church isn't thought of as a thing made by men but the actual Body of Christ and at the same time the Bride of Christ. Paul tells us that we should love our spouse as Christ loved the Church, his Bride since he was willing to give and sacrifice his entire life for her."

"I've never heard of the Church being referred to as a bride. How can the Church be both the bride and the body of Christ?"

"Think of a marriage. We become one but still remain two distinct people who maintain our integrity as individuals. It is a mystery, but in a marriage, the one Church can be both the Bride and the Bridegroom, a term Christ often used when referring to himself."

David leaned back and crossed his arms over his chest. "Very poetic, but what does that have to do with me?"

"Probably the same as it has to do with each of us. Think about the messages and where they are pointing. Do you believe in truth? Do you believe in God? Do you believe in God revealed to us in Christ? And now, do you believe in the Church that Christ left us, so we can know him? I know that all sounds very religious, but it's the crux of what life is all about."

David sighed, "Tom, I wouldn't want anyone trashing my company, so I haven't really said too much about yours, but I have some issues with the Catholic Church. I'm not sure I'm up to listening to why it's so great when I know that quite the opposite is true. I've been seriously conflicted. I have a lot of respect and, believe it or not, admiration for you as a person while on the other hand, I don't understand how someone like you can't see what seems so clearly rotten about your Church."

One of the guys in the next booth said, "This sounds like a heavy conversation for a sports bar. Mind if we listen in?"

Tom shrugged. "If David doesn't mind, I'm okay with it."

David nodded, almost relieved to have other voices included. "Why don't you join us?"

They introduced themselves as Pete and Andy and slid into the booth with Tom and David. Andy said, "We didn't mean to eavesdrop but how often do you hear actual conversations about anything except sports at a bar?"

"I guess this is your first time at Dempsey's."

Tom laughed. "So, what did you hear that piqued your interest?"

Pete answered, "You mentioned something about the Church and about Catholics. I've been studying more these days at my Baptist Church. I was curious where your conversation was going to go. What's the writing on the paper you were talking about?"

David turned the paper so that Pete and Andy could see and told them about the four marks of the Church. Pete said, "Sure, we read that in the Creed all the time. One, holy, catholic and apostolic church, but that doesn't mean the Roman Catholic Church. I'm pretty certain of that."

David glanced over at Tom, but he seemed relaxed and interested in Pete and Andy's perspective.

Tom met Pete's gaze. "How do you feel specifically about the Catholic Church versus say the Baptist Church?"

"I don't want to be negative, but I don't even think Catholics are actually Christian, never mind the one true Church. I really don't think Jesus meant a physical church, but a universal community of followers."

David knew this conversation wasn't headed anywhere good and motioned to Dempsey to bring over another round.

"I appreciate your honesty and your sincere interest in being a follower of my all-time favorite person," Tom said. "I think of us as fellow Christians on the same journey. What would you say are your top issues with the Catholic Church?"

Pete sat back. "Let's see. Where do I start? I think the Catholic Church got lost and focused on power instead of Jesus. It put its own traditions and authority ahead of what's in scripture and put doing works ahead of faith and salvation through Christ alone. Catholics worship Mary, saints, and statues, which is wrong. The Mass is a perverted ceremony to sacrifice Jesus every week, and the Church thinks a piece of bread is the actual body and blood of Christ. Purgatory, indulgences, you name it."

Andy added his own complaints. "Not to pile on, but what about corrupt popes, the Crusades, the Spanish Inquisition, being anti-science, and the current sexual abuse scandal? The Catholic Church is certainly not 'holy'!"

Tom didn't appear to take offense. "Boys, I know exactly how you feel and why you may firmly believe everything you do. I don't know your history or the information you have, but I can remember saying the exact same things you are saying and feeling just as strongly."

"So, what's changed?"

Tom raised his mug. "Me. With the help of some history and the truth. I challenged someone once with pretty much the same list you just rattled off. He asked me just one question—'If this was the one, holy, catholic and apostolic church, would you want to know?' It took me a few weeks of soul searching to ask myself if I would honestly want to know."

David smiled. "So, you were sleeping on Procrustes's magic bed?"

Tom nodded. "Every night, and comfortably too. But following Christ isn't always comfortable. I had to look seriously at why Jesus built a Church and how he did it. He handpicked and trained twelve apostles, representing the twelve scattered tribes of Israel. When he came back from the dead, he trained them some more to make believers and proclaimers of his Good News to all nations. He gave them gifts through the Holy Spirit to teach His authority. Jesus said, 'He who listens to you, listens to me, and he who rejects you, rejects me.' He gave them the ability to perform miracles, to forgive sins, to speak so that people of any language could understand them, to baptize, and to turn simple bread and wine into the true presence of Christ Himself. These were not all educated men, and they went from being afraid to having the courage and gifts to spread the faith in the face of agonizing torture and death. These men couldn't have been acting on their own; they were guided in the fullness of truth and filled with the Holy Spirit."

Pete said, "I agree with some of that."

Tom said, "Some is a good start. It became clear to me that I had to really listen to the words Jesus spoke and the actions he took. I had to do the same when I looked at the words and actions of the early Church that was guided by the Holy Spirit. Jesus said to his apostles, 'I have yet many things to say to you, but you cannot bear them now. When the Holy Spirit of truth comes, he will guide you into all truth.' He also said, "I will build my Church and the gates of hell will not prevail against it,' meaning it will never be destroyed, and never fall away from Him, and will survive under the protection of the Holy Spirit until He returns. Any human organization would've collapsed as all others have. Finally, Jesus said his Church would be the 'light of the world,' 'a city on a hill that cannot hide,' so it would appear to be visible and meet the description in Timothy 3:15 as the 'pillar and foundation of truth.'

"Now, Pete, say you were a simple fisherman and your name was Simon, and Jesus asked you and your friends who you thought He was. And say you were the only one to reveal the truth to everyone by saying, 'You are the Christ, the Son of the Living God.' And then Jesus looks at you and changes your name to Peter, meaning 'rock,' saying, 'Blessed are you, Simon, son of Jonah! For flesh and blood has not revealed this to you, but my Father who is in heaven. And I say also to you, that you are Peter, and on this rock, I will build my church; and the gates of hell shall not prevail against it. And I will give to you the keys of the kingdom of heaven: and whatever you shall bind on earth shall be bound in heaven: whatever you shall loose on earth shall be loosed in heaven.' What are you thinking at that very moment?"

"I wouldn't know what to think," Pete replied.

Tom continued. "But everyone at that time would've known. When a king left the kingdom, there was the office of Prime Minister, and the king would give him the keys as a sign of his power and authority until his return."

"I have never heard that before."

"Take another look through the New Testament and notice how often Peter's name is mentioned versus the other apostles and his role in arbitrating early Church matters. You will see that his name is the only name that is changed by Jesus, which always indicated a change in office as part of a covenant."

"Are you trying to say that I—I mean Peter, was actually the first pope with the authority of Christ until his return?"

"Yes, like the office of the Prime Minister with the keys and authority of the king to arbitrate matters. When Jesus said to Peter, 'whatever you bind on earth or loose on earth will be bound and loosed in heaven,' that seems like a pretty important office, and the early Church treated him and his successors as such."

Andy interrupted. "But you Catholics think the pope is infallible and cannot make mistakes, and yet there have been really bad popes!"

"You're right!" Tom said. "There have been a handful of awful popes put in office through questionable means. There are probably four to seven seriously bad Popes out of over two hundred and sixty, but don't confuse infallibility with impeccability. Many popes lived lives of extraordinary holiness as well, but because we are all sinners, Christ promised that His Church would always be the source of truth and always survive even attacks from within. Christ entrusted important work to sinners and gives teaching authority to those sinners. It is also important to remember that infallibility only means that the Holy Spirit makes sure the Church and the pope never teach against the truth in matters of faith. It doesn't mean that he can't make mistakes. Even those corrupt popes interestingly never taught contrary to the truth when it came to matters of faith. To put it another way, you don't leave Jesus or the Church because of Judas."

David had been sitting quietly, taking it all in, but he was still anxious to know how it all tied to his situation. "So, what do the marks on this paper have to do with it?"

Tom tapped the paper. "In one sense, they give us a sense of the character of the Church. The first mark is that the Church is 'one.' The unity of the Church was important to Jesus when he prayed in the garden to his Father, 'That they may all be one. As you, Father, are in me and I am in you, may they also be one in us, so that the world may know that you have sent me.' Jesus had promised at the outset that 'there would be one flock, one shepherd.' Paul talked often about the unity of the Church and said, 'Because there is one bread, we who are many are one body, for we all partake of one bread.' Today there are close to 40,000 different churches and each one of them has a different version of the truth with no source of authority to determine who has the correct understanding. I personally found nothing in what Jesus prayed for in the early Church that would point to division and conflict in understanding and teaching Christ's message. Doesn't that make you guys wonder at all?"

Andy half-raised his hand. "It does, a little bit, and I agree that we should be more unified if only because it sends a bad message to non-Christians that we can't even agree on our own faith."

"Well said," said Tom, as he moved his finger down the paper. "The next mark is 'holy.' That doesn't mean that all the members are holy because we are all sinners, but it does mean that something is set aside for a special purpose for God and with God as the author. The Church is only holy because it's Christ's Church. According to Paul, the Church is the Body of Christ and we are the members in need of his sanctifying grace."

Tom continued, "And now comes the word that can make my Protestant brethren cringe when they recite the Creed: 'catholic.' Notice, it's a small 'c.' The word catholic basically means universal or according to the whole and lacking nothing. I like to think of what Jesus told his apostles when he gave them the Great Commission: 'I have been given all authority in heaven and on earth. Go, then, to all peoples everywhere and make them my disciples: baptize them in the name of the Father, the Son, and the Holy Spirit, and teach them to obey everything I have commanded you. And I will be with you always, to the end of the age.'

"And finally, the Church is 'apostolic.' Christ founded the Church upon the apostles, saying, 'Did I not choose you, the twelve?' The question to Protestants is this: Did Christ give the power and authority to the apostles to pass on to others what they had received from Jesus? Peter had referred to Judas as a bishop and there was a process to replace Judas with Matthias with the authority to teach. Paul was given the authority to teach and appoint other bishops, including Titus, with the authority to do the same by laying on of hands. Remember that Jesus gave Peter the power and authority to bind or loose on earth, and he said, 'He who hears you, hears me.'

"Protestants, and I myself at one time, hold its only scripture that represents an apostolic succession of the truth, but if you really study the early Church fathers and the history of the Church, everything points to Jesus intending people, with the Holy Spirit, to be a source of authority."

Pete said, "Why don't you believe scripture has the only authority?"

"Holy Scripture is huge, but tell me this—if the written word was the plan, why would Jesus not have written down everything he wanted to pass on? Why would he focus on teaching the twelve? Why would he build his Church on Peter, a person? If the apostles thought the written word was to be the only source of authority, why would they and the Church not be in a rush to pull together those New Testament scriptures? What would be the rationale for waiting four hundred years to compile the Bible?"

Andy said, "That's a good question."

Tom nodded. "Also, how could I trust the Church that believed in an apostolic succession of people, in the real presence of Christ in the Eucharist, the sacraments, and the authority of the pope? How could I trust that same Church that I had soundly rejected as the one true Church to authoritatively put together the scriptures I thought were the only source of truth? I had to get honest with myself and go back and read what the early

Church leaders, from the beginning, were saying. I was surprised to read how alike the beliefs and practices of the early Church were to today's Catholic Church. I was shocked, and I knew I had to make a decision between following the lead of Jesus or what I wanted to believe."

"I would need to check that out," Andy said, "but I still think scripture is the only reliable source of the truth and not some men I don't trust."

Tom held his hands open like a book. "The interesting thing about the *sola scriptura* belief is that it is not biblical, and it's the Bible that calls the Church and not the Bible the 'pillar and ground of truth.' Most of the apostles never wrote, and Paul and John often referred to what they said versus what they wrote. Jesus talks about what people hear and not only what a few of them would write. John said all the books in the world could not hold all the teachings of Christ. The Creed didn't mention the scriptures, and if they were intended to be self-interpreting with the guidance of the Holy Spirit and personal judgment and the only source for truth for individuals, why are there so many interpretations? And why did people have no access to Bibles for 1,500 years? Even Luther himself found out that misinterpretations of the scripture immediately ran rampant, and he quickly declared himself the authority to interpret. Soon after that, there was an explosion of different churches and different interpretations. It wasn't practical; it wasn't historical, nor was it biblical. Paul himself said, 'So then, brethren, stand firm and hold to the traditions which you were taught, whether by word of mouth or by letter from us.' There are several select passages that many Protestants have used to support sola scriptura, but I found these were often out of context or misinterpretations of Greek translations."

Pete said, "I'll go back and do some more reading and checking on this, but to me, the Catholic focus on being saved by works rather than faith seems like the most arrogant and power-driven position that disturbs me."

"It did me as well, but I found that *sola fide* or salvation through faith alone arguments to be problematic when I tested it with reason, history, and biblical scrutiny. What's important to note is that the belief in salvation through faith alone did not exist and wasn't taught anywhere until Martin Luther came up with the idea in the sixteenth century. Martin Luther had some serious and legitimate concerns about things going on by Church officials of his day, no doubt. He also had some personal demons and was tormented by what he described as an angry God of sacrifice, penance, and 'works, works, works.' He hated God for this and lived in dread of judgment by God. He taught that Catholic life was a desperate working to make ourselves pleasing to God, which was impossible since one could never do enough to be saved.

"Then Luther read a passage in Paul to the Romans that said, 'Righteousness of God is revealed. The just shall live by faith.' Luther saw a way to be free of his personal torment as he saw that righteousness was credited, in a binding, legal way, the moment we believe. He didn't read Paul in context when addressing the Romans who were caught up in rigidly following Jewish laws. Everywhere else, Paul talks about faith working through love, about the importance of keeping the commandments to remain in God's love, and that the 'judgment of God who will repay everyone according to his works.' Luther went so far as to insert the word 'alone' after 'faith' in Paul's letter to the Romans and to remove James entirely from the Bible because James had written, 'What profit, my brethren, though a man say he has faith, and have not works? Even so, faith, if it hath not works, is dead.' John writes that no man should add or take away anything from the written scripture, but Luther did."

Pete frowned. "So, we are back to having to earn your salvation because the sacrifice of Christ wasn't good enough?"

"Not at all, Pete. This is one of those 'both/and' situations and not an 'either/or.' The Catholic Church absolutely believes we are saved by Christ's grace alone, but also through faith and works done for charity and inspired by the Holy Spirit. Heck, if it were faith alone, even Satan believes in God, and Hitler would be in heaven despite any amount of evil he did after he believed. Does that make any rational sense? Can we work our way to heaven? Nope. We are saved by grace alone, but we must accept neither by 'faith alone' or 'works alone' but by faith that works in charity. As Paul so beautifully said, 'If I have faith that can move mountains, but have not love, I am nothing.' And Jesus talks about the actions of following his commandments, feeding the hungry, clothing the naked, and visiting those in prison. The bottom line is that all sacrifice comes from the grace of Christ's sacrifice. It is only by the grace of that sacrifice as a free gift we could never earn, but we are called to participate in our salvation which we accept through faith and actions of love."

Pete said, "You are either wearing me out or wearing me down, Tom."

"Sorry to go on like that. There are so many people who hate what they think the Church is, but I have found few who, once they really know the Church, can still feel the same way."

Andy put his hands down on the table. "I need to check some of this out, but I appreciate how non-defensive you were, especially about something you seem to care deeply about."

"Hey, I'm the one who appreciates that you were willing to listen. Most people are so busy countering that they never hear the possibility that something may be different from what they believed it to be."

Later, standing in the cold outside Dempsey's, Tom brought his hands up to his mouth to warm them. "Well, David, I'm sorry the conversation got into all of that."

"I will have to tell you that a lot of what you said just sounds like words to me."

"I can understand not feeling connected, but if there are things getting in the way that you ever want to talk about, without the crowd, just let me know. The things we've been talking about are the things in life that give it meaning and purpose."

David laughed lightly. "If you know how to do that, you could be a very rich man."

Tom grinned. "But I am a very rich man."

They shook hands and headed in opposite directions, towards their respective lives.

Chapter 28

When David arrived home, he felt as if too many issues weighed on him. He didn't want to think about his brother or father. He couldn't reconcile his disconnect between how much he enjoyed Tom and what Tom passionately did for a living. He didn't know how to check in with Jillian after all this time without hurting her more. He was feeling unsettled about Amy and James growing up without really knowing them or helping them to avoid the pitfalls of life. He couldn't, for the life of him, figure out how anyone could be getting into his apartment, past the locks, past Trooper, past the security, and under his very nose. And what were these messages all about?

David sank down into his chair and closed his eyes, letting thoughts fly by at a mile a minute. He knew he should've put Jimmy's diary out of sight, but there it was staring him in the face. He wondered if he really knew Jimmy at all as he reached over and picked up the diary and held it on his lap. He knew he should be going to bed but instead read Jimmy's June entries, scanning them and stopping on the ones that built on what he was beginning to piece together:

June 1: *School is officially done for seniors. Halleluiah! I have no desire to go to graduation next week. Should be able to get full-time hours at Dunbar now.*

June 7: *Dad and Mom take Abbie to the doctors again. Abbie has had problems breathing at times and feeling tired. It looks like a birth defect heart condition called ASD where there is a hole between the chambers, and it is causing pressure in the lungs and less oxygen flow. It looks like the hole has enlarged, and she will need an operation. It will take a lot of money to cover it.*

June 10: *Graduation. I guess this is official. Yes, I went to graduation. Mom and Dad, Pops and Grammy drove down from Maine, and Nonno and Nonna all came, and they looked proud. They all chipped in and bought me a suit. What am I going to do with a suit except wear it to my funeral someday?*

Aug 5: *Nervous today. They held the lottery for the draft. My birthday came up #359. What are the chances next year when the real thing comes up for me? Not feeling good about this. Get this war over!*

Jimmy wanted to have a great summer that year. He had no idea where he'd be the following year or if he would even be alive. He spent his days working at Dunbar with Tommy C, who was now riding the armored car routes regularly. The days were hot that summer in the metal warehouse and the work was boring, but the evenings and weekends were fun. They spent time at their favorite watering holes, hanging around someone's porch in Savin Hill, or on the corner near the Styx bar in the North End. Tommy C came to the North End on one July evening for the San Rocco festival. Then they hung around outside of Styx watching the Sox game and shooting the breeze with some of the other guys. Days like that seemed to have a slow, easy rhythm to them and made Jimmy feel like he was part of something in the neighborhood and was no longer a boy.

Jimmy and Tommy C split a pizza and a pitcher of beer at the old-time pizzeria Regina's on Thatcher Street on the way to the Boston Garden. Jimmy asked Tommy C., "This opportunity that Mo is working on, how comfortable do you feel about it?" Tommy C was chewing his pizza when he said, "I ain't gonna think about it until he can give us more details. He likes you, so I don't think he'd get us into anything too bad. It'd be good to make some dough though. I like driving the truck, but the pay is pretty tight, and we are gonna need to create some other cash flow."

During the summer, it became clear that Abbie would need to have surgery, and that Gianni didn't have the money to pay for it. Her breathing was okay now, but they noticed changes, which were making Annie anxious, especially when she thought about her sister Marie. Gianni told Annie not to worry and that he'd figure out how to earn enough to cover it with overtime and odd jobs. Annie wasn't convinced that Gianni's wages could cover the surgery, so she found a part-time job at a small *groceria* on Salem Street in the North End. The *groceria* was a few doors down from the River Styx Bar. Annie liked the owners and got a discount on anything she bought herself; every bit helped.

After Jimmy graduated, Annie saw him go out almost every night. She assumed it was to be expected but showing up for a quick dinner and then going back out again was difficult for Annie to accept. Annie loved Jimmy from the first second she laid eyes on him and now she felt she was losing him. To add to her stress, Gianni was going out more often at night right after Jimmy left, but they seemed to be fighting less often. Gianni would never tell Annie where he went or why he was out for such long hours.

The *groceria* was open late on Thursday night and sometimes Annie had to work later on those evenings. From the counter, Annie could see out the shop window and watch people walking past or entering the bar. One Thursday night, Annie was surprised to see Gianni walking past the shop.

She moved closer to the window to see where he might be headed without stopping in to say hello. She was taken back when she saw Gianni talking with Mo Diavolo. Gianni didn't seem angry nor was he acting as if he was trying to get away from Mo this time as his left hand rested on the right shoulder of Mo's cream-colored jacket. She could see his other hand moving as he talked to Mo, almost as if he were making a proposition to him. Annie didn't say anything to Gianni when she got home but noticed a difference in his behavior and more secretiveness of late. As they moved into the fall, Annie noticed that Gianni became quieter and was going out more evenings. When she talked to Gianni about Abbie's surgery, he continued to seem confident they would have the money and that she wouldn't have to worry.

David had temporarily drifted off to sleep with the diary in his lap and Trooper sound asleep by his side. When he awoke, he straightened the diary and turned the page to see the rest of the book was blank. The only last bit of handwriting from his brother he did spot was a figure on the back inside cover that read, 96,000 and underneath it was scribbled: Mo's worried about Johnny. He felt as if he had lost access to Jimmy all over again.

David glanced at the clock: 4:14 a.m. He drank a cup of water, but it didn't seem to quench his thirst. He fell asleep and didn't wake until after 8:00 a.m., something he hadn't done on a workday for as far back as he could remember.

At noon David canceled lunch with Quigs and Billy and spent the hour going for a walk to clear his head. He ended up in front of St. Anthony's Church, where all seemed quiet. He decided to see if Tom was in the rectory, but before he could knock on the door, he heard a voice around the corner where the maintenance man was painting a window. "Father Fitzpatrick isn't there."

"Oh. Do you know if he's coming back?" said David.

Angelo answered, "So far he has come back every time, so I suspect he'll come back this time too."

"I mean, do you think he'll be back soon?"

"He's usually over at the food kitchen serving on Thursdays, so I suspect he'll be here in a bit. Did you want to sit in the church and wait?"

David had forgotten it was Thursday already. "No, no, no. I was just passing."

Angelo said, "I'll let him know you dropped by."

On Friday, David took another stroll to the church during lunch. As he walked up to the rectory door, David knocked once before the maintenance man came around the corner.

"He did come back yesterday, but he's back out again now."

"Do you know if he'll be long?"

"Well, he goes out every Friday at the same time, which was just a minute ago, and usually returns in an hour and a half. If you take the Orange Line to Forest Hills and walk down Tower Street to the cemetery, you can probably find him."

David asked, "The cemetery? Is he visiting his mom's grave?"

"His mother's buried in Hyde Park. I'm not sure, but I think it's an old friend."

David thanked him and found himself walking quickly to the T station to hop on the next outbound trolley. The Orange Line trolley cars were old and crowded. David held onto a passenger strap as the trolley screeched and pulled away heading south.

The trolley was full of students from local colleges, older couples coming from one of the various Boston hospitals, and young, single women with one or two kids in tow. It was a motley crew that changed at each stop until he reached Forest Hills and stepped down to the ground as the folding doors slammed shut behind him and the trolley's squeaky wheels pulled way.

David made his way down Tower Street, as Angelo had instructed, until he saw the iron gate leading into the large and impressive Forest Hills Cemetery. There were two beautiful chapels on the grounds, arches, and statues that provided a feeling of beauty and permanence. The fall foliage colored the landscape with bright reds, oranges, and yellows. The plantings and monuments made for a striking setting as well as the interesting task of finding Tom if he were there. He walked the curved paths through the cemetery, working his way up and down the lanes, around a large pond, and past the chapel buildings.

It crossed David's mind that Tom may leave long before he found him. Just then, he saw someone kneeling beside a headstone. He felt awkward about being there and wasn't even sure why he had come. There were trees and bushes along each section of that area and larger monuments that allowed him to move much closer without disturbing Tom or being seen by him. At that point, he realized Tom was sobbing. With a rush, he suddenly felt the tingle of the hairs on the back of his neck standing up in recognition of the pain of a still open wound. This wasn't a momentary tear, but a lamenting cry of grief, sorrow and maybe regret. The always reserved and in control David was now flooded with emotion himself. The pain of the lump in his throat preceded the tears that began to roll down his own cheeks. Tom's vulnerability, his obvious sense of loss and suffering, moved something profoundly deep in David. It wasn't an emotion he could begin to control as he felt his body begin to shake.

Frozen in place, David slumped down on the grass with his back to the monument that blocked him from Tom's sight. The old stone was cold; it made him almost shiver more as the comforting carved angel above him stood with her wings gracefully extended, one hand on her bosom and the other reached out as if to calm him. He sat for several minutes as tears continued to fall more slowly from his eyes. At one point he turned to try to catch a glimpse of Tom, but he was no longer there. He was slow to get up and made sure Tom wasn't in sight. He felt as if he had invaded a very deep and personal part of Tom's life without permission, but Tom was gone, and the cemetery was quiet except for the rustle of the colorful leaves being played with by the gentle fall breeze. He took a step out from behind the angel and saw the modest headstone Tom was leaning on moments before.

David slowly moved to the front of the gravestone until he was standing next to the spot Tom had knelt on. Below the carving of a small angel on the top of the stone, he read:

CORLIE ANN SMITH
May 13, 1964 – Oct 12, 1984
And who can tell but Heaven, at last,
May answer all my thousand prayers,
And bid the future pay the past,
With joy for anguish, smiles for tears?
Anne Bronte

At the base were a single white rose and a smaller bouquet of forget-me-nots. David thought how little a gravestone tells you about someone's life, and that he had never visited the graves of any of the people he knew who had died. They were gone, and the relationship was done, but Tom had been coming to this grave every Friday. She was the same age as Tom, so she probably wasn't his sister. The anguish he had seen on Tom's face was that of someone who had recently lost someone they were deeply close to. David's sincere interest in knowing who this deceased stranger was, among thousands in this burial ground, surprised him. Was it because he really cared about Tom more than he was used to feeling? Had he become so isolated from everyone in his life that entering into someone else's pain out of pure friendship was now a foreign concept to him? He studied the stone, wondering what she was like, why she had died at the beginning of her young adult life, and what the poem meant.

Chapter 29

When David got back to his apartment, he found a note on the front door. *"Are you up for a run tomorrow morning? The weather is supposed to be nice. I'll bring some coffee at 9. (or you can come to Mass and we can leave from there.) :) TF"*

For some reason, David hadn't made any plans for the weekend. It was already nine, and Tom was knocking at the door with two coffees in hand, wearing a tee-shirt, shorts, and running shoes. It was already close to sixty degrees out and shaping up to be a good day for a run. He invited Tom in; Trooper barked until he saw David behind Tom with his hand up. Tom squatted down and took Trooper's head in his hands. "So, you are the vicious attack dog I've been hearing about." Trooper wagged his tail and rubbed his head into Tom's chest. David showed Tom around, and Tom said, "Very nice, and no, I haven't been here before, if you're still wondering."

With a nervous smile, David said, "No. No. No. The thought never even crossed my mind, but if you don't mind, would you empty your pockets on the table?" They both laughed, and David led Tom up to the rooftop terrace.

"So, this is the life," Tom said. "It's quite impressive."

"Thanks. I like that it's comfortable and close."

"Close to work, that is?"

After coffee and a small bite, they left for a run up Beacon Street, then out to the Charles River, running up one side and then down the other until they were sufficiently exhausted. As they walked on the dirt path along the river, Tom said, "Angelo tells me you dropped by this week?"

"Oh, yeah. I was just taking a walk during lunchtime and happened to be walking by."

"So, does a busy executive such as yourself usually take the time to go for a stroll at lunchtime and does that same executive usually find himself on that particular side street?"

"I don't like to get stuck in any routines. So, your maintenance man's name is Angelo? He seems to watch out for you."

"Yeah, he is more than a maintenance man. He takes care of everything and is a great cook, but don't let him talk you into a game of chess. He's sneaky. The odd thing about Angelo is that he does all that for nothing more than a hard cot in the shed and his meals. Just when we really needed someone we couldn't afford, he showed up like a saving angel, fixing things without ever asking. He just saw a need and filled it."

"Are you sure he's just not homeless and looking out for himself?"

"I don't think so. He is too talented and hardworking not to swing a paying job."

David gazed up at the blue sky that held a few puffy white clouds. "Hmm."

They sat on an old, wooden green bench facing the river, watching people running by. "Angelo mentioned that you came by two days in a row?"

"If Thursday and Friday are still next to each other, then yeah, that would probably be two days in a row."

They watched a crew team smoothly make its way down the river under one of the arched bridges that dotted the Charles River between Boston and Cambridge.

"I'm glad you dropped by. Was there anything you wanted to talk about besides just saying hello?"

"Like what?"

"Just checking in as a friend. I don't want to pry, and you may also have plenty of other people you would talk to if you needed to."

David thought he really would have no one else to talk to. He'd never needed to talk to anyone else since he always managed things independently. Why would he need to talk something out with someone who knows him less than he knew himself? "I'm good, but thanks for asking."

"Okay."

"You don't sound convinced."

"You don't have to convince me. It was just a sense I was getting."

David leaned forward with his hands on his thighs. He peered out over the water with the sun now glistening on it as it slowly flowed in the direction of the Boston Harbor. "I do struggle to figure you out."

Tom laughed. "Me? What are you trying to figure out about me except how to stop my killer crossover dribble and drive to my left?"

David joined Tom's laugh. "That is probably the first thing I need to figure out. But you're intelligent, talented, you could do just about anything you wanted in life, yet you chose this. It feels like you've given up your life, for what?"

"Fair question. What am I giving up? Money? Sure. Power? Prestige? Success? Popularity? Stuff? Sex? Yup, I did give that up. You probably know a lot of people who have more of each of those things than they know what to do with. How many of them, do you think, find their lives meaningful and feel a deep sense of satisfaction and joy? Those things gave me a constant sense of emptiness. They never satisfied. I kept convincing myself I just needed more of them to be happy. I tried to preoccupy myself with things to do, entertainment and seeking pleasure, but I found that I was only developing relationships for what I was getting out of them. Someone told me once to love people and use things and not the other way around. It hit me that I was doing the opposite. Did I have good self-esteem? Sure thing. I was all I could think about! I bought into the idea that it was the individual who brought temporary meaning to this existence, so why not focus on myself, do what I wanted and not need anyone? I pursued happiness with a vengeance, but I wasn't happy. I had no story, no narrative, no direction to my life other than myself, and it wasn't working."

David listened intently as Tom relayed his story. "So, what changed?"

"I was coming home on a bus one rainy night. Across from me, there was a mother reading a book to her son and next to me was a tall black man reading his book. I zoned out for the ride home after a long day of selling. I felt so empty and so tired of trying to escape myself in everything I was doing. I listened to the mother reading *The Velveteen Rabbit* to her little boy as he leaned against her body. I had heard the story before but what struck me this time was the line 'Sometimes it hurts to let yourself be loved for real.' She said to her son, 'Love is what makes us real. When someone knows you and loves you, as the boy loved the rabbit, it doesn't matter if you look shabby.' I hadn't noticed before, but the boy had a brace on his leg.

"It made me think as my attention shifted to the man next to me. He was reading a book about Martin Luther King, Jr. He had an index card as a bookmark that was next to his seat. On it was a quotation from Dr. King, 'The end of life is not to be happy, nor to achieve pleasure, and avoid pain, but to do the will of God, come what may.' I can't explain it, but it hit me that God's only will is to love us, and that is what makes us real."

David said, "So, you figured out the secret of life on a bus?"

Tom chuckled. "I had no clue at the time what I had figured out. I just knew I'd been looking in the wrong places and it wasn't working. I figured out long after that bus ride that I'd been looking to create my own self, who always seemed empty and lost. I figured that I had nothing to lose and started reading the Bible and books on God and faith, as long as it wasn't Catholic."

Surprised, David said, "What?"

Tom laughed. "I hated everything about the Catholic Church, or at least what I thought was the Catholic Church. I joined an evangelical Protestant church that was similar to the one I had attended growing up and 'caught the spirit,' as they say."

David shook his head. "How can you go from hating the Catholic Church to joining it? Why didn't you just stay where you were?"

"The evangelical church was great. I haven't found a kinder, more faithful group of people, but as I learned more, I started asking questions, important questions. Why is there so much disagreement between Christian churches? Where is the teaching authority to make the call? Jesus invested quite a bit of time to train and teach specific people and gave them authority. He didn't leave a book, but he built a Church to teach the truth of his message. With no compiled Bible and dead apostles, what happened to the Church between then and the 4th century when we finally had a Bible? How could we trust this Church to compile the authoritative and inspired books of the New Testament unless it was the true Church? What did that early Church, filled with the Holy Spirit, believe and practice when it came to Communion, Baptism, apostolic succession and priests, marriage, *sola scriptura* or salvation by faith alone? I kept getting unsatisfactory answers and recommendations to focus on other things. When I read more and discussed my questions with ministers that had done the same, I found the beliefs and practices of the early Church looked a lot more like the Catholic Church than the one I was in. My church had thrown out so much of what Christ had left us in the Church he had built. It was eye-opening. I started to see a lot of prejudice from bad information to some willful ignorance or—"

David smiled. "—or Procrustes's magic bed syndrome?"

Tom laughed. "A little. So, you do listen."

"A little."

David asked, "So why did you hate the Catholic Church before then?"

"Tell me why you think you do."

"Well," David said, "it's a little complicated. My mother would always be railing against one thing or another. Let's see, she said they were anti-science and only interested in protecting their own power and myths. Then there was the brutality of the Spanish Inquisition, and the millions the Church tortured and executed if they disagreed with them. The Crusades were all about getting riches and power while killing countless people. The corrupt popes, and on and on she'd go. She wasn't the only one who brought those things up either, and now there's the sex abuse scandal and cover-up that are just part of a long list of proofs that this is not the Church Jesus intended."

Tom nodded. "Those were on my list too and to address those I needed to understand the significance of Jesus becoming man and the Church He left us. God loves us unconditionally, without end and without fail. Throughout history, He continuously worked to renew our relationship or covenant with Him, despite how often we turned our backs on Him and found worth in our other gods, whether it be ourselves, or pleasure, power, money, or possessions. When Jesus was born, He took on the flesh of a human being and was both fully human and fully divine. He gave everything, even His life, to show us how much He loved us and wanted us."

David interrupted. "You know, I never did get why God had to make His son die to forgive and save us."

"That is a great question and hard to answer when we assume that God is an angry, revengeful, and cruel God. God can only love. He loved us so much that He gave us the gift of free will to have a relationship with Him. We are children of a loving God and made to love and trust His loving plan for each one of us. When Adam and Eve didn't trust God, the devil convinced them they could be gods and the deciders of what is right and wrong. The problem wasn't with the apple in the tree but with the 'pair' on the ground, who committed an offense against an infinite God."

David smiled at the pun. "Are you saying that there would be no integrity or justice in the relationship if they didn't make amends but because the offense was an infinite one, they really couldn't repay?"

Tom exclaimed, "Wow. Very few people would see that."

"I don't know that I actually believe that there were an Adam and Eve but let me play this out. Since the injustice had to be repaid by man, but couldn't be because man is not infinite, God had to lower Himself to become a man to make the payment because He was God at the same time?"

"David, I think you missed your calling. You should've been a theologian."

"Yeah right, but there is some poetry to this."

"How about this? When Jesus was dragged before Pontius Pilate, Pilate said that he found no guilt in Jesus, but the people called for him to be crucified. There was a tradition once a year to set a prisoner free, and Pilate picked the worst one called Barabbas, thinking that the people would naturally pick Jesus to be let go. But they didn't, and Pilot washed his hands of the case. Most people don't notice the significance of the innocent Jesus standing next to the actual criminal Barabbas and taking his place to die on the cross."

David and Tom were quiet for a second, and then David spoke up. "Do you mean that we are the ones who sin against God and didn't trust Him, but God took our place to serve the punishment and pay the price?"

"Yes, the greatest act of love. Jesus experienced ridicule by many, abandonment by His closest friends and one friend turned Him in for a few coins. He was mocked and experienced stress, incredible suffering. The scourging tore the skin off His back, and finally the most painful form of execution by crucifixion that slowly crushed his lungs under the weight of His collapsing body hanging by nails—all for sins we commit every day without much thought at all."

David sat back and took in a long breath. "That's a lot to think about, but what does that have to do with the Catholic Church?"

"The Church is the Body of Christ. It is like a two-sided coin, messy, sinful, dysfunctional, and corrupt on one side and beautiful, giving, wise, and the source of truth and love on the other side because it's both human, us slobs, and divine, the body of Christ. It's both because Christ took on flesh and was both human and divine, and the Church He left us is both human and, at its core, divine. So, you will see corruption and the failings of the sinners who are in the Church, but the Church itself is the pillar and foundation of truth and love in Christ at the same time. We can't lose sight of that part and that the Church doesn't have the capacity to teach anything but the truth when it comes to faith. The Church does incredible good every day as the single largest provider of social services on the planet, including feeding, clothing and sheltering, educating, providing healthcare, and other services for the poor all around the world. Before I learned about the Catholic Church, that was not something I was aware of."

"That's fine but why are they so anti-science, if not just to hold onto myths and power?"

"The Church has been far from anti-science from the beginning. The Church is focused on truth and has appreciated revealing that truth through art, literature, and yes, science. The Church sponsored science from early on and was responsible for creating the scientific method. It also created the first hospitals to care for the poor and the university system for education. I also found out how many priests were physicists, astronomers, doctors, and scientists—and Catholic scientists such as Copernicus, Descartes, Newton, Kepler, and Pascal were devoutly religious. The Church has always been a promoter of true science since it reveals the beauty, truth and incredible design of the universe, big and small."

"Then why would they torture and imprison Galileo just for discovering the truth about the earth and the universe?"

Tom smiled. "I will admit that it's more of a complex tale than most people want to hear. There were bad decisions on both sides, but the majority of what you and I believed is propaganda that many have been all too willing and even eager to believe. Aristotle taught that the earth was unmoving and the center of creation. Almost all astronomers accepted that view of the cosmos without question, but Galileo was intrigued by

Copernicus's heliocentric theory. With a crude telescope he invented, he began to gain some evidence through observation. While scientists and academics of the day weren't convinced because Galileo had not yet proved his theory by the scientific standards of the day, Galileo moved from proposing it as theory and began proclaiming it as truth.

"Galileo was asked to present his findings to Pope Paul V and Cardinal Robert Bellarmine. Galileo hadn't proved his theory and couldn't answer the strongest argument against it. Despite popular storytelling even to this day, Galileo was actually warmly welcomed and asked to continue working to prove his theory before stating it as an absolute fact, and also not to present it on theological grounds until it was proven. Galileo had agreed but then didn't comply with the pope's request. He also wrote a piece in which the pope felt mocked, and this didn't go over well with a pope who felt betrayed. Galileo wasn't tortured, but he was forced to recant his proclamations about his theory and was put under a comfortable house arrest. There were proponents of Galileo in the Vatican as well as opponents, but it's interesting to note that Galileo ended up being half right and half wrong in his theory since he also proclaimed that the sun was the fixed center of the universe."

"Are you saying that everyone in the Church was clean on their handling of Galileo and in all their actions?"

"I don't think so. Remember that the Church was under a huge amount of upheaval at the time of the Protestant Reformation. They were on the defensive, but as one noted scientist, Alfred Whitehead, said in the age of burning witches by Protestants, 'the worst that happened to the men of science was that Galileo suffered an honorable detention and a mild reproof.' The Church has acknowledged that Galileo's condemnation was wrong. The rejection of his theories, however, were stronger among Protestants and his fellow scientists than the Church."

"Huh. That sounds so different from what I've heard for so many years."

"You mentioned the Crusades and the infamous Spanish Inquisition. Are you up for the skinny on either of those? If you want to read up on the actual history as compared to the tales that have found their way into history textbooks and college professors' lectures, I can get you some."

"I will take the skinny version only, please."

"I will give you the Crusades in one minute. For four centuries, the Muslim expansion by the sword had captured two-thirds of the Christian world and destroyed thousands of churches, including the Church of the Holy Sepulcher, where the tomb of Jesus lay. The Emperor of Constantinople made a desperate plea for aid from the West to help defend the faith and culture itself. This was the birth of the Crusades as Pope

Urban II rallied the knights to push back on the conquest and free the captured Holy Land where Christians suffered torture, slavery, and imprisonment. There were good and bad things that happened in a string of Crusades but the myths that we hear today were developed by anti-Catholic Protestants in the 16th century, and I can say that because I was an anti-Catholic Protestant. In any war, there will be awful things that happen, but the idea that rich knights gave up their treasures and lives for the sake of getting richer isn't historically accurate, and the injustices to Jews during some marches were highly condemned by the Church."

David said, "As long as we are in history class, how do you get around the Spanish Inquisition?"

Tom laughed. "Do you really want more?"

"Let's get it over with."

Tom sat up. "Okay, so try to forget what you think you know from Mel Brooks and Monty Python. A couple of things to keep in mind. First, the 'Black Legend' about the now-infamous Spanish Inquisition was started by Protestants, especially in countries that were enemies of Spain. Secondly, there were two players to think about, the king and the Church. The king was primarily interested in safeguarding his kingdom and the Church was trying to save souls. At that time, faith was in the very fabric of the culture, including science, philosophy, politics and personal identity and salvation. It was about universal truth, and so heresy struck at the heart of truth and tore apart the fabric of the community. Also, kings believed their authority came from God, and neither the king nor the common people had much tolerance for what was a serious crime against the State, not the Church. By Roman law, heresy was a capital offense as was damaging shrubbery in a public garden in London. It was a different time and there was also witch hysteria in Europe that killed 60,000 people because there was no strong court-hearing system in most places. Does that make sense so far? I don't want to put you to sleep."

David looked up at the blue sky and nodded. "Keep going."

"So, the question was how to discern heresy in order to stop unjust executions. You would need people who were well educated and trained in the faith to have a fair trial, because heretics would be considered traitors to God, and therefore, to the king. To the Church, the accused were lost sheep who had strayed. A fair inquisition, which is simply an inquiry, provided a means to escape death and a way to rejoin the community. Since the Church had the only people trained in theology, they were asked to run the inquiry, and they had strict rules on the process but no authority to apply any penalties. They did keep detailed records and most people were acquitted. If the accused were found guilty, they could confess their sin and do penance if they were sincere, but if they were unrepentant, then the Church handed them over to the State authorities. Torture was rare and only done by the State with strict guidelines, limited to fifteen minutes, done with a physician present and recorded by a non-cleric. Any confession had to be repeated the following day to ensure it was sincere. No major court at the time had fewer executions, less than one percent of cases, and they were considered the most humane court and prisons in Europe. The only abuse came when authority slipped from the pope to the kings in the 14th century. During this same time, it was the secular inquisitions that burned thousands in Germany, while places like Italy and Spain that had Church-run inquisitions, found the witchcraft claims false."

Eyebrows furrowed, David asked, "You mean to tell me that the Inquisition was fairer than state trials and helped to save people from unfair convictions and punishment?"

Tom nodded. "In most cases, yes. So, what was the deal in Spain? Spain had conquered the Muslim jihad in the 8th century, so Muslims, Jews, and Christians lived together in a diverse and tolerant way, which was rare in the Middle Ages. However, anti-Semitism did creep into the society over time and baptism or death was forced by the state, not the Church. Church doctrine held that forced baptisms were invalid, thus allowing Jews to return to their religion. However, most Jews didn't go back and voluntarily converted while they still lived like Jews and were called 'Conversos.' The Pope met with Jewish leaders on the situation, but only more Jews converted, which led to more tension.

"By the 15th century, the Conversos had gained power and wealth, which led to anti-Semitic pushback by those believing it was a conspiracy to secretly overtake the country and the Church from within by insincere converts. Most were, in fact, good Catholics who took pride in their bloodline back to Christ. King Ferdinand and Queen Isabelle requested that the Church help them with an inquisition to investigate. The King had full authority in the inquisition to help calm the built-up resentment by both Christians and Jews. Both sides accused large numbers of Conversos, overwhelming the process, but Ferdinand believed the problem of secret Jews was real and needed to be dealt with.

"The process drifted from Church standards, and this resulted in abuse and confusion early on. While most Conversos were acquitted, there were publicized burnings based on clearly false testimonies. Pope Sixtus issued a letter to the local bishops of his concerns about the imprisonment of the innocent, torture, deprivation of goods and property, and unjust executions. The Church ordered bishops to take direct control to ensure well-established norms for justice were respected, that the accused had legal counsel and rights of appeal to ensure fair treatment, and that salvation of souls was the focus. The King didn't follow the Pope's requests, and the process went out of control. I found that the actual history has been greatly distorted in a propaganda effort and few people have felt much incentive to find out what is true and what is fiction when it fit what they wanted to believe."

David nodded. "And I thought you just wanted a run today."

"You brought it up."

"Remind me to not do that again. So how did all that information bring you to decide to do what you do?"

Tom asked, "You mean being a priest?"

"Yes, you know what I mean. What got you to pull the trigger?"

"The stuff about Galileo, the Crusades, and the Inquisition was just getting the garbage out of the way and the foggy glasses off. The real momentum came by learning the truth, listening, getting involved and praying, and then I started to see things better and clearer. I felt freer as I let go of my own notions and trusted God's. When I decided to give my life to this gig, it was the greatest feeling I ever had, and I've felt a deep sense of peace and purpose ever since. This may sound strange but when you become a priest, you are married to the Church in that you give your entire being to her. So, if I have ever seemed a bit zealous in defending the Church, I'm just sticking up for my girl, so to speak. It has been a privilege to be invited into people's lives, their celebrations, their intimate struggles, their joy, and their pains. I love being a parish priest more than anything I've ever done, except, of course, beating you on the court."

They both laughed and watched the world go by for a while longer before begrudgingly getting themselves up.

On their way back, Tom said, "I know you said your mom would regularly criticize the Church, but how do you feel personally?"

David was quiet and then answered, "I don't know anymore. I feel a sense of resentment and resistance to it, and I don't think I trust it. I just know that I don't need it and see no reason to think otherwise."

"Well, thanks for being honest. I'll try not to take it personally, but I've often found that there's usually something deeper involved when people feel a strong sense of resentment toward the Church."

"Like what?"

"Most guys who are either atheists or have a strong resentment towards the Church or God often had relationship issues with their dad. I don't mean to pry, but were you and your dad close?"

David started fidgeting and rubbed his right hand through his hair. He tried to respond but nothing was coming out of his mouth. Tom must've sensed David's high level of discomfort and put his hand on David's shoulder to apologize. David instinctively pulled his shoulder back. "Sorry, I have to go," he said and headed home, leaving Tom standing at the intersection.

Chapter 30

The next morning, David was still feeling angry at Tom for invading an area he didn't want to revisit but embarrassed about abruptly walking away like that. He went to work on Monday feeling no more at peace about it or about his life in general. What was he so afraid of when someone asked about his father? It happened. It's over. He had moved on. But all his time with Tom was making him wonder about the point of his life. So, why had he been so driven, while avoiding close relationships with others, certainly with God? If he met himself, what would he think? Would he want to befriend him? Why did Tom want to be friends with him? Tom never asked him for anything and gave his friendship freely with no advantage to himself. Who else in his life felt that way about him? Until he was eight, he would've said his father. Now, the only other person, besides Tom, seemed to be Kathleen. David had pulled the rug out from underneath her when he walked out, but he felt no hate from her, no revenge, and no repayment for justice. Maybe that was her way of making him feel guilty, but that didn't fit who she was.

His mind was racing, and he told Izzie that he was going to take a walk and she could get him on his phone if she needed him. Once down on the street, he decided to walk over to Tom's to apologize for being so abrupt on Saturday. As he approached, he saw Tom at one of the large wooden doors heading into the church. Tom spotted David out of the corner of his eye and turned to descend the handful of granite stairs with a welcoming smile. Before David could say a word, Tom reached out his hand. "David, it's so good to see you. I wanted to tell you how sorry I am for intruding the other day."

David's eyes welled up for a second before he collected himself. "I think you have it backward. I came here to apologize to you for walking off like that. You've been a good friend and deserve better than a rude reaction like that."

Tom waved toward the church. "I was just going to set up a few things inside. Can you come in and stay a few minutes?"

Outside of his visit to the small church in Stonington, David had intentionally avoided going into a Catholic church, so he expected to feel some sense of hesitation as he crossed the threshold. Again, he felt flooded with thoughts of his father and imagined he was standing beside him instead of Tom. The sunlight was streaming in through the large window over the doors and through the brightly colored stained glass windows along the side. The height of the ceilings and carved columns gave a sense of beauty, of a holy and sacred sanctuary. The wooden pews faced the empty altar at the front of the church and the gold tabernacle that stood behind the altar. Along the walls were statues of apostles and saints, and between the stained-glass windows were wood-carved Stations of the Cross depicting Jesus's last powerful moments. As David was taking it in, Tom faced the altar and went down on one knee, making the Sign of the Cross across his body.

Tom beheld the sight as if it were the first time he had entered this space. "It is beautiful, isn't it?"

David said, "Some might say the money could better be spent elsewhere."

Tom responded, "I understand the thought but have come to a different feeling about the answer. Many of these older churches are the result of sacrifices made by hard-working immigrant families laboring to create something sacred and fitting for Christ, their king. This church belongs to the people who need a sense of beauty and holiness. Beauty brings joy and taps into something deep inside of us we don't need words to understand. Take the vertical architecture. It gives us an immediate sense of God and heaven above. Everything in the church has meaning."

"Everything?"

"Sure. The baptismal font as you enter the church is where we are baptized in death with Jesus and reborn in the living waters as a member of His body. Reconciliation on the way in is to be forgiven for our sins and 'reenter' and turn back towards God."

"What about the statues you pray to?"

"We don't pray to statues and we certainly don't worship them. We are multi-sensory beings who live our faith through all of our senses. We are also reminded of the communion of saints living in heaven, who are one with us as part of the sacrifice of the Mass and model for us Christian virtues. The statues of the apostles remind us that we are an apostolic Church with the truth of Christ passed down to us in a tangible way. The Stations tell us the final journey of Christ in the greatest act of love the world has ever known. While children and immigrants may not always read, they can know the story through these visible scenes."

Tom gazed at the incredible art and color of the stained glass windows along the sides of the church. "David, did you ever notice, from the outside, those windows look dark and ugly, but once you are inside and the light shines through, they are magnificently bright and beautiful, and you begin to see how each window tells a story? That's how the Church was to me, dark and ugly when I was outside, powerful and beautiful on the inside. The crucifix is front and center, not to focus on death but on the great sacrifice and love Christ had for us to show us God's love and mercy for us. It is the greatest act of love and the conquering of death for all of us who choose to follow Him. Jesus tells us He will always be with us and give us Himself in the Eucharist. That is why I knelt in recognition and gratitude of His presence when we came in."

Tom turned around and pointed up. "And this is one of my favorite things about this church; the rose window above the doors where we entered. I love to come in around this time day because the sunlight shines through that window and makes a matching pattern on the floor right here." Tom had walked slowly over to the pattern on the floor that was the replica of the window at which they were now both looking at.

"So, what is different about this window except for its shape?"

Tom's eyes lit up. "I thought you'd never ask. Generally, you see this type of window in Gothic cathedrals. See how Christ is at the center of the window and everything else is beautifully revolving around him? It's the symbol of a well-ordered soul, where your life is ordered with God at the center and all the other things in your life revolve around him. Before I knew God, I put myself, some desire or things in the center and everything was in disharmony. Now I know that nothing else in the center can ever satisfy me the way only God can. We are created for Him. How could anything else satisfy?"

"You know, normally I would be wary that someone was trying to push their ideas on me," David replied with narrowed eyes, "but I can sense that you really believe what you're saying."

"I appreciate that. I like and respect you too much to do that, but I also care about you enough to share what I've come to know as true." Tom and David walked slowly down the aisle with the sound of their steps echoing throughout the church. Tom sat in one of the pews to straighten out some hymnals and when he didn't get back up, David sat down beside him and listened to the quiet, the sense of peace of this space.

After several minutes of quiet, David felt moved to broach a topic he had been avoiding for most of his life. "Tom, you asked about my relationship with my father. I'm sure it was obvious that it wasn't good."

"I would be interested in hearing about it."

David breathed in deeply and then exhaled a few times hesitating to answer. He didn't really want to say anything although he didn't feel the fear he normally experienced when thinking back to his youth.

For the first time in his life since his mother had pushed him, as a young boy, to move forward and never look back, David opened up. "When I was very young, I loved and adored my dad. He made us feel like we were everything, and at the same time, his faith was everything to him. He spent time with me and taught me to believe in myself. He meant the world to me, as did the rest of my family. If I think back, I loved being in my family. That was how I saw the world as an eight-year-old, believing and trusting in my dad. I also looked up to my brother Jimmy, who was ten years older than I was. He'd take the time out to do things with me or just let me know he was watching out for me; I mattered, and he cared.

"The summer of 1971, when we moved to the North End, Jimmy was 18 and started going out at night a lot. Dad went out on those same nights, and Mom trusted him and didn't ask where he was going. She thought he might be getting part-time work to pay for a costly operation that my sister, Abbie, needed. Mom had taken a part-time job to save up as well. She told me later that she saw my father talking to a man called Mo Diavolo, someone whom she was sure my Dad didn't even like. She said they looked as if they were making some agreement. She blames herself for not asking him about it, especially since she thought something was odd."

David breathed in deeply again. His eyes began to well up a little, something that hadn't happened until recently when he saw Tom at the cemetery. "On Columbus Day, we spent the day at the parade and out joining in the festivities, but nothing prepared us for that next day. I guess the long holiday weekend meant a very large sum of cash would be deposited into the Bank of Boston vault that Tuesday morning for a noon pickup by the Dunbar Armored Truck—" David held his breath a moment. "—but something must've gone wrong in the bank. I don't know what it was, but Jimmy was shot and killed along with one of the bank guards. Mom could never figure out why Jimmy was there, but he was there with his security guard uniform on, covered with blood. Mo, two other guys, and my father took off with the cash in a van that had been parked in front of the armored truck. They sped off from police pursuit, leaving Jimmy to bleed to death. Evidently, Mo Diavolo and my father were the masterminds of the heist."

Tom sat frozen and appeared in shock as this story unfolded.

"They made it as far as Virginia, where a gun battle left a police officer dead before they were finally apprehended. The police found an old .38 Colt Police special revolver with a wooden handle that my father had kept hidden above his bedroom closet. It had his fingerprints all over it. This was the same gun that shot and killed my brother and then the police officer. At the trial, Mo Diavolo testified that my father had shot Jimmy by accident and then killed the police officer in the shootout. Despite denials by my father, the accomplice, Gino Cappelletti, confirmed Mo's account of what happened, and my father was sentenced to the death penalty. The furor over the shooting of the police officer brought the case to trial and execution very quickly in Virginia. That was the end of my family as I knew it."

Open-mouthed, Tom stared at David. "I had no idea. I'm so sorry you and your family went through such a tragedy. I can't imagine what you went through as an eight-year-old."

"I think I was just shocked and too young, but my mom felt disgraced, so she moved us to Lynn without telling anyone. We never saw our grandparents after that. Even when they died, we never even attended their funerals." He gazed off to the side, unfocused, adrift in memories. "After that, my mom was a completely different person. She never smiled. She was always tired and short with us. She taught us to be strong and protect ourselves by never looking back. She changed our last names to Kelly and left no trail for anyone who knew her to contact us. She was driven to survive and bury the past with Jimmy."

Tom shook his head. "That's a seriously traumatic experience for a young boy. Broken trust like that can be devastating. It can even prevent us from risking intimate relationships."

David turned to face Tom. "I think I have done okay to get past it and make something of myself."

"You certainly have worked to use the positive energy in your life in an impressive way."

"Isn't that the point, to deal with the difficult things in life and make the best of it?

"One thing I've learned is that we all need to find a way to initially cope with trauma. Some withdraw from people to protect themselves from future hurt, while others take a more proactive approach, building a protective false self, and filling their lives with power, money, or prestige to never get hurt again. There are people who choose more destructive ways to escape, numbing themselves with drugs, alcohol, or sex, because the feeling is so overwhelming at the time. A young person can develop a healthy adaptation to help them cope and survive, but as an adult, those same adaptations can then become mal-adaptations."

"What does that mean?"

"It means that these coping mechanisms of withdrawing, being busy, or creating a protective outer-self can be helpful in the beginning to cope but end up working against us actually living life with real relationships as an adult."

David shrugged. "So, what else can a person do?"

"It really depends," Tom said, gazing at the crucifix, "but they need to relearn to trust, to recognize and accept their true self, and develop healthy relationships with others. Have you heard of something called 'affect tolerance'?"

"What in the world is affect tolerance?"

"Someone once said that our most serious problems come not from our negative emotions or experiences, but from our attempts to avoid or escape them."

David sat in silence, thinking for a moment. "Are you saying that all the ways we come up with to avoid dealing with reality, so we don't get hurt again, are a bigger problem than our actual fears or negative experiences themselves?"

"Something like that. In order to grow, a person needs to be able to bear the discomfort of dealing with a scary or painful feeling. You have to be willing to be displeasing to yourself at times in order to recognize and accept your authentic self and move past your deepest fears and overwhelming feelings. In a situation like yours, where you had a truly traumatic experience of broken trust and loss, it can be a process you do slowly to avoid being too overwhelmed. You regain a sense of your dignity, your unique goodness, self-worth, and challenge some of the 'truths' that drive your emotions and beliefs about yourself and others. I'm throwing a lot at you after you have poured your heart out to me."

"Don't apologize. Somehow, I'm actually feeling that the heaviness has been lifted a bit from my being just by telling you what I have never even said to myself. Up until this summer, I had felt good about everything, but lately, I've started to question the path I've taken over the past years. I've started to notice that I've pulled back from relationships and hurt people I don't want to hurt. I keep wondering if all the effort I put into work and play means anything, or if I'm really just keeping busy until it's all over. I've never known anyone I could share any of this with and I'll say that you have been a pain in the ass pushing me to do so. Oops, sorry. I forgot where we were."

They got up from the pew, stepped into the aisle and walked to the back of the Church. David turned to Tom. "If you could give me one piece of advice, what would it honestly be?"

They had reached the center of the church where the light coming in through the rose window rested on the floor. Tom stopped and pointed up. "I would figure out what goes into the center of your life and then put everything else in relation to that. As a friend, that is what I would honestly recommend. Things make a lot more sense when we do that and you can begin to peel off those protective layers that keep you a prisoner."

They walked outside into the warm sunlight; it felt good to be out in the

184

autumn air. David didn't know how or why he was able to share his family's dark secret with Tom. He had no illusions that he was a changed man. There were too many years of building his safe public self to have a short conversation undo it, but he felt as if he wanted to meet the real David now, even if it hurt to get there.

Chapter 31

Tuesday was a long day of catch up at the office. David didn't leave work until close to 9:00 p.m. and Trooper was glad to see him when he finally showed up at the door. He took Trooper for a walk, and when he returned, searched the house to see if anything was out of place. In some odd way, he was a little disappointed when he didn't find anything. What if he never found out who had left the messages or even more interestingly, how they had managed to get in?

He flipped through Jimmy's diary just to make sure no further messages had been left and walked through the rooms once more but found nothing. He sat at the kitchen table eating a takeout dinner and glanced at the freezer door. Among all the other pictures was the postcard photo of the same old white building that had been left in Jimmy's diary weeks before. How did that card get on his refrigerator? He finished his dinner while continuing to stare at the picture. The large building wasn't attractive. It was made of cement, painted white, with non-descript windows on each side. When he finally got up to pull the postcard off of the freezer, he noticed that the writing on the back wasn't the same as before.

Within these unmoving walls, know that for these many years I have voyaged on an odyssey to make it home to you and to let you know that you have been loved.

As life was unfair to young Telemachus trying to become a man without the love and guidance he deserved, know that he had good reason to remain unwavering in trust as did his lonely mother at her loom.

My hope is that your own journey is one that learns to trust your own weaver and that when you string the bow to remove your false suitors, you will know that I have faith in the son I have always loved.

David glanced down at Trooper, who returned a concerning expression. David sighed, "I guess the journey continues, boy." Trooper nodded in agreement. The next morning David woke up feeling more rested than he had in a while. He no longer dreaded the messages. Now he felt more curious than ever and when he left work early to walk to the church gym at 4:00 p.m., he was feeling a bit lighter.

When he arrived at the school, Sister Helen was inside the doorway as usual. He was expecting the Irish Gestapo treatment again without his chaperone to vouch for him. To his surprise, she gave him a teary-eyed hug and then walked down the hall to help out a student who had been waiting for a parent to come to take her home. A lot of confusing things had happened over the past several weeks, but this had to top them all as he headed to the gym doors while scratching his head and turning back to look at Sister Helen for a clue.

As David opened the doors, he could hear the semi-rhythmic sound of basketballs being dribbled and Tom blowing the whistle to bring them into a huddle. David walked towards them while Tom and a few of the boys smiled as they saw him join the huddle. This week went better with the drills and games. You could tell the boys had been taking the time to work on the basic skills, and it helped with the flow of the practice, making it more enjoyable to the boys. Some boys, however, seemed to continue to be tentative or were holding back to avoid looking bad.

David called the boys over to sit on the first bench of the wooden stands and said he was pleased to see progress but wanted to tell them about an NBA game he had seen. "Everyone knows that the NBA team with the worst record has the best chance to get the top player in the draft, right?" Most of the kids nodded as they leaned forward to listen. Tom watched with curiosity as David continued, "Well, I went to that last game of the season when the Chicago Bulls were playing against the Golden State Warriors. The loser would be the last place team. Everyone was wondering what was going to happen during this game. Usually, players have a competitive spirit that makes them want to win and have too much pride to play to lose, but this game was different."

"So, what happened, coach?"

"The ref held the ball for the opening jump and tossed it up in the air, but neither player jumped to tap it, it dropped to the floor and bounced until it stopped right on the half-court mark. Each team just stood there and didn't touch the ball. The refs couldn't start play because the shot clock wouldn't start until someone took possession of the ball."

"That sounds tense!"

The rest of the boys laughed, but their eyes didn't leave David's face as he continued, "The crowd was completely quiet, the tension built as minutes literally went by and then it happened."

"What happened?"

David remained intense. "One of the players reached down, grabbed the resting ball, and raced to his own basket, laid the basket in, scoring two points for the other team."

That same boy exclaimed, "Is that legal? Can you really do that?"

Tom said with a smile, "Not on our team!"

David said, "Yes, it's legal. Since this was a basket for the Bulls, the

Warriors got to take the ball out again and scored again at their own basket. It didn't take long for the Bulls to catch on, so they started to play defense to stop the Warriors from scoring baskets at their own hoop. Pretty soon each team played aggressive offense, except at the wrong basket and the opposing team played amazing defense to stop them from scoring for them. The fans went crazy and cheered louder on each play. The players on each bench were on their feet rooting for their team to play hard to lose the game."

Billy Maguire shouted, "What happened? Who won? I mean who lost the game?"

"It was one of the best games ever played from a fan's standpoint or one of the worst since no one officially scored an offensive point. The game went into triple overtime until the last play of the third overtime when the Warriors scored an amazing shot at their own basket from half-court just as the clock ran out."

The boys all sat with their mouths open, stunned by the story. David said, "It just shows you that basketball is a lot more fun when you aren't worried about failing, and you just go out and give it your best. Some of you boys who are holding back, work on the things you are less confident about together and don't be afraid to make mistakes. We're here to learn together and not to criticize but to encourage each other. If we work together as a team, and we play as a team, you never know how many games you might win."

Billy said enthusiastically, "Or lose!" Everybody laughed as Tom told them that was all for today.

As David and Tom were putting the balls in the bag. Tom whispered to David, "You're a great coach at heart, but you may need to go to confession after each practice if you keep up these kinds of stories." David laughed as he put the last ball in the bag, but Tom placed his hand under the ball to stop him. David knew what that meant, and he played to win all three games against Tom.

Afterward, they walked over to Dempsey's for a quick bite and cold beer. Dempsey greeted them at the door with a big smile on his rosy cheeks, "Good evening to you, boys. Now you know we have a high-class establishment here, and some patrons are even known to take a shower now and then before they come for the fine cuisine."

Tom glanced over his shoulder. "I think those patrons were just behind us. Now fetch up some grub and a few brewskies beer-tender before I bring the whole sweaty team in to smell up your fine establishment!"

Dempsey laughed. "You are playing with fire, boys. I control the tap and if you don't behave, I'll be shutting you off and it'll be Shirley Temples for the pair of you." David and Tom dropped their heads in shame as they headed over to an open booth.

As they settled their tired bones into their respective seats, David said, "The strangest thing happened today."

"Do you mean stranger than that story you told the boys today?"

"Yes, stranger than that. Sister Helen stopped me at the door to the school again today. Just as I thought she was going to chastise me, she put her arms around me and hugged me!"

Dempsey put down two cold beers as David finished, and without a word, walked back to the bar.

"I would think you would know exactly why she was hugging you."

David shook his head. "No, I really don't."

Tom's facial expression showed a sense of surprise as he asked, "So you're not the one who left a $20,000 donation for the school in an envelope marked 'For dry nuns and appreciated friendship?'"

David shook his head. "I wish I could take credit, but it wasn't from me. Does that amount cover what is needed?"

Tom appeared bewildered. "Well, that's strange and an interesting mystery. It won't cover close to what we need, but it certainly is a lot more than we had the day before. Huh. Well here's to the generous soul," he said, raising his glass to David's. Tom laughed to himself. "I wish I could've been at that game you talked about with the boys today. It was a clever way to get the point across to the boys that are still a bit tentative. I'm glad you came back to coach. It's a lot more fun with you there."

"I hope you know that my rates do go up after the first two sessions, but I'm sure that your rates for deciphering go up as well."

"Another message?"

David slapped the card out on the table and turned it so that Tom could see the picture of the white building again.

"Is this the same card as before?" Then he turned over the card to see the verse on the back and read the first line, "'Within these unmoving walls, know that for these many years I have voyaged on an odyssey to make it home to you and to let you know you have been loved.' Do you know what it means?"

David shook his head. "Not a clue."

"Let's think a bit. The card was left for you, so it could possibly be referring to you, but it is hard to tell. 'Within these unmoving walls,' I wonder what the connection is to the picture on the front, if there is any. I assume that it's not a building you've seen before?" David shook his head as Tom continued reading, "'As life was unfair to young Telemachus trying to become a man without the love and guidance he deserved, know that he had good reason to remain unwavering in trust as did his lonely mother at her loom."

David set his mug down. "Who is Telemachus?"

"The son of Odysseus from Homer's *Odyssey*. The first verse mentions voyaging on an odyssey, so I think it seems like a good possibility."

Tom took a swig of his beer while David stared at the writing. "Why would that story be meaningful to me?"

"Is it?"

"I've heard of it, but I've never read it. I don't even really know the story."

Tom sipped his beer, then set the mug aside. "Odysseus, the king of the Greek island of Ithaca, had been away at war in Troy. The story is about his struggle to get home to his wife, Penelope, and his son, Telemachus, who was only a year old when he left. Odysseus is strong, courageous, and confident, but most of all, he had a cunning intellect. He was a favorite of the goddess Athena, who tried to help him on his journey, but the god of the sea, Poseidon, put obstacles in his way at every turn. Odysseus has a conflict between his pride and desire for glory, and his desire to go home. His journey takes ten years on top of the ten years he was already at war, so Telemachus basically grows up without knowing his father."

"Ah! I remember seeing this book and the *Iliad* as a boy but never knew the stories. Does Odysseus end up getting home? What happens to the son and the mother?"

"Odysseus has many adventures along the way while fighting against both Poseidon's efforts and his own pride. Meanwhile, the house of Odysseus in Ithaca is full of suitors for the hand of Penelope and the power and riches that come with it as they have presumed Odysseus to be dead and Telemachus is not yet the man to stop them. Subsequently, Telemachus ventures out on a journey to find his father, and in the process learns to become a man and trust Athena's guidance. At home, Penelope works to hold off the suitors because she has faith that her husband will return. Penelope is just as cunning as Odysseus. She promises to pick a husband once she has finished weaving a burial shroud for Odysseus, which she weaves by day and then undoes at night so that it will never be completed."

"What happens to the son?"

"Telemachus returns home and as a man. Odysseus finally makes it back to Ithaca and disguises himself as an old beggar. By this time, Penelope has agreed to marry whichever man can string Odysseus's bow and shoot the arrow through a line of twelve axes. When every one of the suitors fails to even string the bow, the old beggar is laughed at when he offers to try. It becomes apparent to the suitors who the beggar is when he's the only one strong enough to not only string the bow but skilled enough to execute the impossible shot through the line of axes. Odysseus and his son, with the help of a few trusted servants, then kill all the unfaithful suitors."

David stared wide-eyed at Tom. "Is that the end?"

Tom shook his head. "When Penelope becomes aware that Odysseus is home, she is leery that the gods are playing a trick on her and asks a servant to move their wedding bed. Odysseus becomes upset saying that the bed has been built from the trunk of an olive tree around which the house was constructed and was immovable. Penelope now knows that this is truly Odysseus come home, and as the bed, their marriage was forever immovable. Odysseus then goes to visit his father, who has aged from worry and grief. His father recognizes Odysseus by the scar on his foot that he had given him as a boy, and Odysseus embraces and kisses the father he hasn't seen for so many years."

Tom put his hand on the postcard and finished reading the message, "'My hope is that your own journey is one that learns to trust your own weaver and that when you string the bow to remove your false suitors, you will know that I have faith in the son I have always loved.' Huh. It sounds like a letter to a son who has had to grow up without the love and guidance of his father, and there's been a good reason for that son to have trusted in the father's love and desire to come home to him. He hopes that the son can trust his own 'weaver' and remove his 'false suitors,' and to know that the father believes in his son and has always loved him."

David sat there visibly breathing out.

"There is really a lot in these three lines. Your own 'weaver' seems to make reference to your maker, God. Removing 'false suitors' could be talking about what we discussed the other day, what other 'gods' we put first at the center of our lives that don't work. What stands out to me is the focus on trust, and that it may have seemed broken but in reality, never really was. Do you have any idea who this might be about?"

David was feeling overcome by all the emotions going on as Tom talked through each line. He just shook his head.

"Please forgive me for asking you another sensitive question, but you did say your dad is no longer alive, correct?"

With more anger in his eyes than sadness, David snapped back, "He's dead, and he is dead for a reason."

Tom nodded and reached over to pat David's shoulder. "Sorry. There just seemed to be something there. Maybe it is from someone who knew your dad? I don't know. I definitely don't know what the picture on the front is about either."

David was quiet as they finished their burgers and beer. He told Tom that he needed to get up early in the morning and called it an early evening. He left the bar with Tom sitting by himself with the postcard of the white stone building on the table.

David ambled back to his apartment, thinking of the *Odyssey* tale and how difficult it would've been for Telemachus and his mother for all those years. Why would someone have left that card on his refrigerator? Who would've known his father well enough to leave this for him after all these years? When he got home, he gave Trooper some attention and then sat down in his chair to think. He got up and went into his room, where the box from his mother's house sat by the closet door. David set the box down on the bed, taking out pictures and letters until he noticed a very old book that looked familiar to him. He saw that it was a small leather-bound copy of Homer's *Odyssey*, something he now remembered his father reading. As he opened the front cover, on the inside was a partially faded inscription: *Gianni, I hope you enjoy the adventures and lessons as much as I have. Love Papa.* He flipped through the old, thin pages until he got to the back cover where he found a news article yellowed by time. The headline of the June 28, 1972, article read:

'Boston Native to be Executed in Virginia Tomorrow'

David had read the article years ago that outlined the story of Giovanni Fidele involved in a $2 million Bank of Boston bank heist in downtown Boston with Mo Diavolo, Gino Cappelletti, and Johnny Maccillo. The operation had been apparently planned for months and went wrong when James Fidele, son of Gianni Fidele was shot and killed along with bank guard Peter Spiro. The armored truck driver testified that neither he nor the younger Fidele was involved or even aware of the robbery plans when they were confronted at the scene. The robbers were involved in a multi-state chase that ended in the shooting death of a state trooper, Sgt. Bernard Kincheloe just across the Virginia border. Fidele's gun, fingerprint evidence, the testimony of eyewitnesses, and corroboration of Fidele's accomplices about the shootings made a very clear case against the North End native, Giovanni Fidele, who would be executed in the electric chair on the morning of June 29, 1972. None of his family members could be reached for comment.

David felt a rush of emotions flooding his body as he read the article to find clues. David had a computer installed in his study a few months ago that he used mainly for work emails and documents, but he had done very little internet surfing because he found it to be a frustratingly slow waste of time. However, he was filled with the need to look up executions in the state of Virginia to see if there was anything about his father's death.

After an hour of searching, the only thing he ran into were articles on the Supreme Court decision in the *Furman vs. Georgia* case, which was one of three cases on the death penalty that the Court was reviewing together. The Court's decision held that a punishment that was "cruel and unusual" would violate the Eighth and Fourteenth Amendments. On June 29, 1972, the Supreme Court effectively voided most death penalty statutes and commuted the sentences of 629 death row inmates around the country and suspended the death penalty nationally. David was sitting in shock as he skimmed through more articles reporting the same Supreme Court decision. He felt panicked as he thought of his father being put to death just hours before the Court decision could have saved his life.

David had never seen an article about his father's actual death. His mother had never discussed his death and there was no funeral he was aware of. Their mother had moved them off stoically to survive in their new life with their new identities and no trail. The new Kelly preoccupation was to shield themselves to lessen the pain and blot out the reality of where they had come from. David sat motionless in his chair. He had no fantasies that his father had been saved by the too-late verdict, but he felt like he needed some sort of closure. At work, David had always taught his sales teams to account for and be ready for all possibilities. David could feel his heartbeat quicken in his chest as possibilities came to mind. He needed to move, and he took Trooper out for a walk, finding himself walking towards Tom's, where he stood outside the rectory door for a few minutes before knocking.

Tom came to the door wearing pants and a tee-shirt—half ready for bed.

"I was feeling a bit restless after our conversation and then I found something at home. I'm really sorry to knock late at night."

Tom waved him in. "Don't be silly. Come on in and bring your good-looking friend in too." Tom fed Trooper a few treats while David took a seat at the kitchen table. "Can I get you anything to drink?"

David shook his head. "No. No. I'm fine."

"So, tell me what you are thinking about."

David stood up again and paced before answering. "I was thinking about the last note and who could've sent it. I could wish it away, but it wouldn't take away the fact that it certainly sounded like it was meant for me and from—" David's voice trailed off. "No one knows me well enough or cares enough to leave these messages without there being something to it. My father presented himself as a man of integrity. Everyone knew his priorities in his life were his faith, his marriage, his family, and his morals. When I found out that everything about him was a sham, I felt shame and then a deserved disdain for him. His life wasn't only a lie, but he killed my brother and destroyed our family. We had to work hard to move on and create a new life, so we'd never be vulnerable to someone like that again. My father's been dead to me for over thirty years, but—" He handed the book and the newspaper clipping to Tom. "I have no proof that he's actually dead."

Tom read through the article before laying it on the table in front of him. "Are you thinking that his execution had been impacted by this last-minute Supreme Court reprieve, and he has been behind these messages?"

David, pacing, shook his head. "You know, I don't know. I really don't know. I don't know if I even want to know."

Tom put his hand out for David to sit down. "What if you found out he was alive? What would you do?"

****

David's face became slightly contorted as he shook his head again. "I would be pissed. Dragging all this up again wouldn't change anything. It wouldn't bring Jimmy back. It wouldn't bring my family back. It wouldn't bring back all those years and I still wouldn't have a father, not one I could trust, or love, or forgive."

Tom could see the anger in David's eyes, and he knew anger was usually driven by fear. He also knew David's reaction wouldn't be the same if he were truly indifferent, which meant David had a reservoir of buried feelings for his dad, which Tom had suspected from early on. It was a signal that a very vulnerable core lay inside of all the success, confidence, and friendly but distant personality. Tom was aware David was at risk of becoming quickly overwhelmed by feelings he had carried inside.

"David, I can't know everything you are feeling, but I think there are probably a lot of conflicting thoughts going through your head right now. I do believe that, no matter what you find, you will be okay. I think the feeling of abandonment and loss of trust in someone you loved and trusted so much as an eight-year-old would be devastating to anyone. In addition, your mom deserted you emotionally, and that could only have made things more painful for you. My heart actually aches to think about how that must've felt, but I also get the sense that both of your parents affirmed you early on in your life, letting you know there is something uniquely good in you, because I can sense it."

David didn't respond to Tom's comments. Tom hesitated to push anything but without thinking, he asked, "If your father were alive, walked in that door, and was sitting down in front of you where I am now, what do you think you would say?"

David sat quietly and lifted his head as he gazed at Tom with his eyes now red around the edges. He got up from the table. "I cannot do this. Don't ask

194

me to do this right now." He grabbed Trooper's leash. "I'm going for a walk. Thanks for talking."

Tom opened the door for David and put his hand on his shoulder as he stepped by him. "You are not alone, David."

Chapter 32

David didn't sleep well on Wednesday or Thursday nights but gave no clues at work that anything serious was on his mind, although it was working overtime.

On Friday, he went for an early run then off to work still feeling unsettled. He worked through lunch and at one o'clock told Izzie that he was going to step out for a bit. Izzie reached to hand him his umbrella, but he ignored her and walked out the door. By the time he ended up at Tom's door, his hair and shoes were drenched.

Tom opened the door before David had a chance to knock. "Come in. Let me get you a towel to dry off."

David sat at the table once again, this time with his wet coat dripping onto the floor. He accepted the towel from Tom and wiped his face and dried his hair.

"I've been thinking of you. How have you been doing dealing with things?"

David raised his head. "How have you been doing dealing with things?"

Tom's head tilted in confusion. "You're a little wet yourself. Where've you been?"

"Oh! I had an appointment and just got back."

"And where, if you don't mind my asking, are you coming from today?"

Tom fell silent, bowing his head toward the table.

"Tom, I have no doubt that you care. And I know you can sometimes ask difficult questions because you care, but I wonder how much you let people into your world."

"David, what's going on?"

"When I ask a simple question like 'Where are you coming from?' you pull back."

Tom was visibly thinking, rubbing one hand down the back of his neck.

"Do you go to the same place every Friday?"

Tom raised his head. "I do. I was coming from the Forest Hills Cemetery in JP. Why do you ask?"

"You expect me to open up to share my childhood pains, but I'm not sure you'd do the same if I asked."

Tom took a deep breath but didn't respond.

"No one is ever really prepared or ready to talk about some things, are they?"

There was a long hesitation before Tom responded, "No. You never really are ready. So which way will we go?"

They sat in deep, pervading silence for several minutes, each inside their own self-imposed prisons. Finally, Tom uttered the first words. "Her name is Corlie. Corlie Ann Smith. We met in my freshman Modern Lit class at BU. I remember walking into the large lecture hall with two hundred other students feeling a bit lost and alone, and then I saw her a few rows over from where I was sitting. There was something about her that intrigued me, but it took over three weeks for me to talk to her. All she said was, 'Why did it take you so long?'"

A smile came to Tom's face but didn't reach his eyes as he drifted back to another time. "I just fell for Corlie right away but didn't tell her until a month later. Then she asked, 'Why did it take you so long?' When she told me she loved me, it began the most incredibly happy time of my life. The world seemed so alive, and I felt such a sense of joy when I was with her that I wanted to feel that way all the time, which meant being with her all the time."

David had never thought of Tom as being in love with a woman, never mind being in a head-over-heels romance.

Tom gazed out the rain-soaked window. "Corlie was close to her family, her mom, dad, brother, and sister. While she was trying to figure life out, her Catholic upbringing in Jamaica Plain was a part of the fabric of who she was. I, on the other hand, thought of faith as a set of archaic myths for those who feared thinking for themselves and living life. I had developed a quiet arrogance about what I believed to be true and was a master of taking in information in a way that fit what I wanted to believe. I'd then confidently convince Corlie of those beliefs out of what I had mistaken as an act love."

David moved forward in his seat. "It sounds like you loved her a great deal."

Tom sighed. "I thought I did, but I had mistaken infatuation, romance, and a big dose of egoism for real love. As much as I had the strongest attraction and feelings for Corlie, I love her more now than I ever did then."

"You shouldn't be so hard on yourself, Tom."

"I try not to, but nothing I did was really loving. I wasn't listening to what she believed. Instead, I spent my energy convincing her to believe what I wanted her to believe. I wasn't 'willing the good of the other' for her with sincere, self-sacrificing love. I wasn't looking at her as a woman with goodness and dignity that had been beautifully made, but looking at the person I wanted her to be for me. Despite her values and a desire to wait, I convinced her to express that love to show she really loved me. Our sexual relationship intensified our feelings and connection together. I convinced her to take the pill, despite the fact that there are a multitude of negative side effects for women and convinced her that it was the loving and moral thing to do."

Tom covered his face with his hands and continued, "I knew it would devastate her family, especially the relationship with her parents, but I was constantly working to convince Corlie to live together that summer after our freshman year. I knew how much she wanted to be together, but I also knew, deep down, that she didn't think it was the right thing to do and didn't want to hurt her parents. She told me that if we were meant to be together, then we'd have our entire lives, and if we weren't, then the answer was easy. Instead of really listening, I convinced her we could live together in an apartment in Brighton without her parents ever knowing. Our friends would be living in the apartment below us. When her parents came over, we would just switch so it would look like the girls were rooming together. I wore her down to do what I wanted and not what she believed was right.

"Ignorantly, I believed birth control meant one hundred percent effective protection, but Corlie found out that this wasn't the case and panicked. I tried to comfort her, but I didn't really listen as I moved into fixing mode instead of empathy and love. She knew in her gut that aborting the baby was wrong, but I again convinced her with my ignorance and selfishness that it was the smart and moral thing to do for her and the baby. I never took the time to know how she really felt. I just wanted to fix the problem. I was a strong proponent of women's rights and abortion rights, but I never took the time to honestly find out what an abortion entailed. I really didn't want to know if the fetus was a living human being whose life we were ending for our convenience. The information, the truth, the facts were all there, but they didn't fit what I wanted to believe, so I dismissed them for the cliché arguments that supported abortion as a good thing; fighting overpopulation, being fair to the baby, being too young or not in a good place to be parents now. I'd rationalize that it would compromise our lives, or that a fetus was a bunch of cells and not a living human being with the right to continue living."

David put his hand out and laid it on Tom's shoulder. "If you honestly believed it was the right thing to do back then, should you blame yourself?"

Tom's eyes welled up as tears rolled down his cheeks. "I blame myself every day for not being responsible, loving or honest. I wasn't truly there for Corlie. I took her to the abortion clinic. They offered no alternatives, so I felt good about what we were doing, even though I could tell that Corlie didn't. I convinced myself that she was just afraid, and I kept telling her it would be over quickly and then we could go back to our lives.

"When we left the clinic, she had that shell-shocked expression on her face that lasted for weeks. I tried to soothe her, humor her, to do anything to make her feel better, but a deep depression began to set into her being. I couldn't figure out what to do. I tried to get her to go to counseling, but she wouldn't go; maybe it was the shame she felt. As it got closer to September, she was no better, and she didn't even want to see her parents or siblings. I was worried but kept thinking it would get better with time. I didn't know the level of darkness, the loss and regret she was feeling. Corlie woke up at night after re-experiencing the abortion in her dreams, feeling overwhelmed by the shame and grief. She never blamed me for any of this, only herself. She tried to go back to classes in September but missed more than she attended. As midterms came around, she was desperately behind and still depressed, with no sleep and no peace."

Tom paused. As he spoke, his voice cracked from the pain in his throat. "She couldn't take it anymore. She believed there was no forgiveness for what she had done. That she'd never see our child whom she had never held and hadn't protected. One afternoon, I came home to our apartment, and I thought she was asleep until I saw the empty bottle of pills and a note next to the bed. Right then, I wanted to die myself to find her and hold her. She didn't deserve the path I worked so hard to lead her down. She was gone, and that was the first moment I actually loved her in the true sense. I would've given my life so she could have hers. I would've done so many things differently to put her and what was good for her ahead of my selfish desires. Two beautiful individuals were dead because of me."

Tom's voice had gotten louder as he went on and the pain on his face was the same pain David witnessed in the cemetery a short time earlier. David realized that Tom had entrusted him with the most painful and sensitive part of his life. David found himself listening empathically and felt as if he were walking in Tom's footsteps as he shared his story and feelings about Corlie. He couldn't think of the last time he allowed himself to feel something through someone else's experience. There was an uncomfortable feeling in his chest as his throat tightened and tears fell for what he now believed was a friend.

Despite feeling as if his own world had been turned on its side in recent months, David was thinking solely about someone outside of himself and not in reference to himself. "I'm sorry that I pushed you like that, and I'm even sorrier for what you've been carrying around with you all these years. There must be a point where you can—"

"Forgive myself?" Tom interjected sharply. "I work on that every day, but two beautiful lives do not exist today because of my selfishness and willful ignorance."

David resisted fixing. "I can imagine that would weigh heavy on your heart. How have you been coping with that?"

"I guess I haven't thought a lot about how I'm coping, but more about how Corlie and the baby are doing. I pray that they are safely in God's loving arms."

"If you honestly believe in God and heaven, then you must know that they're okay, not struggling any longer. You must know that they would want you to let go of the guilt. I would think they would want you to forgive yourself. Remember, you asked me what I'd do if my father were sitting right in front of me, could I forgive him? With all your wisdom, what would you tell me?"

Tom sat in silence for several moments before responding, "I would tell you that mercy and forgiveness are at the heart of God's unconditional love for each one of us. From the beginning of creation, God has been coming to us with forgiveness and mercy time after time, despite our constantly turning our backs on all of his love and not trusting his plans for us. I would tell you he loved us so much that he was willing to send his only Son to repent for the sum of our sins for all time and to pour himself out in the greatest act of love by dying on the cross for me and you personally. I would tell you the story of the Prodigal Son."

"I don't really know the story. Do I want to know it?"

Tom wiped at his eyes and took a deep, cleansing breath. "It's truly the best parable Jesus gave us to understand how much God loves us. Are you sure you really want to hear this?"

"I want to hear it from you."

"Okay, then. The story is about a man who has two sons. The younger, rebellious, independent son demands from his father his share of his inheritance now. The son's breathtaking rudeness is basically saying to the father, hurry up and die and 'Give me my share coming to me.' Despite the son's hurtful behavior, the father gives the son what he asks for and the son goes out into the '*cora makra*,' which in Greek translates to the 'big emptiness.' There the son tries to cling to what he thought was owed to him as he spends it on empty worldly pleasures until he himself is empty, alone, penniless, and starving. The son ends up feeding pigs, an indignity for any Jew, and realizes that his father's servants and even these pigs eat better than he. Finally, he chooses to return to ask forgiveness of his father and hopes he can work for his father as a servant."

David listened with interest. He was thinking about how difficult it must've been for the son to come back to his father and wondered how his father would react.

"The son headed home on foot. Now, remember that he hadn't only spent half of his father's estate on sinful living but also committed the ultimate insult to his father. Because this was seen as an insult to the community as well, it was dangerous for him to walk through the town to reach his father's estate. Jesus tells us that the father had been looking out for his son the entire time he was gone and when he finally saw him off in the distance, he didn't wait for him but runs to greet and protect him. It was considered disrespectful for a father to have to come out to his son, but this showed the father's unconditional love as he embraced him and kissed him. The son said to him, 'Father, I have sinned against heaven and against you. I am no longer worthy to be called your son,' but the father put the best robe on him, a ring on his finger, and sandals on his feet, calling for the fatted calf to be killed for a feast to celebrate his return. The father said, 'For this son of mine was dead and is alive again; he was lost and is found.'"

David knew he couldn't do the same for his father but was still struck by the story.

"That's what I might tell you."

"Thanks. I will say that is quite a story. Now, what would you tell yourself? Is the issue that you won't forgive yourself or that you don't believe God would forgive you?"

Tom sat stunned for a moment. David could tell by the look in his eyes that he hadn't thought of the question being turned back on him.

David got up. "Are you going to be okay?"

"Sure. I appreciate your pushing me in uncomfortable places. That's what friends who care do, and it is good for me to take some of my own medicine to see how it tastes once in a while."

"Unfortunately, I have to get back to work, now that I'm dry in more ways than one."

Tom shook his hand firmly as they opened the door. "I might be a little peeved at you but mostly I'm grateful for your coming by and dripping all over my kitchen floor—in more ways than one."

David smiled and headed back to work as blue skies and sunshine started to break through the previously gray cloud cover.

Chapter 33

When he got up on Saturday, David had a sense of impending confrontation he couldn't calm. He was supposed to take his daughter, Amy, out on Sunday, but she had a tennis tournament on Saturday Kathleen thought he should attend instead.

During the match, Kathleen told David that Amy was continuing to become more and more withdrawn from her and was particularly upset when Kathleen confronted her about a nineteen-year-old boy who was asking her to go out.

David gasped. "What?"

People turned to look at them. David lowered his voice. "Who's asking her out? She's only sixteen. Why's some guy that's almost twenty doing asking a high school girl out? It's usually because they can't get anyone their own age to date them and they know a younger girl is going to be flattered and easy to impress."

Kathleen raised her eyebrows. "Really?"

David knew Kathleen was well aware of the younger women he had dated, including Jillian. David said, "She's just a kid."

Kathleen said, "And a kid that's becoming a young woman and an attractive one if you hadn't noticed yet."

He wished he'd arrived beforehand to talk to Amy. She didn't notice him there until the very end, and she greeted him afterward with a snide attitude. David and Kathleen walked over to congratulate her on her win as she was putting her rackets in the bag. Amy didn't even look up at him.

David repeated, "Great game, Ames."

Amy finished zipping up her bag. "The first games were even better. Too bad you couldn't make it."

"Amy!" Kathleen said in a warning tone.

David put up his hand to let it go for now. They all went back to the house. Amy took a shower while Kathleen and David talked.

Kathleen settled on the sofa. "I was thinking this new attitude would be a passing phase but ever since this boy came into the picture, it seems as if she's been building a wall between herself and everyone else in the family. I know some of this is normal, but I'm getting worried about bad decisions that don't go away."

"I may be the last person who can help right now, but I'll try to see what I can do."

Amy came down the stairs with wet hair, a peach blouse, and a pair of jeans on over her boots. She didn't look like someone who was planning on being great company. David gave Kathleen a "wish me luck" glance as he and Amy headed out the door.

The ride was quiet. David was thinking about how to open up the conversation and at the same time how miserable this date seemed like it was going to be.

David drove down to Snug Harbor in Duxbury, aptly named for its cozy feel and picturesque view of the small town harbor where there were still a number of boats moored. David knew Amy used to love to sit at the harbor as a little girl and hoped she felt the same way today, listening as the waves lapped against the boats and the rigging slapped against the masts from the wind that rocked the boats.

David broke the silence. "I'm sorry I didn't make it to the beginning of your match, but from what I saw, you played very impressively." Amy's eyes focused on the boats in the harbor. David remembered how much she loved to talk as a child, finding joy in everything. Back then, she had admired him. He had hoped the setting would open her up to talk but decided he had to broach the topic himself. "Your mom seems a little concerned about some boy that might be interested in you."

Amy sighed deeply. "He's not just interested in me; we are dating."

"Dating? How old is he?"

"Since when did you worry about an age difference between people dating?"

David didn't appreciate the tone but tried to stay focused. "It is a little different when you are only sixteen, Amy."

"I don't think three years is that different, and a lot less than some women I've seen you with."

"Is he in your high school?"

"He is Justin, and he's a freshman."

"In college?"

She rolled her eyes. "In ninth grade at nineteen?"

"Listen, there's no way you're going out with someone who's in college at sixteen. I don't know him, but two things come to mind. One: why won't someone his own age go out with him? And two: nineteen-year-old boys usually only have one thing in mind."

"He's not dating someone his own age because he loves me. And what do you think he has in mind that's so bad?"

David looked out at the harbor as the Harbormaster was coming in on a hard-bottomed inflatable boat, trying to think of how to respond in a way that was effective since he was well aware of the fact he was losing his audience. "Amy, I think you know what I'm talking about."

Amy nonchalantly said, "You mean sex?"

"I'm glad you feel that comfortable. Even if you think the world of this young man, there's no way you should be dating him at your age, and you are definitely not going to have sex."

Amy was quiet for a minute. "Why not?"

"Why not what?"

"Why not have sex? Isn't is a natural part of a relationship?"

David started to feel uncomfortable, and he knew Amy was testing him as far as she could go. "There are a lot of reasons why you should wait until you find the right man and get married."

Amy laughed. "You sound like the nuns at school. 'Sex is a beautiful and intimate gift and meant for only the person you are going to marry for life,' or 'It's a mortal sin to even think of sex unless you are married and are going to have children' or something like that."

"I'm sure you know how uncomfortable I am right now with this conversation, but the bottom line is that you're not going to have sex with anyone at your age!"

"I don't understand. Is there something wrong with it?"

"No, but you are too young."

"So, if I were a little older, then it's a little more okay?"

David hesitated. Amy was setting traps in his logic. "No. You will still be too young, and a young woman should have some sense of dignity and self-worth."

"I don't know why you have to wait if there's nothing wrong with it. And I don't think it's only wrong for girls and not for boys."

She was getting too quick for David.

"You have sex with women you date, don't you? You don't seem worried about their dignity or honor. They're usually younger than you and not committed to you for life, but you obviously think it's okay. Why would it suddenly be so bad for me? I need to know why I should have to wait."

David hadn't thought about it from this perspective before and started thinking about all the things that Tom had said to him and Luke that night in the North End. Suddenly, it started to make more sense when he thought about someone he cared about and not from just his own vantage point. "I know you probably don't believe this, but I do love you and want the best for you. Dating a college boy, even if you think you 'love' him, isn't going to be the best thing for you, trust me. You are asking really good questions, though."

Amy's eyes widened.

David continued. "I think you are a one-of-a-kind girl. Strike that, you are a young woman who's not only incredibly beautiful, intelligent, gifted, very deep and caring but also someone who deserves everything that God has planned for you."

Amy teared up.

"There's nothing wrong with sex. It is beautiful and intimate and incredibly powerful in making you feel close to someone you care about deeply, but it's more than just that." David was as surprised as Amy must've been as he spoke. "Sex is one way to give yourself fully and completely to another person in a life-giving act of love, a love so great you may have to give it a name nine months later and care for her or him for many years. It would be a lie to give some of yourself and to make that bond something that's not life-giving and not committed, and I don't mean for six months or a year but forever. You deserve that kind of love and that kind of respect from someone who cherishes you and wants the best for you in a way he is willing to sacrifice and wait for because you are worth it– and you are worth it. Amy, trust me, you are more than worth it. This boy may think he loves you, but he doesn't really know what love is yet and certainly isn't really thinking about what's best for you for more than the moment. If he were the right guy for life, he'd be willing to wait for you, when it's right to date you respectfully, when you are ready for a relationship. At your age, this may not seem like it makes sense, but you have to trust your mom and try to trust an old man who is just finding out what it means to care about people enough, to tell the truth."

David fixed his gaze on Amy, expecting to see an angry face, but she had tears rolling down her cheeks. He stretched his right hand out and put it around her shoulders. She turned her face and buried it between David's arm and his chest as her tears began to soak his blue jacket. David held Amy as she cried and pressed into his body with an embrace that seemed so common only six years ago. After several moments, David heard a faint rumble from Amy's stomach and they both laughed a bit as David started the car. "I think I have a cure for that."

David drove a short distance to Farfar's Ice Cream, a place that Amy loved to stop when they took a family drive to Duxbury. The name meant "father's father" in Dutch and the ice cream was rich, creamy, and tasty. Amy always got the Oreo Cookie, and David got his usual Mint Chocolate Chip. They sat outside on the wooden benches where the sun was coming down warmly on their bodies as they enjoyed each lick. David knew the pain he had caused Amy over these years hadn't been suddenly fixed, but today was a start. After dessert, they stopped at the Milepost Tavern for lunch and both had fish and chips in a basket to complete their "summer" fall outing.

Kathleen was at the opened front door as the car pulled into the driveway. Amy gave David a kiss on the cheek as she went upstairs to her room. Kathleen had more than a surprised expression on her face as David turned toward her.

Kathleen's eyes narrowed. "Don't tell me you bought her a car?"

"No. We just spent time together. Is James around?"

"He's still at his friend's house, but I can tell him you were asking. Maybe you can call him tonight?"

"That is a good idea. And how are you doing, Kathleen?"

She seemed surprised at his question. "Me? I'm doing okay. If I can stop worrying about you three, I'll be doing just fine. How about you?"

"I've been having some weird things going on, but I'm doing okay now."

"Weird things?"

"It would take too long to explain. Let Amy tell you how she's feeling."

As he walked to his car, Kathleen said, "Take care, David. Remember to call James so he isn't waiting up all night."

David held his hand to his ear like a phone, then waved goodbye as he got into his car and drove back to his apartment.

He settled down on his sofa and tried to write down the five messages that had been left to see who might be playing this odd joke on him. He wrote them down in order and said them aloud to Trooper, "Truth, God, Jesus, Church, and trust." He thought the first three items, truth, God, and Jesus, were logical statements rather than questions for him, but the last two were definitely still a challenge. Trust had been lost so long ago and only Kathleen and Tom came to mind as people he might be able to trust somewhat, and maybe Izzie with less personal things. With his father, all feelings of trust seemed to have been shattered, and since he had supposedly been a devout Catholic, David had long ago developed a bad attitude towards the Church. If someone was playing games with him, then it was someone who knew him more intimately than he was comfortable with. David had contacted a private investigator and was waiting for some intelligence from him to help resolve the mystery.

Midafternoon Tuesday, Izzie brought in a registered same-day Priority Mail envelope with a postmark from Richmond, Virginia. She hovered by the door, her curiosity plain on her face. He stared at her till she backed out of the room and closed the door.

Tapping the envelope against his open palm as he decided what to do next, he stood up and peered out the large windows in his office and across the Fens, paced around the room, then returned to the window. He wasn't sure he wanted to know the answers inside the thin cardboard envelope, but it seemed silly not to open it after all the money he spent.

After a good ten-minute delay, his heart racing and beating loudly against his chest, he decided to open the envelope. He physically felt a sense of dizziness and panic when he tore the perforated pull tab, and his breathing got shallower and more rapid as he pulled out the sheets of paper. He stared out the window a moment more before fixing his eyes on the top sheet. Then his heart stopped beating for a second.

Dear Mr. Kelly,

Our investigation has confirmed that:

Mr. Giovanni J. Fidele (age 40), of Boston, Massachusetts, was convicted of the murder of his son, Mr. James Fidele, and a State Trooper of the State of Virginia named Sgt. Bernard Kincheloe, by the Commonwealth of Virginia on March 15, 1972.

Mr. Giovanni J. Fidele was scheduled for execution on June 29, 1972, by electrocution.

On June 29, 1972, Giovanni J. Fidele's sentence was commuted to life in prison without parole due to the Supreme Court decision that effectively abolished the death penalty in the United States.

Mr. Giovanni J. Fidele (age 71), is currently alive and serving a life sentence in the Virginia State Penitentiary in Richmond, Virginia. This was confirmed by the prison secretary.

Please let us know if there are any further questions concerning the above findings or additional investigation that you would like our office to attend to.

Best regards,

Paul J. Fastbinder

Fastbinder & Harlow Law

Suddenly, everything that had been under control seemed now in disarray, and everything David thought he knew was now in question. David's mother had told them that their dad was gone. They had all read the article in shock and didn't go out of the house on the day of the execution, June 29, 1972, or the next several days. For David, it seemed now as if the incomprehensible was happening all over again for the Fidele family. David's father may have been dead to his mother, but he'd been alive all these years without any communication. There were no letters, no calls, and no neighbors to say otherwise. Of course, David's mom, Ann, had moved them quietly out of the North End to the North Shore city of Lynn,

Massachusetts, just a few weeks after the actual robbery and Jimmy's death. They were in new schools and Ann had legally changed their names to Kelly. The family never talked with their relatives or old friends again. This new start would make them new people, with the past erased from their memories and their connections gone forever. No one could find them because no one knew where they had gone. David had fallen back into his chair and held onto the empty envelope with one hand and the letter in the other. "My father has been alive this entire time."

Chapter 34

David was having a hard time focusing at work with the flood of questions racing through his mind. How could his father still be alive? Why would his mother let them believe he was dead all these years? Even in her last days, she gave them no hint of the truth. David knew he had to leave work to sort this out and told Izzie to cancel his remaining calls for the afternoon as he left with only his coat—no briefcase or a word about where he was going.

He walked briskly home to a surprised but happy Trooper. After deciding that a long run may help to flush out all the anxiety he was now feeling, he changed into his running gear. Before heading out, he tried to reach Tom at the rectory, but there was no answer and he left no message. He was suddenly very much alone in a private tornado of emotions. He headed out the door and ran as he did when he was a boy, trying to push the confusion out of his mind with physical exertion. He ran along the Charles, not even noticing the faces of the myriads of people he passed, then across Beacon and through the Common, down Haymarket and through the busy streets of the North End. He ran along the waterfront and then back through town until he found himself outside of St. Anthony's front steps. David was physically and mentally exhausted as he hunched over the stone railing breathing deeply and dripping with sweat.

David felt torn: part of him wanted to step into the church and sit to compose himself, and part of him felt as if it were the last place he wanted to be. While he was catching his breath and cooling down, he walked up the empty driveway to the garden behind the rectory. There was a bench next to the trimmed hedge overlooking the garden and a fountain where he sat to calm himself down.

David was startled by Tom's voice.

"David, it's you," Tom said. "I didn't realize you were a garden person. I've got to say, it looks much better since Angelo has been tending it."

David stood up like a young boy who was caught doing something he shouldn't be doing. "Oh. Hi, Tom. I was just out for a run and stopped here to catch my breath. I hope you don't mind."

"Of course not. The grounds are for everyone, and I'm always glad to see you. Is everything all right?" Tom sat down on the bench with David.

David rubbed the side of his face as he thought about what he wanted to share. He started to say everything was fine, but the words wouldn't come out.

"Sometimes I come to just sit here and listen. It is a nice escape in the middle of the hectic city but can end up being the opposite."

David nodded. "You mean busyness is the escape, and the quiet is where you are forced to see things more honestly?"

Tom smiled. "Something like that."

They sat quietly for a while. David knew Tom was biding his time, waiting for him to start the conversation.

David hunched over and stared down at the green grass and the stepping stones that led up to the bench until he drummed up the courage to say it aloud. "I got a letter in the mail today. For some reason, I became overwhelmed with trying to process what it was actually saying. I hired a firm in Virginia to confirm what I already believed to be true about my father, but they came back with information that didn't seem possible. I still don't believe it, really." Three deep breaths. His fingernails bit into the palms of his hands. His heart throbbed in his chest. "The letter said my father's sentence had been commuted at the last minute, and he has been alive this entire time in a Virginia prison." He waited for half a beat, expecting Tom to react, but he didn't; he was waiting, listening. David glared at the heavens. "I'm thinking, 'How is that even possible?' My mother never let on and my father never communicated anything to us over all this time. Not once!"

Tom remained silent a moment, then whispered, "Wow. That is incredible news." He let the words sit for a moment. "What was your first instinctive reaction when you read this?"

"Are you kidding? Reaction? I was frozen. Part of me wanted to see him and part of me was incredibly angry again. I don't think I can or want to go through all the hurt and anger I worked through years ago. It's being drudged up again, and for what?"

"David, you were faced with something that no young boy should have to experience. Your father should've been your rock. Coping with that type of pain and anxiety as a child may have buried the confusion and pain but not really let it go. Now, this unexpected news is putting this right in front of you again to deal with as an adult."

David sharply responded, "Deal with it? Why should I deal with this again? For years, I held on to thinking he was going to come back and tell everyone they had it all wrong, but he never even bothered to contact me, and as far I knew, he was dead. He was no longer part of who I was. My mother worked on me to move from denial to anger and to use that feeling to drive myself in everything I did—to be successful and make myself the person I wanted to be. She moved me past the escape and depression into action and results. I don't know why she wasn't honest with us. She may have just been angry at what he did to Jimmy, or how he lied and what a hypocrite he was. Maybe to her, he was dead as a husband and a father? I don't know, but the idea of contacting him now seems to be bringing up anger from deep inside of me. I hate the feeling, and I don't like the thought of going back to how I felt every night when I lay in my bed as a boy." Tom put his hand on David's back and sat there in silence for a few minutes before David stood up abruptly. "Thanks for listening, but I don't think I really want to talk about this anymore. I need time to figure out what I'm going to do."

"Anytime, David. Don't hesitate to ask. If you need me for anything at all, I'm here."

On the way home, David's mind continued to churn. He felt different about sharing his feelings after Tom had been willing to open up about his own sensitive history. The fact that Tom would trust David with the ugliest parts of his life had made an impact on David. He wasn't ready to go there fully with Tom, but at least he knew he had someone he could trust if that time came.

As he got closer to his Beacon Street apartment steps, he thought there was no way he could see his father without a ton of anger pouring out. *Do I want to see him? What would I even say to him? Hey, Pop, how've you been? Why did you kill my brother and destroy our family? Why was your life a lie and how could you abandon me?*

Trooper greeted him at the door. David squatted down and ran his hands through his fur. "I can always trust you, boy, can't I?" He glanced around. "Anybody break into the apartment today? After all, it is Tuesday." He walked through the rooms looking for another note, then soothed himself in a very long, hot shower.

Clean and more relaxed, David sat in his leather chair with Jimmy's diary. When he flipped to the empty pages, he thought these blank pages represented all he really knew about what happened. The man, who always talked about putting God, marriage, his family first, and the importance of honesty and integrity, was a big lie all along. Even if he went into this for a good reason, how could he involve Jimmy? How could he kill his own son and a police trooper? How could he remain silent all these years? David wiped away a tear as he thought about never seeing Jimmy again. He realized all these questions and feelings weren't going to go away.

As he dozed off, he found himself drifting back into a dream of himself as a young boy running frantically through the dark woods trying to get away from a rabid wolf. He was running barefoot on the unsure ground, dodging trees that came up faster and faster before the ground beneath him opened up and he landed in a deep, dark sinkhole that seemed too deep to escape. As he began to see what was in the hole with him, he panicked and woke up in a cold, uncomfortable sweat.

David went to work in the morning, shutting off his emotions and attacking work with a fervor to fully occupy his mind. Just after lunch, Kevin Walsh dropped by to see him.

Walsh was out of breath and was white as a ghost as he came into David's office.

"Walshy, are you okay?" David asked. "You look as white as a ghost."

"I spent the evening at Dana-Farber with my dad. He's not doin' well."

"Then what are you doing here? What can we do to help?"

"I'm going back this afternoon. I just wanted you to know that I may be in and out for a while." Walsh choked up. "I think we are losin' him and nothin' I have in my bank account can do anythin' to save him. I can't do anythin'. I'm kicking myself for not findin' the time to see him more, to spend time with him. I convinced myself that I was too busy, knowin' all along that it would mean the world to him to see me more often. I just want to sit with him even if he doesn't know I'm there."

David patted Walsh on the shoulder. "Kev, take all the time you need. Just let me know what we need to cover, and you focus on your dad."

Walsh started slowly towards the door. "Thanks, DJ. I can't tell you how much I appreciate your understanding."

"Just take care of him and yourself. Let me know if there's anything else I can do."

David delved back into his work, glancing at the clock once in a while, but not caring that quitting time had come and gone. He didn't want to go home.

Izzie finally poked her head in. "Is everything okay, Mr. Kelly?"

David looked up and nodded.

Izzie said, "You take care tonight. See you in the morning."

Her interruption busted his shield. He decided to leave as well.

Despite having his suit on and knowing the boys' practice was ending, David made his way to the church to let Tom know he was okay.

One of the boys was heading out of the school doors. "We missed you today, Coach. I think Father Tom missed you too."

"Thanks, Hank. How's that jump shot coming?"

The boy grinned. "Oh, it's coming along. I've been practicing using my legs to shoot. It sounded weird when you said it at first, but it makes sense when you do it. You know what I mean, Coach?"

David touched the top of Hank's head. "Keep it up. It gets more natural, with practice, to build muscle memory."

"Will do. I trust you, Coach."

Tom walked out of the door before David turned around. "Hey, stranger. We missed you. Are you up for a Dempsey stop?" David nodded, and they made the short walk to the pub.

Before they could even sit down, Dempsey was at the table with two cold pints and a smile. Tom raised his glass. "How are you doing?"

David tapped his glass against Tom's and took a sip. "It was a rough night, but this helps."

"I hope I'm not overstepping my bounds, but I thought that maybe we both have some opportunities for forgiveness in our lives."

David's tone was more resolved as he put his glass down. "I don't think I can forgive a man who has offered no repentance and was a fraud who destroyed his entire family. I don't see how that would help me or him. Even if he were sorry, I could never forgive what he did. It was too big of a line to cross. I'm feeling a bit better now that I've decided to just leave things as they are."

Tom sat holding his beer. David could tell he was studying him, seeing someone who was retreating for reasons he knew now Tom could identify with.

After several moments of silence, he said, "David, I have information that will come as a shock, but it might shed some light on your mystery."

"What information? What are you talking about?"

"After morning Mass, I was looking for Angelo, to see how the building repairs were going. The shed door to his room was slightly opened, and when I knocked and didn't get a response, I opened the door to see if he was okay. On the wall, I noticed a picture pinned to his wall. It was of the same white building you received on the postcard with two of your messages. I've been curious about Angelo for some time. He showed up out of nowhere, asks for nothing other than work and a room no bigger and no more comfortable than a jail cell." David's head moved forward, and his eyes squinted in response to that last sentence. "I saw a few other things jotted down on papers on his bed and his desk that started to put some pieces of the puzzle in place."

"What puzzle?"

"I know Angelo is a good man and a godsend for me, but I also knew I shouldn't be going through his things like that. I should be showing more trust and respect for him, especially for all he's done. Anyway, I asked Angelo to drop by the pub tonight, if you're okay with that."

David frowned, but nodded his consent.

Just then, Tom saw Angelo outside the pub window and waved him in.

Angelo came in and sat down next to Tom and nodded to David.

Tom said, "Angelo, thanks for joining us. I think you know David Kelly. We have a mystery we were hoping you could help us solve. David has had a number of break-ins to his apartment despite changed locks and a tight security system. Someone has been able to slip in and out each week, but they take nothing from him. In fact, they leave something each time. We've been racking our brains trying to figure out how this is possible. What do you think?"

As both David and Tom anxiously waited for an answer, Angelo put his forearms on the table and pulled forward. "I would say you might have some clever mice to take care of."

David exclaimed, "I don't think mice write messages, carry large stones, or carefully place pictures on a freezer door."

Angelo sat back. "I hear they've been doing amazing things over at that MIT these days."

David hadn't noticed a lot about Angelo when he met him in passing at St. Anthony's, but sitting this close, he saw the look of a hard life on his rough face and stubby, coarse hands. When he looked straight at Angelo, he didn't see that roughness in his eyes, but the look of someone who'd known him for his entire life. With his heart starting to beat rapidly in his chest, David asked, "Angelo, I appreciate your coming over and trust you are an honest man. Have you ever been in my apartment?"

Angelo glanced down at the table and then back up at David. "Possibly."

David half smiled. "Possibly? Could you have possibly been in my apartment on several occasions, leaving things behind?"

Angelo said, "That would also be possible."

Tom nudged Angelo with his shoulder. "Angelo, if we buy you a beer, can you let us know the whole story? It would mean a lot to me, and I think it would be helpful to David."

Angelo leaned back in his seat and was apparently contemplating what to do next as Tom waved to Dempsey for three beers. Angelo thanked Dempsey and took a long sip of his cold brew. "Okay. I may have stopped by your place a few times, and I may have left a few things, as well, but I never disturbed anything and didn't take anything."

David leaned in on his side of the table. "But why and how did you do it?"

Angelo answered, "The 'how' was easy. Your locks, alarms, and that great guard dog of yours weren't really much of a challenge. I spent most of my younger life perfecting my ability to get in and out of places that had things I wanted to borrow long term. Breaking into homes in rich neighborhoods became easy, and little by little you learn the trade. Safes, banks, and high-end security systems became a game I could play with anyone. About thirty years ago, I was involved in a large-scale museum heist in DC that didn't go as planned, and I landed in the Virginia State Pen for a forty spot. After the mandatory solitary confinement, I ended up in a two-by-four of a cell with this guy from Boston, funny accent and all. I wasn't particularly interested in girl talk, and he seemed a bit shell-shocked to even know we were sharing a broken-down toilet, cold cinder block walls and the hard metal beds with smelly old paper-thin mattresses. I was angry at the only person I ever cared about in my life—me. When I realized that this guy was on death row, I saw no benefit for me to get to know him, which is hard to accomplish when you spend that much time in that small of a confine. I quickly realized he was at peace regardless of his fate, even the electric chair. That man is responsible for saving my life and my soul, and I would do anything for him. That man is your father."

David felt dazed as he was trying to process Angelo's story. Here he was sitting across from someone who probably knew his father better than he did.

Angelo now stared at David. "There's no man I've ever met with more integrity, more heart, and more character than Gianni Fidele. David, I know about every minute of your childhood, about your mom, Jimmy, Bobby, and Abbie. Your dad loved each of you so much, and it crushed him to be separated from all of you because he knew how much you needed a dad. Listen, I was a hard-nosed thief with no sense of love or purpose in my life. In spite of my resistance, he patiently taught me the purpose of a well-lived life. From your father, I learned that self-worth comes from God alone. That a real man lives through Christ's example. He wanted so badly to pass all these things on to you, so you could have a life of joy and love, but he had to make do with someone like me."

David noticed that Angelo's eyes had filled with tears as he took another drink of his beer. "I wish I could share your admiration and love, but did he ever tell you what he did to his family?"

Angelo reached out and put his hand on David's forearm and pulled him forward. "David, whatever you think you know about your dad is not the truth. Everyone in the pen claims he was innocent, but your father never did. Even up until that morning of June 29th, 1972, he didn't whine about his innocence, but the truth is that he was innocent. He blamed himself for not saving Jimmy, but don't ever think he was responsible. Your dad didn't like talking about it, but over time I got the story out of him. Everything he told me was confirmed by one of the guys on the heist called Johnny Maccillo, who spent a dime in the pen. Your father was concerned about Jimmy's lack of direction and mistrusted the people he was hanging around with, especially a guy named Mo Diavolo."

"My mother said she saw Pop looking pretty friendly with Mo several times before the robbery, looking like they were making some agreement."

"Your dad never trusted Mo. He tried to get Mo to stop spending time with Jimmy, to stop giving him tickets and letting him in his bar. Mo had supposedly agreed, and that may be what your mother saw. Your dad told me he followed Jimmy when he left the house at night to see where he was going and if he was okay."

David shook his head. "Angelo, I want to believe you, but why was he at the robbery with his gun that killed Jimmy and a cop? His fingerprints were all over that gun."

"Well, your dad continued to follow Jimmy because of the type of places he was hanging out and who he was with. Jimmy had left some notes around about dates and lists of things to take care of that made your dad even more nervous. Putting the pieces together, he figured out that Mo had worked on Jimmy and his friend Tommy Collins for quite some time to convince them they could have a nice payday with little risk to them. According to Mac, when Jimmy pushed back on Mo, Mo told him they didn't have to do anything illegal, that the insurance companies would cover any bank losses, and that he'd be able to help the family out with Abbie's operation."

"Once Jimmy and Tommy were in, they were let in on more of the details of the plan. The target was the Bank of Boston branch closest to the North End, and the pickup would be Tuesday after the large Columbus Day weekend receipts. They estimated about two million to be split between the local family, Mo, and his team. The only thing that Jimmy and Tommy needed to do was provide uniforms to Mo, Mac, and Gino Cappelletti, borrow your dad's .38 Colt from the hiding spot above your father's bedroom closet, and to sit in the Dunbar armored truck while the others took care of the rest and loaded the van parked in front of the armored truck. Your brother, Jimmy, was never supposed to be in the bank."

Angelo stopped to drink his beer. "Jimmy was too young to ride as the 'hopper.' There was another guard who was supposed to ride with Tommy, but he didn't show, and Jimmy filled in. There were two other guards who rode in the back of the truck who had no knowledge of the plans. On the day of the heist, Mo, Mac, and Gino were already parked in the van, dressed in their security guard uniforms. Tommy later pulled up behind them and directly in front of the bank entrance. Tommy acted as if the electronic auto locks were stuck for a bit and told the two security guards in the cargo-hold to be patient. The normal hopper had provided Mo with the security passcode and the official procedure for accessing the money from the bank manager without suspicion. The entire heist was to only take ten minutes from the time the armored truck pulled in front of the bank.

"It all went bust when Gianni showed up to confront Mo and try to save his son from committing a felony. Mo never liked Gianni. He was more than happy to corrupt Jimmy to hurt Gianni, and he had no intention of having his master plan undermined by him. When Gianni didn't see Jimmy in the bank, he started towards the door just as Mo yelled for everyone to hit the floor and keep their faces down. Mo waved your dad's gun at him and yelled to your dad to get down. When he didn't, Mo pointed the gun at your father just as Jimmy rushed into the bank and jumped in front of your father as Mo fired the gun. Jimmy fell bleeding into your dad's arms telling him he was sorry. Mo kept yelling at people to keep their heads down and to not look up as he rushed at your father, whacking him across the temple, then ordering Gino and Mac to load your father into the van with the money."

Stunned, David released a breath he didn't realize he had been holding as Angelo continued the story. "Even with the shots fired, the Mafia boss, Angiulo, had guaranteed Mo that there'd be no police in the area during the heist, so Mo was able to load the van and make a clean getaway. They made it as far as the Virginia border, where they got into a gunfight at a barricade and a State Trooper was shot and killed with Gianni's gun. Mo had cleaned off his fingerprints and put the gun in your dad's right hand to get his fingerprints on it. He then testified that Gianni had planned the heist and was responsible for the two deaths with his own gun. Mo's testimony was convincing, and he strong-armed Gino and Mac to corroborate his version. Even with Gianni's denial, your dad was quickly convicted of two first-degree murders, armed robbery, and endangering the lives of citizens.

"Sometime after Mo had been knifed and killed in prison, Mac confirmed Gianni's story to me and filled in a few more holes."

David, tears in his eyes, directed his gaze to Angelo. "Is this all true?"

Angelo nodded. "Every word of it. Your dad is a good man. Always has been. You may have stopped believing in your dad years ago because of how things looked, but all that pain wasn't based on who your dad was. I don't know why your mom lost faith in him. Maybe the shock of losing her son was too much, but he never stopped loving her or the three of you the entire time. When I got out this past spring, I told him I would try to find you. It wasn't easy because he had no clue where you lived or that you changed your name. When I found out you worked at the Prudential, I found St. Anthony's just a few blocks away and a good friend here in Father Tom. Your dad was overjoyed when I let him know I found you. I told him you were doing well in some ways but seemed lost in others, so I decided to try to use Father Tom to help teach you things that your father had taught me. Your dad was very happy to learn that you two have become friends."

Tom said, "Angelo, did you have anything to do with that donation made to the school?"

Angelo nodded. "That was thirty years' worth of prison wages from David's dad. He wanted the school to have it as a thank you for your being a good friend to his son."

David sat back with his palms flat down on the seat shaking his head. "Angelo, I want to believe everything you just told me, but if that were all true, why didn't he contact me over all this time?"

Angelo finished his beer in one gulp, stood up, and said to David, "Come with me."

David and Tom glanced at each other in puzzlement and got up to follow Angelo back to St. Anthony's, where he led them to his modest quarters. Inside the small room, David saw a cot, a chair, some tools Angelo was working on, a bureau and a small desk. Angelo was down on his knees pulling out two white boxes that looked like they once held work boots and put them on the bed. "Open the lid."

David opened the lid and saw what appeared to be thousands of neatly filed small envelopes. David's eyes squinted slightly as he reached in to pull one of the envelopes out: *Mr. David John Fidele, 16 Lewis St. Apt 3, Boston MA, 02113.* Below the 8 cent Eisenhower stamp were the large red words: *"Return to Sender. No forwarding address."* David stood paralyzed as he held the very thing he had always hoped for, a letter to him from his father. Angelo put the lids back on the boxes, picked them up, and placed them in David's hands, saying, "Take them home, David. They are yours."

When David returned home, he laid the boxes full of letters on the coffee table in front of his leather chair. Trooper sat down next to the chair, encouraging David to sit beside him. David lifted the top of one of the boxes of neatly organized letters to his mother, Bobby, Abbie and him. All were unopened and returned, never reaching their destination, yet his dad kept writing. David opened some of the letters to his mom, letters from a man who was still in love with his bride. He apologized for the pain she must be going through and for not doing enough to follow his instincts to protect Jimmy. David finally sat down with the first letter, taking his time to open it and unfold the thin paper his father had written on thirty-one years earlier.

Dearest David,

You are much too young to make any sense of what has happened. I know that you loved your brother Jimmy and will miss him tremendously. Please know that he is safe, loved, and not in any pain right now in heaven or on his way there. That may not take away the pain you are feeling right now, but it might help as time goes by. Also, please know in your heart that much of what you might hear about what happened is not going to be true. I would never hurt your brother or anyone in the family. It will be hard, but it is important that you trust that I love your mom, Jimmy, Bobby, Abbie and especially you.

I don't know how long it will take but I will see you again. In the meantime, try to be strong and believe that you are loved and that I'm very proud of you. Also, believe that God loves you no matter what and you can always ask him for help with anything at any time. I will try to write to you often and hope you can write to me as well. Please tell your mom, brother, and sister that I love them too. I miss you, David, but trust that I will see you again.

Much Love,

Dad

David wept.

He couldn't remember crying like this since he was a boy, but the events of the last several weeks had touched a place deep inside of him. To David, crying had seemed like a weakness, not something a man should do. But thinking of his father physically writing this letter to him reached right through the walls he worked so hard to build. There were so many letters. David felt ashamed that his father had never given up on him while he had lost trust in him so easily. Not only had he lost trust in his dad, but he even came to feel hate and indifference as he grew up and charted his own controlled path in life.

David stayed up the entire evening reading one letter after another. It was as if Gianni had tried to be the father and role model he was meant to be through his writing since he could not be there in person. He would write about things he wanted David to know as he grew up to see how wonderfully made he was, to enjoy the wonder of the world, to be a young man he'd be proud of, and to practice virtues. David's dad also gave him pointers on how to build confidence in himself, how to stand when hitting a baseball or shooting a basketball and recommended great books to read for his age. He even drew pictures to illustrate his messages. In some letters, he told jokes or included riddles to solve, but most of all, he let David know that he was always thinking of him and would always love him. As the weeks approached the date for Gianni's scheduled execution, the letters to David's mom got more emotional, describing an intense fear paralleled with a sense of peace that God would take care of him.

David sobbed uncontrollably. For the first time in his life, he felt a bond with his dad as a human being with feelings of happiness and joy, but also fear and anxiety. His chest shook as he tried to catch his breath. He felt himself wanting to cry out for his father as if he could hear him through all the years.

As years of letters went by, David's dad tried to teach him about how important his faith would be throughout his life, how much God truly loved him and had a plan for him. He taught him about being a man of honesty, courage, fortitude, love, joy, faith, and family. Each letter felt as if it were written in love and would touch on one or two points to let it sink in. David could tell from his father's letters how much he missed each one of them, and how often he thought of them and prayed for them—and despite the returns, he never stopped writing.

His dad wrote about the man who shared his cell. The relationship was difficult and rocky in the beginning as his dad tried to forge a friendship with a hardened criminal. Angelo Salvato was a thief from an early age, growing up in a loveless family. He lost his dad early in life and tried to fend for himself. He buried any sense of conscience he may have had and became an extremely skilled criminal, spending his time with other criminals. There was no love, no happiness, and no sense of direction in Angelo's life, and as far as he knew, it was over when he began his forty-year sentence with someone who didn't think as he did. Angelo was no longer feeling bitter, but feeling nothing at all, looking forward to nothing but existing each day. He wasn't interested in hearing about anything that went beyond that reality. David was curious how this man his father described became the man that he shared a beer with at Dempsey's.

Chapter 35

David was so engrossed with the letters, the night passed into the morning without sleep. On the way to work, his thoughts volleyed back and forth from the good news that his dad was alive and innocent to the old familiar feeling of hurt, betrayal, and wishing he hadn't found out. Instead of not feeling much of anything, David felt overloaded with a battle of conflicted feelings and headed over to St. Anthony's without realizing his change in direction. Tom was outside greeting people as they were entering the church for morning Mass. As Tom shook the hand of a man in a dark suit, he noticed David walking towards him and moved to greet him. "Hi, David. How are you after last night?"

"I stayed up all night reading letter after letter. I know I should be feeling incredibly happy right now, but instead, I'm feeling confused. I know this isn't a good time."

"I do need to say Mass in a few minutes, but I want to hear about your feelings. Try not to be hard on yourself. Remember that you just received shocking news. You're probably still mentally processing it against a deeply felt experience as a boy that is completely different and the basis for everything you've believed to be true."

"Thanks, Tom. I'm a bit ashamed of how I feel and maybe even about who I am. I don't know. If you have some time later, I'd appreciate an ear."

"Any time after four is good for me, and David, I truly believe that things are going to be more than okay for you."

David halfway smiled, thanked Tom, and headed towards work.

After a day in which David felt as if he was barely present, he told Izzie that he was leaving a bit early for an appointment. He walked into the empty driveway at St. Anthony's and knocked on the door of the rectory, but there was no answer. David was a little early, so he walked around the building towards the garden and noticed the door was open to Angelo's small quarters. He peered in, knocked on the old wooden door, and Angelo appeared with a welcoming smile.

"David! I hope that I didn't drop too much on you all at once last night. It's good news, yes?"

"Don't worry, Angelo. You've been a loyal friend to my father to do everything you have, and I can't begin to tell you how much I appreciate it. I read the letters most of the night. It was quite an emotional ride. I do have a question for you, though, if you don't mind my asking?"

"For Gianni's son, I'd be happy to answer any question."

Angelo sat on the edge of his bed as David took the only chair in the room. David scanned the simple quarters Angelo had been living in. He could understand, after living in a small, cold cell of cinder blocks and steel bars for thirty years it must have felt homier, regardless of how it compared to David's high-end, spacious apartment. At the same time, it hit David that it may have felt lonely after sharing a space every day with his dad.

"So, tell me what you want to know."

David took a deep breath. "As much as I'd like to know everything about my father, I did read something in one of the letters that made me curious about you. He described the man who first came to share his cell, but you seem to be a very different man from that man he described."

Angelo sat forward and chuckled. "That's because I am a very different man than that man. That man was self-made on the outside and empty on the inside, and far from the person he was created to be, far from his true authentic self, and mind you, still working on it.

"David, your dad is the best man I've ever met, but I didn't like a thing about him when I first entered that cell. Despite his prison sentence, he was a good man who suffered a great injustice and never complained. I, on the other hand, had decided to be anything but a good man and cared about no one but myself. I was bitter, angry, and had a heart of stone. Your father never pushed but showed interest just beyond what I felt like sharing. At first, he would try to get me to talk about sports or some safe topic. Over time he realized that I was reconciled with the fact I was going to hell because Satan at least wanted me, and I was fairly certain that God didn't. Now mind you, your father would read stories like the *Iliad* and the *Odyssey, Lord of the Rings, Don Quixote*, or poems by Elliot, Yeats, Poe, and Shakespeare. I'd never heard them before, and it would pass the time. When he began to understand my belief that Satan wanted me and cared more about me than God did, he got Dante's *Divine Comedy* out of the library. He told me it was a story by an Italian writer whose true love had died. Your dad carefully read the opening line: 'Midway on our life's journey, I found myself, in dark woods, the right road lost.'"

"You see, your dad was smart," Angelo said as he pointed to his head. "He knew it might strike a chord."

David smiled as Angelo continued.

"Dante was taking a journey with the poet Virgil into the depths of hell to see sin for what it really was. Now, there were nine circles in the inferno, each tighter and narrower than the previous showing the narrowing of the soul that comes from sin and turning inwards with self-preoccupation. In the first circles, Dante was chased by three beasts, representing the sins of self-indulgence, like lust and gluttony. The circles moved then to greed, anger, heresy, and violence, and finally the sins of maliciousness such as fraud and betrayal being the worst. The punishments were not arbitrary cruelty but expressions of justice with each sinner experiencing the negatives that are natural results of the person's dysfunctional behavior.

"What struck me was what sins were the gravest. Fraud, that violated the natural trust between people, and betrayal, which violates a special trust in a relationship where loyalty is critical. These last sins of betrayal act against the nature of love, God's greatest gift to man, and they saw the worst sinners: Brutus, Cassius, and Judas. Finally, at the center, the narrowest part of the cone-shaped inferno, was Satan himself. I used to think he would be waiting there anxiously for me, but no! Instead, he was pathetically stuck in solid ice with huge wings that would take him nowhere as he was locked in the narrow confines of his own ego. I realized right then and there that he was completely indifferent and uninterested in me. I don't know how your father knew that image would shake me to my core, but it did."

David was thinking about the betrayal of trust in a close relationship being considered the worst of all sins, and how that might be why he struggled so much with his broken relationship with his father. That broken trust felt like a heavy door that shut him off from any relationships getting too intimate, too close to risk that pain again. Angelo asked, "Are you okay, David?"

David shook his head. "Oh, sure. You were saying that Dante escaped hell, which is a neat trick."

"Your dad continued the story the next day when Dante and Virgil entered purgatory, where there was a seven-story mountain to climb with seven terraces representing the seven deadly sins." Angelo rattled them off with the help of his fingers. "Pride, envy, wrath, sloth, avarice, gluttony, and lust. You see, pride is the worst and the basis for all other sins. Pride is distorted will and self-trust, putting yourself at the center instead of God. Pride prevents you from seeing that you have something to learn and that you don't determine what's true. When Dante came across the prideful penitents, he saw that they were carrying massive weights on their backs and were permanently hunched over, to bring them down to earth."

Angelo waved a hand for emphasis. "Your father didn't judge me. He helped me see my sin of pride. The opposite of pride is humility, and he showed me its strength by his example. Humility ended up not being the weakness I thought it was. He showed me that humility was not thinking less of yourself, but thinking less about yourself, recognizing your strengths and where they came from. The enemy of intelligence is failing to realize that you have more to know and pride had kept me from asking questions.

"Purgatory means hope because of God's unceasing love and mercy. I just needed to see myself as I was and repent about where I had turned my back on Him. Sin had made me less, it made me blind, and it made me think of myself as less. Little by little your dad and I talked about truth, God, Christ, and love. The story ends as Dante finally reaches heaven, where he meets a woman he recognizes named Piccarda. She explains to Dante that the essence of heaven is to dwell in God's holy will, 'In his will is our peace.' That line really hit me after I understood it. It took me a lot of years, but I'm no longer the man your father first described. I'm now or at least trying to be, the man God made me to be. I owe my life to your father, and that's why I'd do anything for him or his family. Anything."

David was genuinely moved by Angelo's story, and despite normally being wary of fully trusting anyone, he completely believed every word Angelo spoke. Suddenly, David realized that a good deal of time had passed as it was getting darker outside Angelo's window. He thanked Angelo for sharing his story and insights into his father.

Angelo unexpectedly stood up and hugged David. "I'm not much of a hugger, but I promised that one from your dad."

David smiled unreservedly as he peered directly into Angelo's eyes, wondering if he was getting a tiny glimpse of his dad.

David made his way back to the rectory and found a note on the door that said Father Tom was in the church. David thought of just heading back to work or home, but at the end of the driveway, the doors were staring right at him. He slowly climbed the seven stairs and gently opened the large wooden door to the church. The inside was lit and seemed both magnificently beautiful and quietly peaceful. David walked up the side aisle looking at each station, the statues, and paintings of those that had dedicated or given their lives to the Church. When David reached the front of the tabernacle, he felt a tug to do something but continued to walk slowly across the altar as Tom came out from the sacristy.

"Ah, David, I thought you might've changed your mind. I'm glad that you came in." He peered up at the strikingly beautiful ceilings and across the church. "It's nice this time of night, isn't it?"

"Yes, it is. Sorry if I kept you waiting. I was talking with Angelo for a while. I think I'm getting to like him after all."

Tom stepped down from the altar area to the pews where David was now standing and shook his hand. "How did you fare today?"

"I was okay. Just a little restless, I guess. My talk with Angelo made me feel a bit better."

Tom gently squeezed his shoulder. "Well, that's good to hear. I was thinking of you all day. I was actually praying for you much of the day." David just rolled his eyes a little but didn't protest.

Tom sat in the pew and David joined him.

"You said you were feeling a lot of conflicting emotions. How are you now?"

"Still confused. How can I find out my father is alive, that he's actually innocent, but feel leery of seeing him and angry he is alive?"

Tom straightened out some hymnals in the bench before responding. "We started talking a bit about this earlier. You had no small traumatic event for a young boy, and most likely looked for ways to cope with the pain of incredible broken trust and feeling of abandonment. From what you told me, that abandonment wasn't just physical but emotional from both your parents. Your mom was probably trying to cope herself and protect you and your siblings at the same time. My guess is that she truly believed letting you know he was alive would open up those painful wounds again. People find different ways to cope with fear and a sense of shame or self-worthlessness."

He paused, and the quiet of the church settled around them. "I talk with many people who feel a deep sense of emptiness and anxiety they try to fill with socially approved venues like work, exercise, power, wealth, success, or popularity, others by addictions to drugs, alcohol, or sex, but they never cure the emptiness or soothe the anxiety for long. Avoidance tactics taken to protect oneself tend to amplify the conflict and negative emotions, so people look to soothe or escape themselves more. I don't know if any of this applies to your situation, but it would be completely understandable with what you experienced."

"It sounds like a vicious cycle. As you get further from who you really are, you feel more anxiety, so you double down on building those protective walls and escapes. I don't know if I've ever seen myself that way, but I know a number of people who work for me that might fit the bill."

Tom smiled. "The reality is that we all do it to some extent. We all have some amount of emotional insecurity that creates a sense of self-rejection or worthlessness. That feeling of emptiness or shame is highly uncomfortable, so instead of tolerating some level of discomfort to deal with it or find out the truth, we find ourselves constantly avoiding it. It's really the avoidance that causes the most problems. We get busy and look for distractions from our inner voices, but we know, deep inside, something is calling us to something more, something outside of ourselves that can help us see who we really are." Tom glanced up at the large crucifix hanging over the altar and said, "It took me a long time to find out we weren't meant to face it alone. I felt like a man stuck in darkness and no one who passed by could get me out until someone jumped in that pit and said, 'I have been here before, and I can help you find the way out.' Jesus joined us in our suffering to help us find the way out."

"Ask me how I feel about my father."

Tom turned in his seat, towards David. "Okay, how do you feel about your father?"

"I don't know."

"Do you love him?"

"I don't know."

"Do you trust him?"

"I don't know."

"Do you want to see him?"

David sighed. "I really don't know."

"David, I don't think you should feel bad about that or think it is abnormal."

"What? I don't know if I even want to see my own father and that's not abnormal?"

"Think about it. You haven't seen him in person since you were eight, and you just learned he's alive. On top of that, the effects of your tragedy were experienced through all your senses over a very long time and that doesn't just go away. The perceived 'truths' you may have built your whole life upon would take anyone possibly years to unlearn and replace with the actual truth. No, I don't think it's abnormal, even if you subconsciously hoped you never heard the news."

David stared straight ahead. "Huh."

"Think of the feelings that could come up that might feel overwhelming, outside the controls you've put in place."

David rubbed his chin as he thought about what Tom was saying.

"Are you afraid that you might not recognize or even reject your dad when you see him? After all, your only memory is when he was thirty years younger through the eyes of a young boy. Maybe you fear that prison has changed him, or that you're not sure who the real Gianni Fidele is? Or maybe –"

"Or maybe what?"

"Nothing. I was just rattling."

"Tom, you never just rattle. What were you about to say?"

Tom focused on the altar. "I was thinking about the question you asked me when we talked about Corlie. You were on the mark with your instincts. What I was wondering is, do you think you might be afraid your dad would reject you? Loss of trust or abandonment can feel very much like a form of rejection to a child. Rejection of who you are inside, instead of the public self you created to protect that real self—that now very vulnerable self?"

As David processed Tom's question, he felt as if there were suddenly holes in his carefully built armored self. He hadn't consciously thought of it that way, but the question seemed to pierce through his armor like an arrow shot from the bow of Odysseus himself. Tom's pause lasted just long enough to let the feeling of fear sink into David's very being.

"I have no idea if this is the feeling going on deep inside, but knowing you, I can see no way that your father would feel anything but love and pride towards you. The important thing to remember is that you are going to be tempted to pull back and desperately avoid the discomfort. I have found it's important to be able to tolerate some level of discomfort to move forward, to truly relieve the anxiety and to find peace in your true self."

After sitting for a few minutes in the welcomed silence of the church, David said, " I don't think I want to run anymore. I don't think it would be humanly possible to busy myself enough to quiet down the voices in my head now, and I don't think I could be at peace by avoiding what I need to do. I think I'm going to take a walk and think a bit if you don't mind."

Tom stood up with David and accompanied him to the back and out onto the quiet street in front of St. Anthony's. He patted David on the back and told him to take care as David walked and reflected until he found himself on the streets of his old neighborhood in the North End. He hadn't realized until he saw the masked superheroes, ghosts, and other characters, that it was Halloween night.

David was thinking how hard it would be to tell who hid behind some of these more elaborate costumes on both the children trick-or-treating and the adults out to party for the evening. How long had he been hiding his own self behind his expensive suits, respected position, and protective wealth? How many people had he hurt along the way, ensuring that no one got too close a peek behind his mask? Would his father reject who he truly was or who he had become? Would he be proud of him? His father had nothing, not even his freedom, yet Angelo still had a deep, abiding respect for him.

Suddenly everything David had built up to protect himself seemed meaningless. Would his father be proud of his salary, his houses, his car, his club, his position, or his golf score? Thirty years and these are the fruits he had to share with a man that measured things by a very different yardstick and had a very different idea of what a man was.

David walked by the pub Mo Diavolo once owned. The neon River Styx Bar sign was no longer there, and it was now a restaurant called Pisano's Café. Mo had built and left nothing that lasted but an old story and years of pain for many families.

David now realized what was bothering him so much and started back home.

Chapter 36

David sat at his kitchen table and started to write out a list of everything he thought was important in life and another list of where he actually spent his time. He stared down at the paper for a while, looking at what was essentially his life and how he defined himself. He repeated the exercise, guessing what his father would put down as important and where he spent his time, and then placed the two lists side by side. Outside of being a hard worker, he saw little if any overlap. He sat tapping his fingers on the page and then got up to walk off some nervous energy before going into the den and picking up the second box of letters. Every letter from his father included something about how much he loved and missed him, but he was thinking his father didn't know him as an adult and might indeed feel very differently about the man he had become.

Disappointment seemed a certainty. His dad talked about a faith-sharing group he had begun, which had grown over the years. He described what a gift it was to see Angelo grow over time, the peace it brought him, and how Angelo was able to do the same for him. He hoped David had such a friend to trust and grow with. David was happy that his father had someone over all these years in prison.

The next day, after work, he hustled over to St. Anthony's, where he heard folk music coming from an open basement door under the church. After a few songs, David could hear students saying goodbye and heading off in different directions, their laughing drifting into the dark with them. David walked down the stairs to the basement, where a few people stood packing up their guitars and saying goodbye to Tom. Tom caught sight of David at the entrance and waved him over to introduce him to the young vocalist. David told him he enjoyed his music before stepping away with Tom.

Tom guided him to chairs in the far corner. "So, how is it going today?"

"Self-made David isn't doing well, but that may not be a bad thing. Do you have plans for the rest of the evening?"

Tom said softly, "If you don't mind Luke's company as well. We haven't eaten yet and we're going to go for some Chinese food at a place just over on Mass Ave."

They walked a few blocks over to an old Chinese establishment called Ling's Bamboo House and sat in one of the old, high-backed, U-shaped booths. Luke ordered a mock Mai Tai, while David and Tom both had a Shancheng beer to toast themselves. Luke joined in with, "The three struggling philosophers are back together again."

David smirked at the notion of him being a philosopher. "I agree with the struggling part."

They clinked glasses in agreement.

Tom said, "David, I hope you don't mind, but I was telling Luke about the news of your dad being alive after all this time. I didn't share anything else but wanted you to know that."

"No problem. Luke, your brother's right. My family suffered a tragedy when I was a boy that took the life of my brother, Jimmy, and sentenced my father to the electric chair for killing him and a police officer. Until this week, I didn't know he was innocent and still alive in Virginia."

Luke stared open-mouthed at David. "Holy crap! I can't imagine how devastated you must've been over all these years. What are you feeling?"

Tom's mug hit the table. "Luke!"

"It's okay, Tom," David said with a wave of his hand. "I'm trying to figure out that question myself."

Luke leaned back in his seat. "I'm sorry, David. I've never heard anything like this. Wow. How old were you when this happened?"

"I was eight, and I thought there was nobody like my father. I admired and loved him, and in one act I couldn't comprehend, I lost all respect, all trust, and all love for him. My family changed forever. Each one of us changed in almost every way imaginable. Despite that, I thought I was doing okay until some guy driving an old, broken-down Honda dropped his basketball, which happened to roll in my direction."

Tom, studying his menu, kiddingly acted as if he wasn't listening.

"When I told your brother, I had mixed feelings about the news of my father, wondering if I could really trust him, forgive him or even love him. Your brother asked me if I might be more afraid that it would be my father who would reject me. It challenged me to think past my initial instincts and fears. I had to think if he'd be proud of me and what would he be proud of."

Luke blurted, "I can't believe you asked him that."

"I think he asked me that because he cared about me like a true friend. I realized it wasn't an easy question to ask, but the right one to help me stop avoiding it."

Tom looked at David with affection.

"So, I wrote down all the things in life I thought were important, and then where I actually spent my time and energy. Trying to be humble here, but I'm fairly successful at my work. I have made more money than I can probably spend, own two expensive homes, own part of a club, have the sports car I dreamed of as a kid, can date most women I pursue, enjoy expensive restaurants, golf clubs, and entertainment events. Why wouldn't a father be incredibly proud of that success? Then I started thinking about what my father cared most about and what he thought a man was. I realized none of those things would be on his list. I don't really know him outside of vague memories as a young boy, but I experienced a man who put his faith and family first, long before he thought of himself. He worked hard, but as a means to take care of his family and not as an end for himself. Listening to Angelo and reading my father's letters, I saw a man who doesn't complain or think the world owes him anything but looks to how he can continue to serve others. I also saw—"

David cleared his throat and collected himself. "I saw a man who never gave up on me even though I so easily gave up on him. If I saw him right now, I couldn't give him back a man whom he'd be proud of because I'm not proud of who I am."

After a thoughtful pause, Luke said, "David, I don't know you very well, and I don't know your dad at all, but I think he'd understand and think you are being too hard on yourself. How could he not be proud of you?"

David rubbed his forehead. "I appreciate that, Luke, but I'm self-focused. As a matter of fact, I'm all I can think about, as your brother would say." He sighed. "I left my wife and kids. The minute I get close to someone special, I pull back and hurt her, knowing full well when I start any relationship that that's the plan. I have more money and stuff than one person needs, and I do little good with it outside of my own entertainment. I buried my own mother this summer and felt nothing. I have a brother and a sister I rarely speak, and a daughter and son I barely know. I spent thirty years hating my father when it should've been the other way around. No, I don't think I'm being too hard on myself at all, Luke."

He shifted his attention to Tom. "I want to see my father, but I want to see him as a man he can be proud of, someone he can be glad he never gave up on. I need to be humble here and ask you for advice on how I can begin to be that kind of man."

"I can only tell you what I know, but your path can and will be different."

"I trust your wisdom and need all the help I can get."

Tom glanced at his brother and back to David. "All right. First of all, don't do this because you think your father will love you or love you more because of it. If he's anything like the man Angelo describes, his love isn't conditional. It's not based on what you do or don't do, or what you accomplish or don't accomplish. He loves you because you are his son, period.

"Secondly, I think you've already taken the biggest step to move outside of your personal pride. Our culture isn't big on humility, and it's what we need. Pride is a man's most difficult hurdle and assumes you need no one else, including God, to become a self-made man. The problem is this self-made man isn't the one God created and not your true self. We remain disconnected from our role in God's plan for us, which is something much greater with purpose and meaning. I don't claim to have all the answers you need, but your question tonight says you're doing what too few men do—being courageous enough to get past your ego and pride, to think about who you really are as a man made for others."

David was listening with purpose. "You know, I don't think that would've resonated with me several weeks back, but I think I get what you mean. I understand you can't do this overnight, but what else do you think?"

"The next one is tough."

David glanced at Luke and realized from the look of concentration on his face that Luke was seriously absorbing their conversation.

"The greatest trap in life is self-rejection, and greatest failure is to not love who you are and what you are. Each of us has been created, not as just an 'average man' in the eyes of the world, but as a beloved and precious man in the eyes of God. Most people don't see their self-worth through God's eyes. If they did, they'd know He is the only source that can satisfy our desire to know we are worthy of love. So, we look for validation in places that can never satisfy. We look desperately for others' approval and validation, but it doesn't satisfy. We look to popularity, success, power, wealth, pleasure, or busyness to fill the empty void, but it only makes us more distant from ourselves and more anxious. Instead of pursuing fewer of those things that were never made to work, we tend to pursue them even harder. As young children, we look to our parents' gaze to tell us they can see in us the goodness and beauty God put there. In that gaze, we see that we are very much worth loving, but even that only leads us to look to the only source that can satisfy, God himself."

Luke asked, "Tom, do you really think most people suffer from self-rejection?"

"I think we all do somewhat, and the more we buy into the world's view of what's important, the more we feel as if we are less. I don't think most people do this on purpose. They are trying to fill a gnawing feeling, an empty void, or to avoid a fear that may not be their fault and only their subconscious might understand. Suffering the loss of trust and experiencing abandonment as a young child would shake anyone's sense of self-worth."

David asked, "How do you start to believe in yourself?"

With a half-grin, Tom said, "Good question. I'm working on this myself, but I have to keep reminding myself life isn't about trying to make ourselves worthy of God's love but to recognize he has already made us worthy. In knowing that, we are called to live our lives with the dignity of who we are, beloved sons and daughters of God."

Luke put down his drink. "Are you saying we don't have to do anything or even be good people?"

"Not exactly. I'm saying we shouldn't do it to earn love but because we are loved. God can only love us, and love is something you don't keep, but give away, so we are called to give that love away to others and to trust fully in God's plan and love for us. It's the point where you begin to realize your life isn't actually about you, and you begin to be truly free to be yourself.

"David, I'm sorry for not getting directly to your question, but the essence of being a man is all about self-giving love, of which Jesus gave us the greatest example. You can't really give something you don't have to give. A man needs to have a sense of his true self and know where it comes from, to be able to give himself to another. If we live an empty, self-absorbed life, we aren't giving ourselves made in the image of God. Love is the greatest gift God gave us. Not the feeling of love, but the act of love, of truly willing the good for another. If someone threw a hand grenade into a room with innocent women and children, what would a real man do?"

Luke said, "He would throw himself on it and give his life for the others."

"When people turned their backs on God in sin and selfishness, what did He do?"

David said, "He gave us His only son."

"Correct and correct. Let me give you an example of how backward we tend to have things in today's world. While Jesus, the man, poured himself out to give His body up for us, most men today ask women to give their bodies up for them. We use people instead of loving them."

Luke said, "That puts selfishness in perspective."

"Once you remove the self-referential nature of 'loving' someone and truly want the good for them, with 'no strings attached,' then you are getting closer to the kind of love God has for us. To truly live, you have to die of yourself, your ego. To receive what matters, you have to give everything away. To receive love, you have to give it away. What do you think the opposite of love is?"

David replied, "Hate."

Luke smirked as if he had heard this riddle before.

Tom said, "Try selfishness. Jesus came to show us God's love and how to love each other. True love doesn't focus on itself but on the other. I think Paul said it best in a letter when he wrote to the Corinthians. 'Love is patient and kind; love is not jealous or boastful; it is not arrogant or rude.

Love does not insist on its own way; it is not irritable or resentful; it does not rejoice at wrong but rejoices in the right. Love bears all things, believes all things, hopes all things, and endures all things. Love never ends.' He said faith, hope, and love were the greatest virtues, but it is love that endures since we will no longer need faith or hope in heaven."

David took a sip of his drink and asked, "Tom, I assume you just laid out an important foundation for answering my question?"

Tom made eye contact with David. "I know, 'What things should you be doing to be a man your father can love and be proud of?' Remember when we were in the church and we were looking at the rose window?'"

"I remember."

"Do you remember our conversation about it?"

"Um, we talked about not putting ourselves or any other priorities in the center that don't belong there. We said life only works when we put God or Christ at the center and then order our lives around that center, recognizing who made us and whose will we should trust and follow."

"You actually paid attention, huh? If you try doing that and thinking about what we talked about tonight, I don't think you need me to tell you anything you can't figure out for yourself."

David's instincts told him Tom was most likely right, so he didn't argue back as the waiter set the food on the table.

"Ah," Tom said, "We can finally get down to important things like some egg roll, low mein, and hong sue gai chicken."

All three laughed.

David valued what Tom had said, but the laughter was a good break from the serious conversation.

Chapter 37

Back at his apartment, David poured himself a glass of water then sat in his favorite leather chair with a pen and a lined pad of paper, while Trooper lay by his side. He had planned on writing a list of a new set of priorities but felt immobilized when it came to listing the most important priority, so he laid the pad down on the coffee table. Then he closed his eyes, imagined the stained glass rose window, and visually tried to empty out the center of all he had placed there over the years.

He remembered his father telling him once that he would know God was thinking of him if his heart was beating and his lungs were breathing. He started to talk out loud, "I know we haven't talked for a very long time. I'm really not sure exactly what to say, but I think I need Your help. I know I need Your help. I know I need to keep You at the center of my life, but I still don't understand why You let all this happen to my family. I think we were a good family. I truly don't understand Your plan here, and I know I need to think about it now. Please take care of my father. Please help me to change and be who You want me to be." He sat with his eyes closed trying to listen for a responding voice in the silence. He listened for quite some time and heard nothing but the quiet of his apartment. Then he felt an unusual sense of peace that everything was going to be okay. This wasn't a feeling he had experienced since he was very young, back when he felt as if things would always be all right as long as his father was around.

David kept his eyes closed, and in the dark, he began to see the light of the rose window in front of him. He could feel himself moving his own self out of the center and letting go of control long enough to feel God in the center. Around the center, he could see three smaller stained glass sections. He was trying to imagine who the figures were in these sections. He couldn't see the figures, but he had a strong sense that his father and family were in one of them. It wasn't just the living members of his family, but all of them, including Jimmy and his mother, and neither seemed angry nor unforgiving. He didn't want to move, but his eyes floated to the next section, and he had a strong sense Kathleen, Amy, and James were there waiting for him. When his mind's eye moved to the third section, he couldn't get any sense of who or what resided here. It wasn't a sense that it was empty, but that he couldn't make out the image. He felt his eyes beginning to open to the light of the room, and it took him a second to adjust and focus on Trooper, who was watching him with much curiosity.

He picked up the pad of paper from the table and began to write on one line and then the next with a feeling of purpose.

David slept deeply that night without any of the restlessness he had been experiencing recently. When he woke up close to nine, he felt a different energy in his stride as he took off for a run that ended up near St. Anthony's. He had intended to stop by to see if Tom were available, but he noticed him talking with someone who seemed familiar. As he got closer, he could see it was Jillian talking to Tom just outside the rectory door. Even though he felt exhausted at that point, he picked up the pace and passed them unnoticed on the other side of the road. He was finding the same old pattern of questions starting to run through his head. Why were they talking? Were they talking about him behind his back? Why hadn't Tom said anything to him about Jillian before? Could he trust him completely? None of the questions were making him feel comfortable as he headed back home. After much angst, he knew he had to find out what Tom knew about Jillian, but it took him two weeks to finally walk over to the church on a Sunday night. Tom had Mass at 7:00 and David noticed a lot of college students socializing out front of the church afterward.

David entered the church as someone was putting a few things away from the altar when he noticed Tom in the back. The lights were dimmed and soft against the walls and columns. Tom had taken off his vestments and was wearing his more traditional black shirt and collar, black pants, shoes, and a friendly smile. Tom walked towards the back of the church as David slowly walked towards him until they met in the middle where they had stood many weeks ago. Tom reached out his hand to David. "David, I've missed you. I hope everything's all right."

David didn't reach out to shake Tom's hand. "I actually came by a few Saturdays ago but you were busy talking with someone outside your rectory door."

David watched Tom's face as he made the connection. Nodding, Tom said, "I assume we are talking about someone you know?"

"Yes, and I think you know who I'm talking about. Why would you be seeing Jillian Miller?"

Tom nodded in an understanding gesture. "I'm sure you can appreciate that I can't talk about any of the conversations I have had with Jillian."

"Conversations? How often do you see her?"

"Originally, she had come to see me out of concern for you after that September 11 anniversary, when you left her after seeing me. She came back for herself. She wasn't doing well with the sudden change in her relationship with you. We just talked through some things. I didn't disclose anything about you, and she respected that. She just wanted to know if you were okay and if she had caused anything that happened. I let her know you were all right, that I thought you needed time with family matters that had suddenly come up, and that you were torn between wanting to see that she was okay and not wanting to hurt her more. I hope all that was okay, David. I didn't feel as if I could leave her to fall into a pit of self-rejection and blame."

David sat down and stared blankly at the empty bench in front of him for several moments. "I'm sorry, Tom. I should never doubt you or your intentions. For some reason, my instincts keep sending me in the wrong direction. Thanks for being honest and for taking good care of Jillian. I would want her to have someone to talk with, and I'm glad she chose you."

"Thanks for understanding and caring. I do think she's going to be okay." He sat down next to David. "You said you came by a few weeks ago. Were you coming to see me for anything in particular?"

"I did. I was thinking about what you said when we were out with your brother that Friday night. You said I could figure out my priorities on my own if I got the foundational things right. I, um, I don't know if I prayed, but I actually tried talking with God for the first time since I was a boy, and maybe that time when Amy had been in an accident with her bike that sent her to the hospital."

Tom looked fondly at him. "David, talking to God is praying. It's a relationship and like any friendship, you need to spend time together, to reveal yourself, to be heard, and to really take the time to listen. The answers may not come in the form you expect, but they come. How did it go?"

"I don't really know, but I asked for help and tried to be still, which isn't easy for me. I visualized the rose window you talked about, to unclutter the center, and then put God in that spot. Then I just waited to see how the rest sorted itself out. I only got a short glimpse of two of the three sections around the center."

"Do you remember what they were?"

David nodded. "They had to do with my family growing up and with my family now, Amy and James. I got a sense I should focus there and think about what a man would do. In terms of my father, would a real man give up on his dad? Would he see him and be there for him? I decided I want to ask him to forgive me for not trusting in him. I want him to know he's not alone, that I'm going to be there for him. But I also think it would mean a lot to him if I was the man he had always hoped I would be."

David stared up at the ceiling as his eyes filled with tears. "I want him to be proud of his son. If you read his letters, he never gave up on me and tried to teach me what it was to be a man, to be humble and strong at the same time in my faith. To be the kind of father who makes a difference to his own children, letting them know how much they are valued and loved while challenging them to be who they really are. He'd want me to reach out more to my brother and sister. My whole life has been about me, about work and success, about stuff and staying busy enough to ignore that I'm not a man at all but a selfish and frightened boy avoiding pain instead of dealing with it."

Tom put his hand on David's shoulder. "I can imagine none of that feels very good right now. While I'm not going to disagree with everything you said, I do think you are being very hard on yourself."

David turned to Tom. "Yeah, look at you. You are giving your life to others. What am I doing with my work but serving myself?"

"Okay. I think of your job as serving quite a few people. You have a gift you are using to teach and build an incredibly good sales force that brings in business."

"Wow, really earthshaking."

"Think about it. That success helps to create tens of thousands of jobs, giving an opportunity for all those people to have families and to provide for them. In turn, all the companies that do business with IMG then grow and offer the same opportunity to their employees. Think of how many people's lives you actually touch in a meaningful way. Many more than I do in my little corner."

"Thanks, Tom. I'll have to think about that a little more, but I know I'm falling short with my family. I grew up without a father for so many years, and I should know better than anyone that sending a check and going out to dinner or a game a handful of times a year isn't the same thing as being there!"

"As I said, I'm not going to disagree with everything you said. We're not perfect and we get off the track many times in life. The good news is this is one thing you can do something about. You can't change the past, but you can start today to avoid making it the only thing they remember. This is one of the most important roles a man has in life, so I'd give yourself some credit for seeing it now. You'd be surprised how many men don't come to this realization until after they retire, and they've had time to reflect."

"Thanks for being straight with me. I need your honesty even if it stings a bit. I don't know exactly how I'm going to start, but I'm going to see what I can do."

"David, I'm not a father like yourself, but I've learned over the years that kids don't expect or even need their parents to be perfect, they just need to know they matter enough for you to care and love them. I have a feeling that, whatever you do, you will touch their hearts in a really good way."

David sat forward. "I hope so. As I said, I just wanted to let you know where I am on things and to thank you for being a friend. I hope I'm not becoming a nuisance or a drain on you."

"Quite the opposite. Your friendship is a great joy to me and your courage to be so openly honest with yourself and caring about where you're heading is an inspiration to me. One thing I'd keep on doing is taking just a few moments each day to have that talk with God, and in the silence, try to hear His voice and look for it all around you. I'm going to keep praying for you and for your family, including your dad. I hope you will feel comfortable to see him sometime soon."

They both stood up and walked to the entrance doors. "I'll give it a try and will blame your praying if it doesn't work."

Tom laughed and turned towards the front of the church, genuflected and made the Sign of the Cross before turning back to walk out with David. David took Tom's hand this time and gave it a firm shake as they said goodnight and headed towards their respective homes.

As David walked away, he could hear Tom yell out, "The boys are missing their favorite coach!" David didn't turn but smiled and put his arm up to wave, acknowledging he heard him.

Chapter 38

On Wednesday afternoon, David walked to St. Anthony's with his sports bag in hand. As he headed to the school entrance doors, David could see Sister Helen in the lobby. He hadn't seen her since the time she hugged him. When he got to the door, she blushed, and he could tell. He gave her a smile that told her he wouldn't let this moment go by without maximum leverage.

"Good afternoon, Sister. Now I know a Christian woman such as yourself wouldn't show someone love and affection that was conditional or could be bought."

Sister Helen blushed. "No, Mr. Kelly, it was an honest—"

She stopped as David pulled out an envelope and placed it in her hand. "No explanation is necessary, but it was nice to get a hug." He started towards the gym doors as she opened the envelope to find a check to St. Anthony's School for one hundred thousand dollars.

She called out and quickly caught up with David. "I don't understand! What is this for?"

He grinned. "I hoped it might help out here with some repairs. The first gift you received was a much larger one, though."

She tilted her head, confused. "I don't follow. This is five times the amount of that gift. How could it be much greater?"

David took notice of her sincere face. "I think there's something in the Bible Tom explained to me. You know, about a widow's offering from the little she had. In this case, that widow was my father. That was a much greater gift than I just gave you, but this is a start." Sister Helen's eyes were now puddles, and she put both of her arms around David and thanked him. David hugged her back with a look of fondness to let her know how much he appreciated it.

When David opened the door to the gym, a few of the boys ran over to him eager to tell him about the progress they were making on their dribbling, shooting, and boxing-out skills. Tom was working with a group of boys on a few fundamental plays and gave a thumbs up when he saw David organizing the boys at the other end of the court.

After practice, David and Tom played one-on-one until they were exhausted and agreed it was a good night to stop at Dempsey's for a burger and a cold beer.

Dempsey was glad to see them back after several weeks. He came over to the booth with two beers. "So, you're finally thirsty enough to come back, or did the cat just drag you in?"

David took his beer. "We just missed that beautiful face and your amazing cooking. We'll have two burgers."

Tom raised his glass to Dempsey and agreed he had a beautiful face, and then added with a brogue, "that only a mother could love."

As Dempsey walked away, Tom and David tapped their glasses. "It was good to have you back today. The boys really missed you after being stuck with just me for a few weeks. So, how are you doing?"

"I'm fine. I had a very long conversation with Kathleen, my ex-wife, about Amy and James and how I can become more involved. I give her a lot of credit; she didn't use the conversation to let me know how absent I've been. She was happy to hear I was ready to step up to the plate. When I thought of my dad, I felt ashamed about how easy it was to distance myself from them and from my responsibility. It's embarrassing to admit, but I know it's the right thing to do."

"I have a good feeling you'll give them a great gift and one you'll cherish as well."

"Thanks, Tom. I have to say I'm more than a little nervous, but I'll give it my best. I also got to thinking about Kathleen."

"I haven't heard you talk much about her. Are things friendly between you or is there friction?"

David stared down into his beer. "Things are fine. We don't have arguments or anything, and I didn't argue about support or the house, so there is no friction. We've been apart for six years now, and from what Amy's told me, she hasn't dated once. She's smart, thoughtful, kind, fun to be with and still very attractive, and yet she seems to choose to be alone. I don't really understand why."

"Does that make you feel guilty?"

"I don't know. Maybe a little, but she deserves to be happy."

"Is faith important to Kathleen at all?"

"You would love Kathleen. She grew up Catholic and always went to church growing up. After we were married, she started reading and going to classes to learn more about her faith, and she became very devout. She always took the kids to church and didn't make it an issue that I didn't go."

"Hmm."

"What?"

"Did this become an issue for you in the relationship?"

"It may have bothered me a bit, but as I said, she wasn't in my face about it. I just thought women tended to like going to church more than men."

"David, if Kathleen is a devout Catholic, then she most likely won't date."

241

"We're divorced. Why couldn't she date?"

"The Church teaches that marriage is a commitment for life and not just as long as things are going well."

"That's not really practical. People fall out of love, things change, and you can't expect people to be miserable for the rest of their lives. That makes no sense at all. It sounds almost cruel."

Tom took a swig of his beer and set the mug down on the table. "One of the things the Church does is listen to what Jesus taught us about His Father's plans, and then always trust He had a very good reason behind that plan, something we don't always understand until we trust it fully." Tom pulled a small book out of his jacket pocket and flipped through until he came to the passage marked Matthew 19.

"What's this about?"

"Possibly the answer to why Kathleen believes what she does. Jesus is being asked here about divorce. He replies, 'Have you not read that he who made them from the beginning made them male and female, and said, 'For this reason, a man shall leave his father and mother and be joined to his wife, and the two shall become one'? So they are no longer two but one. What therefore God has joined together, let no man put asunder. And I say to you: whoever divorces his wife, except for unchastity, and marries another, commits adultery; and he who marries a divorced woman, commits adultery.'"

David was silent for several moments and then asked, "What does that mean?"

"Jesus is saying that God created man and woman for the covenant of marriage in which they become one. He tells us man cannot take apart what God has joined together, and that marriage is for life. A lot of people see marriage as just a civil arrangement or a breakable contract. In a contract, two parties enter into a mutually beneficial agreement exchanging goods and services. The guarantee is the 'word' of both parties where you sign your name on the bottom line. On your honor, you agree to fulfill the terms of the agreement. A contract can be dissolved by either party if it's no longer beneficial, and the terms are usually stipulated."

"That sounds right. Why doesn't that describe a marriage agreement?"

"A marriage isn't just a contract but a covenant."

David ran his fingers up and down his mug. "What's the difference?"

"A covenant is different in some really important ways. From the beginning of time, it was how you established family bonds when there was no blood relationship. Instead of exchanging goods and services, you exchange persons. The very nature of giving yourself means the arrangement is permanently binding. In a marriage, I give myself to you and I'm no longer mine but yours, so I can no longer give myself to anyone else. Does that difference make any sense?"

"I guess I can sort of see the distinction you are making."

"Think about a civil contract where your honor or word is required in the agreement, but a covenant is so profound it requires an oath or a vow calling on God's honor and name to be the guarantor of the covenant."

"Huh. So, you are saying marriage is different and not breakable?"

"Exactly! Marriage is the ultimate example of a covenant and why it's permanent since you've given yourself to someone. That covenant is made permanent when you give yourselves to each other on your wedding night. Sexual expression isn't only fun but is actually where we intimately and sacramentally become one as we fully give ourselves in an act that bonds and can create life, a new family."

David, mouth open, was shocked. "No one ever told me this."

"It's a shame when couples don't really understand what they've gotten themselves into or really committed themselves to. Think about this. The real purpose of life is to know and experience God's unconditional love for us and then give it to others. That's the only way we're going to be truly happy. Marriage is a relationship where we can see unconditional love in each other and get a glimpse of the face of God in that love."

Tom let several seconds pass. "David, marriage is no small thing in God's plans, and he has really good reasons for it. When Jesus was born, he revealed to us that God is three persons in one, a community of self-giving love. Think of marriage as a relationship that most closely reveals that community of love as two people become one while maintaining the dignity of each individual. It's in that intimate relationship that you can fully discover your true self, love, and happiness through the total and sincere gift of self to each other."

David was attentively listening as Tom continued. "Say you believe marriage is a breakable contract. Can you see how that would completely change the character of what a marriage is and how the two individuals relate to each other, never fully giving themselves to the other?"

"How's that?"

"We all come to a relationship with some baggage, fears, and insecurities. Think of what a relationship would be like if you could really share anything and everything about yourself without fear of that person rejecting you or leaving you, no matter what. We don't know where that journey will take us, but imagine taking it with someone we can trust with unconditional love, holding nothing back and without fear of rejection."

David sat stunned at the thought. "Total trust?"

"Total. In a marriage, you die to self and give yourself fully to the other in a commitment of love for life, not because you expect something back. Think about how that changes your ability to be completely vulnerable and trust another person to love you unconditionally no matter what they find out about you. Being truly intimate involves being truly seen and still loved by another the way God sees and loves us. Letting someone truly into your life in a shared reality can be really difficult and requires that unconditional love, which allows you to trust that person to see your authentic self, the person you yourself may not have yet fully accepted. Marriage, in the real sense of the word, allows each of you to see the dignity, beauty, and value with which each of you was created—without hiding parts of yourself."

David nodded thoughtfully, only too aware of his hidden self. Tom continued, "Wedding vows say you will love them in good times and in bad, in sickness and in health, for richer or poorer, all the days of your life. Love isn't willing the good for yourself through the other. Love is self-gift, about willing the good for the other, an unconditional and unending active love. The boy falls in love but when the infatuation stage is over, the boy leaves, and the real man will love."

"So, you think Kathleen still believes she's married and cannot date or marry again?"

"I think it's very likely that she does."

"But I thought Catholics had their own version of divorce. What's that called?"

"I think you are referring to the annulment process. It is actually nothing like a divorce. Divorce is a legal process that looks at how a marriage ended. Annulment is a process too but to understand if a true marriage commitment ever took place in the beginning. It originated with royals being forced to marry purely for political reasons, to join kingdoms. The couples never chose each other. They weren't married with a commitment based on love.

"Nowadays, there remain reasons why a couple may not have been capable of making a sacramental commitment. The couple may have been too immature or one of the parties may not have been free to marry or they were emotionally incapable of making a true marriage commitment. If the process reveals that a sacramental marriage commitment never happened, then they were never truly married to begin with. It doesn't mean they didn't have a relationship, or they never loved each other, but that a true commitment to sacramental marriage didn't take place. As Jesus said, divorce and then remarriage isn't possible since the divorced person can't break a union God had joined, and they would be in a state of adultery. God knows the path that leads to true love, joy, and peace. Our human tendency is to take our own path instead."

"It sounds almost impossible for two people to live that out for a lifetime, don't you think?"

To David's visible surprise Tom said, "I agree." Tom sipped his beer. "That's why it really has to be a marriage of three: wife, husband, and God being the strength and glue that makes the impossible possible."

David smiled at Tom's sincerity in what he was saying. "Tom, you have never been married. No disrespect, but how can you really know what it's like to be married?"

"No disrespect was taken. It's a fair question and one that isn't always asked so politely. I'm sure you won't be surprised if I say that it all starts with God. God is truth, and God is love and always giving love. Since marriage is all about experiencing all the ups and downs of life together in the context of that love, I can share that with the hundreds of couples and people I talk with every day who share their struggles, falls, and concerns with me. I'm inside the marriages and families of so many people. It's an experience few people have the opportunity to know. Despite popular belief, priests are human and grow up in families and experience their parents' marriages firsthand. Books that share experiences and thoughts on marriage and studying human psychology for years is helpful, but it's the person-to-person contact that makes it real. I agree it's not the same as living it day to day, through the joy, intimacy, and laughs, and also through the hurts, anger, arguments, and disappointments."

David said, "I never thought about how many marriages you get to see up close."

"You'd be amazed. The priesthood itself is like a marriage. Remember when I said that Jesus is the bridegroom of his bride, the Church. A priest gives himself in love to the Church to serve as a husband cherishes his bride. It's a commitment for life, in good times and in bad, in which he is called to give himself fully in service to the Church and to God. The only difference is, when a priest has a problem in his relationship with God, he knows who the problem is with."

David laughed. "Well, that makes things easy. But I think you left out giving up something else as well?"

Tom nodded. "I know what you are talking about, but it's really a small sacrifice for what I receive in return."

"But you give up sex, a wife, and kids!"

Tom stared into his almost empty mug. After a few minutes, he whispered, "Those I lost twenty years ago."

David knew immediately what he meant and shared the silence with Tom.

After paying and saying goodnight to Dempsey, David and Tom found themselves in a familiar spot outside the front door of the pub. Tom patted David on the shoulder. "It was good to see you. I'm glad you came by the gym. It looks like we'll have a team to start the season in a few weeks."

"They are a good group of boys and I'm enjoying them. And as usual, I appreciate your listening to my drivel."

"It's not drivel, David."

"Well, it's uncharted territory for me to say the least."

"True for all of us. Tell me, have you had any more thoughts about seeing your dad?"

"No, not really," he replied, then laughed. "Actually, I don't know if I've thought of anything else but that, lately. I want to get a few things in place before I contact him. I was hoping to catch Angelo to ask him not to say anything."

"I'm sure Angelo would honor your wishes."

On the way home, David thought of the way his life was about to change.

Chapter 39

It would be a difficult balancing act for David to meet the demands of delivering the all-important fourth-quarter sales results while refocusing his personal priorities. He saw Amy and James every weekend that didn't conflict with their schedules. Amy was still a bit wary of her father's motives and commitment, but James was all too happy to take advantage of the newfound time with his dad. When the St. Anthony's team played scrimmage games on Saturdays with the other local Catholic schools, James came to be the ball boy and shoot around before the games. David also helped out at My Brother's Table when he could and brought Kathleen and Amy to help serve one time. He even convinced some of his crew at work to volunteer at a few lunches during November and for Thanksgiving Day. Both Kathleen and Amy, as well as the guys from work, saw a side of David that they didn't recognize. He was also noticing this unknown side of himself and felt more confident about seeing his dad.

David filled out the required prison visit application, and more importantly, he wrote to his dad for the first time. It took him several evenings to write what he wanted to say, and he still felt unsure that he had it right.

Dear Pop,

I guess the above greeting narrows down who this letter is from. I met your friend Angelo, and he brought me the news I never thought was possible, despite wishing it were so all my life. I still can't believe you are alive and doing well, under the circumstances. Angelo also brought me a gift that was only second to the news you are alive, and that was your loving and faithful letters. I have spent many nights reading each one with tears in my eyes—not only from reading what you wrote but also missing life with you over each of those years.

I thought you might also like to know you have two grandchildren from me and one from Abbie. My oldest, Amy, is sixteen and sometimes too intelligent and beautiful for her own good but you will really like her. James is seven and just starting to gain some confidence in himself. He loves baseball and he will hopefully take after his grandfather. I'm sure you're aware by now mom passed away this August. She was buried next to her sister Marie as she always wanted. She worked hard to keep the family together and provided for us growing up. I don't know why she didn't accept all the loving letters you sent to each of us without fail. The only thing we knew or thought we knew was you were both dead and guilty of all the charges. I wish she knew the truth as Angelo has graciously divulged to me.

My wish is to come down to Virginia to see you in person if you are ok with that. I will have to admit I am a little nervous to meet you, but I'm more excited than anything else. At times I think of myself as eight years old again and meeting you as a young boy, instead of a thirty-nine-year-old man. I received approval to come down any weekend you would like. If there is anything I can bring or do for you, please let me know. I look forward to hearing back from you and even more to finally seeing you again.

Much love,
David

David sent the letter express and received a prompt reply from his father, who seemed to be overjoyed by the prospect of seeing his son. David scheduled his flight for Friday. Once on the plane to Richmond, part of David regretted not having flown down the day before to spend Thanksgiving with his father, but he also felt as if he needed more time to prepare himself emotionally. At the hotel, anxiety and anger took turns playing with him. How would he feel when he finally saw his father face-to-face? Would his anger evaporate now that he knew the truth? He tried his best to sleep, but dreams of the week his brother died, his father being arrested, the police, the newspaper reporters who came to the family's North End apartment more times than he could count, all flooded his mind and kept him awake most of the night.

The night seemed to last forever, but the morning did come. The State Penitentiary ran a strict visitation schedule, and David was to meet his father for a scheduled one-hour slot from eleven to twelve o'clock, arriving one hour earlier in order to pass through security. He drove towards the prison, and reality started to sink in when he recognized the white building that sat behind the walls and barbed wire fences from the postcard Angelo had left in his apartment.

He brought his approved visitor papers and one of the guards escorted him into the facility with its cold hard walls and steel bars. He emptied his pockets of all his belongings except for pictures of Amy and James and was patted down in his security check. As he was moved further into the building to the visiting area, he could hear the unsettling sound of the sliding doors with thick metal bars slamming shut behind him. There was nothing about the prison building that felt anything but cold, hard, and uncomfortably empty of life. It made him appreciate his life, and at the same time, wonder how his father was able to be unbroken by such hardness for thirty years.

The visitors were led to a waiting area and his heart was beating at an incredibly fast pace as he waited to be moved into the visiting room where he'd see a man without even knowing what he looked like. Finally, the heavy-barred gate to the visiting room opened, and one by one, each visitor was led into a specific booth with a seat, a small counter space, and a telephone on each side of the thick pane of glass that separated them. There would be no embrace or even a handshake today or maybe ever. He sat down and waited for what seemed like an eternity until the prisoners were brought in one at a time and escorted to the other side of the glass from their visitor. They all wore the same blue denim shirts and pants, and he couldn't tell which man his father was until a guard brought one of the prisoners to where he was sitting. The man, visibly older than David had pictured, had black and gray-peppered hair, and wore a prison shirt with the number 316 over his pocket. It was obvious this may have been his first time in the visiting room as well, since it didn't look routine to him either.

As the man lowered himself slowly into his chair, a smile made its way to the man's face as his eyes radiated the love and joy he felt seeing his long-lost son. A tear rolled down Gianni's cheek as he continued to gaze at David with nothing but love in his eyes. It took a moment for David to compose himself, and he pointed to the phone so that they could talk. David spoke to his father for the first time in thirty-one years. "Hello, Pop. I'm sorry it took so long."

Gianni shook his head as tears freely fell down his cheeks. "David, we've waited so long, much too long. I can't tell you how happy I am to see you." Gianni's right hand was facing towards David with the palm side up and moving back and forth as he said, "I can't believe my eyes that this is the young boy I left behind. I'm so sorry for all the days, all the years, we have missed. I've missed you each and every one of them."

"All these years, I thought it was only me who missed you, Pop. It was such a shock, believing that you were dead and to find out that you've been alive, after all this time." David smiled. "I have to admit I was expecting that time had stood still, and you were still about the age I am now, but you look good and it's so good to hear your voice. I can't believe we are this close, but we still have a wall between us."

"There are walls and bars everywhere here, but you learn to see past them."

There was an awkward moment of silence. "David, when I first went to prison, I don't know if you knew this, but your mother did come down to visit. She was so devastated and hurt about Jimmy. I could see she was angry and had lost trust in me. She was using her resentment and maybe even hate to deal with the pain. When she left, I think she was convinced I was responsible for Jimmy's death and in one way she was right. Your brother died trying to save my life. Whether or not I had actually pulled the trigger, I was responsible, and I don't think your mother could handle the death of her firstborn after losing her only sister as a young girl. I couldn't blame her for how she was feeling. I was devastated myself. I couldn't find a way to convince her that I still loved you all. As one letter after another came back unopened, I knew our bond of trust had been broken. What I'm trying to say, David, is if you lost faith in me or felt abandoned, I can understand why. I'm so sorry for any pain this caused you and even more sorry for not being there for you when you were growing up."

Tears welled in David's eyes. "Pop, thanks for saying that, but you're the one who's been wronged. We should never have lost faith in you. I should've trusted in the man you were."

"How old did you say your son James is?"

"Seven, going on eight soon."

"About the same age you were when all this happened. Would you expect James to be able to figure out all these conflicting things going on at his age?"

David understood his question and just shook his head in response.

"Tell me more about your life."

"What would you like to know, Pop?"

"Well, can I ask about your family? You mentioned Amy and James, tell me about their mother."

"Their mother's name is Kathleen, and you'd like her quite a bit. She has a strong devotion to her faith and family."

"That's so good to hear. I hope your faith has served you well too. What about Amy and James? You told me a little in your letter."

David told Gianni about things the kids were involved in and about their personalities, and about things he had been doing with them over the past month. David didn't mention he had divorced Kathleen and that he hadn't been living with them for the past six years. He talked about volunteering at the food kitchen, coaching, and about how well things were going for him work-wise. David figured leaving work until last would show his father a good sense of priorities. He asked about how Gianni had been coping with prison life and the injustice of his conviction. Gianni displayed remarkable perspective and ability to make the best of a difficult situation.

"My biggest regret is losing my family for so long. The other two regrets are not feeling the sunshine and ocean breeze on my face and not having some real Italian cooking once in a while."

David laughed at the last one and the conversation flowed more naturally until the five-minute signal light came on all too soon. When the guard came to get Gianni, he silently stood up placing his palm on the window, and David did the same as they said goodbye.

Walking back out into the sunshine, David was surprised that his emotions had been more under control than he had anticipated, almost to the point of not feeling much emotion at all. It wasn't apparent to him what mechanisms were in play, but he had expected more volcanic emotions at seeing his father. He hadn't gone into the visiting room as the eight-year-old David, but the managed thirty-nine-year-old self-made man. He felt more as if he had dodged a bullet of disappointing his father instead of emotionally resting in a loving father's embrace, and that this feeling was coming solely from himself and not from anything his father had done. Had he expected too much? Was he holding back to avoid taking an emotional risk? Was he even fully recognizing that this was actually his father he had just met with? He couldn't answer any of his own questions and wasn't sure, at the moment, if he even wanted to.

When David exited the gangway at Logan Airport, he noticed someone sitting there waiting—Tom. David shook his head in disbelief. "What the heck are you doing here?"

"I was thinking of a tropical vacation, but I couldn't decide which island to fly to, so I've just been sitting here frozen in Boston."

David sat down next to him. "Sure. Sure. And I have a sure bet at the track for you. So, what are you really doing here?"

"I know how much you hate riding in those limos, so I thought I'd offer you the ride you really deserve, in your favorite broken-down Honda hatchback."

David laughed. "I hope you're not expecting a big tip."

On the way home, David told Tom all about his visit with his father and his observations about his own unexpected feelings. Tom listened and let David talk his feelings out. Within twenty minutes they were in front of David's Beacon Street apartment. He thanked Tom for the luxury ride and grabbed his bag.

Tom rolled down the passenger side window. "Thanks for the company, but you weren't much help with my tropical island dilemma."

"I will see what I can come up with. Thanks for the ride and for listening."

Tom leaned towards the passenger window. "It's a start, David. Let the relationship and your feelings unfold naturally." David smiled before unlocking the door to his apartment.

Chapter 40

James had asked to have Thanksgiving "leftovers" together, so David drove to Hingham on Sunday to be with his family. David forgot how much he missed Kathleen's knack for making simple foods taste great. The turkey was tasty, as were the stuffing, potatoes, peas, bread, and homemade eggnog. By the time the squash pie was attacked and conquered, everyone leaned back stuffed and happy.

When they were alone, David talked to Kathleen about the shocking news and his visit to see his father on Saturday. Kathleen sat quietly for a minute then tears welled in her eyes and rolled down her cheeks. David put his arm around her before calling Amy and James down to share the story of the grandfather they never knew. Neither David nor Kathleen had ever talked to the kids about their grandfather's conviction and assumed death.

As Amy and James sat on the couch, David could tell that Amy knew something was up as she obviously noticed that her mother had been crying. "Amy, James, I have some news to share with you that I only learned of myself a short time ago. You probably noticed that I've never really spoken before about your grandfather, my father, other than that he was no longer alive. I found out this fall that he is actually alive. I visited him yesterday, and we talked about both of you, which made him very happy."

Amy froze in open-mouthed shock. James jumped up. "I have two grandfathers!"

David laughed.

Amy said, "How could you not know your father was alive? Was he missing from the war?"

"It's a long story," David said as began to tell them about his family life as a young boy and the events that changed the course of his life when he was eight and finally how he came to know the truth.

"Wow," James said, "that is so cool! Can I tell my friends?"

Amy said, "That's unbelievable! If he's innocent, when can he get out? When can we meet him?"

Kathleen placed a hand on her shoulder. "Amy, we know the truth about Grandpa Fidele's innocence, but there may not be any living witnesses that could testify to it in court."

"That's not fair!" Amy cried at the injustice. "How can you keep an innocent man in prison? There must be something we can do?"

David replied, "We will do everything possible, Amy. Everything."

"Why did you call him Grandpa Fidele instead of Kelly?" Amy asked.

"That was his name. My mother had our last names legally changed to her maiden name after the conviction, and I've been a Kelly for so long that—"

"My name is really Amy Fidele?"

James said, "Maybe we can have two last names!"

After dinner, David helped Kathleen with the dishes. As they stood side by side at the kitchen sink, David stared out the window and then caught Kathleen gazing at him as she had when they first married.

Suddenly, in that look, David saw their history; destruction of the most important relationship in her life, breaking an important commitment to the children, and losing someone she loved for a reason she still did not truly understand. It had all been devastating to Kathleen, and yet, she'd never displayed anger or resentment towards David, only pity for someone she still cared deeply about. During the years of their marriage, he had slowly pulled back from the discomfort of closeness, that invasion of his managed self. In response, she got busier with the kids, Church, and the community, but that had led him to feel quite alone at times, an aloneness he sought and feared at the same time.

Normally, on the way home, David felt a subconscious sense of relief, but this evening he felt lonely. Once in his apartment, the feeling of emptiness was only broken by Trooper. Once in his chair, he thought back to dating Kathleen in college. Things seemed simpler then. He was focused on college, working at a small restaurant in town, and at odd jobs in Lynn cutting lawns in the summer and shoveling snow in the winter, playing basketball, and seeing Kathleen as much as possible. Her parents wished he had a foundation in faith, but they liked him and knew Kathleen believed in him and loved him deeply. He began working internships when IMG was a start-up and did so well at his inside sales assignments that he became an assistant sales rep before finishing his senior year, making more money than his mother did full-time at the General Electric in Lynn. Things seemed to be finally going well for David.

Although he and Kathleen had been dating for over four years, David hadn't been thinking about getting married at this point in his life, but after sharing Thanksgiving dinner with Kathleen's family in 1984, he decided that he wanted to ask Kathleen for her hand. He owned an old Chevy Malibu car by then, and on December 13, kidnapped Kathleen out of her Art History class to take her for a ride up the winding North Shore roads through the old towns of Beverly, Essex, and then Manchester-by-the-Sea until they parked at a beautiful beach called Singing Beach. Despite the time of year, the temperature was in the mid-sixties, and it was a perfect break from the shorter, colder and more intense days of study. The small half-mile beach was in the shape of a horseshoe, with rugged Maine-like rocks acting as protection on either end and sand in between that made a bird-like singing sound with each slide of their feet. David had never taken Kathleen there, but he knew she'd love it. They bought ice cream cones at a small shop up the road and walked barefoot with arms around each other's waist while enjoying their cones and the sounds of the waves beside them.

David loved making Kathleen smile, and as she took deep breaths of the ocean air and let the sun rest on her grinning face with her eyes closed, he knew she was happy. As they walked, David said, "You know, Kat, there's a legend that dangerous pirates from the Barbary Coast landed on this very beach several hundred years ago and buried their treasure here to escape their hunters."

Kathleen laughed. "I'll bet there's as much chance of there being pirate's treasure on this beach as there is that you even know where the Barbary Coast is!"

David didn't answer but stopped in his tracks, putting his arm out to stop Kathleen from walking further. David stared down at a spot in the sand.

"David, what is it?"

David dropped to his knees, and said in a serious tone, "I don't know." His hand started to brush aside the sand, and he finally said, "I guess it was nothing. I thought I saw something. Wait, hold on a second." David brushed the coarse sand very gently. Kathleen squatted down next to him, waiting for David to show her what he found. David had his right knee in the sand as he uncovered something. He gazed up into Kathleen's eyes and lifted his hand eye-height. "Would a most incredible and beautiful young woman named Kathleen O'Shea ever consider spending the rest of her life with a poor, shy boy who will try his very best to love her, honor her, and be by her side?"

Breathless, Kathleen's eyes filled with tears as he held up the diamond ring in his sandy hand. She put her arms around him. "Yes! Kathleen O'Shea would very much love to spend every day of her life with David Kelly." She held David, kissed him and held him some more. "I don't know if I ever imagined being this happy. I love you, David."

David knew Kathleen had always dreamed of a September wedding, and they set the date for September 14, 1985. He was kept in the dark about where they were going for their honeymoon, which was the prime source of joking during the reception. Kathleen paid for the tickets and friends of her parents helped with a timeshare they had in the Bahamas. Kathleen even bought clothes for warm beach weather and packed for David. With a six-hour flight that was delayed and the heavy rains when they finally got to their destination in the pitch black, both David and Kathleen were dead tired and fell soundly to sleep on their wedding bed without their first anticipated moments of physical intimacy. Waiting for marriage was something that meant a great deal to Kathleen that David didn't fully understand but honored during their courting. As the bright morning sunlight made its way into their honeymoon suite, David woke up on a large, comfortable bed in a bamboo hut with a thatched roof. The sunshine was streaming in through the bamboo doors, showing glimpses of a palm tree and the tropical ocean water outside. As he turned his head, Kathleen's side of the bed was empty, and he quickly tried to collect his thoughts about last night. He opened the door to what could only be described as a private island oasis, but this didn't match the sight of his young bride at the end of the hut's private dock.

As incredibly beautiful as everything was surrounding him on the tropical island, nothing compared to seeing Kathleen's feminine body for the first time. The sun on her long brown hair and shoulders, the curve of her back, the perfect symmetry of her form and her shapely bare legs made for a moment that David could have melted into for eternity.

Kathleen playfully dove into the clear emerald water and came up turning towards David with an invitation to join. It didn't take David more than a fraction of a second to dive off the pier. She wrapped her arms around David's shoulders, kissed him passionately, and they made love for the first time in the tropical morning waters of their own private beach and then again when they got back into their small bamboo bungalow hut. Kathleen was as in love as she had ever hoped for, and David felt the hope of more than he had ever thought possible for himself as they began their life journey together.

David sat back in his chair trying to follow what could take him from that moment to walking out the door ten years later. He had become more involved in his work and driven by success. Kathleen was more involved with the kids and the community. Later nights and weekends, frequent trips and work becoming more of the priority in his life, all seemed justified to David as he provided a safe future for his family. Any conversations or arguments over his logic with Kathleen led to David putting a quick end to the discussions. As he became less and less involved and spent less and less time at home, David became a stranger to the kids, and they became strangers to him.

On their tenth anniversary, David came home after midnight due to negotiating a large customer deal, which didn't lead to a loving conversation that night. David ended up driving back into town to spend the night at a hotel, and then the next night until he came home to tell Kathleen that he was going to live in town for a while. Most of his sales team had gone through divorces of their own and only helped to convince David that he needed to separate from Kathleen. Within six months, David purchased his Beacon Street apartment and offered Kathleen a very comfortable settlement of divorce she didn't accept, not for more money but because she didn't believe in divorce or that their marriage was over. She was more worried about David than angry because, as much as she believed in David, she knew him well enough to understand that he was running away from life, not towards it.

David's thoughts shifted to visiting his father and why there was more of a level of discomfort than joy in finally seeing him. David thought about the things he should be doing as a man. Telling his dad he left a woman like Kathleen for no good reason other than selfishness and a long list of meaningless priorities left David with a feeling of shame and failure. He couldn't justify what he had done to Kathleen, Amy, and James in exchange for success, power, pleasure, and possessions.

Somewhere in his train of thought, Tom's words about Kathleen believing they were still married finally hit him. It wasn't only that Kathleen believed they were still married, but that Tom was also saying he was too. How could this concept have slipped by him so easily? David's instincts from his years in business quickly led him to look at identifying the problem and the best solutions based on the best inputs. *What would my father tell me to do next? What would God want me to do?* David was surprised by those first two new sources of direction. He finally thought, *What would an authentic man of honor do?*

David sat and thought for quite a while, then called her.

Kathleen answered. "Hello."

"Hello, Kat, it's David."

"Is everything okay? Did you get home all right?"

"Yes. Yes. I got here safe and sound."

Kathleen hesitated. "Did you leave something?"

"I guess you could say that. I wanted to talk to you about something and wondered if you might be available for dinner tomorrow?"

Her voice wavered. "I think my evening is open, but could you tell me what you want to talk about?"

"Sure. I will let you know tomorrow at seven. Sleep well."

He hung up, took a deep breath, and headed to bed.

Chapter 41

David left a message that he'd bring a pizza by for the kids and arrived a little before seven o'clock to pick up Kathleen. He was holding the hot pizza when James greeted him at the door, wrapping his arms around his father's waist. Amy came down with a more reserved greeting and a quizzical expression on her face. Finally, Kathleen descended the stairs looking as attractive as she had when David first met her on campus, dressed nicely but not too formally, since she had no idea what the get-together was all about. They chatted in the foyer for a minute, then drove only a few minutes down the road before he pulled in front a spot familiar to both of them. The quaint Button Island Café was the first place that David and Kathleen had shared a meal when purchasing their home in Hingham.

They sat at a corner table, overlooking the harbor and tiny Button Island, which would only have been visible if the lights of a boat shone behind it. He ordered a house merlot, and he raised his glass to Kathleen over the small table candle as she did the same, waiting for him to provide some clue for the dinner invitation. Finally, David said, "Thanks for being willing to see me tonight. I know this was out of the blue, and I didn't even let you know what I wanted to talk about."

"No, you didn't, but I trusted that you wouldn't have called if there wasn't a good reason."

He leaned forward, just slightly, his fingers playing with the stem of the wine glass. "How could you trust anything I say anymore? I made the most important promises to you and broke them, and I know I've hurt you and the kids deeply."

Kathleen gazed at him several moments without speaking or her face exposing the chaotic thoughts that probably whirled in her brain.

Finally, she replied. "As much as I want to tell you not to be too hard on yourself, I'm not going to argue with you on this."

"I understand. Well, what I wanted to talk to you about relates to a new friend."

The narrowing of Kathleen's eyes, of her whole face, made David pause, and it dawned on him why: she thought he meant a female friend. He shook his head without even thinking about it. "A priest. This person is a priest. His name is Tom, or I guess it would be Father Tom to you."

Kathleen's eyes widened. "Really?"

"Yes, really, but don't get any wrong ideas. Anyway, Tom and I were talking about you."

"About me? What were you saying about me to a total stranger?"

David smiled. "Trust me, he is no stranger. I was talking about you and well—um, he was talking about how you might be viewing marriage differently from me, and that is why, as far as I know, you haven't dated since we separated."

Kathleen shook her head, appearing more confused. "I'm not sure where you're going with this, and to be perfectly straight on one thing, we didn't separate, you left."

"You're right. I want to apologize for not being the man I promised you on our wedding day. I didn't live up to my vows. I didn't love you as you deserved and still deserve. I deserted you and the kids, thinking solely about myself and not the impact it would have on the family. You would think that I, above all people, should've known what broken trust and abandonment can do to a child's life. Tom tried to tell me what true marriage is and why it's meant to be forever and not just some nice words to say at the wedding."

Kathleen's eyes filled with tears. "David, what are you trying to say?"

"I told you that I met my father for the first time in thirty-one years. He made me think about what being a man means and what things in life are important. Almost nothing I've filled my life with was on that list except for the time I was with you and the children. I want to be a real man, Kathleen, one that I and my father can be proud of. I don't know if you would even consider this, but could you ever find it in your heart to forgive me and trust me again after all the pain I've caused? Father Tom said you may believe we are still married in the eyes of God, regardless of any legal paperwork. I didn't know if that would also mean you could love me again as your husband."

Whatever their talk may have been about, Kathleen would've probably never anticipated it would be this nor been emotionally prepared. A surge of emotions played across her features—disbelief, agony, joy, love, and disbelief again. She quickly excused herself to go into the ladies' room.

David stood as she left, then collapsed in his chair. What had he expected? Immediate reconciliation? What was he thinking?! Here, in a restaurant, where showing her emotions openly was impossible. He should've known. He should've thought it through, gone to a secluded spot where they could've talked alone.

Finally, Kathleen stepped back into the Café and rejoined David at the table. He could tell she'd been crying, as her eyes were puffy and her face red, almost shaking. Once she sat down, she just stared at him and closed her eyes for a few moments before putting her thoughts into words. "I'm—I'm not sure what's going to come out of my mouth, so forgive me if this isn't all that coherent. First of all, yes, I believe we are still married, and, yes, I am still very much in love with the David that I married. I think Amy and James desperately need a family with a dad, but I could never subject them to another separation. It would be too devastating to them, and to me. I want to trust you, and I want to believe that you truly believe what you're saying, but I have to be honest that I'm extremely nervous about where this might go. I need time to let it sink in."

David gazed into her eyes. They were even bluer than he remembered. In them, he saw the girl he had fallen deeply for in college. He had dated a number of women since their separation, but none were like Kathleen. "Kathleen, I know you needed no time to answer the first time but take all the time you need now. I don't blame you for being wary. As a matter of fact, I am glad you are and I'm willing to do whatever you need to help make your decision."

Kathleen, her eyes tear-filled, nodded as she exhaled through her tightened lips.

They had some not-so-fancy fish and chips for dinner and shared a bowl of Indian pudding with vanilla ice cream for dessert. Afterward, David helped Kathleen on with her coat, and they stepped outside into the crisp evening air. As they approached the car, David took her hand and they turned towards each other. She gazed up at him. "David, before I give you an answer, I will need three things."

"Anything! What?"

Suddenly, Kathleen made a step back and then whacked David on his left shoulder and then several times in the chest with all the force she had. It didn't hurt David, but he could feel her years of pain, the pain he had caused by his disloyalty, being let loose. He knew this because part of him wanted to do the same thing last Saturday against the thick glass at the prison that separated him and his father. Regardless of knowing that his father didn't intend to hurt him, he had experienced the pain of being abandoned, a pain that still remained deep in the emptiness of his very soul.

She stepped back and gasped, "David, I'm so sorry. I don't know where that came from."

He put his hands on each of her shoulders. "It's okay. It's okay, Kat. I deserved that and a lot more. I want to make up everything to you and the kids." Then he grinned. "I am a little afraid to ask about the other two things you need!"

David's comment broke the tension, and they both laughed. Then, to his surprise, Kathleen raised herself up on her toes and kissed him softly on the lips. He put his arms around her and kissed her back as a light snow began to fall.

David drove her home and gave her a goodnight kiss at the door. "I'm sorry to spring this question on you. Let me know what you need to feel comfortable with the right answer for all of us. I don't want to hurt anyone, but I don't want to foolishly let you and the kids out of my life again."

"Part of me needs no time at all but another needs some time to process everything. I don't know what that will mean, but I appreciate your understanding of how important it is. The third thing is to know that the kids won't be hurt again. I need to know that Amy and James will not be hurt if this isn't a permanent proposal. I need to trust that you will also take the time to be sure of yourself as well, regardless of how I feel. I need to put them first."

David gazed deeply into Kathleen's eyes until she returned the gesture. "I give my word. I'll do everything in my power to never hurt any of you again, as long as I live."

Kathleen nestled her head into David's shoulder and chest as he held her close in an embrace they hadn't shared for many years.

Chapter 42

During the first week of December, David made sure that all the large deals were being managed and moving through the proper process. He also worked with the basketball team practice on Wednesday and a scrimmage game on Friday afternoon. David and Tom's patience working with the boys was paying off as they got more competitive each game they played.

On Saturday morning, David took an early flight to Richmond and visited his father for the second time. David felt more at ease this visit and could offer more to the conversation by talking about his family, coaching, the food shelter, and very little about his work. Gianni's eyes were always full of love for the short sixty minutes he had to gaze upon his son, but David noticed that he seemed a little older than he had noticed on his first visit. David wanted to make him as happy as possible and making him proud of his son seemed to be one thing he could offer.

Gianni didn't preach at David, but he did try to let him know where his own strength, peace, and purpose continued to come from, despite the harsh prison life. He gave David names of some books he thought would be helpful and encouraged him to stay connected with Angelo and Tom. He felt his father wasn't judging and rejecting him, but inside he felt as if he needed to earn that trust and love.

During the second week of December, Kathleen called David to see if he'd be willing to stay in the guestroom at the house a few days a week to see how he felt about things. James loved having David come on Sunday, after they went to Mass, and stay until Tuesday morning. Amy continued to have mixed feelings and was most likely being protective of James, her mom, and herself. David was aware she was watching how he and Kathleen interacted together, and how much her mom was obviously still in love with him, despite his abandonment and infidelity. He overheard Kathleen talking to Amy about marriage commitment, forgiveness, and making sure a young woman expects and demands to be treated with respect and dignity. He was sure it must be confusing for Amy to reconcile those things when she didn't know if she could trust him yet. They were both well aware that there was considerable risk involved, and that the stakes were large when people opened up their hearts fully.

David made another trip down to Richmond on December 21. While the old prison facility was never going to feel comfortable, he was getting used to the routine and became familiar with the guards and other regular visitors. Gianni mentioned that only a handful of prisoners tended to get any visitors since they were often too far away from family or friends. Gianni told him that life had taken its time to go from unbearable to being at peace with his life. David couldn't see how that was possible, but Gianni told him, with great conviction, how much his faith has saved him mentally and spiritually.

Gianni told David that he didn't want to see him for Christmas because he wanted him to spend that time with his family. David argued a bit but knew his father was right, so he said he'd be back within a week or two.

David drove down to Hingham late that Sunday morning before Christmas. The houses along the way into town were decorated with wreaths, lights, manger scenes, and Santa's sleighs. David had strung the outdoor lights a few weeks before and today they were picking out a tree at a local farm. James picked out a "Charlie Brown" tree that made everyone else glance at each other, but he was so enthusiastic that he had found the perfect tree, no one said a word other than, "We have the perfect tree!"

When they got home, David put up the tree, while Kathleen made sure the roast and vegetables were making good progress for Sunday dinner. James helped David bring down the boxes of ornaments and lights. David handed him two packages of tinsel he had snuck into the house knowing Kathleen was adamantly against the silver, glittery strands on the tree. David smiled as he got the expression he was expecting from Kathleen, and while she tried to maintain a more serious look, she couldn't hold back her smile.

After a dinner with excited conversation, all four of them moved into the living room to begin the much-anticipated tree decorating. Even Amy seemed to relax as they trimmed the tree while listening to Christmas music in the background. Finally, when David turned on the lights to make it official, they all agreed that James did indeed pick out the perfect tree. Kathleen made some hot chocolate while David arranged the logs in the fireplace for a fire. They sat together to watch *It's a Wonderful Life* and at the end, James proclaimed, "See, their dad was lost, but came home for Christmas too!"

David put his arm around him. "That's right, James, and if you ring a bell, I will grow wings as well." At that, James' eyes became big enough to fall out of his head and everyone laughed.

Kathleen clapped her hands. "School tomorrow, so this party will have to continue in your dreams."

David helped bring in the mugs, washed and dried the dishes with Kathleen in the kitchen while telling her about his visit to Gianni, and how nice it was to be home for the tree trimming. Kathleen was quiet, and David noticed tears coming down her cheeks. He quickly dried his hands and turned her towards him. "What is it, Kat? What's the matter?"

Kathleen shook her head as she tried to wipe the tears with her hand.

"Look at me. I'm ready. I want this, and I want you. I'm ready to make a man's commitment to you and the kids. I'm ready to love you in good times and in bad, in sickness and in health, all the days of my life."

Kathleen closed her eyes, exhaled a deep breath, then looked up at David with emotions she couldn't control, and she pulled herself towards him. "Every part of me wants this and every part of me is terrified at the same time."

David held her close. "I told you to take all the time you need. I'm ready to be your partner, your friend, your champion, your love and to be faithful and committed to not only you but to us. I completely understand if you are still hurt or feel unsure that you can really trust me, and I'm willing to do whatever it is to work through those feelings."

Kathleen remained in David's arms and let her head rest against his chest until her tears finally slowed, and she could collect herself enough to speak. "David, I believe in you, and I so want to trust the beautiful words you are saying. I really do with all my heart. I think we were meant to be truly married and grow old together. I think God meant for us to be together, and I know I still love you and will always love only you. The man I loved and admired left us without an explanation and no reason. That doesn't mean that you didn't have a reason in your heart, but I don't understand it. I'm so afraid of believing you, that your promise that may seem right to you today but not five years from now. I can't do that to us or to you without believing your heart."

One of the reasons David was so drawn to Kathleen was her depth of honesty and insight into a situation and the people involved. This wasn't an objective work situation but deeply personal and emotional, and Kathleen had the ability to know all that was at stake, not just for now, but in the future. David didn't feel hurt or as if he wished he hadn't let Kathleen know how he felt, but he did feel as if he should go home tonight and give Kathleen some room. "Kat. I have no plans on letting you go, now or ever, but I completely understand what you're saying. I think we should find a way to talk through each concern until you feel more confident you can trust me. Don't take this the wrong way, but it might be better if I went home tonight to give you some time. I'd still like to be here for Christmas if you're okay with that?"

Kathleen nodded. "I would like that."

As they finished cleaning up together, David asked Kathleen to explain to the kids why he wasn't there in the morning. On the way home, David thought about everything Kathleen had said, agreeing that she was asking the right questions and doing the right thing.

Despite this being the end of the quarter push for sales, David had planned on taking off Christmas Eve to volunteer at My Brother's Table with several of the guys at work. Afterward, he would drive down to Hingham for a Christmas Eve party at the house where they had invited neighbors and friends. He was hoping to convince Tom to come down to meet Kathleen. He did drop by the next day at lunchtime and caught Tom in the church watching Sister Helen and a number of the students practice the nativity for Christmas Eve. David stood in the back and watched until Tom noticed him and moved to the back as he continued to watch and make a few gestures. "Happy Christmas, David. Did you want to try out for a part in the play? I think we're still looking for a realistic looking donkey."

"Do you make all of your parishioners feel this welcomed, Father Tom?"

"Only the ones that bray. What brings you by?"

"I wanted to invite you to a party at my family's house in Hingham."

Tom said with an exaggerated accent, "I would love to come to the Sowth Showa. When is this gala event?"

As soon as David said, "Christmas Eve," Tom's face dropped.

Tom could obviously see the disappointment on David's face as he said, "David, I'm sorry but Christmas Eve and Day are like the Super Bowl for priests."

"I should've thought of that. When are your Masses?"

"We have a 4:00 and then a midnight Mass."

David smiled. "Perfect! That gives you plenty of time in between."

"Right. Let me see what I can do."

Chapter 43

On Christmas Eve morning, David drove into work with his car loaded down with gifts for Izzie's family and his sales team. Despite Kathleen's response to David's "proposal," he was feeling almost relieved to have more time. About eleven, he headed over to My Brother's Table with several people from work, including Izzie, who brought Joseph, Isabelle, and Jenny with her. Sam had a big smile as David brought in the troops and assigned each their responsibilities for lunch. Later, when David handed out one hundred new winter coats, Izzie stood aghast. "Mr. Kelly, I'd swear you were Santa Claus." He shared a quick drink with Sean and Kevin at Dempsey's and was feeling a different kind of good.

He drove down to Hingham and got there just as the caterers arrived with the traditional Italian Christmas Eve menu of seven types of fishes, appetizers, drinks, and desserts. He spared no expense to make this a festive party for neighbors and friends who came—and they came. Kathleen, David, Amy, and James could hardly move in and out of the kitchen to the rooms where people were talking loudly, laughing, and enjoying themselves. At about a quarter of seven, David noticed Tom making his way through the front door, and he worked his way over to greet him. By the time he reached him to shake his hand and thank him for coming, he noticed that Angelo had accompanied him as well. Angelo gave David a hug. "I hope you don't mind my crashing, but Father Tom wouldn't take no for an answer."

David clapped Angelo on the back. "You're welcome here anytime, and I'm glad you came. The food is in the next room, but first, can I get you two a drink before you turn into pumpkins?"

Tom and Angelo both said together, "Yes," and they made their way into the room where the food and Christmas tree were. David made sure they were set and asked them to not move until he got back.

Somehow, David squeezed his way into the kitchen where Kathleen was organizing refills of the food trays. She was wearing a Santa hat and a big smile when she saw David's head above the crowd. Kathleen loved people and holiday parties and felt especially good that everyone seemed to be having a good time. He asked for someone to take over filling the trays as he grabbed Kathleen's hand and headed back out to find Tom and Angelo. When they finally got there, Amy and James were already talking with them. Angelo was playing a game with James to see if he could guess which hand held a prize.

David put his hand on Tom's shoulder. "It looks as if you've already met Amy and James. Tom. Angelo. This is Kathleen. She is responsible for all this Christmas cheer."

Kathleen looked into Tom's eyes and pursed her lips to keep from crying because she probably knew that he was the reason for the change in David. Kathleen's perception wouldn't have missed the depth and kindness in him. Kathleen wiped her hand on her apron and put it out to shake Tom's, saying, "Is it, Father Tom?"

Tom took her hand.

Kathleen said, "I can't tell you how good it is to finally meet you. I've heard so much about you from David and couldn't be more pleased that you came, especially when it's such a busy time for you."

Tom swallowed his bite of lobster. "Not too busy for David, and I've been looking forward to meeting you too."

David turned slightly. "This is Angelo, a longtime dear friend of my father. He's the reason I know about Pop. I could never repay him for what he means to both Pop and me." With the kindest eyes, Kathleen greeted Angelo and thanked him for being such a friend to Gianni. David grabbed two drinks from the table, and they all raised their glasses and wished Gianni a holy Christmas.

Tom and Angelo stayed at the party for a couple of hours before they had to return to St. Anthony's. They caught Kathleen and David near the door to say goodbye and thanked them for inviting them. She started to shake Tom's hand again, but then spontaneously gave him a hug and kissed him on the cheek. "Thank you so much and Merry Christmas."

By 10:30, most people had left to head back to their homes or go to evening Christmas services. Finally, by eleven everyone was gone and the four of them collapsed on the large couch in front of the tree. Kathleen said to the kids, "That was fun. Now, do we want to go to the midnight Mass tonight or go tomorrow morning?"

Amy said, "I'm tired but I would rather go tonight and not have to rush tomorrow."

James nodded, and to everyone's surprise, David said, "I guess I could come along."

They had to get ready and leave quickly to have any chance of finding seats at this Mass at St. Paul's Church in Hingham Center.

The choir was singing Christmas carols while people filed in and greeted each other. A friend who spotted Kathleen waved them over to a pew with space for three, which they promptly took, since few remaining spots were available. James sat happily on David's lap as they sang along with the choir until Mass began. Everything looked and sounded beautiful, but it all seemed like ritualistic pomp and circumstance to David. He hadn't been to Mass since he was eight, and that was not by mistake. He spent as much time as James just looking at the different people around them. When it came time for Communion, David stepped into the aisle and let everyone file out of the pew to receive as he sat back down until they returned. One thing that David did notice was how much this meant to Kathleen, and David had no clue why. Amy even seemed especially reverent when receiving as well.

Everyone was tired but happy as they traveled home, staring at all the homes lit up, and anticipating Christmas morning. It even started to snow just enough to give the ride a quiet, intimate feeling. When they got home, James ran upstairs and then back down with four stockings to put by the fireplace. David noticed that one of them had his name on it.

After the kids went to bed, David put his arms around Kathleen. "Are you happy, Kat?"

"I'm happy tonight just because you're here."

"Hopefully you'll get better presents than just me."

Kathleen gazed into David's eyes. "You know what I mean."

David kissed her softly, and then more passionately than they had for many years.

David knew what would be a perfect way to end the evening, but Kathleen slipped under his grasp. "You'd better watch out, you'd better not cry, you'd better not pout, and I'm telling you why," and as she reached her room she said, "Santa Claus is coming to town." David smiled as he grabbed one of Santa's cookies, leaving the crumbs on the plate that James would be sure to check in the morning, and went to his own room to sleep soundly.

James was up before daybreak and immediately woke everyone else. Kathleen put on some coffee and Amy turned on the tree lights while David lit the fire to help warm the room. They took turns opening the presents in their stockings until they reached the traditional clementine at the bottom. Amy was excited about her first cell phone, which Kathleen wasn't completely sold on. The last package under the tree was for Amy, a large, wrapped box with a series of smaller boxes inside, which she unwrapped until she finally revealed a jewelry box made of attractive woven silver. Amy thought it was beautiful, and Kathleen looked on curiously as she opened it to find a small silver card, which she read aloud, "This gift entitles the beautiful and gifted young holder of this card to a magical trip to Italy."

Kathleen gave David a look that let him know that they needed to talk.

David nodded, while, Amy squealing with delight, hugged him before he turned to help James set up his new racetrack set.

He stayed most of the day but needed to get back that evening to be at work fairly early to tend to two major deals still in the closing process. He felt as if he had a good day, and that everyone enjoyed their Christmas. Kathleen echoed the same as she helped pack up his things, bumping him with her hip. "I never got a trip to Italy."

"I would be happy to take you on a trip around the world. It was Pop's idea."

"Dad?"

"Yes. I was talking to him about Amy being at an important point in her life for making decisions that can be life-changing. Since we really don't know each other well, and she's in a difficult stage to really connect with, he said it might be good to just go somewhere and spend dedicated time together."

"New Hampshire is somewhere. Italy? And how do I know what decision path you are planning on helping her to explore?"

"I get it, and I won't take her unless you're totally comfortable with both."

"That's a promise I'll make you keep."

David hugged and kissed everyone goodbye, despite James' pleas to stay, and made his trip back to his apartment and furry companion.

Chapter 44

David caught an early flight on Saturday morning to Richmond and arrived at the prison early. He exchanged Merry Christmas greetings with the guards out front and presented his approved papers at the desk inside the visitor entrance. The desk guard smiled at David and brought his papers into an office and reemerged with his senior officer, Sergeant Bo Dillon, who asked David if he didn't mind coming into his office. David was sure his visit approvals were still valid as he followed the sergeant into his austere office. "Is everything okay with my paperwork, Sergeant Dillon?"

"Yes. There are no administrative issues. I wanted to let you know you won't be able to see your dad today."

David's eyes widened as he sat forward in his seat. "Is he all right? Did something happen to him?"

There was a hesitation in Dillon's response. "David, your father means a great deal to most of the men and guards in this prison. Everyone was saddened when he was diagnosed this past summer."

"Diagnosed? Diagnosed with what?"

Dillon walked and put his hand on David's shoulder. "I'm sorry if you didn't know, David, but your father was diagnosed with cancer. He's already gone through a series of treatments. Evidently, he may have had a relapse this week or may just be worn down."

Suddenly, David felt as if his world had turned upside down again and was in shock as he left the prison facility. Dillon wasn't able to tell him much about his father's actual medical status but did let him know the local hospital where he was being treated. He headed over to find out what he could. At the reception desk, he asked if there was anyone he could talk to about Gianni Fidele. The receptionist immediately knew his name and directed him to the nurse's station outside the room where his father had stayed. David met several nurses who had only kind words to say about Gianni and they asked David to sit in the waiting room while they flagged down Dr. Finn.

Sometime later, a tall, lanky man in a white doctor's coat stood in front of him. "Mr. Fidele, it's good to meet you. I'm Dr. Finn. I can't tell you how much of a privilege it's been to care for your father, and that's not something I often experience with patients from the prison. Please don't take that the wrong way."

David didn't bother to correct or explain the difference in last names.

"No. No problem. Can you tell me what he has, and what's being done for him?"

The doctor sat down. "Mr. Fidele, I'm sorry for this news, but there's not much more we can do for your dad. He has an advanced stage of cancer that's entering his spine."

David just sat in shock for a full minute. "How long are we talking about?"

The doctor shook his head. "I wish I could tell you. Honestly, I didn't expect him to make it through the summer, but he is both a stubborn and incredibly positive man. His will to live has been so strong that I think he has refused to let it beat him so far. It was almost as if he had something to finish in his life."

David left the hospital in a daze and a strong sense of denial that his father was sick. Nothing seemed fair after all these years of loss. Would he only get to see his father for a handful of weeks and then be left again? How could God be so cruel twice in his life, twice to a man like his father? There was little David could do over the weekend, so he took his scheduled flight home to figure out what he was going to do.

At home, he called Kathleen to let her know he wouldn't be over on the weekend and to trust that it was for a good reason. David felt as if he needed to shake this feeling of malaise that filled his head and heart. On Sunday, David called a friend at a top law firm for some advice on getting his father a release based on a medical exception. He told David that this wasn't common, but they'd begin working with their team in Virginia to put together a plea for Gianni's release into David's custody due to the immediate circumstances. He'd make his dad's case a priority, knowing that time was precious, and that David would cover any expense.

During the week, David could feel his entire being pulling back to the safe haven of the world he built over the past several decades. He'd normally have organized a New Year's Eve party for the office at Dante's, and then go down to the Cape for an extended weekend after closing out the quarter, but he did none of those. Nor did he spend New Year's with his family or see Tom. He felt like he finally had a focus and something to live for, but he knew once his father was taken from him again, that would be all gone. For the next few weeks, he worked, exercised, read, slept or just sat in his apartment waiting until he heard from the law firm and from prison that his father was up to having visitors.

On Friday afternoon, he was in his office finishing up a conference call when Izzie walked in to get his attention. He just held his hand up not to interrupt the call. Before he knew it, twelve boys in basketball uniforms walked into his office. Billy Maguire and Double J Johnson held up a warm-up jacket with the letters "ST. ANTHONY'S" stitched on a curve across the front. Before David could say anything, they turned the jacket around and the back read, "COACH KELLY." Billy handed the jacket to him. "Coach, we have a big game this afternoon and we need you there. We learned a lot from you because we believed in you and stuck with you. Now you're stuck with us."

David looked down at all the faces that had become familiar to him over the past several months. He smiled when he caught the smirk on Izzie's face. He said, "Boys, if you promise to play like we've practiced and give it your best, I'll be there cheering you on."

Double J said, "And coaching us on. We still need some work!"

Tom poked his head into David's office as the boys filed past him. "See you at the game, coach!"

David arrived at the game in his finely tailored suit and realized he probably looked more like a highly-paid NBA coach wannabe than a kids' coach. He took off his jacket and tie and slipped on his new coaching jacket to cheer the boys on. The game was fun as the team started off slowly but stayed on their game plan to fight their way back and actually won on the last play. To celebrate, they went out for pizza and arrived home full, with a feeling of satisfaction.

After the kids were dropped off back home, Tom asked David if he wanted to catch up for a bit. David was tempted to say "No," but went back to the rectory with Tom.

"We have orange tonic or some good ole—"

David smiled and exclaimed, "Moxie! I don't think I've had that stuff since my father tried to poison me with it as a kid. Do you actually drink that?"

"It is an acquired taste and this way I know Luke won't drink it up on me."

"That's for sure. It would grow some hair on his chest."

David opted for the orange soda, and Tom went for the high-test Moxie.

"How is Luke doing these days?"

"Well, he has been showing up at the Friday coffeehouses, so I've been seeing him on a more regular basis. He's such a young man now, but I worry about him in this culture."

"Now that I'm spending more time with Amy and James, I can understand your concerns, but I think you've provided a light to follow."

"Thanks. That means a lot. So, tell me how have you been? I haven't heard from you for several weeks and that's not always a good sign."

David sat back and stared at the table as he ran his fingers across it feeling as if he were at a fork in the road; one would lead him to an emotional response, the other to a managed response. He decided to take a risk. "I went down to visit my dad the Saturday after Christmas, and they said he was too sick for visitors—he has late-stage cancer they can no longer treat."

Tom's mouth fell open in shock.

"I'm working to see if they might consider a release for medical reasons, but that may take time he doesn't have. I really don't know what's going to happen here. I just know I finally got to see my father after being robbed of him for all those years and now—" David took a deep, shaky breath. "And now he is leaving me again. Why? Why would God be this cruel to him?"

"David, I'm so, so sorry. I can't imagine how devastating a blow this must be after you finally got to be with him. I can't tell you why, but I can tell you that God can never be cruel. God can only ever act out of love."

David scowled at Tom. "Well, this doesn't seem very loving."

Tom let the moment sit for a bit before responding, "You said your dad had a very strong faith, right?"

David nodded.

"To him, this life is just a small part of our entire existence, an existence which doesn't end. Like it or not, we're not made to live forever here but forever with God. Our only real decision in life is if we want to live in God's love or not. God isn't The Godfather who makes us an offer we can't refuse. He gives us the dignity of free will, and in that free will we can refuse his love."

"So, what?"

"I think your father's entire life has been a very resounding 'yes' to that offer and I believe that whatever happens from here on, he will be in very good hands. The question is, how will you be?"

David rubbed his forehead. "I don't know, but what I do know is that I'm going to do everything I can to get him released and let him have the best care I can. If I can get him back to Boston, I'd like you to meet him and show him where he put thirty years of his earnings."

Earnestly, Tom replied, "I'd be honored to meet him—and to thank him in person for his generosity and for his son as my friend. Is there anything I can do?"

David glanced up at the ceiling. "Yes. Yes, there is, Tom."

Tom sat straight up and with his palms open. "Anything. What can I do?"

David took a deep breath. "I want to become Catholic. I want to be able to take my father to Mass. I think that would make him happier than anything else I could do for him."

"Is this something that is in your heart, David, or something you want to do for your dad?"

"What? What does it matter? This is something we can do for him, and you said you would do anything."

Tom stood up and walked several steps back and forth and then sat back down and placed a hand on David's shoulder. "We can only do this if it's sincere, truly sincere. He would only want you to do this if it was. I'm impressed with all you've been doing over these past several months with the food kitchen, your generosity to the school and the boys, the time you are spending with your family, and your courage to care about your dad. For whatever reason, these are good things, but they are even better if they are done out of authentic self-giving love."

David was taken aback. "Why else would I re-prioritize my entire life and do all this if it weren't real?"

Tom said, "I didn't say it wasn't real. The question is, do we do things to feel better about ourselves or to have others accept and love us? We can even do this with God, trying to make ourselves 'good enough' for him to love. I think both God and your father love you already for who you truly are and not conditionally for what you might or might not do."

"Of course, I'm sincere. I want to do this."

"David, do you know where the word sincere comes from?"

David shook his head.

"It comes from the Latin words 'sine', meaning without, and 'cera,' meaning wax. Ancient merchants who were dishonest would use wax to hide defects or cracks in their pottery to make it look more valuable and to sell it for a higher price under false pretense. The reputable merchants would hang signs over their stalls with the term 'sine cera' or 'without wax.'"

David's forehead tightened with confusion. "So? What does this have to do with anything?"

"We all have defects, and we work really hard to make sure that no one can see them and sometimes think we are worthless because of them. We want to sell a better version of ourselves than our authentic selves. Jesus didn't come to love, teach, and save the perfect, but sinners like us. He wanted to transform us from selfish sellers of ourselves into the sincere lovers of others. We need to be able to let go and trust enough to hide nothing and know we will never be rejected or valued less. If you want to truly come into the Church that Jesus built, you need to hang a sign around your neck that reads, 'sine cera.' You need to do it for authentic belief in Christ and His Body, not as a tool to make your father proud."

Tom got up to pour them some more tonic and to give David room to think.

David was tapping his hands on the table trying to figure out his next move. "Technically, Tom, I already am a Catholic, right?"

"Were you baptized a Catholic?"

"I think so."

"Did you receive your First Communion?"

"Yeah. I did, the spring before Jimmy's death."

Tom smiled. "I'd say that you are still a 'baby Catholic.' If you are sincere about this, I would be the happiest man in Boston, but you'd still need to do a few things. You'd need to make a full confession of your serious sins to receive the sacrament of the Eucharist, basically say you repent the things that turned you away from God and that you want to be in his loving grace. Then, you would need to be confirmed in the faith. I assume you didn't receive your Confirmation?"

David shook his head. "No, but can we do it all this weekend?"

"I love the enthusiasm, but there are classes that started this past September called RCIA or Rite of Christian Initiation for Adults and I think they would help you. There are four really great people in the class, and it finishes at Easter when you would all be fully received into the Church."

David got up and started pacing. "No. No. I don't want to go to class or wait until the end of April. I don't have that kind of time. Can you just forgive my sins and do whatever ceremony is necessary for Confirmation?"

Tom softly spoke, "David. This is a bigger deal than even marriage. You need to understand what you are getting into to be truly in it. The Church isn't a solo endeavor, but a community of believers. Jesus said, 'Where two or more of you are gathered in my name, there I am among them.' How about this? How about if we meet once a week and catch up on what the RCIA group has covered so far this fall and see what you think?"

David said, "Okay. How about twice a week, to go a little faster?"

Tom laughed. "All right. Wednesday and Friday nights after basketball for the enthusiastic catechumen."

"The cata-what?"

Tom laughed louder.

Chapter 45

On that next Wednesday, David checked in with the law firm to see if they made any progress and also with the prison to see if his father was up for visitors. Both answers were negative. He went to the gym for basketball practice, and after the last boy left, he asked Tom where they were going for his first class. Tom was holding the ball at the top of the key.

"Here is fine," He shot with one hand and the ball went through the basket. "David, you know how important it has been for the boys to have the right attitude when they came to learn about the game?"

David nodded.

"At work with your sales teams, how important it is that they really listen to your instruction to 'get it' versus assuming there's nothing new to learn?"

"Okay, I understand."

"You don't ask them not to think or not to ask questions, but you ask that they listen with the right frame of mind to learn. The same goes for anything we talk about with the Church."

"I gotcha, chief. Where do we start?"

Tom held the ball in his hand again. "When you are playing basketball, what is always, always, always the focal point of the game?"

David pointed to the ball. "The basketball."

"Right. I'll probably get into trouble for this analogy but, in everything we talk about, think of Christ as the ball and keep your eye on him. Jesus said, 'I am the way, and the truth, and the life; no one comes to the Father but by me.' Did you ever hear of the term 'Incarnation'?"

"Nope."

"Most of us either take it for granted or just don't believe it, but the Incarnation is that God took on flesh and became one of us, so we could become like Him. Jesus is God Whom we can see, touch, and know, and Who experienced everything we experience as He gave His entire self for us. The Incarnation reveals to us things we wouldn't have known about God otherwise. It reveals to us that God is a community of love in the Trinity, three persons in one God. It's not an easy concept to get your head around, but Jesus told us He and the Father were one, 'When you see me, you see the Father.' In Genesis, it talks about God creating the universe and when it came to creating man, the Word reads, 'And God said, Let us make man in our image, after our likeness.'"

"Did you say, 'Let us?'"

"Yes, us. God is the Father, Son, and Holy Spirit, and we are made for God in Their image to be with God. He made us with worth, purpose, and for His love. We just need to trust in His loving plan for us, in His unconditional and never-failing love. Jesus is the Word of God made flesh, so what He does and what He says is the truth and shows us what life is all about. God gave Adam and Eve everything, but they failed to trust in His love. They grasped for the forbidden fruit in the desire to be God, to be the deciders of what is right and what is wrong for themselves, because they thought God was holding out on them. Jesus shows us that God holds nothing back, not even His only Son, who pours Himself out for us in mercy and love."

"Huh."

"Who let go and trusted God when faced with an incredible ask?"

"I guess Jesus?"

"Sure, but who else?"

"I don't know. Who?"

"Mary. Mary was asked as a young girl to become the mother of God. She said, 'Yes,' fully trusting in God's plan without knowing what was going to happen to her. She was the new Eve and Jesus – "

David interrupted. "And Jesus was the new Adam?"

Tom smiled. "Yes! Jesus was fully divine but also fully human, so He felt the physical and emotional pain and the doubt, yet still trusted fully.

"Think of this—God made Adam. Then Eve came from Adam's side. Now the new Adam comes from the new Eve through the Holy Spirit. Perfect symmetry, if you ask me. So, you know the story, Jesus was born as the new King under the most humble of circumstances. He grows up to teach of God's love for us and what we must do. He gave His life so we may have a life with God in heaven. But what did He do before He ascended into heaven?"

"Tom, ask me some questions I can answer."

"He taught and trained His apostles. He gave them not only instructions but the authority to teach in His name, to perform miracles, to forgive sins, and to bring us the presence of Christ in the breaking of the bread and in the wine. He built His Church. 'And I tell you, you are Peter, and on this rock, I will build my church, and the gates of hell will not prevail against it.' Lastly, Jesus promised them the gift of the Holy Spirit which we fully receive in Confirmation. He told His apostles, 'I have yet many things to say to you, but you cannot bear them now. When the Holy Spirit of truth comes, He will guide you into all truth."

Tom took a shot and put it through the net without touching any iron. "That's probably enough for our first class, young man. Everything we talk about going forward will have this as the foundation, so it is important for this to sink in, even a little bit. Are you up for a quick bite? I promise not to talk shop."

David replied, "I'm starving, but I might have a few questions if you don't mind working overtime."

As much as they enjoyed Dempsey's, they both agreed that tonight Chinese was in order and meandered over as Luke walked toward them. He greeted them with an upbeat smile and hug as he turned to walk with them.

"Good to see you, Luke," Tom said. "Are you up for some lo mein?"

"I'd love to, but I just dropped by to let you know I'm planning on going to Peru for the spring semester. I'll be leaving on Saturday."

Tom exclaimed, "Peru! Why Peru? What's this all about?"

Luke had both of his hands in his pockets and was moving his feet back and forth to stay warm. "Okay, I'm going down with a girl from school." As soon as he saw Tom's entire being sink out of concern and disappointment, Luke's hands came out of his pockets to hold his brother's arms. "It's not what you think. This girl is really different."

Tom shook his head.

"Tom, we're going on a mission trip for the semester. Her name is Kathryn. We'll be properly chaperoned. She'll be staying in the convent with the Dominican Sisters while I'm staying with a family who's involved in this mission work to help build homes, medical clinics, schools, and small farms. Kathryn flew down during spring break last year with a Catholic group from school, so you should love her."

Tom closed his eyes and let out a sigh of relief.

"I really like this girl, and I won't say that it's not a big part of why I'm going. There's something deep and real about Kathryn I haven't run into before. She has a strong set of morals and doesn't apologize for it. She has a conviction about herself and what is important in life, which I love. So, you don't have to worry about us shacking-up because she's already let me know she wants the real thing. She told me on our first date, 'Women were called to inspire, not to seduce.' I'll be okay, and I think this will be a good thing for me."

Tom put his arm around his younger brother and pulled him close. "You never cease to surprise me, Luke. I'll pray for you, though, and you have to promise to write, a lot. Do you need any money for the trip?"

"Thanks, Tom. I'm okay for money. I'll let you know how things are going at least once a week."

They hugged, and Luke headed back in the direction of his school as Tom and David headed off for some Mandarin cuisine.

Over the next several days, David wrestled with his conflicting feelings about his dad and some things Tom had said. As they sat in the two cushioned chairs in Tom's office on Friday night, David wasn't sure if Church was what he wanted to talk about.

Tom asked, "How have you been this week?"

David sighed. "I'm not so sure. I was thinking about some things you had said about knowing what motives were really behind my decisions."

Tom sat patiently, probably waiting for David to expound, but David only continued to stare at the floor.

"How do you feel about this news concerning your father?"

"I think I'm mostly in shock."

"Are you angry?"

"I don't know. I guess that I should be."

"This won't sound right, and I'm not saying this because you don't care but because I know you do, but do you feel any sense of relief?"

David shot a cold glare at Tom while inside he knew he had experienced a feeling of relief and was ashamed of it.

"Here's my concern for you, David. You had what I would call a traumatic event over a long period of time—something you couldn't just flip the switch on after thirty years. It would be natural to believe the reason you were abandoned might have even been your fault. You might even suffer from a fear of rejection of your true self, whom you are protecting. A lifetime could be spent trying to prove to yourself that you aren't worthless through a strong drive to be successful, powerful and protected by material things. Deep inside, though, those things don't remove the fear that you actually deserved to be abandoned or rejected. It would be a natural subconscious relief to not have to face those feelings head-on. Does that make any sense?"

"I think I put all those issues in the rearview mirror a long, long time ago."

"I understand, but that doesn't always mean you've really dealt with them. Often it means working overtime to avoid them, impacting our ability to accept our true selves. This, in turn, affects our ability to be intimate and open with others, to be at peace. I'm not trying to tell you what you feel. I can't know that, but I think you've experienced some pretty sharp pull-backs since we've known each other and in your major relationships. I think it could be helpful to see if there are opportunities to peel that well-constructed onion back a few layers. What do you think?"

"I don't think so."

"Well, it's always up to you, but we tend to resist changing things, even if they cause incredible anxiety or even deep depression."

David laughed. "Are you trying to say that I'm depressed?"

"No, not at all. I am saying our minds work to fool us at times in ways we think are helping and protecting us, but actually, keep us from living life. Remember when I said that the adaptations we used to cope when we were young tend to become maladaptations when we move into adulthood. If a person is abused when they are young, withdrawal may be an effective way to cope and protect themselves as a child, but then that withdrawal habit can compromise their life as an adult. People subconsciously resist doing things to remove depression, anxiety, or other uncomfortable feelings because they think those feelings somehow provide protection or that they even deserve those feelings. They may also think, if they removed that coping mechanism, they would be vulnerable, or it would minimize what had happened to them. That resistance can be very strong and is very common."

"I'm not resistant, I'm just not interested."

"Or willing to take the risk or pay the price?"

David stood up and shot back, "Do you mean like you and Corlie?"

David knew this would hurt, but there were no signs that Tom took this lash-back personally. David rushed out of the rectory without saying another word. He felt a high level of discomfort with the conversation. Who was Tom to be poking at his mental state when he had his own baggage and uncomfortable truths? What would be the point in talking about how he had felt as a boy? He wasn't a boy anymore and couldn't change the past, but only deal with the present. Maybe his life was built on avoiding sensitive areas from his past, but it also provided motivation to drive himself to be the man he was today, and he was working to correct the mistakes he'd made. The more he walked, the more he was starting to feel agitated and uncomfortable with the unsolicited conversation. David found himself replaying the conversation back and forth to himself.

After an hour of walking, David had flushed out most of the agitation and moved to an honest recognition that he had impacted people with his avoidance and probably was doing things to gain his father's approval. He started asking himself if spending time with his kids and promising his wife a real commitment was more to show his dad he was worthy of his love than out of a true act of love. One thing David was beginning to be sure of was that he wasn't all that sure of anything right now.

Trooper was waiting for him at the door, seeming as if he knew exactly how David felt.

Chapter 46

The next morning, after another night of tossing and turning, David took a morning run with the intent of seeing Tom. Once he got there, he resisted the desire to turn around. David crossed the street and slowly approached Tom, who was saying goodbye to parishioners from morning Mass. The two stood silently before David said, "I'm sorry for leaving so abruptly, again."

He shook David's hand. "Not a problem. I was poking in uncomfortable territory."

"I feel a bit lost. I have no desire to go where I need to go, and I think I need help."

Tom gave a subtle nod. "I know some really good counselors—"

"No! I'll only talk to you. I need someone I can trust."

Tom put his hands on David's shoulders and peered curiously into David's eyes. "You trust me, David? You know, it's not a good idea for a friend to be your counselor. To make any progress, you may have to go to very uncomfortable places and withstand the trials of seeing the ugliest parts of yourself, to be displeasing to yourself. That can be very difficult to do with someone you know; it could end the friendship."

David smirked. "I'm willing to lose you, but isn't it you who said true love is being able to show yourself, warts and all, and know you will still be loved unconditionally?"

Tom nodded, and David took off on his run without a word.

Wednesday afternoon, David enjoyed himself working with the boys on new plays and thought of nothing else but his interactions with the boys. After practice was over, David wasn't sure what to expect next. After collecting the balls, Tom said, "I have an idea. What do you think about continuing to study the Catholic faith on Wednesdays and then use Fridays for what we discussed Saturday morning?"

"So that I can have the weekend to put myself back together?"

"Something like that. Do you mind going over to the church for tonight's class?"

David frowned. "I kind of like thinking of a basketball gym as my church."

"We could do that, but tonight the church might work better for this."

Tom opened the doors of the church and waved David in. "I don't know if you've ever heard of G.K. Chesterton, but he would've loved the pub debates we've been having. He once said, 'When he has entered the Church, he finds the Church is much larger inside than it is outside.' One of the first things to know about the Church is that it's not this building or any building; it's not even what people might think of as a human organization that is a coming together of like-minded people for some mundane purpose."

David stared at the high arches of the church and the rare beauty of its architecture. "Why do they call this building a 'church' then?"

"This is the sacred space where members of the Church gather and where most of the sacraments are celebrated. This is where we come together as a community, to hear the word of God himself, to be strengthened by his grace, guided by truth, and to be in the real presence of Christ and he in us. So, in some ways, it is just a building, but in other ways, it's part of something special."

"Okay, but there seems to be a heck of a lot of made-up rituals and noise. If you want to be spiritual, why do you need a building or all this religion to get in the way of keeping it simple and more direct?"

Tom smiled.

"Do you think my question is funny?"

"No. No. It's one of the most common questions I get. 'Spiritual, but not religious.' We talked about this a few months back at the pub. I think personal spiritual seeking can be a good thing. We should seek the truth about ourselves and God. The problem is that we're very human and our solo journeys of faith usually don't work and usually are rooted in a flawed approach. Ask a hundred people who are 'spiritual but not religious' how it's going so far, and most will say they haven't really gotten fully into it. When we seek God, we have a human tendency to do it on our own terms and begin to create a God in our image. When we put ourselves in charge, we see what our limited imagination can see, and we choose the parts of God we want to see. The key to the spiritual life is to understand it is God Himself who seeks us and chooses us, and not the other way around. God has revealed Himself to us through His Word, through the Incarnation, the teaching and loving example of Jesus, through the Holy Spirit, and the Church Jesus built and left for us as the 'pillar and foundation of truth.'"

Tom held his hands open. "Here is the tough part. Think of the Church as not a building or organization but as the Body of Christ Himself. He told us we are members of His body and we see God more fully through his eyes and words than anything that comes from our limited human understanding or imagination. Jesus gave a hard time to the religious people who weren't spiritual, but as a very religious man Himself, He taught that the two go indispensably together. He knew our human side and our needs better than anyone, so He left us Himself in a Church that understood that need.

"Jesus said, 'I will build my Church and the gates of hell will not prevail against it.' Do you think any human organization with all the corruption of individuals in it would've done anything but collapse a long time ago? He said His Church would be the light of the world, a city on a hill that cannot hide and that the Holy Spirit would guide it in truth. The other side of the coin is that the Church is also us, and we have our problems. It's a community of sinners, so we will always have failings at all levels in the Church, but at its core, it is the Body of Christ and can never fail to be true. Jesus said He is the vine, and we are branches and a branch cannot bear fruit unless it abides in the vine. That is why it's so important for us to belong to His Body, to be part of his Church."

Tom's words weren't totally resonating with him. David said, "Okay, but that doesn't answer my questions about all the rituals and ceremony, the rules and regulations."

"Give me an example."

They were still standing in the back of the church. "How about all the things you have to do to 'get in,' like Baptism and Confirmation. Why do you need to go through those ceremonies to be acceptable?"

"I think that's a very fair question. At work, if a sales rep asked you why they needed to go through your training, spend time with customers, learn the products, or be at work to be on your team, what would you say?"

"I'd tell him to find another place to work."

"But what if I told you that he was really good at selling and would be a top member of your team?"

David saw his point and frowned. "Then I'd tell him to keep an open mind and trust my guidance that they'll come to see why these things were important to help combine what he needed with the skills he brought."

"Okay. Now God knows He has already made you acceptable, but He also knows you need His grace to follow and be in Him. Jesus knew we are human and initiated sacraments to help give us the grace, strength, and understanding we need so we could know God's love and plan for us. These sacraments aren't useless noise but practical and important ways for us to become holy and close to God."

David followed Tom up the center aisle. "All right, I'll ask the plant question for the class. What actually is a sacrament? You mention the term like it's something essential like I would use the term 'selling value' in my sales training. What the heck is a sacrament?"

Tom slipped David a dollar bill from his pocket. "Good question!" Tom stopped beside the Baptismal font. "Think of sacraments this way. We are both physical and spiritual beings. Instead of just talking in flowery intellectual words, as I might tend to do, Jesus used stories, and He also used very physical things such as water, bread, wine, fish, and even mud to make His points, perform miracles, and to leave us with sacraments. Sacraments are visible signs from Jesus which give us spiritual grace and help us when it comes to God's love and plans for us. Some are more of an initiation into the faith like Baptism, Confirmation, and Eucharist; some are for healing such as Reconciliation and Anointing of the Sick; and some are for service and mission, such as Matrimony and Holy Orders. Each one came from Jesus Himself and was carried on by the apostles from the early Church to the present."

Tom cupped his hand in the water of the Baptismal font. "What sacrament uses water as a sign?"

David laughed. "Do I get to phone a friend?"

"Nope, because I know that you know this one."

"Okay, Baptism. It washes the stain of sin from a baby who couldn't have committed any sins. How practical is that?"

"You're correct that this newborn couldn't commit sin, so why does it need Baptism to wash away sin? When a baby is born to a mother who is addicted to drugs, does that have an effect on the baby?"

"Sure."

"Was it because of anything the baby did or the result of the condition they were born into?"

"From their parents. Okay, I get the analogy, but what does Baptism really do for the baby?"

"Did you notice that the Baptismal font is located here at the back, or entrance of the church?"

David noticed the font and the surroundings. "Sure. I thought maybe there wasn't enough room in the front?"

Tom smiled at David's subtle sarcasm. "Baptism is like the door to the spiritual life of God. Jesus said, 'No one can enter the kingdom of heaven without being born of water and spirit.' While Jesus didn't need to be baptized, he went to the river where John the Baptist was baptizing people repenting and confessing their sins in order to come back to God. When he saw his cousin, Jesus, coming to be baptized, he balked but did what Jesus asked; a voice from heaven was heard saying, 'This is my beloved Son in whom I am well pleased.'"

David was working to listen and connect this to himself. Tom said, "David, Baptism is the grace that brings us into sharing the divine life.

While we are called to be morally good people, this is an unearned gift through God's love to be beloved adopted sons and daughters of God with whom He is well pleased. It's not something we do or earn in Baptism, but rather God breaking into our lives and fundamentally changing us as we are born again or born from above. Remember Jesus saying that what is born of the flesh is flesh and what is born of Spirit is spirit? This isn't saying flesh or nature is bad, but that grace builds on nature to bring flesh and spirit together, like Christ himself. It takes the ordinary and allows it to participate in the divine. When we are blessed in the name of the Father, the Son, and the Holy Spirit, we are marked as adopted sons and daughters of God, as we're made in their image."

David looked into the waters of the font. "Yes. Are you saying it's not that we are bad and need to be cleaned to be good enough, but that we are made good and baptism brings us into God's family in a spiritual way?"

"I think you're getting it. We need to be born again in washing away the sins of our fallen nature, but you're right that we are now officially in the family." Tom pointed up at the Rose window. "Do you remember when we talked about the problems of putting power, wealth, sex, success, or anything material at the center of our lives?"

David's face dropped a bit as he begrudgingly said, "Yeees."

"What if I told you none of those things were considered bad?"

David leaned forward, confused. "Come again?"

"Sexual expression of love and your oneness with your wife isn't bad but good and beautiful because it's part of God's design and intent and done for His glory. Power and wealth can be good things if used not for self-serving reasons or as an end in themselves but for good and for God's plan. God wants us to know the joy of an abundant life, but we can only really experience this when we give of ourselves by loving as God would love. Baptism brings us into that divine life with meaning and purpose. I think if you want something with a return like that, it's a pretty practical pool to jump into."

Tom blessed himself with the holy water from the font and then made a Sign of the Cross on David's head with his wet thumb. "I think that's enough for tonight. Any questions will have to wait for a burger at Dempsey's."

David clasped his own throat. "Thirsty!"

They both laughed, and Tom genuflected towards the front of the church before they left.

"So," Tom said once they were outside and walking towards Dempsey's, "now can you see why the font is at the entrance as you come into church with a reminder of your Baptism?"

"I'm getting the idea that everything in Church is intentional and has a meaning I didn't understand before."

"Kind of like when that new sales rep finally starts to get what you're trying to have him see or one of the boys on the basketball team?"

"Kind of."

"And, whether you knew it or not, because you are baptized, you are on the team."

David nodded.

Tom grinned. "And I know how much you hate sitting on the bench."

Chapter 47

On Friday, David woke up feeling a little nervous in anticipation of his talk with Tom that evening. The day at work was busy, and coaching the game right afterward made it a little easier not to think too much about it, but as he walked into the rectory, the underlying panic started to creep into him, with nervous tension in his chest and the jim-jams in his stomach. Tom had gone to the kitchen to get something for them to drink while David sat in Tom's office. On Tom's desk was a small block of wood with a saying that read: *What is the first business of philosophy? To part with self-conceit.... It is impossible for anyone to begin to learn what he thinks he already knows. – Epictetus (c. 100 A.D.)* When David spun the block around there was a saying on the other side: *The greatest trap in life is self-rejection. Henri Nouwen.*

Tom came into the office probably feeling almost as nervous as David. David figured that balancing friendship and his responsibilities as a therapist was a difficult task. The risk a patient had to take in being really honest can feel terrifying, embarrassing, and even shameful at first. Leaning into fear is much easier to talk about than to actually do, but Tom had told him that a lifetime of avoiding fears was a hundred times harder than actually facing them.

"Tough game tonight, but I see a lot of progress with some kids. Why don't we sit over here?" Tom motioned to the upholstered wing chairs by the bookcase.

David glanced at all the books on psychology, philosophy, and faith. There were also biographies and books by people who had faced steeper challenges than he had. He cleared his throat. "So how does this go, doc?"

Chuckling, Tom said, "You might be able to tell me. What are some things that you think you might want to be different?"

"I don't know if I need anything to be different. I'm just trying my best to make people in my life happy and do a better job of being honest with myself."

Tom nodded. "Okay, remember you only have to share what you are willing to. I may push you a bit at times but you're still in charge of the direction you take and the waves you dive into."

"Waves?"

"Do you remember when you were at the beach as a kid and a large wave rose up? You tried to outrun it, but it was always faster than you.

Sometimes emotions are scary, and we spend our lives running from them versus diving through them to the other side. Leaning into uncomfortable feelings can be difficult, and we naturally resist. We need to figure out what those fears are and what the perceived truths and thoughts are that drive them. We can only do that by confronting them."

David said, "So, you are saying I'm not going to like this, and I'm going to want to leave or possibly take it out on you?"

"Maybe."

David sat quietly for a moment. "I thought the patient just tells you his troubles and you listen sympathetically so that he feels better knowing someone finally cares and understands them?"

"Empathetic listening is an important part of the process. The person needs to feel understood and that they can trust the therapist, but that, in itself, isn't really therapy. Think of someone who has been coming every week for years to talk with a counselor. They feel listened to, but they remain depressed or anxious or any number of things. At some point, they may actually feel worse, as if their situation is hopeless. That's why more is needed than just empathetic listening and understanding. Unfortunately, most therapists out there may be doing more harm than good for their patients by fostering the philosophies that led to the feelings of emptiness and self-rejection in the first place.

"I'm sure you won't be surprised if I tell you that our sense of self-worth can't ultimately come from anything or even anyone one except the One Who made us. There's something inside of us that desires to know we are valuable and loveable for our true selves and not our manufactured self, nor our accomplishments, our wealth or power, our popularity or approval from others. None of those last or fill the emptiness we feel by chasing them. Many of today's therapists have bought into the self-bounded individualism where we ourselves determine what is true and right based on how we feel. I wanted you to know I could only offer you what I believe to be true and what has really worked for people. You're still in charge of what decisions you make, though."

David took a deep breath, absorbing what Tom was saying. "I'm good with that, plus I could tell if you weren't being genuine. I heard some very positive things from people in the Newton office about how Jillian has been doing, so I trust that you know what you are doing. What do you want to know first?"

Tom grinned. "Thanks. I also have to trust you'll tell me when you feel as if I'm getting out of line. Okay? Let's start with the things you think have the greatest impact on you and your relationships."

David said, "Like what?"

Tom handed David a notebook and pen. "Just spend a little time with it and write down things you do or feel that may be something you might like to free yourself from, change or even just understand."

David sat for quite a while letting different thoughts flow through his mind and some ideas came to mind that wouldn't leave. Now, David had to decide if he actually wanted to write them down.

Eventually, Tom spoke. "David, that is your notebook. Nothing you write in there ever has to be seen by me or anyone else, so even if you write something down, it doesn't mean we need to talk about it then or ever."

That freed David to start writing what came to mind. On the first page he wrote:

TRUST

FATHER - MOTHER

ALONE

And then he stopped and closed the notebook, looked up at the ceiling and then closed his eyes as he breathed in deeply.

Tom didn't say anything, probably to allow David time to sit with his thoughts for as long as he needed. Finally, David opened his eyes and collected himself with another deep breath. "Okay. What happens next?"

"That depends on how comfortable you feel sharing anything that came up."

"I don't know if I feel comfortable yet."

"That's okay. Let's do this. Can you take the notebook and draw a line down the middle of the page for each of the things you wrote and write down the benefits and costs of feeling the way you do?"

"Do you want me to do this now?"

Tom answered, "Only if you want or you can do it at home."

David said, "Let me try the first one," and he started to write down the benefits and costs for the fact that he had a hard time trusting anyone.

Benefits	Costs
Protection from pain	Absence of close relationships
Avoid abandonment	Being alone
Avoid fear	No intimacy or love
	Loss of family Hurt Jillian
	Abandoning Kat, Amy, James
	No close friendships

David felt as if he could keep going in the Costs column but kept coming up with blanks for the Benefits column even though the items he wrote were no small things to him over the years. David wasn't ready to share these thoughts with Tom, at least not now. He closed the notebook. "I think I've written what I can for tonight."

"Great. It's not always easy but can be very insightful. Did you want to talk about anything you wrote down or anything else that comes to mind?"

David shook his head. "Not tonight. I need to think about things for a bit and see where I want to go."

Without any sign of disappointment in his tone, Tom said, "That's perfectly fine. You just let me know when and how you would like to proceed."

"I appreciate that. I think I'll head home if you don't mind."

"I'll always honor what is best for you, David. I'll be praying for you."

David thanked him and carried his notebook home, thinking of all the things he had traded in to live a life free from fear of abandonment. Had the costs of not trusting been too high, not only to himself but to everyone else in his life?

When he arrived home, he squatted down and rubbed his hands through Trooper's fur and looked him in the eyes to let him know how much he appreciated his companionship.

When David got up to get something for Trooper and himself to eat, he noticed the message light blinking on his phone. He half listened to the messages as he was preparing supper until he heard Dr. Finn's voice.

"Mr. Fidele, I've tried to call a few times today to let you know we will be operating on your father later today to remove a tumor we located next to your father's spine. We're hoping this will help to alleviate the pain he's been experiencing the past few weeks. Please give me a call before six p.m. today or tomorrow after nine a.m., and I can update you on his status. My number is 804-555-0513. I look forward to talking with you."

Not knowing how the surgery went, David felt a sense of panic in his chest. He needed his father to be healthy, to be alive. To be honest, he needed his father to know his son was someone he could be proud of before he died. He had a lot to do to get to that point before he lost his chance.

He couldn't wait until the morning. He called the hospital surgical unit, but the doctor wasn't available, and they couldn't give him much information but did let him know his father was doing okay. He stayed up late and nodded off occasionally, slipping into disturbing dreams chasing his father and not being able to catch him and then having his father chase him as he ran faster and faster away from him until he woke himself.

In the morning, David took a long run and still had to wait for a half-hour, which seemed to last an eternity, before he could call the doctor back. Finally, he reached him, and Dr. Finn told David the operation had gone well, and Gianni was already feeling relief. He also said that he wouldn't be ready for a visit for a few more weeks but assured him Gianni would be well cared for.

David spent a lot of that Saturday thinking about the short list he had written down: TRUST, FATHER-MOTHER, ALONE. He wasn't sure why he had written 'mother' or the word 'alone' down on the list. He wasn't uncomfortable spending time alone. As a matter a fact, he kept his distance intentionally, so he'd never be too close to another individual. There must've been a reason for including each item on his list, but he couldn't figure out why only the predictable and enjoyable life he had been living just five short months ago seemed to have been turned on its head. He needed to get things sorted out, and soon. It struck him that this was the first time he wasn't able to handle something on his own.

Chapter 48

By Wednesday, David was feeling ambivalent about going to the boys' practice and his "religion class," but the thought of seeing his father in a few weeks compelled him to go.

Practices were running smoother. Several of the boys were beginning to take on leadership roles, making sure everyone was giving each drill his full attention and effort until it became second nature, not only individually, but also as a team. After practice, Tom asked David if he was up for class because David "would never forgive himself if he missed this one!" David didn't know what Tom meant but followed him over to the church, where once inside, Tom led him over to the confessional box. David wasn't sure what was up, but he opened the door next to the one Tom had just slipped into. Inside was a seat, a kneeler, and some small pamphlets on the Sacrament of Reconciliation. There was a screen in front of him and he could hear Tom slide over the wooden screen on the other side of the partition. David still couldn't see Tom, but now they could hear each other. Tom said, "Aren't you glad you came tonight?"

"You aren't supposed to know who I am, are you?"

"Normally, people like to sit face-to-face for this sacrament, but some feel freer to talk about difficult things with privacy. This may not be something that hits you immediately, but the Sacrament of Reconciliation may be one of the most beautiful and unique things about Catholicism."

David was silent as Tom continued, "One of the most extraordinary things about God's love is that it's unconditional and abundant in mercy, which is really good because we need it. Jesus knows we will fall, and that we will sin, every one of us, time and time again. In the Sacrament of Reconciliation, we receive the grace, strength, and clarity of sight to see ourselves honestly and humbly. We always have the opportunity to reconcile our hearts and lives with God. Does that make sense?"

David said, "Sort of, but why do we have to confess to a priest? Why not just directly to God?"

"One thing Jesus knew was what we needed. Humans tend to be a bit weak when it comes to an honest and regular examination of conscience, truly repenting for our sins, and knowing we are totally forgiven. He knew our need to confess our sins out loud, to have guidance and to hear those words of forgiveness. That's why one of the gifts and authority He gave His apostles was to forgive sins. He didn't give them the authority to judge individuals, but to look at our actions and to administer the grace of this sacrament."

David said, "When did He do that?"

"If you read the Gospel of John, Jesus said to the apostles, 'Peace be with you. As the Father has sent me, even so, I send you.' And when he said this, he breathed on them, and said to them, 'Receive the Holy Spirit. If you forgive the sins of any, they are forgiven; if you retain the sins of any, they are retained.' Tom was silent for a minute to let that sink in then said, "Unless you want to make any confession tonight, we can step out of the box."

David quickly stepped out of the intimate quarters once Tom did the same. Tom said, "Remember when we talked about the Prodigal Son, and the father came running to his son with love and mercy? That is what reconciliation is about. Most people think God is the one who is changing in this process and He'll be willing to forgive us if we can prove we deserve it, but God never withholds His love or mercy. God initiates and offers forgiveness; we just need to believe that healing gift is there to receive it and be truly sorry for our sins.

"Many people hold onto a child's immature view of sin, thinking they did something bad or they are bad and need to be punished for God to love them again. Sin is anything that turns us inward on ourselves and away from God. It puts up a barrier that clouds our vision and understanding of truth, of God, and of ourselves. God gives us His laws, not to set us up to fail, but because He knows what will bring us true joy and happiness. He knows self-focused desire turns our hearts away from Him, believing we know better than God what is good for us. If God wasn't loving and merciful, He wouldn't have sacrificed His only Son to take on the sins of the world in forgiveness."

David reflected about that for a moment. "I still don't get why Jesus had to die so brutally just to satisfy God's anger and disappointment in our sinning."

"Think about your son. You know that being honest, responsible, and caring isn't only the right thing to do but will also make him much happier than being the opposite. Would your rules and teaching be out of love? Or would they be traps you set for him to fail?"

"It would be for him and not me."

"What if you found him lying, skipping school, and stealing things he wanted from the neighbors? Would you just fix it for him and move on?"

"Of course not! If I did that, I wouldn't be doing the best thing for him."

"What would you do?"

David thought for a second. "I would give him some consequences, make him apologize, and return what he stole. I would teach him to understand why I was concerned and why it's important to do the right thing."

"Well," Tom said, "God loves us even more. It's true our sins against God deserve justice that we could never repay on our own. Since Jesus was both human and divine, He could make the ultimate sacrifice for our sins by giving His own human life in love for us and showing us the way by trusting and honoring His Father's will. When we're baptized, our sins are washed away, and we are invited into God's life, but we're not made perfect. As human beings, with God's grace, we can join His body in the Church, and participate in our salvation with our free will to sin or not, to repent or not. If God didn't give us free will, He wouldn't be respecting our true dignity in a loving relationship, and He wouldn't be showing us real love just as you wouldn't be for James if you just 'took care' of it for him without any personal responsibility on his part. Your son couldn't do it without you any more than we can do it without God's grace and guidance."

David sat in one of the pews. "Jesus died for the sins of everyone living then and before Him, but how does that help us?"

"I like questions, and that is a good one. The Father, Son, and Holy Spirit live outside of time, unlike us. Jesus' sacrifice for us was for all people and all sins throughout all time, and that includes you and me."

David glanced up at the crucifix above the altar. "Are you saying my sins now were responsible for putting Him on that cross, suffering and dying a death like that?"

Tom looked up with David and replied softly as his eyes welled up. "And mine too, David. And mine too. I think about that so many times, especially during Lent. When Jesus, the innocent man, stood next to Barabbas, the criminal, He took His place on the cross, just as He gives His life for us."

"Then why would God ever love us?"

"God is love, so He can only give love. He wants our lives filled with joy, love, and peace and to live life abundantly. God is always ready to run down the road to greet us, put a robe around us, and have a feast in celebration when we turn back towards Him. He never turns His back on us. Sin kills the wonderful person He created, and in our turning back to Him, we are no longer dead but alive again—even if it takes us till our last breath of life on this earth to get it."

David sat quietly taking in the church's soft and peaceful lights and all the saints surrounding him and cheering him on. Finally, he pointed to the crucifix. "Do you really believe making a confession of all my sins is important to Him?"

"I do. And it's just as important that we are willing to forgive others."

David's mouth fell open. "Forgive who?"

"Anyone who sins against us."

David tilted his head, confused. "No matter what?"

"No matter what. Do you know the Our Father?"

"I think I know some of it."

"Jesus actually told us that this is how we should pray to the Father, and it's quite extraordinary. 'Our Father, Who art in Heaven, hallowed be Thy name; Thy Kingdom come, Thy will be done on earth as it is in Heaven. Give us this day our daily bread; and forgive us our trespasses as we forgive those who trespass against us; and lead us not into temptation but deliver us from evil.' What stands out to you?"

"I don't know. What should stand out?"

"Lots of things, but three always strike me. The first is Jesus using the word 'our' at the beginning. He is telling us we are His brothers and sisters and God is 'our' loving father."

David said, "That's interesting. What's the second thing?"

"'Thy will be done.' Jesus said this in His agony in the garden, the night before He would die on the cross and modeled this for us His entire life. Mary showed us this so perfectly in trusting God's will over her own fears and desires when she said 'Yes'. I think about that line every time I say the prayer and that is as often as I can."

"I'll have to work on that one. Not understanding it but trying to actually do it. And the third?"

"The third one is really important as well, and we should be careful about what we ask for. 'Forgive us our trespasses as we forgive those who trespass against us.' Think about that. If we don't forgive others completely, we are asking God to not forgive us completely." David's eyes widened with surprise, and his mind flashed back to all the people he hadn't forgiven over the years.

David squinted. "Don't worry, David. God doesn't drop us off on earth and say, 'Life is hard. Good luck. Hope to see you in heaven!'"

David laughed, but it was partially a nervous laugh. Tom said, "Really. Don't worry, David. You have a lot of people rooting for you, including the Big Guy." Tom leaned over and whispered, "I heard He likes you."

David smiled. "Oh, okay. I will try to put in a good word for you then."

"I'd appreciate that," Tom laughed, "and maybe a cold one if you're up for it?"

"Do you take the rest of the candidates out for a beer?"

"No, and I was hoping you were taking me out tonight."

David said, "Only if I can get a 'get out of jail card' from you and the Big Guy. I don't think anyone would want to spend that much time in the confessional with me. There must be a Fast Pass or something."

Tom laughed again as he closed the church door. "I think He likes the old-fashioned way, low-tech humbleness and straightforward honesty." As they walked and chatted on this chilly night, David was glad Tom didn't mention anything from last Friday night. Tom didn't bring anything up at Dempsey's either, and David appreciated the respect Tom was showing him.

Chapter 49

After a solid basketball win by the boys' team on Friday night, David left Tom to bag up the basketballs and slipped away without him noticing. Tom understood that David may not be ready to open up after last week's session.

When Tom entered the rectory, David was sitting in the winged chair by his desk.

Tom jerked at the sight of him. "Oh! I thought you left."

"And miss another night of fun and excitement? Are you kidding me?"

Tom took a seat. David's notebook was on his lap. "Have you had any updates on your dad?"

"Not since I spoke to the doctor on Saturday. They think it will be a few weeks of recovery before I can go back down to see him. Thanks for asking."

"I hope the surgery helps, and he does well. How do you feel about seeing him when he is doing better?"

"I just want him to get better."

"But how do you feel about seeing him?"

"I'm looking forward to seeing him. Why wouldn't I?"

"Do you have any other feelings floating around?"

"What are you getting at? Sure, I'm excited and a little nervous as well."

"Okay. Why do you feel nervous about seeing him?"

David moved in his chair. "I don't know. It's hard to get to know someone you haven't seen for thirty years through half-inch thick glass on a phone line. It's awkward and I don't know how he'll be after his surgery."

"I can imagine that setup being difficult and almost impersonal. If it were me, I'd want a big old bear hug. I see you brought your notebook today."

"I didn't think it was optional. I think what you really want to ask is if I did the exercise you asked me to do."

Grinning, Tom asked, "Now that you mention it, were you able to spend some time with it?"

David opened the book to the pages he had written. "I did. I didn't want to do it. I hadn't planned to do it, but putting my thoughts on paper made me think about things a bit."

"That's good, and that's the intent. Is there anything you'd like to share?"

David hesitated but finally answered, "I was thinking I was ready, but I'm not so sure right now."

Tom nodded. "Let me ask you this. Do you ever feel anxious about anything?"

"Sometimes. Doesn't everyone feel a little nervous or anxious before a big event?"

"Sure. What types of situations make you feel the most anxious?"

*****

David had to think a bit. He had never admitted these feelings to anyone before.

"Were you nervous or anxious before that tournament basketball game in high school?"

David wanted to say he was just a little nervous, but out came, "Anxious. I was very anxious going into that game."

"You played like a demon on fire in that game. I don't think I've seen that level of fight from anyone else. It was a great game, but why do you think you felt so anxious before the game?"

"I don't know." David shrugged. "I didn't want to lose."

"You're very competitive. There is healthy anxiety and unhealthy anxiety. Think of running into a grizzly bear on a camping trip—healthy anxiety, whereas unhealthy anxiety comes from our thoughts that are a bit distorted. Our feelings come from our thoughts and our thoughts come from our beliefs. It's that underlying belief that is often the culprit of our anxieties."

"I never thought about the connection."

"So, the thought of losing the game made you feel highly anxious. What would've happened if you lost the game?"

David chuckled. "We did. I thought if we lost the game people would think I was to blame and I wasn't as good a player as they thought."

"So, what if you lost, and it was your fault, or you weren't as good as everyone believed, how would that make you feel?"

"If I didn't succeed, and I wasn't the player they thought, then people would see me differently."

"So, what if they saw you differently? What if they thought less of you? How would that make you feel?"

David hesitated. "I'd feel like a loser. Like I was less."

"How about at work, now? You are incredibly successful and respected. Do you ever get anxious at work?"

David took a deep breath and exhaled slowly. "Sure."

"When do you feel the most anxious?"

"Mostly before each new quarter when we have to produce results again."

"But I heard you beat your plan every single quarter and by higher margins than anyone else in the company."

"Sure, but if I missed a quarter—"

Tom shrugged. "What if you missed a quarter? How would you feel?"

"Like people would see I'd been lucky or a phony all along and I wasn't as good as they thought."

"So, what if you were just like everyone else, doing his best but not always succeeding?"

David stared ahead blankly. "I'd feel like a loser, as though I was less than everyone else." David knew he hid these feelings so well, he expected Tom to be floored by this admission and that he would see him in a lesser light, but Tom didn't seem surprised.

"Feelings of anxiety and depression have been growing by leaps and bounds in the world with more and more people feeling disconnected, empty, and without a sense of meaning to give them a reason for being. Part of your drive and fear of failure may come from what you suffered as a boy. I do know one thing that you may not know."

David said, "And what's that?"

"You could never be a loser or less than anyone else."

David clenched his teeth for a moment, debating whether to speak his mind, but who better to say it to than Tom? "What has been confusing me is the distinction between being a winner and being respected. It all seemed to have gotten turned upside down when I saw my father. I went from 'What do I not have?' to 'What kind of man am I, in terms of what really matters?' All my effort and success up to this point suddenly seems worthless next to the values that my father has lived by. It's getting harder to process my life lately." Saying it aloud didn't have the sense of relief he expected. Instead, he tensed at having shown his vulnerability. Just putting it out there made his flaws more real, made his life look worthless.

Tom watched him closely. "While that may feel uncomfortable, it may actually indicate good things going on." They both sat mulling things over for a few minutes, then Tom pointed to David's notebook. "Do you feel any more comfortable to share your exercise?"

The anxiety and indecision percolating in David rose up. He'd already said enough. He felt worse for the discussion, not better. "I already said no!"

Tom leaned back and relaxed in his chair. "That's okay. You have to be ready to participate in making any inroads. Why don't we stop for today? Maybe you could spend the week thinking about what you wrote and any other areas that are bothering you or making you anxious and write them down. Also, see if you could write down two or three goals in terms of what you would like to make better."

"Why are we cutting this off so early?"

"I think this is hard stuff. I don't think you've ever been shy about hard work, but it's also scary stuff and resistance to really participating and doing the work is a fairly normal instinct. See if you can spend some time writing out more about what bothers you the most and what thoughts are behind those feelings. Then peel the onion back another layer or two to see what feeling comes up if you ask yourself, 'What if that thought were true?' Finally, decide what benefits and costs there are to avoiding those feelings and what goals you have for this therapy. When you're ready to do that, we can get back together and see what's what. Did you ever see the movie *The Untouchables*?"

As David was putting on his coat, he asked, "The one with Costner, Connery, and DeNiro?"

"That's the one. Do you remember what Sean Connery said to Kevin Costner when he wanted to break up Capone's ring?"

David nodded as he started heading out the door. "Yes, I do."

Tom's best Sean Connery impersonation followed him out the door. "What are you prepared to do?"

Chapter 50

David walked home feeling agitated but couldn't understand why. He went into his study with Trooper and then took out his notebook and pen. "So, Trooper, what do you think bothers me the most?"

Trooper tilted his head with worried eyes. David started writing whatever came into his mind.

WHEN PEOPLE LIE
PEOPLE WHO DON'T DO WHAT THEY PROMISE
MISSING A COMMITMENT
LOSING AT ANYTHING

Then David thought about each one. He wrote: *How do I feel when someone lies? I feel impatient. Why do I feel impatient when people lie?* He had to think about that for a while before he wrote: *I think when you lie to someone, you don't have respect for them. How does that make me feel? I feel more upset and even angry. Why do I feel angry? I DON'T KNOW.* David had similar results with the other items on his list. How could he write goals if he didn't know what the problem was? He tried anyway to keep Tom happy.

GOALS
LEARN TO TRUST PEOPLE CLOSE TO ME
BE LESS ANXIOUS ABOUT THINGS
BE THE MAN MY FATHER WOULD BE PROUD OF

David closed his notebook but didn't feel any better. He tried working out in his exercise room to get tired enough to sleep, but he tossed and turned throughout the night.

The morning arrived crisp and cold, and David thought a run might do him good and help him to get out of his head. He ran a five-mile loop around town, up and down different streets until he stopped at the Eastside to warm up and get a cup of coffee. When he walked into the cafe, Linda dropped her ordering pad and her jaw, and with an exaggerated eye-roll yelled to the kitchen. "Well, well, well, look who the cat dragged in! I thought you fell off the face of the earth."

David sat at the counter. "Linda, I'm crawling back on my knees. How could I desert you? Where else would I get this kind of friendly service?"

Linda picked up her order pad, leaned on the counter, and peered at David over her glasses.

David knew the routine. "The usual."

Linda said, "The usual you have been having the past several months or the usual usual?"

"The usual usual."

Linda came back with his coffee and shortly afterward his two eggs over easy, rye toast, and home fries. The comfort of familiarity was making him feel better.

David had no plans and was starting to feel anxious about spending the day alone with unresolved feelings. He knew he couldn't wait until the following week to address his conflicting feelings, so he showered and changed quickly, grabbed his notebook, and headed over to St. Anthony's to see if Tom could spare a few moments.

Tom paused at the sight of him. "Are you really this much of a glutton for punishment?"

"I'm sorry for showing up like this, but I just need a few minutes to talk."

Tom waved toward the door. "Let's go in so we don't freeze before you get to say what's on your mind." Tom made some coffee and they moved into his office to sit.

"So, what's on your mind? You seem a bit upset."

"I know I've been resisting your help. I don't know why, but I did try to do the exercises you gave me, and it only got me more confused and agitated. Shouldn't I be feeling better looking under the covers a bit?"

"Absolutely not. If you were feeling nice and comfortable at this point, you wouldn't be seriously looking at anything meaningful." Tom pointed to David's notebook. "Do you know why you brought that with you today?"

"Well, as much as I don't feel like doing this, I think I should share what I've written."

Tom sat forward in his chair and took a sip of his coffee. "Why the change of heart?"

"Does it really matter?"

"It could matter, but let's not dwell on it."

David opened his notebook. "You asked me to write down what things I'd like to free myself from, change, or just understand. I wrote, 'Trust, Father, Mother and Alone.' I don't know why I wrote those down, they just came out. I started with 'trust' and looked at the benefits and the costs, and what I wrote in each column struck me."

"What struck you the most?"

"If I have to be honest with myself, the benefits of not trusting people was all about protecting myself and the costs were all about the loss of close relationships and hurting people who have tried to love me. I was surprised by the costs."

"That's impressively honest and insightful. What does it make you want to do?"

"I don't know. That's why I'm here."

"Do you think that 'trust' and 'alone' are connected to the other words you wrote?"

"I really don't know. I don't know why I wrote them down either."

"You said that things with both your dad and mom were good before the tragedy; do I have that right?"

David thought back to those days when his family was together and relationships seemed safe. "This is a child's memory, but it was good. It felt safe, and I was happy. I loved my parents, and I always felt like they loved me."

"That's a good way to feel. After Jimmy's death and your father was charged, tell me what changed."

David stared at the wall. "Everything changed. The world tipped upside down. It felt so confusing, and I felt paralyzed that this can't be happening. I felt physically ill for the longest time. I remember my heart feeling as if it were ripped right out of my chest and was being stomped on by the people around me. Before that, I trusted my father more than anyone in the world. Then, everything felt like a fraud, as though I'd been lied to all along. It didn't make any sense to me. Nothing did."

Tom said, "You told me once that your mother changed."

"I didn't recognize her. Her smile, her laugh, her softness and affection all left her. She became bitter and almost cold with my brother, sister, and me. She'd say, 'Be strong and succeed, and no one can hurt you again.' Her anger at my father was always close to the surface and her feelings about God or anything Catholic were always overtly negative."

"What were the strongest feelings you were having at that time?"

David crossed his arms and held his jaw in his left hand as he thought back and pictured himself with the charred remains of his family.

David answered, "I don't know. She told us we were moving out of Boston, to Lynn, and our old life was dead. We never saw our grandparents or anyone who knew us from the neighborhoods in the North End or Savin Hill again, kind of like the witness protection program. We changed our name and never talked about what happened, to anyone. Mom went to work full-time at GE and made sure we had food on the table."

"I can imagine that being overwhelming for anybody, never mind when you were only eight. Do you remember any feelings you had specifically about your mom other than noticing a sharp change in her personality and your relationship?"

David knew he'd been overloaded or flooded with feelings at that time and worked hard, even to this day, to avoid that emotional flooding. "I don't really know what I felt towards her. I felt lost. The transition to the new neighborhood and school was tough. After several years, I remember reaching the point where I had to make a decision about pushing to move forward with strength or continue to wallow and sink further into the pit. Hard work and a focus on success became all-consuming and seemed to resonate with my mother. It was the only time I felt accepted by her. I felt as if I were on my own to make it in the world. I focused on excelling in sports, school, and anything else I began to do. It felt empowering and safe. I stopped feeling like a victim; I could be in charge of my life."

"David, are you saying you felt nothing in relationship to your mom during this period?"

He didn't know what the feelings were, but he knew they were there. David shook his head and felt as though he was drifting off to avoid thinking about it.

Tom raised his mug. "Do you need any more coffee or anything?"

David shook his head.

"Do you remember your feelings about your dad right after the event?"

David could remember himself feeling numb and completely disoriented in the days after Jimmy's death and his father's arrest. Police were coming in and out, questioning family members, questions he couldn't answer.

David glanced up at Tom. "Immediately afterward, I felt devastated, confused, and shocked. I didn't know what I felt towards my father other than confusion and conflict. I think those feelings moved to dislike and indifference as I started focusing on my own success—more like an island that was solid enough to survive any storm that passed its way."

Tom stood up for a minute and went to look out the window. "I can understand the incredible shock of what happened to you as a very young boy. There wasn't only a break in trust, but you lost your brother, your father, and in no small way, your mother and siblings. You also lost all of your sense of community and extended family connections, all at the same time. You may have experienced very strong withdrawal to cope and emotionally survive, but it doesn't mean that strong feelings weren't there." Tom sat back down. "Tell me your feelings when your mother passed away."

"I'm not proud to say this, but I didn't feel anything really, except feeling bad for her since I don't think she could enjoy life for all those years."

"Take nothing I ask as a sign of disrespect, but did you feel any sense of relief when she passed away?"

David stared down at the floor for quite a while and finally said, "Yes."

"For her or for yourself?"

David hesitated, feeling ashamed. "For me."

"When you found out that your father had terminal cancer, did any part of you feel a similar sense of relief?"

David was taken aback by his question. "I'm sorry, what are you asking me?"

"Our feelings are just that. They're not a judgment of you or your father. I was just curious if you felt any sense of relief, not because you don't care about him or want him to die. There are many layers of things going on—joy that he is alive and innocent, but also the challenge of trying to get to know someone that is somewhat of a stranger and someone you want desperately to be proud of you. I'd expect that you'd have a million thoughts and feelings going in different directions at the same time."

David nodded almost imperceptibly. "I did. I felt a sense of relief and panic at the same time because there may be so little time left. I felt ashamed once I found out about his condition."

Tom made a few notes on the pad he had on his lap. "Have you ever experienced stronger feelings than a dislike for either your father or your mother?"

"What do you mean exactly by stronger feelings?"

"I don't know exactly. Love, trust, and security are so important to a young boy. You may have felt ashamed, betrayed, hurt, and afraid. It is also possible that anyone in this situation would even feel hate for their parents, wishing they were dead."

David was feeling highly uncomfortable and he didn't want to continue the discussion down that path. He sat silently composing himself before responding. "I don't know where this is going. Why would I ever hate my parents or wish they were dead?"

"I'm very sorry if that question seemed out of line. I'm only poking at some possible, and common, feelings that can come up when someone has gone through what you have. I'm asking because our emotions can be masked over when we don't recognize the reality of what we felt, even if it makes us feel ugly or ashamed in the process."

David looked straight at Tom. "I believe you are trying to help, but I need to take a break for today. Don't worry, I'm not running away. I just need some fresh air and a break to think."

"Whatever you need is what you should do. We may run into things that are highly uncomfortable at times, and I may be unintentionally out of line at times."

David put on his coat and shook Tom's hand, heading out the door as Tom sat down and closed his eyes as to calm himself. While the session had been difficult for David, it had also been difficult for Tom as his friend.

*****

After a while, Tom went into the church to pray. Through the dim light, he could make out a person in the front pew—David

Without turning around, David said, "It's okay to talk to me." Tom walked up to the pew where David was sitting and took a seat next to him where they sat in silence for over ten minutes. Looking straight ahead, David whispered, "Did you know you actually cannot lie to God? We perfect our ability to lie to ourselves and others, but you can't lie to God. It just hit me that he already knows the truth. He knows us better than we do, so we can't tell him anything he doesn't already know."

"I think you hit on a very simple but a deep truth."

David continued to sit, looking up at the empty altar and a large crucifix high above it. "You asked if I ever felt hate for either of my parents. I know that I hated what he did and that he left us alone. I know that I hated that my mother turned off any sense of emotion for us. I think that may have been when I started hating God. He didn't take care of us. He let it happen and ignored my prayers when I needed him. I thought if they were all dead, I could be stronger and move along with my own life, chiseled carefully out of a granite exterior and that no one could disappoint me again. I trusted them to be there, and they both abandoned us for no reason I could understand."

"A lot of times we bury intense feelings we think we aren't supposed to have."

*****

David stared at the floor. "I've been trying to sit here and drop all my armor, all my defenses and know what I actually feel." Tears welled in David's eyes as the feelings rushed in through the walled levy that had separated him from that hurt.

Tom said, "Did you feel angry?"

A lump grew sharply in his throat as he struggled to speak. "Yes. I felt angry. Angry at the world. I felt a rage at times that was aimed at my parents and especially at God. I felt as if I couldn't and didn't want to survive the dark pit I'd been plunged into with no one to help me understand it. Do you want to know how I felt then? I felt damn angry. Do you want to know what I feel now? Angry and pissed. Yes, I'm glad my father is alive, but I'm angry that I need to prove myself to him when he was the one who lied and left me. Now, just when he gets me to open that door just a little, he'll abandon me again. I know not all of that is true, but that's how I feel!"

David's emotions were like toxic sensations running through every vein and every nerve in his body. He felt himself miles down the pit yelling into the void for help that would never arrive. His chest and limbs were literally shaking as he tried vainly to calm himself down. If Tom weren't sitting on the end of the pew they were in, he would've rushed out the door back to the safety of his old, heavily managed routine and busyness, but he was trapped.

"I know you're experiencing what probably feels overwhelming, but I'm going to ask you if you know why you felt so angry?"

David turned sharply toward Tom. "Why? Why did I feel angry? How can you ask that?"

Tom peered into David's eyes with a tone of empathetic friendship. "David, it's okay to be angry. It's not wrong to be angry even at God; he can take it. I want to know what it means to you to be angry. Some of our feelings are like a two-sided coin and certain feelings always go together. Anger is a strong emotion that many people, especially nice people, think they should never feel, which can cause a lot of anxiety. The flip side of that same coin is fear. Where there is anger, there is always something we're intensely afraid of. I want to know what you felt most afraid of when you were the angriest then and angry now."

David's emotions continued to run high, and he was feeling more uncomfortable than he could remember ever feeling as an adult. He fought against the emotions flooding him as he tried to think about what he was afraid of, not only as a child but still today. He never thought of himself as afraid of anything, other than being too close to another person. Tom was the only person who was allowed this far into these secret rooms of his inner self.

Tom repeated the question. "David, what did you feel most afraid of?" immersing David in the uncomfortable feelings he had worked so tirelessly to avoid and stopping him from thinking with his subconscious defense mechanisms.

"I was afraid that they would leave me, and I'd be all alone!"

"Okay, what if they left you, and you were alone; what would that mean?"

David was again taken aback by the question. "Wasn't being abandoned and alone enough?"

"What would that mean if you were abandoned? What are you afraid that it would mean?"

David couldn't think as he moved uncomfortably in his seat, looking up at the spiral ceilings of the church to find an escape. He could feel a wall come tumbling down as he blurted, "It would mean that they didn't care enough about me to stay!"

Tom pushed one more time. "And what if they didn't care about you enough to stay?"

David's entire body was shaking more than ever, and his heart felt as though it were burning and pounding through his ribcage as he yelled out, "It would mean that I was worthless! That I was nothing!"

Tom put his arm around David as he was breathing in and out with quick but deep breaths to calm his entire being.

David had gone to a place he vowed to never go, to a place he was sure would confirm his worst fear and be the fatal blow to his very existence.

Tears poured uncontrollably from David, tears and emotions that had been built up for over thirty years were now free to escape the prison they had been held in for just as long as David's father had endured his own prison sentence.

Tom cried silently as he held his arm around David's shaking body. David had experienced his descent into his personal hell, all the way to the bottom of the black pit. He had experienced constant nightmares about this, and now he survived the journey. As emotionally exhausted and drained as he felt, David started to realize that he'd survived and felt not only a great relief but a sense that his underlying fear had disappeared. He hadn't addressed his feelings of worthlessness or being nothing, but he no longer felt as vulnerable. Under any other circumstances, David would've felt embarrassed by his exposed feelings, but, instead, he felt relief and freedom.

Tom squeezed his shoulder. "I'm sorry we had to push so hard. You really showed a ton of courage and strength to break through some serious emotional walls." His voice quavered as it caught in his throat. "I'm truly proud to have you as such a close friend."

His sincere show of emotion touched David deeply. This was the first conscious challenge to his fear of being worthless, the fear that had stoked so much incentive and drive to always succeed and excel, to present a perceived sense of value to the outside world, while he carefully hid his real self deep inside.

Tom joked, "This probably wasn't the Saturday morning you had planned."

David stood up and shook his head, placed his hand on Tom's shoulder, and together they walked toward the doors as the sun streamed in through the rose window overhead.

Outside in the crisp, cool January air, David took a deep cleansing breath "What now?"

Tom smiled. "We still have work to do. Now that you know what that hidden emotion and belief have been, you need to challenge it and crush it with the truth. Self-rejection is the robber of life and the reason why we try so desperately to fill that sense of emptiness with all the things that never satisfy."

"Because our sense of self-worth can only come from one place?"

Tom chuckled. "Maybe there's hope for you yet. I'll see you Wednesday, but call me anytime you need to talk."

David reached out to shake Tom's hand and then decided to embrace him instead as Tom returned the embrace until they separated quickly, humorously acting as if it didn't happen.

David arrived home feeling exhausted, but lighter, starting a new journey without the weight of his imagined world on his shoulders.

Chapter 51

For six weeks, David met with Tom on Wednesday nights to learn about the faith and the Church. They discussed faith and reason, the meaning of the commandments, morality, sin and forgiveness, the dignity of life, who Jesus was, His teachings, and His loving sacrifice. They studied scripture and how the New Testament fulfills the Old Testament in the salvation story, the early Church, the role of its members, and the final things in life. With Tom's encouragement, David became comfortable enough to ask lots of questions and to challenge things, such as the reliability of the Bible, or the authority of the Church. The conversations were lively, deep, and eye-opening for David as he came to find meaning and purpose behind so much that he once thought to be quite the opposite. Faith wasn't another thing you did on the side, but something that ran deep into the fabric of a person, creating rhythm and purpose to everyday life, transforming even ordinary things into instruments of grace. David had started this process for the sole purpose of making his father happy and proud of him, but now learning about the actual history and meaning of the faith had given him a desire to learn more.

During that time, David continued to meet with Tom on Friday nights to undo David's strong but distorted truths that had built up, his fears of a lack of intrinsic self-worth, and false beliefs that the source of self-worth came from the validation or approval of others, or from his achievements and perceptions of success. It was a difficult task to crush "truths" that David had believed at his core for so many years.

By using several techniques of cognitive behavior therapy, Tom worked with him to challenge those beliefs over and over. Developing a deep sense of his own intrinsic value as a person also involved looking hard at the false-self David had built over time to protect his authentic-self. It had created a vicious cycle of becoming more anxious as the disparity between his actual-self and false-self grew. The phrase Tom used that caught David's attention was, "I am what I am not," which made it clear how denying your real self can do nothing but create ever-increasing subconscious unrest. In the end, the source of a person's self-worth and value can only be satisfied by God Himself, our creator. We are made in God's image and are made with unconditional love for the purpose of being part of God's plan and part of God Himself as His adopted son or daughter.

At the end of one of the Friday night sessions, David paused while putting on his coat. "Tom, can I ask you a question?"

"Sure. What's up?"

"We've been meeting on Wednesday nights for one thing and Friday nights for another. It finally hit me that, in the end, they're not really different discussions, are they?"

Tom grinned. "Nope. In the end, they are very much the same."

David smiled as he nodded back.

*****

David's weeks started taking on a rhythm with basketball and RCIA on Wednesdays; working as a regular now at My Brother's Table on Thursdays for lunch; basketball and therapy with Tom on Fridays; and spending Sundays with Amy, James, and Kathleen. When David was finally given the clearance to fly down to Richmond to see his father, something felt different—as if he were going freely, without looking to prove his worth through his father's approval and without the anger and mistrust he once carried.

David approached him with a broad smile that made his eyes squint. Gianni walked a little more gingerly to his seat but looked much better than David had anticipated. As Gianni picked up his receiver, David said, "Pop, it's so good to see you. You look really good. How are you feeling?"

Smiling, Gianni answered, "How could I be doing any better than when I'm seeing my son? You seem good."

David laughed. "You could be doing better if you were home with me. I should've asked you first, but I hired a law firm to see if you can be released due to extenuating circumstances."

Gianni gave a little smile as if he were sure it couldn't come true. "That would be really nice, son."

David was honest with his father this trip, talking openly about his life and about his feelings.

Gianni nodded, and tears came to his eyes several times as David talked about his emotional breakthroughs, his lessons on his faith, and the work he was doing to be the father his children needed.

Gianni and David both smiled as they shared the line from *The Godfather*. "A man who doesn't spend time with his family can never be a real man."

As usual, the time allotted never seemed like enough, but it was also unlike David's first visits.

On the last Friday of February, David met with Tom, as usual. After their session, Tom asked, "David, I have a favor to ask of you. I would like you to join the rest of the RCIA team on Monday nights if you are available."

David was surprised by the request. He preferred the one-on-one format. "Tom, I don't know. Monday nights are tough." Tom continued to smile at David without saying a word until David responded. "Why don't we just keep going the way we have?"

"Two reasons: one, we agreed to have your own classes until you were caught up, and two, our faith isn't really meant to be a solitary act. Our personal relationship with God is the main thing but doing this in community is what the Church is all about. Plus, I think you'll like the four elderly women who will be joining the Church at the same time as you."

"I know I have to trust God and my father, but we never said I had to trust you."

Tom laughed. "I think that's a very wise strategy."

When David arrived at the church on Monday night, he was surprised to see the RCIA team already standing at the back of the church with Tom and more surprised to see that they were not four little old ladies with whom he might feel out of place.

Tom greeted him with a wave as he approached the group. "I would like to introduce David Kelly. This is Pooja, Marge, Mike, and Ben."

David leaned over to whisper in Tom's ear, "Four elderly women, huh? I owe you one." David shook each of their hands and stopped in front of Ben, a Patriots football player, six foot three inches and almost 300 pounds, with a shaved head. "It's Ben Harris, correct? We actually met briefly at an event at the stadium last year. I've enjoyed watching you play."

The others had their own stories: Mike seemed like a normal guy who had grown up with no faith and was probably in his mid-forties. Pooja, raised Hindu, was an attractive woman in her twenties who was dating a Catholic man. Marge was the old lady in the group, a lifetime Presbyterian who was converting and was full of energy and character. David was feeling more comfortable joining the group after spending time with them.

Tom asked the group, "Does anyone know what's special about this week?"

David didn't have a clue.

Ben raised his large arm. "Ash Wednesday is this week, then Lent begins."

Tom nodded. "Great. Who can tell me what day of the week Ash Wednesday falls on?"

David's hand shot up. "The day after Fat Tuesday?"

Everyone laughed.

"And we'll call this smart-aleck Monday. As you may know, this is the beginning of Lent, and for me, this is a great time to focus on things in my life and my relationship with Christ. Before Jesus started his ministry, he went into the desert for how many days?"

Ben said, "Forty days. He fasted, prayed, and was tested by Satan."

Tom said, "Excellent, and it's a great time for us to fast, to repent for our sins, and for spiritual renewal through prayer, fasting, and good works. What happens on Ash Wednesday?"

Mike answered, "People have ashes on their foreheads to show their faith?"

Tom nodded. "It indicates the beginning of a time of reflection and sacrifice and the priest will mark your forehead with ashes in the Sign of the Cross saying, 'Turn away from sin and be faithful to the Gospel.'"

David asked, "Why do people give up stuff? Sometimes it seems as if they just want to look holier than someone else."

Tom sat straight in his chair. "The intent is not to let on that you're fasting or making a sacrifice. It's good for the soul and brings solidarity with other Christians all over the world. For me, giving something up or doing something different provides a nice daily reminder that this period is different, a great time for spiritual growth."

Tom stood in the middle of the five candidates and said, "We will talk more about Lent and how important Easter is to us as we go along. Does anyone know when the period of Lent ends?"

Marge said, "Easy one—Easter."

Tom replied, "Close. It actually ends when Holy Thursday Mass begins. Part of what is called the Triduum: Holy Thursday, Good Friday, and Easter is what I wanted to talk about today. Can anyone guess what that is?"

David kidded, "I'm guessing that it's not chocolate Easter bunnies?"

Tom pointed to David. "You are correct, it's not chocolate Easter bunnies. It's the center of our worship and the source and summit of our faith. This was as true for the early Church as it is today." The group was silent, and Tom continued, "I want to talk about the celebration of the Mass. Sounds like a party, huh? Let me know if these descriptions of going to Mass sound familiar - boring, confusing, meaningless ritualistic, routine, et cetera."

David said, "I'll have to admit that I don't get the Mass, and it does seem a lot like those descriptions."

Tom replied, "Good. I like honesty. Well, let me see if I can give a little context and meaning to what is happening in the Mass and see if that changes anything for you; kind of like knowing the game of football to really appreciate and enjoy it."

Tom stood at the back of the church facing the altar. "Think of the Mass as having four main parts. In the first part, we come together to worship and spend time with God as a community. Now, follow me down the aisle." When they reached the front, Tom knelt on one knee to make the Sign of the Cross. "I'll let you know why I did that in a bit, but normally people come into the church and spend a few moments getting their heart ready for Mass by kneeling and praying. Note that there are no divisions or preferences for anyone worshiping, the rich and poor, all ethnic backgrounds, young and old, male and female, all pray together because we are all members of the Body of Christ. The priest will wear vestments to cover his own self to act '*in persona Christi*' or as Christ at the Mass. That doesn't mean he is Christ or better than anyone else, but a successor of the apostles given the authority for this role. At the beginning of the Mass, what do we do first?"

Pooja responded, "We sing an entrance song."

Tom smiled. "That's correct, but I was thinking about how the Mass itself begins. We all make the Sign of the Cross together."

Mike asked, "Why do we make the Sign of the Cross so much?"

Tom answered, "A really good question. We make the Sign of the Cross in the name of the Father, the Son, and the Holy Spirit to remind ourselves of our baptism and that we belong to God, putting ourselves in his loving protection. In this moment you realize the important truth that your life is about God and not about you."

Tom seemed to let that point sink in for a moment. "At this point, we continue standing together to call to mind our sins, realizing we are a community of sinners and that we can only be saved by God's grace and forgiveness. God never gives up on us and wants to forgive us. The second part of the Mass is the Liturgy of the Word, where we hear the sacred stories from the Old Testament or the story of God and Israel, then one of the Psalms, followed by a reading from the New Testament, such as the letters of Paul. Finally, we stand to hear the Gospel stories and teachings of Jesus Himself, showing how the Old Testament is fulfilled in Jesus. Catholics believe these readings are not only the inspired words of God, but that the Word is God Himself. The very first verse of the Gospel of John says. 'In the beginning was the Word, and the Word was with God, and the Word was God.' Following the readings, the priest's homily hopefully provides some insights to the scripture readings and how they relate to our lives today. This part of the Mass is completed by everyone standing and saying the Creed, in which we make a statement of what we believe as Christians."

Marge raised her hand. "A lot of this is done in the Presbyterian Church: songs, readings and a homily. We even read the Apostles' Creed sometimes.

We don't kneel or have the statues, incense, and crucifixes."

Tom smiled. "Does anyone know why you see these things in Catholic churches?"

David remembered Tom talking about them but remained silent.

"Remember that most people didn't read or write until the sixteenth or seventeenth century and the poor are often not educated, even today. We are human beings and Catholics who take in and live the faith through all of our senses. The pictures, carvings, and statues teach about the faith and the saints to children and adults. The sense of sight, smell, touch, sound, and even taste are all used to take in and live the faith through our whole being. It also reminds us we celebrate the Mass as one Body of Christ, not only around the world but with the community of saints in heaven.

"This is a great lead into the next part of the Mass, the Liturgy of the Eucharist, which literally means to 'give thanks,' just as Jesus celebrated the Passover meal in the Last Supper the night before he died on the cross. Simple gifts of bread and wine, for the Eucharistic meal and sacrifice, represent the entirety of creation to be offered up to God and are literally changed into the true presence of Jesus Himself. This is the tough part for most people to absorb and believe, but it is the most incredible gift Jesus left for us—Himself."

Pooja asked in a soft voice, "Father Tom, do you think most Catholics truly believe in this? I would think if they did, they'd come every day and would come to the altar on their knees to receive Christ into themselves."

Everyone was very quiet, and Tom was very taken with the depth of her inquiry. "Pooja, that is a beautifully stated question and a very important one. Unfortunately, I agree that many Catholics don't fully realize what the Eucharist is. Most don't even practice or come to Mass because they've found something else to be the center of their lives. That is why it's so important for us to be a visible witness to others and share this gift."

David raised his hand. "So, if you don't believe this is possible, does that mean you can't become Catholic?"

"You certainly shouldn't receive something you don't believe in. This is a critically important part of the faith of the Church from the earliest days."

David queried, "How is it even possible for bread and wine to magically turn into the actual body and blood of Jesus and still look and taste like plain old bread wafers and inexpensive wine?"

Moving in closer to the group, Tom continued, "Do you believe in God?" Everyone nodded and then Tom asked, "Is anything impossible with God?"

David looked ahead and said, "No."

"Then it would be possible if God wanted it to be so, right?"

Everyone said, "Yes."

David pondered aloud. "Okay, anything is possible, but how do we know this bread and wine actually changes into the actual body and blood of Christ? How do we know this just isn't a pagan ritual that the Church has told us to believe?"

Tom glanced from face to face. "Does everyone wonder even a bit about what David just asked? It's an important question to ask, so don't feel embarrassed. Be honest."

Heads were nodding, and Ben said, "It's a tough one to try to explain, especially coming from a Baptist church that doesn't have a great opinion of the Catholic faith. How do we know, Father Tom?"

"We've been through the Gospels and why it makes sense for us to trust them. At the Last Supper, Jesus knows this is His last night with the closest people in His life whom He had been teaching and living with for three years. It only makes sense that everything He says or does on this night has significant meaning." All heads nodded in agreement.

"Think of what has happened this week for Jesus. It was the week of the Jewish Passover when they celebrate this feast as a commemoration of their liberation by God from slavery in Egypt. On the tenth day of Nisan, the lambs are brought into Jerusalem to be inspected and only those without blemish would be sacrificed at the Passover meal to commemorate God's protection of the Jewish homes with the blood of the lamb marked on their doorposts. On this same day, Jesus came riding on a donkey and is greeted as a king, but He is also the lamb being brought in for inspection and the ultimate sacrifice."

Mike said, "I've heard of Jesus being referred to as the Lamb of God, but I didn't know what that meant before. And I'm not sure I totally get it yet either."

Tom offered, "Let's keep going with the events of the week, and I think it may become clearer. So, the Jewish people are bringing in their lambs for inspection for a sacrifice to God, but an imperfect sacrifice to be sure. Jesus is led in at the exact same time. During this week, He is being inspected by the people, and by the high priests with questions, traps, and finally a demand for his arrest and death. Being good Jews, Jesus and His apostles plan to celebrate the Passover meal, but the apostles don't get the true meaning of what is about to happen. If you remember, Jesus tells the apostles that one of them will betray Him that night, and Judas 'leaves Mass early' to do just that."

Everyone laughed softly but listened intently as Tom continued. "Judas is paid thirty pieces of silver, same as the price to release a slave from bondage and says he will identify Jesus to the guards. In the meantime, Jesus is breaking unleavened bread and sharing the four cups of blessing in the wine, as was the Passover tradition. Jesus breaks the bread and says to His apostles at the meal of sacrifice and celebration, 'Take this, all of you, and eat it, this is my body which is given up for you. Do this in memory of me.' And then Jesus takes the wine and says, 'Take this, all of you, and drink from it, this is the cup of my blood of the new and everlasting covenant. It will be shed for you and for all so that sins may be forgiven. Do this in memory of me.'

Tom took a few seconds before asking, "What words stand out to you?"

Ben answered, "Is."

Mike glanced over at Ben with a puzzled face and asked, "Is?"

Ben turned to Mike. "Jesus said, 'This is my body,' and 'This is my blood.' He didn't say to think of it as or it's a symbol of— One of His last acts was to change those simple things—bread and wine—to something else. How else would you interpret His saying 'is'? It seems pretty clear."

Mike responded, "Oh. That's a good point."

Marge added, "I heard, 'It will be shed for you.' It makes me think of that song, 'I'll never know how much it cost, to see my sins upon that cross.' It gets me every time I hear it. Even though Jesus gave His life two thousand years ago, He did it for my sins today. It makes me feel ashamed and thankful at the same time."

A silent pause fell over them until Pooja spoke. "He said, 'Do this.' I guess if He only meant for this to happen once, He wouldn't have told the apostles to 'do this.'" Everyone could see from the expression on Tom's face he was very pleased and impressed with what they said.

Tom said, "Now, the Passover celebration begins after dusk on the fourteenth day of Nisan and ends at dusk the next day. Before they could drink from the final cup or the 'consummation cup,' the Passover feast is interrupted. Jesus knows His hour has come and experiences the agony in the garden. Think of the Garden of Eden. Jesus isn't only the sacrificial lamb but the new Adam who fully trusts in God's will. Jesus asks for the apostles to stay awake with Him saying, 'My soul is overwhelmed with sorrow to the point of death. Stay here and watch with me,' but they fell asleep in his hour of agony as He sweats blood from His brow, something that happens at the time of extreme anxiety. Remember that Jesus is man and divine, so He has two wills. His human will may have been weak and afraid but needed to trust and follow along with His divine will. In the garden, He says, 'My Father if it is possible, may this cup be taken from me. Yet not as I will, but as you will.' Notice that Jesus had not taken the fourth cup of the Passover meal saying, 'I shall not drink from the cup until the day I drink it new with you in my Father's kingdom.'

"Judas betrays Jesus and turns Him over to the guards and Peter denies

Him three times that evening. The high priest questions him and charges Him with blasphemy in believing himself to be the Son of God, and they turn him over to Herod, and then to Pilate to have him convicted and executed. Pilate questions Jesus and concludes, 'I see no fault in this man.' Remember that Jesus is the true Lamb of God and only those Passover lambs without a blemish, 'without fault,' are acceptable for sacrifice. Jesus is beaten severely and then Pilate washes his hands of the affair as the people chose to free the murderer Barabbas over Jesus. Jesus, without sin, took the place of the real sinner on the cross as He does for us. On the cross, Jesus refuses the wine mockingly placed up to His lips, but as vinegar is placed on the hyssop branch to His lips, He gives himself over saying, 'It is finished,' with this final cup of consummation." Tom stared up at the crucifix at the ultimate act of love by God and Jesus and closed his eyes for a full minute.

Tom then said, "Spend some time with John's Gospel on the Bread of Life. Jesus talks about the Old Testament's reference to the manna or bread from heaven brought by Moses and then says the true bread from heaven that gives life is from His Father. Jesus says to His followers, 'Truly, truly, I say to you, unless you eat the flesh of the Son of Man, and drink his blood, you have no life in you; he who eats my flesh and drinks my blood has eternal life, and I will raise him up at the last day. For my flesh is food indeed, and my blood is drink indeed. He who eats my flesh and drinks my blood abides in me, and I in him.' You can imagine the reaction from Jews who wouldn't even eat meat unless it had the blood completely drawn from it because they believed you became what you ate the blood of, and animals were lower than man."

Pooja asked, "But Jesus would be higher than man and we would want to become like Jesus, to have Him in our bodies and souls, wouldn't we?"

Tom replied, "Beautifully said. People grumbled, though, at what Jesus was saying and asked, 'Who is this man that offers us his flesh? How can this man give us his flesh to eat?' Many disciples said, 'This is a hard teaching. Who can accept it'? And they left. Now, if the Bread of Life was meant to be just a symbol, what do you think Jesus would've done as many disciples started to leave him over this?"

After a few seconds of silence, David said, "He would've called them back to tell them not to worry, that this wasn't really His flesh and blood to eat."

"Right, and the word He used in Aramaic for eating translates as 'to gnaw,' so he truly meant to eat in a real way. At the Passover meal, the people ate the flesh of the lamb of sacrifice as a meal of communion. Instead of calling them back, He turned and asked the others if His teaching of truth offended them and they turned their backs on Jesus who turned then to His apostles and asked, 'You do not want to leave too, do you?' Jesus was willing to let people leave over this important truth."

Ben said, "It would seem as if He were telling all His followers they needed to do this and not just the apostles at the Last Supper. What did the earliest Church believe?"

"Good question, Ben. When Jesus came back after His resurrection, he spent time with the apostles teaching and instructing them and giving them the authority to speak and act as Christ. He also told them He would send the Holy Spirit, who would remind them of all He taught them and guide them in truth. When Jesus was on the road to Emmaus, He traveled with some of His apostles, who didn't recognize Him until the 'breaking of the bread' with them; there He was revealed. The early Church celebrated the Liturgy of the Word, sharing teachings and stories of Jesus, which became the Gospels and other scriptural readings. They also celebrated the Eucharist, sharing the communion meal of bread and wine. You can read the earliest Church fathers and see they absolutely believed in the real presence of Christ in bread and wine at Communion. Jesus said this was essential to their eternal life and didn't intend to make that offer only to the twelve apostles and no one else."

Marge asked, "Father Tom, isn't doing something in memory of someone just a recollection of them?"

"Well, when Jesus said to 'do this in remembrance of me,' the Jewish understanding of that word was not just to reminisce or to re-sacrifice Jesus but to make that moment present at this moment. God, Jesus, and the Holy Spirit do not live in time but outside of time. The Mass is making the sacrifice of love that Jesus made truly present to us now, forgiving our sins now, not only to the people in this particular church but to the entire community of believers on earth and in heaven. It is truly a mind-blowing moment, and once I understood what the Mass was, I've never found the Mass to be boring, routine or meaningless again.

"Did you know," Tom continued, "it's not the priest who changes the bread and wine into the true presence of Christ but Jesus Himself acting through the priest? It's a holy moment, and that's why we kneel or bow before the tabernacle to honor Christ's presence, a presence He knew we needed. The Bible tells us we'll go to heaven in body and soul, and we need to nourish both to live. We need to let go of our human resistance to what seems hard to believe and trust completely in what Jesus teaches us.

"Jesus started His public ministry at a wedding feast. The Mass is like a wedding feast where the lamb is revealed to be the bridegroom and the Church, his Bride. Just as in a marriage, where man and woman give themselves completely to each other and to God, Jesus also gives Himself completely to us."

Marge said, "And we receive Him completely."

"Absolutely, Marge. Jesus asks us to give our lives for others, which isn't only hard but impossible without the grace and strength we receive each week at this celebration of the Mass."

Tom took the team through the actual Liturgy of the Eucharist, using the words of Jesus, saying the Our Father together, giving the sign of peace to each other, and finally at the end of the Mass where they are 'sent out' to share the Good News with others and live the life Jesus came to give us. The group talked for quite a while after Tom finished, asking questions and sharing their thoughts about the things they hadn't understood before. All were encouraged to come to Mass each week, even though they would have to wait until they were received fully into the Church at Easter Vigil to receive Communion themselves. David was the only one who would be eligible to receive, but he knew he needed to reconcile himself first to be fully in communion with God. David and Tom talked about this several times, one-on-one, to help comprehend the importance of sincerely being ready to receive Christ.

When David returned home that evening, he was glad he met the other candidates and was actively rethinking his negative feelings about the Mass and other beliefs he had rejected over the years. He thought about his father and Kathleen and how much their Catholic faith meant, and he was now beginning to understand why it was so important to them.

Chapter 52

On Wednesday, David received a phone call from the law office working on his father's appeal for a medical release. They were ready to present the full medical records for justification and a number of character witnesses to vouch for Gianni's character. Angelo had helped to identify nineteen other prisoners who were now out of prison and would provide often remarkable accounts of their change in life after being part of Gianni's men's faith group. After their release, men who were hardened criminals, drug addicts, murderers, and lost souls had started businesses, gone back to reconcile with their wives and families, and all seemed to be immersed in giving back to the community and their faith. Their testimonies were emailed to David, and his heart was deeply moved by the written accounts of the impact his father had on each of their lives, including Angelo.

Tears welled, and a sense of pride and love for his father enveloped him. It was as if he was finally beginning to know his father as a man and how it took nothing but Gianni's faith, truth, and love to impact these men, their families, and society in a way that David could never match with all his success and achievements. Finally, the lawyers were able to get written testimony from Gino Cappelletti stating that Gianni Fidele was indeed innocent of all charges. Gino was putting himself in danger by his testimony, but he had lived with the weight of this lie for too long, and the lawyers sealed the deal with him when they explained the circumstances.

David paced all day in his office waiting for the news from the hearing in Richmond. By six o'clock he had heard nothing from the lawyers. Concerned, he called the office only to hear the team hadn't yet returned from the hearing and there was no news. David couldn't wait at the office any longer and needed to get out. He went over to see Angelo to thank him for all he'd done to help with the supporting arguments and for the letter he'd personally written.

When he reached St. Anthony's at seven o'clock, Angelo wasn't in his tiny quarters, but David could see the lights on in the church. He quietly opened the large entrance door and saw the church full of parishioners. When he saw Izzie with ashes on her forehead in the morning, it should've dawned on him that it was Ash Wednesday. David hesitated to go in but saw a familiar large man with a bald head at the end of the aisle close to the back—Ben Harris, who had slowly turned his head to see what the sound was from the back. He smiled broadly when he saw David and waved him to come and sit with him. David walked quietly to the pew and stepped in as Ben squeezed closer to the person on his right. Ben shook hands with David and then continued singing the entrance song to the Mass, which had just begun. For the first time, both of them actually knew what was happening and why, and now the Mass took on a different quality of beauty than they had ever known before.

After the examination of conscience and prayer of confession, the parishioners started filing out of each pew and walking towards the altar to receive the Sign of the Cross on their forehead with ashes. When David and Ben reached the front, where Tom was administering the ashes, Tom smiled broadly and made a Sign of the Cross on David's forehead saying, "Turn away from sin and be faithful to the Gospel."

As David walked back up the aisle, he remembered walking back to the pew with his father as a boy and reaching up to touch the ashes on his forehead to know what they felt like. He almost felt the same urge as he reached the pew to touch the ashes and see the residue on his thumb, but he resisted this time. As they sat down, he could feel his phone buzzing in his pocket, but he knew he couldn't pick it up during Mass.

When the time for Communion came around, David and Ben walked back down the aisle and folded their hands across their chests as Tom had instructed, since they weren't receiving the Body of Christ this night. David finally understood that this wasn't meant as a denial or a punishment but out of recognition that this was indeed the real presence of Christ to be received in full communion with the Church body, which now felt right to him. Once he had thought the people looked like mindless cattle filing down the aisle, but now, with an understanding of what was actually happening, there was a beauty and peace to the procession of the congregation to become one in Christ.

After Communion, the Mass ended fairly quickly, and the last song was sung. The altar servers, Eucharistic ministers, lector, and lastly Father Tom left the now empty altar and walked towards the back. Tom winked at David and Ben as he walked by and went to the back entrance to shake hands and say goodbye to the parishioners as they left.

Not being able to wait any longer to find out who called, David slowly slipped his Blackberry out of his jacket pocket. He glanced down, as his thumb clicked on the display button and read a text from the law office which simply said, "HE IS COMING HOME!" By the time David got to Tom, he could hardly hide his joy. "David, what happened? I feel like something's going on."

David felt frozen and couldn't respond for a second. Then he blurted out, "My father. They're going to let him come home."

Tom made no hesitation to put his arms around David. "That's such great news! When did you find out?"

"Just a second ago. I was waiting all day, and after hearing nothing, I came here to see Angelo. When I poked my head in the church, Ben saw me and pulled me in by the collar." Ben came up to David and Tom just in time to catch the end of their laughter and asked what was happening. David explained the long story to him in the rectory with Tom.

David got home and found himself actually saying a prayer of thanks to God for the news, leaving him with only a good feeling about seeing his father.

Chapter 53

David called his father the next morning to share the good news. Gianni was happy, but he also knew he was dying and was at peace with whatever happened for the remaining days or months of his life. David had set up his own bedroom for his father because it was the room filled with morning sunshine. He moved his clothes and things into one of the guest bedrooms and didn't tell his father he had moved. David flew down to Richmond and Gianni was feeling good for the flight back to Boston. This was the first time he had been on a plane since his military service in the Korean conflict. Gianni couldn't believe he was back in his hometown and would be able to see his good friend Angelo again. He also couldn't believe the size and impressiveness of David's Beacon Street apartment. When David showed his father his bedroom, Gianni felt the same kind of discomfort Angelo had experienced and had asked David if there was anything smaller. David said, "Pop, let's just try this for now, and we can change if it doesn't work out." Gianni smiled weakly and gave in.

David had ordered food from his father's favorite restaurant in the North End to be delivered and had asked Angelo to come in with the delivery man acting as if he was a restaurant employee. When Gianni finally realized what was going on, he stood up and gave his old friend Angelo a teary hug. They ate, talked, and laughed until Gianni was feeling worn and was ready to sleep in a real bed.

Angelo said, "I had to sleep on the floor for the first several weeks before I could be comfortable in a bed, but you've been pampered in the hospital for some time now, so you should be okay, Gianni."

Gianni smiled and nodded as he walked to his room more slowly than Angelo may have remembered. Angelo helped him change and gave him a kiss on the forehead as he left the bedroom. He thanked David for having him to dinner to see Gianni and said he could be available anytime to come over and help out or be with Gianni while David was at work or traveling. David knew Angelo was making a sincere offer and that he'd probably need his help. After Angelo left, David sat by Gianni's bed and talked with him for a while about being home, about the changes in Boston, and about things Gianni would like to do. Gianni said he'd like to attend Mass in the morning, and David nodded, understanding how important this was to his father.

Gianni was up earlier than David, and David found him sitting on his bed, dressed and ready for Mass when he got up. When they entered the church, Gianni blessed himself from the baptismal font, and then went as far as he could to genuflect towards the altar.

During the Mass, David watched his father and realized how much this meant to him. He was living his life for Christ and here he was with Him in the Word and in the breaking of the Bread. He saw a tear come down his father's cheek as Tom held the consecrated Eucharist in his hands and raised it high above his head. After the Mass, Gianni wanted to stay seated in the pew for a while, which gave Tom the opportunity to come back in to meet Gianni. "Father Tom, it's always good to meet a good friend of my son. I've heard a lot about you over the past several months."

Tom laughed while still shaking Gianni's hand. "We'll have to compare notes because I may have heard more about you from your son and Angelo. I've been trying to teach him how to play basketball, but I think it may be a hopeless cause. I'm very honored to finally meet you and have you come to St. Anthony's for Mass."

Gianni smiled, and they walked towards the back of the church. "This is quite a beautiful church. It must've been built by—"

Tom interrupted, "Yes, it was built in large part by those generous, talented, and faithful Italians. They certainly have an eye for and a commitment to aesthetics and beauty."

Gianni smiled. "And the Irish have a commitment to the faith itself."

David realized it would be a lot for his father to travel down to Hingham, but he wanted him to meet Kathleen and his grandchildren. He had called Kathleen the evening before and asked if she minded coming to the apartment to meet Gianni.

There was no hesitation in Kathleen's response.

Even though he and Kathleen had been separated for over six years, only Amy and James had actually ever been to David's apartment. When David and Gianni got home, David put a roast in the oven for a Sunday dinner for the family. Lucy had brought back Trooper from his overnight, and he was predictably agitated to find a stranger in the apartment. He barked loudly until David calmed him down and assured him that his father was one of the good guys. While Gianni was lying down for a short nap, David set the table and prepared dinner.

Early in the afternoon, Kathleen arrived with the kids. David worried about Trooper waking his father but to his surprise, Trooper went right up to Kathleen, who squatted down in her blue dress and rubbed her hands through the fur on both sides of Trooper's neck. "That's a good boy. Aren't you a good boy, Topper? Yes, you are."

David took their coats and then checked on his dad and found him sitting on the end of his bed with his eyes closed. "Pop, Kathleen and the kids are here."

Gianni stood up and walked out to the living room. Kathleen shot up. "Dad," she said and gave him a long and teary hug.

"Beautiful outside is no question," Gianni said, "and David has let me know how beautiful a person you are on the inside and what a wonderful mother you are to these two beautiful children. But what am I saying? They are almost grown up now. I think I can guess which one is Amy and which one is James." Gianni opened his arms, and with that, both Amy and James walked comfortably into his embrace.

Kathleen helped David with the meal while Gianni talked and played with his granddaughter and grandson for the very first time. At one point, Gianni pulled out two coins from his pocket and gave one to each of them. "These are very old coins my grandfather had given to me when I was a boy. Tell me, did you go to Mass this morning?"

James nodded.

"Do you remember the Gospel reading at all?"

James shook his head, while Amy said, "It was something about Caesar."

"Very good. The Pharisees were trying to trap Jesus with a question about paying taxes that would get him in trouble if he answered 'Yes' or 'No,' but he was too smart for them. What did he do?"

Amy said, "He asked for a coin and then asked whose image was on it."

"That's excellent. Whose image was on it?"

"Caesar. I remember what Jesus said. It was something like, give to Caesar what is Caesar's."

"Right. So, we give to Caesar the things that bear his image. Can you guess what bears the image of God?"

Amy and James were silent as they thought of any coins that had God on them.

"I'll give you a clue. The answer is in this room."

They looked around their father's apartment and then again at the coins he gave them. "I don't know, Grandpa."

"Okay, I don't want to keep you from dinner. It's you. And me. We are made in the image of God and we belong to God. Instead of falling into the trap, Jesus always teaches a bigger lesson that will make us happy. If we give ourselves completely to him, we will be happy because we belong to him. He made both of you and loves you very much."

David and Kathleen smiled as they heard the end of the conversation.

At dinner, David loved watching how comfortable the conversation flowed between Kathleen, Gianni, and the kids. It was almost as if he were watching them in slow motion with no sound as he took in each moment. He couldn't help watching Kathleen's smile and loving blue eyes as she laughed and talked.

He almost felt like a boy in grade school who had become infatuated with the girl who sat several rows over from him in his English class, then it finally hit him like a ton of bricks. When David had left the family to live on his own, he found Trooper outside his door with no owner in sight. Trooper only had a medallion on his collar with his name on it written in script, "Topper." He tried to find the owner to no avail and decided to take him in as his roommate, so he changed his name to "Trooper." When Kathleen entered his apartment today, Trooper greeted her as an old friend instead of his normally instinctive barking at a stranger.

Here David was abandoning Kathleen with a ten-year-old and a one-year-old, while she was worried about his being alone. Kathleen knew David was okay conquering the world on his own, but she also knew, deep down inside, he was afraid of being truly alone. His heart and mind were both racing as he scrambled to ask himself what the other possible options were when everyone stopped talking and Kathleen asked, "David, are you having your own private conversation?"

That brought David back to the moment. "No. No. I was just thinking about something. Hey, is everyone ready for some cannoli for dessert?"

After Kathleen left with Amy and James, David sat with his father in the den, reminiscing about some happy times. David finally managed to bring up his thoughts about Kathleen and Trooper. Gianni smiled, unsurprised. "Son, can you not see the love in that girl's eyes, in her actions, and in her heart? It sounds like you believe love is a conditional thing—if I feel good, I love you; if I'm upset with you, I don't love you. I'm sure Kathleen was very hurt, if not devastated, by being left, much like you must've felt all those years ago. But love is much more than how we feel. It's wanting the absolute best for the other person no matter how imperfect their love is at the moment. Think about how we treat God every day, and how he never gives up on us, loving us and being ready to hold us again. I think Kathleen is a very special woman and has that kind of love for you and the kids more than you realize. I wouldn't be surprised in the least if your theory about her was right on the mark, not surprised at all."

David told Gianni that he needed to step out briefly to take care of something. Gianni had a good idea of what David was taking care of as David drove down to Hingham and knocked on the door on a cool, star-filled evening.

Kathleen stared open-mouthed at him. "Is something—?

"I just had a question for you."

Kathleen grabbed her warm coat and a white knitted hat and stepped outside to listen to David's mystery question.

David shoved his hands into his pockets. "Kat, you've never been in the apartment before today, right?"

"That's right."

"Have you ever been on the front stoop of the apartment before?"

Kathleen hesitated.

"Have you?"

"It's possible."

David nodded as he gazed up at the stars.

"Why are you asking?"

"Today wasn't the first time you met Trooper, was it? Trooper has been a great companion and a fierce defender of the homestead. When you came to the door, he acted like you were an old friend, and then, when you called him Topper, it took me a bit, but the lights finally came on."

"Okay, I won't tell you I was happy when you walked out on your commitment to me and your own children, but I knew you were probably struggling internally. I didn't think it would be good for you to be alone, so I stopped in at the animal rescue, and when I saw Topper, something just told me to take him. The rescue people said he'd been a good companion for someone in the West End before a break-in robbery to his house that left the owner dead and Topper wounded. That may be why Topper, I mean Trooper, tends to be overprotective with strangers."

David gazed deeply into Kathleen's eyes and deeper into her soul. This act of selfless love on Kathleen's part seemed far beyond anything he thought he deserved. How had he missed this? The humbling answer came to him: he had never cared enough to know her that deeply before. David thanked Kathleen for being honest and for being so kind, but on the way home, he felt strangely disoriented about the world of relationships he thought he had finally figured out.

Chapter 54

Before David knew it, it was the last Monday meeting of the RCIA group before Holy Week, and he was about to become a full member of the Church that he had long misunderstood and condemned. The more the group covered the many questions each candidate had struggled with, the more they all felt energized and at home with their new faith. As a group, they went out into the community by helping the poor, sick, and those in prison, to make their faith one of service to others. David had become good friends with everyone in the group, now seeing them with a new sense of depth and appreciation, but he became closest to Ben, who would sometimes come out with David and Tom for a beer at Dempsey's after class.

Afterwards, David told Tom that he was ready to make his confession and receive the Sacrament of Reconciliation, something he'd been hesitant to do so far. Ben had talked to David about his own first confession, saying "Definitely not something I wanted to do, but I figured that the more you need it, the less you want to do it, so I just followed Father Tom's lead, and you know what? I'm glad we have Reconciliation. It was quite an experience. I felt lighter, cleaner, almost like I had a fresh start and a heavy weight had been taken off my shoulders."

That Wednesday, David sat down in Tom's office while Tom heated up some tea. Instead of David's mind being flooded with a list of things he needed to confess, his mind was almost blank. Tom came in and handed David his cup and sat down saying, "Is it hard to believe it's already here?"

David tried to think of what Tom meant. "Oh, you mean Easter?"

Tom smiled. "No, the Red Sox home opener is on Monday!"

David nodded, knowing Tom was trying to put his mind at ease.

David said, "So what are we supposed to do here?"

"Well, it would be good to have a sense of what the Sacrament of Reconciliation is all about. The Church believes, and I believe, that it's an important habit to examine our choices and actions in life and to see which ones are healthy for us and for our relationships, especially our relationship with God. David, how do you feel about Amy and James?"

"What do you mean? I love them."

"Do you want the best for them?"

"Sure."

"And would you try to pass on your wisdom and give them guidelines you know would be the healthiest for them?"

David nodded.

"What if they defied your teachings, and you knew they were heading into unhealthy or dangerous territory because of it, would you turn your back on them or welcome them with open arms if they recognized it and apologized?"

David said, "Welcome them with no hesitation."

"And that is how God feels about you."

Tom got up and walked to the window, where he paused and then turned to David. "Who are you?"

David lifted his shoulders, puzzled. "What do you mean?"

Tom asked again, "Who is David Kelly?"

"Um, I'm ahhh... I'm me, a father, a salesman, a friend, what do you mean?"

"At your very core, who *are* you?"

David shrugged his shoulders, confused. Tom sat on the edge of his desk and said, "Who created you?"

"Oh, okay. God created me, and as He did you, by the way."

Tom said, "Who was Jesus?"

"Jesus was the Son of God."

"What did Jesus call God?"

"He called Him Father."

"And when He taught us how to pray to God, what was the prayer?"

David thought for a second. "Our Father."

"Perfect. What is the first word?"

"Our."

Tom said, "Exactly. You, David, are the Father's son too. To God, you are His son, and He knows you better than you know yourself, and He loves you unconditionally—even more than you love and want what is best for Amy and James. With His love also came His plan for you and His commandments to help you live the life He knows is best for you. When we break those commandments or don't trust God and choose our own will over His, we are turning away from God, as did the Prodigal Son when he didn't honor his father. He knows we are human and will fail over and over again, so we need His mercy and grace on the journey. When the apostles asked Jesus how to love Him, He told them: 'Whoever keeps my commandments and observes them is the one who loves me. And whoever loves me will be loved by my father, and I will love him.'"

"I'm not sure if I could even name all the commandments."

Tom said, "We can review them. We can only sin when we are aware of what we are doing, but we're also responsible for forming and developing our conscience, to find out what is right and wrong. Remember, no matter what we do, no matter how bad we think it is, God will always forgive us because He never stops loving us and wanting us to know that."

David said, "I would think there are some things we can do that couldn't be forgiven, even by God. What about the people who killed Jesus?"

Tom said, "On the cross, Jesus said, 'Forgive them, for they know not what they do.' So, even that was forgivable. When you think of God, think of His mercy so you never have to hide or think you are no longer acceptable to God. Think about how much you would want Amy and James to be reconciled, no matter what."

Tom sat back down. "Jesus taught how life on earth was about love, mercy, and forgiveness. You can see that Jesus gave His apostles the authority to teach, baptize, and even to forgive sins in His name. 'Peace be with you. As the Father has sent me, so I send you. Receive the Holy Spirit. If you forgive the sins of any, they are forgiven them; if you retain the sins of any, they are retained.' When we do sin, we should apologize directly to God as well, but He has given us a gift of this sacrament to receive His grace and forgiveness in a tangible way. Jesus knew we are human and need to make our confession verbally and to hear we are forgiven through our ears. The priest can help us with our examination of conscience, provide guidance and support, and acts in the person of Christ in absolving us from our sins. The more we sin, the less we tend to see that we are in sin because we are turning away from God. It is a lot like a pane of glass that is dirty. If we hold it up to the light, it's pretty clear where the spots are, but if we turn it away from the light, it's hard to tell where those spots are."

David talked to his father about his examination of conscience, and he seemed happy to hear that David was taking this sacrament to heart. When David came back on Friday, he felt nervous but ready to meet with Tom for his first confession in over thirty years. As he talked through his life and his stumbles, David found himself to be surprisingly open and honest to a fault with Tom. David wasn't proud of how he had treated people along the way, how he had often ignored those in need, abandoned his own family after feeling unjustly abandoned by his own parents, how he had been dishonest with himself for so many years, how he had hated God and not loved and honored Him throughout his life, how he had used women in relationships and in thought, and how he hadn't used his gifts, resources and time to make a difference in the lives of others as he had been completely self-focused and selfish for most of his life. It was an act of great humility for David to be so forthcoming about his choices and actions, and to his own surprise, truly repentant about each sin he had confessed. Tom asked David if he were truly sorry for the sins he confessed, and David bowed his head. "Yes, I am."

Tom had David recite the Act of Contrition. Then, putting his hand on David's head, he said, "God, the Father of mercies, through the death and resurrection of His Son has reconciled the world to Himself and sent the Holy Spirit among us for the forgiveness of sins; through the ministry of the Church may God give you pardon and peace, and I absolve you from your sins in the name of the Father, and of the Son, and of the Holy Spirit."

David was trying to let what he just heard register in his heart. He was truly forgiven. He was starting with a fresh slate with God and with himself without the growing burden that had weighed on his conscience for so many years. He had expected to feel nothing, but there was a definite feeling of freedom and desire in his soul.

"Tom, despite believing I'm forgiven, I'm still struggling to know what the right thing to do for Jillian is. It's a casualty of my selfishness that I don't know how to make it up to her without hurting her more."

Tom stood up and opened his desk drawer and pulled out an envelope with only David's first name written on the front. "I was asked to give this to you at a time that seemed right."

David tightened his forehead, confused as he took the envelope from Tom and unsealed it to find a letter from Jillian.

Dear David,

I'm writing this letter to let you know that I'll be moving to Pennsylvania and on with my life. I won't say that I wasn't deeply hurt when I was feeling very much in love with you, but Father Tom has helped me to get to a better place. I'll continue to work on myself and avoid some of the relationship pitfalls I've found myself repeating. I want you to know that I'm not angry with you and now know that you were never free to be mine in the first place—something I didn't understand before. I don't want you to blame yourself since we were both coming to the relationship without a healthy understanding of a lot of things. It's important to me to move forward and for you not to try to contact me. It would hurt much more than it would help me, and I hope you can respect and understand that. I hope and pray that your life is full of everything you deserve and I'm confident now that I'll be okay.

Take care and bless you,

Jillian

When Tom came back into the room, David was deep in thought about Jillian and how he wished he hadn't hurt her so deeply. She deserved so much better than being a victim of his ignorance and self-preoccupation.

Jim Sano

His sins may have been forgiven but the consequences to others hadn't disappeared, and Jillian was telling him that he couldn't fix this one with her. He could only make sure he treated those in his life with dignity and self-giving love.

Chapter 55

David took his father to the Palm Sunday service to start Holy Week. After Mass, they walked over to the Eastside for breakfast, where David introduced Gianni to the harried Linda. Linda just looked at Gianni and said, "I guess this explains things," to which both David and Gianni laughed.

David said, "Pop. You've been feeling pretty good lately, right?"

Gianni nodded. "I can't complain."

"I know it's early in the season, and I know it's Holy Week, but I heard the temperature is supposed to get to 81 degrees on Tuesday, and I wondered if—"

Gianni interrupted David. "I'd love to go to the game with you. They're playing Tampa Bay. What kind of baseball town is that?"

Tuesday was a warm spring day for the game and it happily reminded them both of the time they sat together at Fenway when David was just a boy. Later that day, they sat in the den relaxing while David asked his father, "Pop, I want to receive Communion on Holy Thursday. Tom spent a lot of time teaching us about the Eucharist. I get it in my head, but when I see you at Communion, it seems as if it touches your heart. What am I missing?"

"It might be one of those things that will make sense when you receive. There are a lot of things we can't really understand on our own, which is why we need Christ as a real part of us, in our hearts, in our souls, and in our bodies."

David said, "Maybe. I guess I'm like a doubting Thomas; I need to see to believe it."

Gianni chuckled and asked, "Have you ever been to Italy?"

"I did visit Rome for a sales meeting several years ago. It's a beautiful city. Why do you ask?"

Gianni said, "Just a few hours east of Rome is a town called Lanciano. It was the birthplace of Longinus, the Roman centurion who pierced the side and heart of Christ at the crucifixion. The name Lanciano means 'lance' or 'of the spear' in Italian."

David asked, "Pop, is this connected to what we're talking about?"

Gianni answered, "I hope so. In 700 AD, there was a priest-monk at the Monastery of St. Longinus who was having heavy doubts about the true presence of Christ in the Eucharist. So, it's okay to have doubts or questions. One day, the monk was saying Mass, and as he raised the host up at the consecration, the host turned into actual flesh and the wine into visible blood. The flesh remained intact, and the blood divided into five clot globules, some believing this related to the five wounds of Christ, two in his hands, two in his feet and one in his side."

"Pop, how do we know what really happened 1300 years ago and that this isn't just a story or hoax?"

"Fair question. Both the flesh and the droplets of blood still exist today, not changed in appearance or corrupted. Neither of those things can be explained by science even to this day. In 1970, the most detailed tests were made by noted scientists—hematologists, anatomists, pathologists, histologists, biochemists, and on and on, including the renowned Dr. Odoardo Linoli, an expert scientist on anatomy and pathological histology."

David said, "Okay, I'm impressed with the expertise and objectivity of the scientists, but what did they find?"

"They found several things that confirmed that the flesh was striated muscular human tissue from the heart of a male, and without being hermetically sealed or with any traces of preservatives, it hadn't decomposed. Nor could a human hand have cut this sample that encircled the decayed bread at the center. The team found that the five globules of blood were also not corrupted and had the same proportions of proteins, chloride, phosphorus, magnesium, potassium, sodium and calcium as fresh blood, which is normally gone within twenty minutes of exposure. The five pellets of blood weighed the same as one pellet or any combination of the globules, again not scientifically explainable. The possibility of fraud was conclusively excluded."

"If what they found wasn't scientifically possible and there was no fraud involved, how can this miracle not be huge news?"

"For those who don't want to believe, they dismiss it and move on. For those who do believe, this is a simple confirmation of what they had faith in all along. For me, I trust the words of Christ and the beliefs of the early Church guided in truth by the Holy Spirit. The apostles believed in the real presence of Christ in the breaking of the Eucharistic Bread because of divine revelation. The Miracle of Lanciano might be helpful to a Doubting Thomas because it shows that anything is possible with God, even the seemingly impossible."

On Holy Thursday evening, David attended Mass at St. Anthony's. It was the end of Lent and the beginning of the Triduum, something that was never previously a part of David's conscious world. David sat in the second row with his father and sponsor. Ben, Mike, Pooja, and Marge all sat with them as well, as the church began to fill up to celebrate the Lord's Supper. Throughout the Mass, there was a sense of simplicity, peace, and beauty that brought David into the present in a way he hadn't experienced before. When Tom washed the feet of twelve parishioners, there was something profound about the humble act of service that Jesus wanted to show by example to his apostles.

As the naked altar was covered with cloth and the simple gifts of bread and wine were brought up and placed upon it, there was a sense of expectation that Jesus would be there with them. David remembered that Tom had said, in that timeless moment, Christ was present in his sacrifice with the entire community of the Church on earth and in heaven. It was a powerful moment for him as a tingle ran up the back of his neck and his eyes welled up at the moment of consecration.

When David approached the altar to receive Communion after his father, he felt an impulse to bow in recognition of Whom he was about to receive into his very being. At that moment, it made so much sense and he was glad he had made his reconciliation. Tom smiled as he held out the host to David. "Body of Christ," and David said, "Amen," as he held out his hand and took the Eucharist and placed it in his mouth and made the Sign of the Cross.

On Good Friday, Gianni asked if David would bring him to the church at noon to walk the Stations of the Cross. The Stations depicted fourteen moments of Christ's passion from conviction to crucifixion and death for our sins. David took a half day from work and went to the Stations with his father, and for the first time in his life put himself in the footsteps of Christ and what He actually went through out of love for us and trust in His Father. David hadn't had a moment of revelation like this in his entire life, simultaneously feeling a sense of shame and incredible gratitude. He had simply come to see to his own father's wishes and was taken by surprise to think about the human person of Christ experiencing betrayal, abandonment, false accusations, mocking torture, aloneness, and the most painful form of execution devised, and all for love and mercy for him. This experience made the Good Friday service and passion readings all that more moving, and David felt exhausted when he returned home with Gianni afterward.

Saturday was a quiet day. David made a late breakfast for Gianni and himself, which they ate at the sunlit kitchen table. Gianni had sent letters to Bobby and Abbie, to see if they could either come to Boston or he could travel out to see them, but there was no response. David had called Abbie, and she was hesitant to open up the wound again. Gianni said, "David, I know I'm doing pretty well at the moment, but things can change quickly. I can't force anything on your sister or brother, but I do want to try to see them somehow this spring."

David said, "I spend my days convincing people why they should do things; I'll see what I can do. I think there's a lot of pain there that they don't want to face. I've tried to let them know the truth and how lucky I am to know the man I'm blessed to be with now."

That evening, anticipating a large crowd for the Easter Vigil, David and Gianni got to the church early. Pooja, Marge, Mike, and Ben arrived with their sponsors early as well, so they were all able to sit together. As Kathleen, Amy, and James arrived to sit behind them, David could feel his emotions breaking out of his normally controlled nature. Then Izzie and her children Joseph, Isabelle, and Jenny came in and sat with Kevin Walsh, who smiled at David in a way that broke the tension. Angelo came and sat with Kathleen. David was most moved when, to his surprise, the entire boys' basketball team came in, all wearing dress pants, shirts, and ties. Despite the respect and popularity he had, in reality, David lived a life alone, without true intimacy or friendships. Seeing these people he had gotten close to and now cared about sitting together at the Vigil overwhelmed him and made him feel anything but alone.

The service began in total darkness, just as before the creation of the universe. The new paschal candle was lit and dipped into the baptismal font. From that candle, each person lit the candle he was holding and shared the light with the person next to them until the church was filled with the candlelight. There was something intimate and unifying as the readings and songs moved the service from the Creation to the Fall, through the covenant relationship between God and Israel, until the life, death, and resurrection of Christ in fulfillment of the early scriptures. Gianni stood with David next to him, his hand on David's shoulder as Tom confirmed David into the faith, marking his forehead with the Sign of the Cross in the holy oil of Chrism. "David John Giovanni Kelly Fidele, be sealed with the gift of the Holy Spirit."

David responded, "Amen," as he was now a confirmed member of the Church that Jesus built and graced with the gifts of the Holy Spirit to help build it up.

After the Mass and the final song to celebrate that Christ was risen and had conquered death for all, the parishioners met in the basement for a social gathering and food to break the fast. James came running up to hug his father, as David was congratulating Ben and the others, which was soon followed by hugs from Amy and Kathleen. David introduced Izzie and her family to everyone. The boys from the basketball team, sporting their new black jackets with red writing on the back that said, "St. Anthony's Basketball, Conference Champs," all said hello to Coach Kelly as they had moved their way through the noisy, festive and packed hall. As David was talking with his father and Angelo, he noticed Kevin Walsh standing about ten feet away with some coffee in one hand and a cheese Danish in the other. David wiggled his way through the crowd and reached Kevin just as he was taking a bite out of the Danish. David patted Kevin on the back. "Of all the people I wouldn't expect to be here tonight!"

Kevin said, "I think I would've said the same thing to you not too long ago. Izzie told me what was happening, and I thought, 'I have to see this.' It's been a long time since I've been to Easter Mass, and I'll have to say that I like what you have."

David looked Kevin in the eyes. "It's what has been missing in my life. I really appreciate your coming."

Kevin said, "Don't let me take you away from your family, but let's go out to dinner sometime soon, and you can tell me what has really been going on with you."

David put his arm around Kevin's shoulder and replied, "It's a promise." David made his way back to his family and friends and remembered feeling much like he did on Christmas Eve with his family and neighbors those many years ago.

As people left, and the hall thinned out, David stayed and helped put away chairs and clean up in the kitchen, as did Kathleen, Amy, and others, while James sat and talked with his grandfather. David and Tom hadn't had a chance to talk all day and as they folded some tables together, David said, "You must be exhausted, but these were three incredible days. I want to thank you for everything, and I mean everything you've done as both a friend and a good priest."

Tom lifted the table with David. "I appreciate the kind words, but none of this has been a one-way street. Our friendship means a great deal to me. It also means a lot to me to see you with your family and in a good place with yourself. When I finally joined the Church, it felt as though I had come home. I hope it feels that way for you. A lot of people are running around these days chasing happiness, but I think joy is a deeper feeling that comes from putting Christ at the center. It's a great gift I'm glad we can share."

David gave Tom a hug. "I think it's time to get Pop home and let the family get back to Hingham."

Kathleen kissed Gianni goodnight as she put her coat on. "We're looking forward to seeing you tomorrow for Easter dinner, and I'll have that lamb simmering in the oven when you arrive."

The next day was one of the best Easter dinners anyone in the family could remember.

Chapter 56

While life felt completely different to David now, things seemed to get back into a simpler routine. There were no more Monday or Friday night meetings at St. Anthony's and no basketball coaching. David now had more time to spend with Amy and James and with his father. His brother, Bobby, hadn't responded to any calls or letters from Gianni and David, but Abbie had finally agreed to have them come out to Minnesota to visit Memorial Day weekend. She told David she was anxious about seeing their father, given the anger she harbored for so long, but David convinced her that she'd be very glad she saw him.

Although Gianni didn't say anything, David suspected he was feeling more pain in his back, especially when he walked for any length of time. He was also experiencing weakness and numbness in his chest and down his legs. Four days before their flight to see Abbie, the pain became more severe, and after another night of no sleep, Gianni told David he needed to go to the hospital.

David flushed with panic, but he forced himself to remain calm. "Okay, Pop. I know a doctor at Dana-Farber who is really good. I can take you over this morning."

"I'd appreciate that, son. I'm sorry about this."

"Why are you sorry, Pop?"

"I'm sorry to put you through what may be coming, and I was so looking forward to seeing Abbie this weekend."

David had called ahead to Dr. Richard Heigel, someone he'd met through social functions and fundraisers, and felt he could trust with his father's care. When they reached the hospital, there was a wheelchair ready at the door that David gently assisted Gianni into. Gianni looked up at David. "I won't break. I'm just feeling a bit of discomfort."

David put a hand on his father's shoulder as he registered him and took him up to Dr. Heigel's office where the doctor examined Gianni and asked him to describe what he was experiencing and his history. He then ordered a PET scan for Gianni while David stayed in the office to talk about his observations and where they could get Gianni's medical records. After a few hours of waiting, Dr. Heigel called David and Gianni back into his office to discuss the scans. "Without having your records or the results of the bone scans or needle biopsy, I can't give you a definitive diagnosis yet."

Gianni calmly said, "We all know I have cancer that includes spinal tumors. I'm assuming from the symptoms that there's at least one new tumor beginning to grow and pressing on the spine. Is that fair to say, Dr. Heigel?"

Dr. Heigel glanced at David and then back to Gianni. "Mr. Fidele, I'm sorry to say that is most likely the case. I'm seeing several growths that look like tumors in areas that would be difficult if not impossible to operate. I do want to wait for your full records and the remaining lab results before we make a plan of treatment."

"I completely understand. I've been dealing with this for some time now, and I'm past the point of chemotherapy and radiation. The expectation was that the tumors would return and spread into the spine itself. What I'm hoping for is that you can help with the pain management and if you have other recommendations after you've seen the other test results. I'd appreciate that. Thank you for seeing me on such short notice, Dr. Heigel. I suspect it's not easy to get onto your busy schedule."

"You're welcome, Mr. Fidele. It helps me to know your awareness of your situation and I will absolutely let you know as soon as I have more information." Dr. Heigel wrote on a small pad of paper. "In the meantime, I would fill this prescription to relieve some of your current pain. After the results, we can discuss the possibility of a spinal pump for more effective pain management or the use of nerve blockers. It is hard to know yet what the best options are, but we will do everything we can to give you the best care."

"Rich," David said, "I truly appreciate this, and spare no cost to do whatever you can. I just want my father to have whatever he needs."

Back home, David called Abbie to tell her that the trip looked like it needed to be canceled, but Abbie wasn't sure if she could arrange a trip to Boston.

David also called Angelo to let him know, and Angelo came over that afternoon to visit, allowing David to visit Tom. "I had to take Pop to the hospital," he explained to Tom with a choked voice, "and it looks like the tumors are back already and may not be operable."

Tom reached his hand out to grasp David's arm. "I'm so so sorry. Is he in the hospital now or home?"

David's eyes were red and puffy. "He's home and Angelo is with him. He never complains, but he told me that the pain was strong. I feel so cheated. Things were going great. We were building a really nice relationship together and with Kathleen and the kids. Why does this have to happen so soon? Why can't God show his mercy now?"

"I understand. I can't give you a magic answer. I don't know the plan for your dad or for you, but I do know there is one. I also know he will be more than okay in God's hands, but today he's in yours and glad of it. I can see it in his eyes when he looks at you. There will be plenty of time to be angry at God, but let's give him a chance to show us more."

A feeling of abandonment and fear came over David again, but he felt comforted by the empathetic look of his best friend.

Tom suggested David walk over to the church with him. The statue of Mary gazed down with a look of love and peace. In front of her were several rows of prayer candles, and Tom picked out two long wicks, giving one to David. "Let's each light a candle for your father and say a prayer for him."

David hadn't lit any of the candles before. Now in the quiet of the night in the house of God, it seemed natural to light the candles and say a prayer for Gianni.

Tom said, "Holy Mary, please hear our prayer. Dear Lord, we pray this evening for Your most faithful and gentle servant, Giovanni Fidele. He has continued to put his trust in You and do Your will as he suffers from this insidious disease. May he be strengthened in joining his suffering with Christ, and may he be healed in His name. Whatever Your plans are for Gianni and David, may they know of Your never-failing love and Your boundless mercy as they never lose trust in You and Your will. We pray for strength, guidance, and healing, in Your name. Amen."

"Amen. Thank you, Tom. That meant a lot."

They sat together for another fifteen minutes in silence, praying and letting God fill their hearts with peace.

When David returned home, Gianni was already in bed, and Angelo was sitting at the kitchen table waiting for David. They talked about making sure Gianni had someone available while David was at work, and Angelo offered to remain available, which made David feel much better.

After a week and no news on the PET scans, David was getting impatient and drove to Dana-Farber to see Dr. Heigel. "David, it's good to see you. I actually talked to your dad yesterday when he called me."

David was surprised. "You already talked to him?"

Dr. Heigel said, "I planned on having you both in later this week, but I had a call from him. I have to tell you he's very much on top of what's going on with his condition and options. He sounds like someone who does his research and asks the right questions."

"I'm not surprised, but can you tell me what you've found out?"

Dr. Heigel was somber. "I can tell you that the tumors are malignant in nature and there are several. It may be just a matter of time before it metastasizes in the spine itself. I'm very sorry to give you this news, David.

Your father seems to be a very strong individual and at peace with his situation, but I think he's worried about you."

"Worried about me? How can someone with spinal cancer be worried about me?"

Dr. Heigel took off his glasses and pinched the bridge of his nose. "David, your father is most likely entering the final stages of battling his cancer. It may be only a matter of a few months, and he is very aware of this terrible reality. I don't think he's worried about himself but those he cares about deeply whom he leaves behind."

David stood up and paced a bit before turning. "There must be something we can try. I cannot believe there's nothing that can be done. All this money for research and innovations and you are saying that there's nothing we can do for my father?"

Dr. Heigel stood and walked around to the front of his desk. "David, there have been some great advances in treating cancer. I hope we'll look back on treatments such as radiation, chemotherapy, and surgery as crude and barbaric, but right now they remain the only options available in many cases. Your father has been through several rounds of chemo and radiation treatment, and while there may be some palliative benefit to additional treatment, we are at a point where they will not eradicate his cancer. I believe your father's preference is not to spend his last days in hospitals but spend that time with family at home. I know that's very difficult to hear, and it may feel like giving up, but I don't believe that this is the case for your father. From a professional standpoint, I respect your father's wishes and agree with his decision. As a friend of yours, I can completely understand the pain and how hard this news must be for you. I am so sorry to be telling you all of this, David."

David shook his head in disbelief and sat back down without saying a word as he stared down at the floor trying to process what he was hearing.

"David, we don't know yet what will happen. As I said, he is very strong for his age, but he also has been through a lot, and it does take something out of you. The important thing is that we are there for him and monitor him closely. There are options to help with the pain that can be quite strong when it comes to spinal cancers. We will make sure he has everything he needs, and that you and your family are included as well. It can be very hard for sons and daughters to do this when their parents are sick, but the best advice I can give you is to put yourself in your father's place and think about what you would want. It's your best guide to doing the right thing for your dad."

"I appreciate your being straightforward with me. This isn't easy for me to hear, but I can imagine that it's not the easiest part of your job either. I just want to make sure he's as comfortable as he can be and has the best care available. I also want to be trained to be there for him through this as well. If you can help with that at all, I would appreciate it."

Dr. Heigel said, "Absolutely. Family involvement is really important, and I think that will be especially true for your dad."

David got up and shook Dr. Heigel's hand and thanked him as he left his office feeling dazed and unsure of the road ahead.

Over the next few months, David made sure Gianni had company and the care he needed. It was always hard to tell because Gianni wasn't one to complain, but he was generally doing well with the pain medication he was taking and was able to spend time with David and Angelo and to see Kathleen, Amy and James at least once or twice a week. It meant a lot to Gianni to be able to develop relationships with his remaining family even though he knew it would be a more painful goodbye in the end. He had always thought he'd rather suffer the pain of loss and know he really had something to miss than to avoid relationships just to avoid the pain of loss later on. He hoped that his family would feel the same way in the end.

Many days, Gianni took advantage of getting outside whenever he could, sometimes walking and other times in his wheelchair with someone he cared about pushing from behind. Gianni told David how grateful he was to have this chance to be home with his family, to experience the sights, sounds, and smells of early summer. He talked openly about dying but drew people to him with his sense of humor and his joy of life itself. When he felt able, he went to daily Mass. It was something that brought him great peace and strength. When he wasn't able to attend, Father Tom would drop by to bring him Communion and visit with the family.

They celebrated James's birthday with a fishing trip on a boat David rented, and on the Fourth of July, they had a picnic on the Common during the earlier family fireworks. Gianni was fully present for each moment he could be, but by mid-July, the pain became severe and constant. David took his father back to the Dana-Farber unit to do another round of scans that revealed the growth of the tumors and cancer metastasizing to his spine. Dr. Heigel wanted to introduce a low dose of morphine taken orally to ease the pain and have a nurse spend several hours each day with Gianni to provide therapeutic massage and monitor his status. David cut back his hours at work and worked from home to be with his father and learn everything the nurse was doing to help Gianni. Time had passed far too quickly for David. He was feeling the anticipated loss of his father and he was not ready to lose him again.

On the third Saturday of July, Gianni was sitting up in the adjustable bed David had brought in and they were watching the Red Sox game together on the television. The Sox were playing the Yankees that afternoon at Fenway and were only a few games behind. David was happy Gianni was feeling well enough to enjoy the game with him.

Gianni said, "I don't know if this four-to-nothing lead is safe, but I think they'll win today."

David said, "After losing by one run in the ninth last night, I hope you're right. Maybe they'll finally win the whole thing for you this year."

Gianni smiled fondly at David's still youthful enthusiasm for this rivalry. "That would be nice for you and James."

In that comment, David didn't miss his father's awareness he wouldn't be here to watch the games at the end of this season.

"David, I have a large favor to ask of you. It's something I've been thinking about and would like to do."

David put his hand on his father's. "What is it, Pop? Anything you want."

"I feel a bit selfish, but I would like to be in Maine for my last days and then be with your mom."

David stared down at the back of his hand holding his father's as he tried to process the reality of what his father was saying. "Pop, if that is where you want to be, I'll make sure that's where we are."

"It would mean a lot to me, son. Could we have Kathleen and the kids over tomorrow because I want to see them before we go."

David felt the weight of those words on his entire being as he realized that his father was feeling his death more imminent than David wanted to admit. "Sure, Pop. I'm sure they'd love to come over tomorrow. Let me give Kathleen a call in a bit." Meanwhile, the Yankees scored two runs in the seventh and eighth innings to tie the game, but the Sox returned the favor from last night and scored in the ninth to win by one. As David was about to cheer in celebration, he noticed that his father had fallen asleep. The tears David had been holding back now streamed from his eyes as he gazed at his father's face.

After talking to Kathleen about Sunday dinner, he called a realtor to see if there was a house available on the island he could rent for an extended period despite the late notice at high season. David explained his father's situation to the realtor, Ray Shepherd. Ray had been on the island his whole life and knew the Kelly family growing up. His aunt had passed away the previous year, and she had a cottage that wasn't being used that Ray thought might be a good solution. After hearing about the location, David thanked him and told him he'd wire money to hold it, but Ray said not to worry about it, he could pay when he arrived in Stonington. Ray said he'd have the place clean and stocked with key essentials for them.

Gianni made the effort to sit at the dinner table when Kathleen, Amy, and

James came to visit on Sunday. Kathleen had brought dinner, and Gianni complimented her ability to get the lasagna just right. "You know, some of the best Italian cooks are Irish girls." During the visit, Kathleen watched David's loving and notably attentive manner with his father. David had told her that Gianni wanted to be in Maine, and he sensed that his time was short. She didn't want to believe it but couldn't help noticing the periodic changes of expression on Gianni's face as he closed his eyes and drew in a deep breath, visibly enduring a strong sensation of pain run through his spine.

David could tell that Kathleen was trying in vain to hide the tears that came to her eyes as she noticed this reaction repeat itself a few times that afternoon. He also noticed Gianni catch her loving concern when he opened his eyes again and smiled gently back at her. Before leaving, Gianni gave her, and then Amy and finally James, a long and emotional hug. At the door, David thanked Kathleen for coming and taking care of dinner on short notice, but she only shook her head saying, "Please take care of him and yourself." David nodded as he said goodbye, thinking about everything he needed to do.

Chapter 57

When David told Tom his plans, Tom suggested having someone from hospice help him while in Maine. There was a Catholic hospice agency on the mainland, and David scheduled a phone interview during the week to talk to someone who might be available. A woman called Maggie returned his call. She told him what types of things she'd help take care of, including administering palliative medication and taking care of Gianni both physically and spiritually. David was glad to hear there was someone who knew what they were doing available at this remote location.

On Tuesday morning, July 29, David had everything packed and ready for the long drive to Stonington, almost a year since he was there last. On the way, Gianni fell asleep while David's thoughts jumped from one thing to another. He thought about his last ride to the island with Jillian, and with it, his mixed feelings about how much he enjoyed her company while he had been so unknowingly unfair and harmful to her. He felt ashamed and a deep sense of regret, not that he knew Jillian, but that he hadn't treated her with dignity and respect. David thought about what Tom had said to Luke and him that night in the North End. "Our hearts weren't meant for these 'mini-marriages." He knew for sure that Jillian's was not.

Before David knew it, he was driving the Jeep over the bridge spanning the glistening waters of Eggemoggin Reach. It was a cloudless summer day as the Jeep hugged the curvy roads winding through the small village of Deer Isle before taking a turn at the tiny post office towards the snug cove of Southwest Harbor.

The dirt road sloped gently downhill with a scattering of homes on either side. David pulled into the gravel driveway of a small, gray-painted cottage that fit the description Ray Shepherd had provided over the phone. The cottage sat on the hill overlooking the protected cove where the sun would paint the sky with strokes of purple, pink, orange, and red at sunset. From the Jeep, David could see the path from the cottage down to the small rustic boathouse and rugged beach. Ray had left the door open and the keys on the dining table as promised. David looked around the simple one-floor cottage, with a living room and kitchen facing the water and two bedrooms in the back. There was an old, black rotary phone on the table next to the doorway and a bumped-out area with the dining table had a view of the quaint cove, a handful of moored boats, and a few small islands.

David was relieved that the home was clean, bright, and had an instantly peaceful feel. The large bedroom had windows on both sides, a few watercolor paintings of the island on the walls, and the bed he had ordered for his dad already in place. When David went to help his father into the house, he found Gianni smiling as he peered out from his passenger side window at the sun dancing on the ocean cove and smelled the salt air he had missed for so long. David knew that Gianni never had vacations growing up, and the summer getaways he had enjoyed with Annie and his family on this peaceful island with its magnificent shoreline, fragrant pines, and many walking paths to the unspoiled spots of nature, were something that Gianni enjoyed and appreciated, especially because he knew how very much Annie loved this spot.

David helped Gianni across the uneven grassed front yard and up the five steps to the front porch, where there were wicker chairs to sit and enjoy the summer days and evenings. Gianni paused to look out again over the beauty of the cove and at Sheep's Head Island that protected that inlet, and then they entered the cottage, which was brightened by the golden sunlight streaming through the windows. As Gianni sat in a chair next to the living room window, David opened a window to let in a gentle ocean breeze. "David, this spot is just right. Thank you and thank you for being here with me. It means more to me than you may ever know."

A half-smile came to David's face. "Pop, whatever you need, just let me know. I have no better place on earth to be."

"I would like two things if you don't mind?"

"Sure. What, Pop?"

Gianni moved his body around to be more comfortable. "I would like to visit your mom's grave tomorrow while I still can, and I'd like to have some fresh lobster or crabmeat while I still have the taste for it."

David's smile grew broader with the last request. "We'll go tomorrow, and I could go for some local shellfish myself."

Gianni smiled and looked peacefully out at the shoreline and the strikingly blue-colored sky that was dotted with soft, puffy white clouds. David guessed he had often dreamed about such a scene while confined in the hard, cold, windowless cell for all those years.

The next morning, there was a tapping on the front door, and David noticed someone standing outside through the laced curtained window of the door. When he opened the door, a short but sturdy woman in her fifties with medium-length brown and gray hair, wearing a blue top and white pants said, "Mr. Kelly, I'm Maggie Haskell. It's a pleasure to meet you on such a day." The tanned skin on Maggie's face was almost coarse with lines of years of hard work, but her eyes and smile were full of joy and friendliness.

"Come on in, Maggie, and thank you for being available on such short notice."

"There's no other kind of notice for us, and I feel honored to be here with you and your dad. I'd love to meet him today, if possible. Have you talked to your dad about having hospice and what we do?"

"I haven't had a chance to talk with him yet. I have no experience with what you do firsthand, but I assume you try to make him as comfortable as possible through this?"

Maggie said, "That is definitely a big part of it. I'm a registered nurse and will make sure that all his medical and pain management needs are met. I believe you specifically contacted us as a Catholic hospice provider, so I'm assuming that you care about making sure we're following ethical procedures, but hopefully also about the spiritual part of the process?"

David nodded. "Pop has a strong faith, which is one reason he doesn't want to spend his remaining time in a spiritually-sterile hospital."

Maggie squinted as she smiled. "And neither do you."

At that moment they could hear a shuffle of Gianni's feet moving across the linoleum floor as he came out of the bedroom.

Maggie crossed the room to him. "Mr. Fidele, I'm Maggie Haskell. I'm a nurse and I'm going to be around to help out with anything you and Mr. Kelly may need." Maggie shook Gianni's hand and got a smile when she said, "I always love it when they send me to homes with handsome men." As Gianni sat down slowly, Maggie said, "Mr. Fidele, how have you been feeling this week? Only honest answers accepted."

Gianni said, "Despite the prognosis, I'm doing pretty well up here," pointing to his head, "but the pain is pretty constant and can be intense at times. The medication is taking the bite off, so I feel like I can be good company right now."

Maggie put her hand on Gianni's back and moved it downward. "Well, we'll be the judge of that. You haven't even told me one good joke yet." Gianni smiled at Maggie's comment and David could tell that her hand on his back felt good. Maggie took out her stethoscope and blood pressure wrap. Maggie asked Gianni to breathe in and out as she listened through the stethoscope at various locations on his back and chest. Maggie asked, "Mr. Fidele, is it painful when you breathe in deeply like that?"

Gianni nodded. "A little bit," Maggie asked Gianni to lie on the couch to see if some light massage was helpful, and then asked David to do an errand so that she could talk to Gianni. By the time David was back, Gianni was sitting in the chair near the window, and Maggie was saying goodbye, telling Gianni that she might consider coming back if he could promise a joke for next time. Gianni smiled and nodded as she stepped out on the porch and then down to the front lawn with David.

David stood almost a foot taller than Maggie, but she made up for the height with personality and straightforwardness. "David, do you have any expectations about this process or how long your father may have?"

"It's all I think about, but I don't think I could answer either of those questions."

"Your dad is a very strong man, and I mean physically, mentally and spiritually. I also think he's at peace with what's ahead of him, which is quite a gift, not just for him, but for you too. That being said, it's really hard to say how things will progress. Cancer tends to spread aggressively in this situation, but hopefully, he'll have the time he needs, and that you'll have the time with him you need. It will never be the time you want or feel you need, but hopefully, it allows you to let him go with some sense of peace. This process can be trying and difficult, but it can also be powerfully moving if you believe God is bringing him home."

"I can see that my father is already comfortable with you, and I like that you are straightforward in your approach. I don't know how I'll be, but I'd like you to show me how to take care of him and the things that need to be done."

Maggie put her hand on David's arm. "We will be the best team your father's ever seen. I don't think you'll need me tomorrow, so I'll plan on coming by Friday morning. Here's my number whenever you need me. I'm just a few towns over the bridge, so I can be here in about thirty minutes."

David said, "Thank you and thanks for coming today."

Maggie said, "This is often a profound two-way gift, and we are never doing this alone." Maggie got into her well-worn Subaru and shouted out from the window as she pulled away. "Enjoy your lobsters tonight!"

When David returned to the house, Gianni looked up at him. "Looks like we won't have to bring this one out of her shell."

"Did you like her? I thought she seemed really good."

In his best Maine accent, Gianni said, "Ayuh. Son, would you mind taking me into Stonington while I feel up to it?"

"I think that's a great idea."

As they drove the winding road from Sunset to the small downtown area of Stonington, past the pier, the old Opera House, and finally the Inn on the Harbor where David had stayed with Jillian, David had a rush of feelings and thoughts run through his head from his childhood, to being with Jillian, to all the events of the past year.

Gianni scanned left and right as they made their way through town. "I really missed this place all those years. Would you be able to drive by Green

Head where we used to stay? It's back that way."

"I know, Pop. I actually took a run by the house when I was here for Mom's burial. The house hasn't changed very much, even with the new owners."

Gianni gazed quietly as they slowed down to a crawl, passing by the house where so many family memories were made.

David turned the car around and parked so they could look at the view of the harbor, the same view they had enjoyed from the porch of their vacation home. They sat for a while listening to the sounds of the quiet harbor as a lobster boat pulled in, and a seagull called from her perch on the heavy posts anchoring the pier. Gianni breathed in the smell of salt air and fish, drinking in the sights and sounds. "Do you remember sitting here for hours with your line in the water waiting to catch a fish?"

David laughed. "Now that you bring it up, I think I do. I was thinking about the time you took me out on the lobster boat with Bert and Ernie. I remember feeling happy when it was just the two of us doing something together."

"I truly wish it hadn't been interrupted for so long."

"Me too, Pop. Me too. We should probably go down to the Co-op and pick out some fresh lobsters for tonight."

David drove back through the main street in the village and up a steep hill where the small white church of St. Mary's sat looking over creation. Before David made the crest of the hill, Gianni said, "Son, do you mind if we stop?" David pulled the Jeep into a spot next to the steepled church, and they walked through the open door. David held Gianni's arm as he worked to genuflect towards the small tabernacle holding the Body of Christ and then helped him to stand back up. The feel of the church was exactly the same to David as when he inexplicably dropped by the previous summer. The church was brightened only by the hazy sunlight streaming through the stained-glass windows, and David imagined that the posted numbers for the songs for the past week's Mass were probably the only things that were different.

Gianni said, "Let's sit for a few minutes and pray for your mother and Jimmy."

As they sat, David's mind was too busy to pray; he couldn't stop thinking about what it meant to be with his dad.

After a while, Gianni reached over and touched David's arm to let him know he was ready. Gianni bowed toward the tabernacle and looked around the church that had been a part of his life.

He deeply breathed in the smell of the church and turned towards the entrance door in the back, looking now at the wooden, carved statue of

Mary occupying her usual spot. Gianni walked over to the statue with David standing beside him to support him.

David said, "I actually remember the last time we were here together, just you and I standing right here."

Gianni nodded, and David knew his father remembered that moment. "I guess if I held your hand, and you were half your height, we would have it right. What did we talk about?"

"You told me—" and then a small lump grew in David's throat as he hesitated, and his voice quavered, "You told me that if I ever felt lost or needed to be strong, to think of Mary. You said she trusted God completely, and that He gave her the guidance and strength she needed."

Gianni took David's hand with a firm grip and smiled as he nodded.

Less than a half mile down the hill was the Stonington Lobster Co-op, a red shingle building that sold fresh fish and lobsters at a better price than the retail stores. They walked out onto the dock where wooden crates were tied together, floating in the harbor waters. Two lobstermen were standing on the dock with rubber boots; worn jeans; loose, stained tee-shirts; and baseball hats with "Stonington Co-op" printed in red across the front. The shorter one said, "What can we do for ya, gentlemen?"

David glanced at Gianni and then back at the man. "Hard-shell. Let's do three two-pounders."

The man said, "All rightie. Let's see what we got here," as he pulled up one of the crates filled with lobsters with blue-green colored shells. He lifted up one with a huge right claw and put it on a plastic tray, saying. "That's a nice one but may be bigger than you want."

David said, "Bigger is no problem. She looks like a beauty." The man proceeded to pull out two more decent-sized lobsters and brought them up to the Co-op building to weigh them for David. Gianni sat on a short post while David paid and carried them out in a Styrofoam container filled with ice to keep them fresh.

On the way back, David pulled the car alongside the Evergreen Cemetery. When he had left the gravesite that day with Jillian and Emma Brown, David had thought he would never return, and here he was with the father who he thought, at that time, was dead and deserved to be so. David accompanied his dad across the uneven path to his mother's gravesite. There was a plot space for Gianni next to Annie because he had promised that she'd rest with her sister when the time came. Gianni read the gravestone: "Beloved sister, Marie A. Kelly, Apr 1, 1934–Aug 13, 1946." Below was carved "Ann E. Kelly, Apr 1, 1934 -." David was surprised that the date of death hadn't been taken care of in all this time, but he was almost glad it wasn't there.

David glanced over and saw his father quietly crying. It hadn't hit him until now how much his father still very much loved his bride, despite all the years of rejection while he was in prison. He didn't have to forgive her because he never blamed her or resented her for losing faith in him. He just kept doing what he vowed to do when he made his commitment to love her in good times and in bad, all the days of his life. Gianni gently nodded as he wiped his wet cheeks. "Your mother was such a beautiful, loving, and fun woman. I never met anyone like her until you introduced me to Kathleen. I see that depth and a spark in her. I know your mother was devastated about Jimmy, and she may not have been the same afterward, but try to remember her when she could be herself, as I'm sure she is right now with God in heaven."

David had to admit to himself that he hadn't thought a lot about his mom since the funeral, not even where she might be, but he could tell his father had prayed a lot about it with a love that never died.

When they got back to the cottage, Gianni took a nap while David put away some supplies they picked up. By late afternoon, they were both hungry, and David started boiling the water for the lobsters and shucking the corn. Over dinner, they reminisced about eating lobsters together at David's grandparents' house, and how he was taught to pick a lobster. Although Gianni's appetite had diminished, he took his time enjoying the taste of each bite, smiling as he watched David's own healthy appetite at work.

As the early evening light took over the colors of the sky, Gianni asked David if they could walk down the hill to the shore. David grabbed a couple of high beach chairs and held his other arm out for Gianni to hold as they slowly descended the road to the shore while noticing the scampering chipmunks and unpicked raspberries along the way. At the foot of the hill was a flat spot in front of large, jagged rocks that used to hold a pier when the cove was once filled with fishing boats. They met a neighbor who was watching her dog run freely on the beach chasing the small pieces of driftwood she tossed for him to fetch, and David put the chairs out to sit.

They sat and took in the sights and sounds of the quiet cove. Two fishermen, still moored in the cove, were attending to their gear as David and Gianni watched. Gianni said, "There are few things as beautiful as this place. Growing up in the city or being in prison for that matter, your eye only sees what man has made, and it never comes close to the beauty of God's natural creation."

"You're right, Pop. It does bring a different sense of peace and satisfaction than a high-rise building ever seems to invoke."

"It's interesting to watch these fishermen taking care of things at the end of a long day. It reminds me of a reading from Luke that I was just reflecting on."

David wasn't a Bible guy but knew this meant something to his father. "I know you want to tell me, Pop, so I'm open to anything tonight."

"Okay, so Jesus saw some fishermen washing out their nets, having no luck after a long day of fishing. Jesus walked onto Simon's boat. 'Put out into the deep water and let down your nets for a catch.' Simon shook his head telling Jesus that there were no fish to be had but agreed to go out and let down the nets one more time. When they pulled them up there were so many fish that the nets were bursting, and they needed help from another boat. Both boats were filled to the brim and were almost sinking. Simon felt ashamed that he hadn't trusted Jesus. Jesus said to Simon, James, and John, 'Do not be afraid; from now on you will be catching men,' and they left everything and followed him."

"So, what's the main point of the story?"

"Most people, including myself for so many years, hang safely around the shallow part of the water, kind of committing ourselves but not really trusting enough to let go of everything that holds us back. We're afraid that we are giving up something or afraid to jump into the deep water with both feet because we don't think we can do it alone. But that's the point, we'll never do it alone, and when we fully trust in God, the return is abundant and overwhelming. We think God asks too much of us to commit everything, but what we can do and what we can give will be so much more than we thought because it doesn't come from us but from God. 'I can do all things through Him who strengthens me.'"

Shortly before sunset, there were streaks of orange, red, and purple starting to color the underside of thousands of cotton ball clouds in the evening sky. Gianni looked up and said quietly, "It took me a long time to get it, but I finally jumped in and everything finally made sense." David knew he had been cautious about doing any more than dipping his toe in up until now but taking this leave from work to be with his dad felt like a leap out of his once-normal comfort zone.

Chapter 58

The next day, they played cards and talked about things David did when he was a boy and how difficult it had been growing up. Outside of getting tired easily, Gianni seemed good despite the obvious episodes of pain that would seem to freeze the moment as he endured them with deep breaths and pushing his hand against his thigh, the mattress, or the arm of the chair he was sitting in. When he took naps, David had time to think about life, which was something he couldn't recall ever having done before. He was appreciating this time with his dad. They sat out on the porch in the evening listening to Red Sox games on the radio as the crickets made their sounds heard and the fireflies flashed in the dark of the night. David stepped off the porch to stare in wonder at the sheer number of stars shining brightly, vastly more than he could see from his Boston rooftop because of the glow of the city lights. At night, Gianni retired early to bed and David sat with no one but himself. Surprisingly, he didn't feel alone or lonely. There was no television, and cell phone reception was non-existent on this side of the island. It was peaceful.

Maggie returned with washcloths, basins, medical-care items and equipment to administer morphine through an IV. She also brought some fruit and a CD player with some spiritual music for Gianni. "How are we doing today, Mr. Fidele?" Maggie asked. "Has your son been taking good care of you or do we have to exchange him for someone new?"

Gianni smiled as Maggie ran the palm of her hand slowly up and down his back. "Couldn't ask for better company." Gianni glanced up at David and then back at Maggie. "But it came anyway."

David laughed and was glad his father remained in good humor, and that it was Maggie who was their hospice nurse that arrived at the door. Maggie listened to Gianni's breathing and took his vitals as she asked him to describe how he was feeling and if he needed more pain relief. She massaged his back as he lay down, and it seemed to be helpful. She worked with him on breathing exercises and other strategies to help him get through the tougher moments of pain. She also reviewed his pain medications, the doses, and intervals for taking them. Maggie explained how morphine would bind to the opioid receptors in the nerve cells along the spine and the brain to calm down the nerves that carried pain signals. It wouldn't do anything to the underlying medical issue nor speed up the process of dying.

Maggie said, "It can cause constipation, stomach pain, anxiety, and drowsiness. I need to know if you ever feel your heart beating slower or faster, if your breathing becomes shallow or if you feel extremely drowsy or light-headed, so we can watch the dosage. Anything out of the ordinary, just let me know. Everybody okay with that fun stuff?"

Maggie showed David how to massage and apply the heat packs, how to bathe him, and eventually how to clean his father when he could no longer do so. David hadn't thought about the level of intimacy that was going to be involved in Gianni's care. What Maggie couldn't show David by instruction, but only by example, was the level of compassion and dignity she showed for his father. Most people would run from this type of work and dealing with the reality of the dying process, but Maggie found a purpose in her work with each individual she came to know in their last weeks or days. Old people are supposed to be ugly and death nothing short of repulsive in this world that valued youth and the superficialities of life, but Maggie seemed to see the beauty in each wrinkle that marked a lived life, in the process of letting go, and being ready to meet God Who has loved them from before their first moment. David watched Maggie hold Gianni's hand as he squeezed it during his reoccurring sensations of pain, gently massaged his back and shoulders, or caressed his face with a look of love and a recognition of his value.

As the days passed, it started to sink in for David that his father's fate was a reality. They would sit and talk, or David would sit in the chair next to Gianni's bed as he rested and listened to music that would lift his soul and bring a sense of peace. David could tell that the sunlight brightening the room and the gentle shore breeze that made the lace curtains float in the air was a thousand times better than lying in a hospital. David read passages from the Bible each morning and chapters from Homer's *Odyssey* or Tolkien's *Lord of the Rings* that he had checked out of the tiny library in town. Gianni smiled as he listened and drifted off in a moment of peace.

Gianni was able to make it once to Mass at St. Mary's and meet the priest who would soon co-celebrate his funeral Mass. Father Robert Mullen had come to Stonington as a boy and shared stories with Gianni as they were close to the same age. Father Bob had a gift for a good sermon that made even the most lukewarm Mass-goers never look at their watch. He came to visit Gianni several times a week to bring him Communion, and also to administer the Sacrament of the Anointing of the Sick, with prayers and a blessing with holy oil intended to bring comfort, peace, and courage to the individual. There was a group of women from the church who had met Gianni and David at Mass, and they dropped by several times with food, fresh flowers, and offers to clean or to stay with Gianni if David needed to do an errand or take a break. The neighbor they had met down the road would also drop by with her dog to see how Gianni was doing.

Late on the Saturday morning of August 9, there was an unexpected knock on the screen door. David came out of Gianni's room and noticed more than one person on the porch outside the door. When David opened the door, his heart felt a burst of joy to see Tom, Angelo, and Kathleen standing there smiling just on the other side of the screen. David stepped onto the porch to greet the most cherished people in his life. He hugged Kathleen and reached out to shake Tom's hand and then gave him and Angelo a hug as well. "I can't believe you are here. How did you even find this place? And you came all this way! I can't tell you how happy I am to see all of you."

Kathleen smiled. "We weren't sure how things were going or if this would even be a good time, but we just had to see you and Dad."

Angelo asked, "Could I ask how he is?"

"He's doing well for what he is going through. Each day, I can tell he loses a little bit, and gets more tired and unfortunately has had more frequent pain throughout his back. The good news is we've been blessed with a great hospice nurse who has been wonderful to him and has shown me how to care for him."

David opened the door to let everyone in. "Let's see if we can say hello. I just gave him his medication."

As David peeked in the door, they heard Gianni say, "I'm always up for company. Who's come to visit?"

Angelo poked his head in Gianni's room and tears of joy came to Gianni's face. He was smiling broadly, and his emotions overwhelmed him as he reached out his hand. "Angelo, Angelo, it's so good to see you. I'm so glad you're here. I was afraid I might not see you again before…well, it's just good to see you." Angelo leaned over and hugged Gianni gently. "I won't break, Angelo." Then Gianni's eyes widened as he saw Kathleen and Tom at the doorway. "I should've put on my party clothes. Did you all make the long drive up today?"

Kathleen was unsuccessfully fighting back her own tears as she came over, kissed Gianni, touching his cheek with her hand. "Dad, I hope this is a good time. I hear you're being well taken care of. It's such a delight to see your smile. Amy and James send their love."

Tom came over and shook Gianni's hand and squeezed his shoulder with the other saying, "You're looking good, Gianni. We've been praying for you and David every day and decided we wanted to do it in person."

Gianni was smiling but then everyone could tell that a rush of pain overcame him as he closed his eyes and breathed in deeply. David quickly held his hand as he put his forehead against his father's and waited for the wave to pass. Gianni finally released his grip and his eyes opened with a noticeable tear on his eyelid. Tears welled in Kathleen's eyes as she watched David's loving compassion as he straightened his father's pillow, whispering something in his ear to which Gianni nodded. When Gianni was more comfortable, he glanced up at everyone and said, "I hope you don't mind visiting with David while I just close my eyes for a bit."

Angelo and Tom stepped onto the porch, but Kathleen stopped in the living room and turned to David, looking up into his eyes with tears still in hers. "David, you are treating your dad with such love and compassion. This can't be easy on him or you, but I can only imagine that it means the world to Dad to have you here with him. It means a lot to me, too."

"I've been blessed to be here and to have this time with him. I really want him to have everything he needs."

Kathleen moved closer to David and hugged him. "How are you doing emotionally? I've been thinking of you every day."

David gently moved closer. "Thank you. I can use all the prayers I can get, but please save some for Pop. He's been incredibly strong. I thought I'd feel cheated, but instead, it's been such a gift to have this time alone with him, to talk with him, and care for him."

David and Kathleen joined Tom and Angelo on the porch with iced tea, cheese, and crackers. They sat and talked about Gianni, the beauty of this small slice of heaven they were looking at, and about all the people on the island who were being so supportive. About an hour later, an old Subaru wagon pulled up, and Maggie got out of the car with her medical bag and opened her hatchback. David helped her carry in several bags of groceries, pausing on the porch to introduce Maggie to everyone.

Maggie said, "I have been doing hospice work for many years and these two make it so easy. I don't feel like they even need me."

David quickly said, "Maggie has been nothing less than heaven-sent. She is so wonderful with Pop and has been trying her best to bring me along."

Maggie chuckled and visited for several minutes before she went in to put things away and to check in on Gianni. Kathleen went in to help and talk with Maggie. David saw himself through another lens as he overheard bits and pieces of Maggie saying, "Mr. Fidele is an incredible man and such a sweetheart and Mr. Kelly has been so good with him. He really loves his dad in a way I don't often see. Most people don't want to be this close to the dying process. It's difficult, messy, and emotional. I've watched Mr. Kelly sit with him, read to him, wash him, massage him, share the pain with him, and even clean him without pulling back. It's been quite an honor to witness such a testament of a son's love for his father."

After Gianni's nap, Maggie went in to check on him and take his vitals. He was able to get up and sit at the table with everyone through a talkative dinner as they all enjoyed the evening's sunset that was nothing less than spectacular. As Gianni was ready to head back to bed, David looked at Tom. "Where did you guys find a place for tonight?"

Tom turned to Kathleen and Angelo. "Ah hum, well, we didn't exactly think our plans through. This island is smaller than we thought and the few places to stay are full."

David shook his head and laughed. "Ohhh okay. Let's see. There are two cots in the room I'm in and the couch here.

"I can sleep in the car or on the floor here," Angelo said.

Maggie waved toward the door. "I'm heading home, and I always keep a blow-up air mattress in my car with sheets, so you're covered. Bring one of the cots out here, put the mattress over there, and let Kathleen have the bedroom. Problem solved, see you sometime tomorrow."

Everybody laughed and decided it was the best solution at this time of night and thanked Maggie.

The next day, Angelo stayed with Gianni while Tom, Kathleen, and David went to Mass at St. Mary's in Stonington. Tom and Kathleen met Father Bob after Mass, and then they went to breakfast at the Harbor Cafe. The waitress asked David how his father was doing. David thanked her for asking. Kathleen said, "David, you must've loved coming up here as a young boy. It is really something special. I can see why Dad would want to be here." Tom agreed as the three of them enjoyed socializing during breakfast. David enjoyed the break, not from his father but from the process itself, a break he knew Gianni could not have himself.

They drove around the island to see the striking views and then back to the cottage in Sunset where they thanked Angelo for the time. Angelo said, "The thanks are for you. It was really nice to spend the time with my dear friend." They stayed and visited with Gianni for a while before they had to leave for the drive home. Gianni blessed all of them and thanked them for coming the long way to see him, but no one had a single thought that the ride was a burden.

As they stood outside saying goodbye, Kathleen gave David a long embrace and told him she loved him. Tom smiled at David and his eyes misted as he said, "He's proud of you, and so am I. Stay strong; you're not alone." David stood at the end of the driveway and watched their car climb the hill and then disappear from sight as he wished them safely home.

Over the next several days, Gianni's pain and fatigue intensified. He told Maggie that he would need more relief but still wanted to be present and awake. Maggie told David that it was time to set his father up with an intravenous morphine drip, which would deliver the appropriate doses at prescribed intervals. Gianni would be able to pump an additional dose to help him tolerate the periods of breakthrough pain. Maggie closely monitored Gianni's alertness and any symptoms that might indicate a need to adjust the doses he was receiving. Gianni was able to walk for short intervals around the cottage or to sit on the porch for a bit with David, but he was increasingly confined to his bed. Having the adjustable bed made it easier to change positions, and to visit or to sleep when he needed throughout the day. Gianni had generally lost the taste for food, but Maggie found ways to give him small doses of concoctions she had made up that provided nutrients and hydration.

David continued to sit by his side, reading, listening to music, talking or just being together and holding his father's hand as he nodded off. David admired Maggie's reverence for his father and how her patience and kindness made such a difference for Gianni and for him. He learned a lot about self-giving love by watching her with his father and watching his father with her.

The intervals between doses of morphine became shorter, and it was apparent that cancer had spread throughout the spine and possibly into the lower sections of the brain. Gianni would at times be very lucid and engaging and other times dizzy or forgetful, once talking about taking a trip with David to Italy. As difficult as it was to watch his father's obvious decline and the inevitable coming to claim him, David was still glad he was able to be with him. He had called both Abbie and Bobby a few times, but Bobby didn't respond, and Abbie still felt like she wasn't emotionally ready to see him, despite David's pleas to not wait until it was too late.

The following week, David was sitting with Gianni, reading the scripture for the day and Gianni asked, "What day is today?"

David stopped and answered, "It's Wednesday, Pop."

"But what day is it?"

"It's August 13. Why do you ask?"

Gianni nodded, and a half smile rose to his face, and then a single tear to the corner of his eye. After a few minutes, David was embarrassed as he realized what the day was and why his father had asked. It was the first anniversary of David's mother's death, and somehow Gianni could sense it or his conditioning from prison to count each and every day had stayed with him.

"Pop, you were thinking about Ma. You remembered the day, and you were thinking about her."

"I always think of her. I want to make sure I can always see her smiling face. I don't want to be wandering around in heaven and not able to find her because I forgot what she looked like."

"You've plenty of time before you have to worry about that."

"I think the time is short. I can sense it, and I feel ready now."

Emotions flooded through David. "Well, I'm not ready. I don't want to lose you, Pop. I really don't feel like I can lose you again."

Gianni reached out his hand to David, and David took it in his, holding it tight.

"I don't want to see you in pain, but it doesn't seem fair to have him take someone like you."

"David, this life is all about knowing God loves you. He wants you to live life abundantly here, but then finally in heaven. I don't feel worthy, but I've been so looking forward to seeing God in heaven and seeing your mother and Jimmy. I don't want to leave you. I love you, David, more than I love myself. This time with you has been such a gift. It has made me so happy that all those years in prison seem worth it now that I've found you. You are my son, and I am your father, but in many ways, you are on loan to me."

David shook his head, confused. "What do you mean?"

"When I'm no longer here, you won't be left alone without a father. God is your father. God loves you as a father in ways that I'm too limited to give, even when I give you everything I have. He is with you always, and His love is never ending, never fails and never dies. No matter how many times you fall and forget this, He will never give up on you. Yes, you are my son, but it's more important to know you are His beloved son—and just as I am, I know He is well pleased with you."

That was the last real conversation David had with his father. The headaches and back pain increased as did the morphine to offset the discomfort. In the days ahead, Gianni was asleep most of the time. Watching him have trouble breathing and wincing at times with breakthrough pain was more than difficult to watch, but Maggie never left him or treated him with any less respect or dignity. David sat up with him as he slept during the day and then rolled in the cot to sleep next to him at night to make sure he was okay. Gianni stopped eating and had trouble drinking from a cup with a straw, so Maggie set him up with intravenous fluids to keep him hydrated.

On that Friday afternoon, David was sitting with his father, holding his hand and reading the scriptures for the day about Mary visiting Elizabeth and proclaiming her "Blessed among women," but the last line of the reading from Paul stood out for David. "The last enemy to be destroyed is death, for 'he subjected everything under his feet.'" His father knew he would die, but to him, there was nothing to fear because it wouldn't end his life with God. David looked up from his father's Bible and around the room he had spent so many hours with his father. The sunlight was streaming in through the windows on one side of the room as David looked to where it touched the floor in front of him. The fine lace curtains that adorned the windows were blowing inward from the gentle sea breeze coming into the room, and there was an overwhelming sense of peace in every corner of the bedroom. David felt a sudden squeeze from his father's hand and a shortened breath inward and then no grip at all as his father's hand seemed to slip out of his as David held on tighter.

Gianni died as peacefully as he had wished, in the place he wanted to be, holding onto the hand of the son he loved and who loved him. A sudden pickup in the breeze that came into Gianni's bedroom at that moment seemed to have swept Gianni's soul out of David's grasp and into the arms of his loving Father in heaven. David got up and put his hands on each of his father's shoulders. "Pop. Pop. Don't go! Please don't leave me so soon! Pop!"

David wailed and sobbed. Maggie finally came in, and her hands felt comforting on David's back as he continued to hold his father. David's head was on Gianni's shoulder as he wept, feeling as if life had been drained from his own body as well. His throat was tight and ached as his cries shook his body. When David finally lifted himself and let go of his father's hand, he turned toward Maggie with his eyes now red and shining from the tears that dripped from his puffed eyelids, and she put her arms around him, hugging him for several minutes. She whispered, "If I had a son, I would be blessed if he were like you, if he loved me as you have so loved your dad."

Chapter 59

After some time had passed, David walked down to the shore where he had sat with his father on one of those first nights when they had watched the fishing boats being anchored down for the evening. He had expected to be angry with God, to move away from Him again when his father died, but he could only see the beauty of creation in front of him just as his dad had. The ache in his heart was raw and painful, but he had this strange sense that his father's soul wasn't gone nor had he abandoned him as he had felt as a child. For all those years, his father had only existed in the hate and anger he felt toward him, but that had all vanished. Now, David felt like his father was still with him, inside of him and in the beauty surrounding him. Somehow, David had escaped the black hole of egoism that had gripped him for so long. Now, he had lived for someone else, and it had changed him. He had somehow leaped outside of himself and experienced the love of another, and that love didn't seem to end when his father's physical being had gone.

Maggie was back at the house, washing and cleaning Gianni's face and body with a warm cloth. She moved all the medical equipment out of the way, and when David came back up the hill, she joined him on the porch with the sun feeling good on their faces. A pair of butterflies were fluttering around the front yard, and the woman from the bottom of the hill was walking back down with her Jack Russell terrier that they now knew was named Pepper. Maggie turned to David. "Mr. Kelly, I only wish everyone could have a father like yours, even if for only a short while. At least they would know they were loved and valued."

"Thank you, Maggie. You've been so wonderful to both of us. I don't know how my father could have lived his last days the way he wished without you. You were heaven-sent, to be sure."

"That's my job, but I believe you're the one who made the difference here. You know what love is all about now."

After sitting for a bit, David went inside and dialed the Colby-Duke Funeral Home. When John Colby asked David if he wanted the same arrangements as he had for his mom, a pain stabbed through him at the thought of how little he had done for his mother's funeral. David told him that he wanted nothing like that this time and that there would be a Mass at St. Mary's for his dad.

Next, David called Kathleen and Tom, tearfully relaying the news, and then he called Abbie and Bobby to let them know their father had died. Abbie wasn't emotional but said she wanted to come out for the funeral. David actually reached Bobby, but he was protectively cold in his response. David tried to tell him he understood his feelings completely, but that he had learned the truth and got past the hurt. Bobby said he was happy for David, but that this wouldn't happen for him. Despite there being no one who knew his father anymore on the island, David planned to have a vigil and the funeral Mass and burial on the next day. He met with Father Bob about what readings and songs he wanted at the services for his father.

Father Bob said, "Your father was a great example to all of us. It's always an interesting sign when a man like your father dies on that feast day."

"John Colby mentioned that. What day was the fifteenth?"

"The Feast of the Assumption of Mary. I know your father was very devout in honoring Mary and admired her strength and courage to trust God. I always think of her when I need a reminder to ask God for the strength to trust in his plan instead of following my own pride and my own plan. It's a constant struggle, and she's a great inspiration as our mother."

David smiled.

"Do you mind if I ask what's behind that smile, David?"

"It's just that my father told me the same thing many years ago in this very church."

On Monday night, David was surprised at the number of people who came to the vigil service. Tom and Angelo brought Kathleen, Amy, and James. Maggie came with her husband. Several of the women who came to the house from St. Mary's brought food and flowers. The woman who lived down the road from the cottage had come with another neighbor. Even Emma Brown had found out about Gianni's passing and came to pay her respects.

After the vigil prayer service, David took everyone out for dinner at the Fisherman's Friend and noticed Kathleen looking at him differently, maybe because he was different.

When they got back to the cottage, the bright moon and the starlit sky shone off the still waters of the cove. David was unfolding a few more cots he had brought to the cottage when he heard the sound of a truck or something making its way down the dirt road before stopping right in front of the cottage. David and James stepped out on the porch, and the others followed as they saw a half-sized bus with "ST. ANTHONY'S SCHOOL" across the side. Driving the bus was Sister Helen and inside filling the passenger seats were twelve boys from the basketball team, complete with sleeping bags and tents for the evening. When Sister Helen got out and marched the boys out of the bus, David glanced at Tom, who shrugged his shoulders and made a face. He approached Sister Helen and the boys. "Are you people lost?"

One of the boys said in a loud voice, "No, Coach. You were there when we needed you, and now we are here to be with you."

The next morning, the church was lit with candles and adorned with flowers as David came down the aisle behind his father's coffin. With him were Kathleen, Amy, and James. He couldn't help but be moved by the people who had come to the Mass for his father. He hadn't expected people to make the long trek up to the island, but Izzie and her family were there as well as most of the men on his immediate staff, including Kevin Walsh. Several people from the island, including Emma Brown, the women from the Church who had been so gracious, and some people they had met in Sunset were there as well. Sam from My Brother's Table was sitting on the aisle and shook David's hand as he walked by, and then he finally saw his sister, Abbie, in the second row, and shared a teary embrace.

The Mass, readings by Angelo and Kathleen and a homily by Father Bob all felt right for honoring Gianni's life and meaningful for all who attended. After the Mass was officially over, David stood up in front of the church to say a few words. He had never had trouble speaking in front of any size audience, but none of that practice seemed to help as he stood in silence for several moments to collect himself. "I could keep you all here for the rest of the day telling you about this wonderful and faithful man that was my father. I love my dad, and I am so proud to be fortunate enough to be his son." David hesitated for another moment as he looked over at his father's casket and a tear ran down his cheek. He closed his eyes and let out a deep breath. "But I don't think I could get through it all, so I will just tell you this: He used his last ounce of energy to teach what every father should teach their child: that they are loved – that I was loved and cherished no matter what. He taught me that life is all about relationships, truth, and love. To truly live life, he taught me that God had to be at the center, trusting in His love for us, knowing we are irreplaceable in His eyes and that He is always there for us. Once that seemed like a lot of meaningless words to me while I buried myself with all the things in life that didn't matter. Now, for the first time in my life, I think I feel truly free and, finally, understand what he meant. I want to thank each one of you here for coming today, but more than anything I want to thank you for the love you've shown. I've been so touched and so blessed by having a relationship with each one of you, and I hope I can return that feeling back to each of you." David looked down at his family, tears streaming down his face. "I was stupid enough to walk away from the three most precious people in my life—" He tried to collect himself but couldn't finish as Kathleen stood up, crying, and hugged David.

Everyone gathered at the gravesite, and Tom offered prayers and words that comforted but also left those in attendance with the sense of inspiration that was Gianni's life. David could feel his father's presence beside him and urging him to be where he now belonged, with his family. After the final blessing from Tom, they all headed back to the church hall for lunch. All the time, David watched Kathleen, who was graciously helping with sandwiches and drinks and talking with the guests, including David's sister, Abbie. He made his way over to Kathleen and took her by the hand, leading her to the garden next to the church. Kathleen didn't ask David why, but just gazed at him with that look from their early dating that he'd never forgotten. David said, "Kat, this is probably completely inappropriate but would you—"

Kathleen didn't let David finish. "Yes. Yes, I will marry you. Yes, I will spend the rest of my life with you. And, yes, I will love you all the days of my life."

David put his hand behind Kathleen and gently pulled her towards him and kissed her deeply as they held each other close. "Kat, why did you turn me down at Christmas but now you're saying yes?"

"I've always wanted you to come back, but I had to know you were asking for the right reason and that you knew what marriage was about. The man I see today is the man I knew you were inside when we married. David, I feel that now you know what love is, what commitment is, and what marriage is. I watched you love your dad with self-giving love that can only come from a man who has really let God into his life and isn't afraid to be and accept who he really is. I couldn't let the kids or myself be hurt again like we were, and now every part of me tells me I don't need to be afraid any longer. I love you, David. I always have and I always will. I want to be your wife and spend my life with you."

For the first time in his adult life, David felt a sense of deep joy as he held Kathleen and somehow knew his father was looking down at him with a smile and loving approval. David also felt a strong sense that God was doing the same. As he kissed and hugged Kathleen again, they suddenly heard clapping and turned to notice that everyone had quietly moved from the hall to the edge of the garden grass and was smiling and applauding. James ran up to his parents, with Amy close behind.

Kathleen said, "I know this may sound confusing, but your father just proposed to me for the third time in his life, and I said yes!"

James said, "That's great because I really need some more work on my baseball!"

David smiled and pulled James closer to him and looked at Amy saying, "Are you good with this, Ames?"

Amy nodded and gave her father a kiss on the cheek. "It's about time." The rest of the people at the reception circled around, and David asked Tom if it was inappropriate or disrespectful to his father if they renewed their vows.

Tom grinned. "I already checked with the man upstairs, and he gave his approval." David wasn't sure if he meant God or his father, but he thought the blessings of either one would work.

Kathleen and Amy went back into the church rectory to take care of a few things as David stayed outside in the garden with a marble statue of Mary behind him and James at his side as his best man. Everyone else went to the basement and carried chairs out to the garden and waited for the bride. Tom put on his vestments, brought out his book, and stood by David. "Don't worry, David, since you're already married, you can't mess this up. Oh, and congratulations."

David laughed and turned to see Amy approaching, and Kathleen a few paces behind. He gazed in wonder at how beautiful Kathleen looked walking down the aisle to take his hand once more. Her dark brown hair softly lifting in the light breeze, and her sapphire blue eyes radiating her inner beauty. Kathleen was over twenty years older than when he had first met her, but she seemed more beautiful than ever before, and he felt so lucky that he hadn't lost her forever.

When Kathleen reached David, he took her hand and turned towards Tom, who spoke for all to hear. "I'm very happy to be here to renew the marriage vows of these two wonderful friends. You have come together, in this Church, so that God may seal and strengthen your love in the presence of this community. Christ abundantly blesses this love, a love that most closely reveals God's unconditional self-sacrificing love for us; a love that delights in the truth, a love that allows each of us the trust to see ourselves as God sees us, and a love where two individuals truly become one in a permanent commitment of their hearts, minds, and souls. Christ has already consecrated you in Baptism, and now he enriches and strengthens you by this special sacrament you are renewing today so that you may assume the duties of marriage in mutual and lasting fidelity. And so, in the presence of Christ and his Church, I ask you to state your intentions."

Tom continued, "David and Kathleen, have you come here freely and without reservation to give yourselves to each other in marriage?"

David and Kathleen both nodded. "We do."

"Will you love and honor each other as husband and wife for the rest of your lives?"

Continuing to gaze at each other, they replied, "We will."

"Since it is your intention to renew this marriage vow, please join your right hands and declare your consent before God and the Church. David, do you take Kathleen to be your wife?"

David looked deeply into Kathleen's blue eyes with more appreciation for her than he had ever felt before and loudly proclaimed, "I do!"

"Do you promise to be true to her in good times and in bad, in sickness and in health, to love her and honor her all the days of your life?"

David said even louder, "I really do." There was some laughter from those watching intently.

After Kathleen had also said "I do" to the vows, Tom said, "You have declared your consent before the Church, and this community. May God, in his goodness, strengthen your consent and fill you both with his blessings. David, you may now kiss your bride."

David put his arms around Kathleen and kissed her deeply with the true love and commitment he now had. Tom turned David and Kathleen towards the gathering. "May I present to you, David and Kathleen Kelly. What God has joined; may no man separate. Congratulations!"

Everyone came up to congratulate David and Kathleen, as well as Amy and James. David would miss his dad in ways he didn't even comprehend yet, but he felt so blessed to have had this time with him. It taught him an invaluable lesson to attend to his relationships with self-forgetting love for the other. But, at this moment, he didn't feel the loss, only the gratitude for having a second chance at life, his marriage, his children, and his relationship with God and with his father. David was living in the moment as his arm was around Kathleen, and he glanced at Tom with a thankful smile for the friendship he had given.

Acknowledgments

Writing a deeply engaging, thought-provoking, funny, and personally moving story has always been a dream of mine, but it was clear that journey from an idea to a published book would take the help and encouragement of a lot of people in my life. Special thanks need to go to my wife, Joanne, for her patient, loving, and thoughtful support, feedback and editing. Thanks also to Michelle Buchman for not only providing her incredibly valuable editing services but also for being such an encouraging mentor. I would also like to thank my publishers at Full Quiver Publishing, Ellen and James Hrkach, for their guidance, support, and expertise to make this dream a reality.

Many thanks to those beta readers who provided insightful, rich, and honest feedback to improve the quality of writing and the story itself, Florence Henderson, Richard Henderson, Jerry Sano, John Sano, Eileen Perrelli, Elaine Morisi, Cassie Sano, John O'Connell, Emily Sano, Father John Culloty, Cathy Knipper, Ron Bolster, and Michael Lavigne.

I also want to acknowledge the many teachers that make themselves available for others and provided wisdom and insights woven into this story of one man's journey from brokenness to wholeness. Thank you, Bishop Robert Barron, Fr. John Riccardo, Scott Hahn, Peter Kreeft, Alex Jones, Stephen Ray, Frank Sheed, Trent Horn, Viktor Frankl, Ken Hensley, Henri Nouwen, Thomas Merton, Rosalind Moss, Jim Blackburn, Jeff Cavins, David Franks, Greg Kolodziejczak, G.K. Chesterton, David Burns, Jason Evert, Jean Vanier, and Pope John Paul II.

Finally, I found writing this novel to be a profound and enjoyable experience. The greatest reason was experiencing a strong presence of the Holy Spirit, guiding the story, characters, and lessons of love, friendship, forgiveness, and redemption—all making the teachings and life of Jesus real and tangible to each of our lives today.

About the Author

Jim Sano grew up in an Irish/Italian family in Massachusetts. Jim is a husband, father, lifelong Catholic and has worked as a teacher, consultant, and businessman. He has degrees from Boston College and Bentley University and is currently attending Franciscan University for a master's degree in Catechetics and Evangelization. He has also attended certificate programs as The Theological Institute for the New Evangelization at St. John's Seminary and the Apologetics Academy. Jim is a member of the Catholic Writers Guild and has enjoyed growing in his faith and now sharing it through writing novels. *The Father's Son* is his first novel.

Jim resides in Medfield, Massachusetts with his wife, Joanne, and has two daughters, Emily and Megan.

Published by Full Quiver Publishing

PO Box 244

Pakenham, ON K0A2X0

Canada

www.fullquiverpublishing.com

Made in the USA
Middletown, DE
19 December 2020

28825677R00209